SHIELD OF SEA AND SPACE

The Chaos Knight

BOOK THREE

ERIN HOFFMAN

an imprint of **Prometheus Books**
Amherst, NY

Published 2013 by Pyr®, an imprint of Prometheus Books

Cover illustration © Dehong He
Cover design by Jacqueline Nasso Cooke
Andovar World map by Erin Hoffman

Inquiries should be addressed to

Pyr
59 John Glenn Drive
Amherst, New York 14228–2119
VOICE: 716–691–0133
FAX: 716–691–0137
WWW.PYRSF.COM

17 16 15 14 13   5 4 3 2 1

Library of Congress Cataloging-in-Publication Data

Hoffman, Erin, 1981–
    Shield of sea and space / by Erin Hoffman.
        pages cm. — (The chaos knight ; bk. 3)
    ISBN 978–1–61614–769–3 (pbk.)
    ISBN 978–1–61614–770–9 (ebook)
    1. Ship captains—Fiction. 2. Women priests—Fiction. 3. Magic—Fiction. I. Title.
PS3608.O47768S55 2013
813'.6—dc23

2013001485

Printed in the United States of America

To Jay
(Of course.)

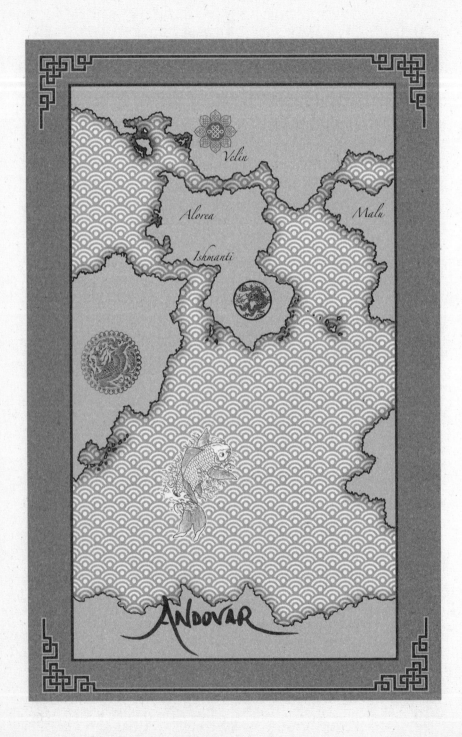

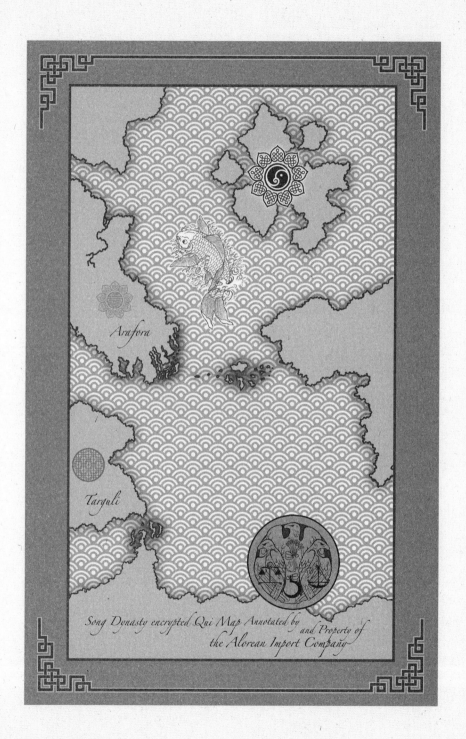

Arafora

Targuli

Song Dynasty encrypted Qui Map Annotated by and Property of
the Alorean Import Company

"I love those who do not know how to live for today."
—Friedrich Nietzsche

CONTENTS

Part Three: Song of Light

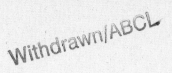

PART ONE

MAZE OF DREAMS

Chapter One
An Auspicious Birth

The halls of the imperial palace were empty, not just this predawn hour but for many months before it, and so only the most loyal imperial stewards remained to hear the labor cries. Deep within the royal apartments, where they'd retreated after the court's exodus, was the birthing chamber where generations of Alorean emperors and empresses had been born.

Only the mother's wails—brave, determined—echoed through the vacant halls; the rest, over a dozen gathered and more waiting anxiously beyond, gave their earnestness in silent prayer. They hoped to witness the birth of another imperial heir.

Ariadel knelt at the bedside, her fingers laced with Calphille's and locked tight, whispering encouragement between the screams. She brushed a sweat-soaked strand of hair from Calphille's forehead gently, then spared a look at Vidarian. He started at the worry in her eyes, then realized it was directed at him: she remembered, no doubt, how it had nearly killed him to watch her birth their daughter only four months earlier. The memory caused his stomach to flip, but he smiled back, and she returned her attention to Calphille.

As was his habit every unattended moment, he thought of Ailenne, and whether she was safe. At four months old she was already showing signs that Endera swore were unmistakably fire priestess gifts, though even the gryphons could not explain why she was showing them so early. The mystery resulted in an assortment of fire gryphons passing in and out of the palace to observe his daughter—an honor, but also a little unsettling.

The high, throaty wail of a newborn pierced through his thoughts. "A girl," Ariadel told Calphille, and the whispers passed behind them with an edge of excitement: "an empress!" Alorea had not had an empress in over a century.

"What shall she be called, my lady?" Whereas before Ariadel had spoken for Calphille alone, now she raised her voice so that the listeners in the hall could hear.

"Revelle," Calphille said, hoarse but clear. "Revelle Aslaire."

Renard, now head steward, glanced around the room, then knelt, hands raised toward Calphille and the babe. "Hail Empress Revelle, heir to the Aslaire dynasty, Empress of Alorea!"

Vidarian had to blink sudden water from his eyes at the knowing smiles Ariadel and Calphille turned on him. Revelle had been his mother's name. Hers was an old Alorean family, devout in their dedication to the empire.

The other stewards took up the call, kneeling in rows:

"Hail, Empress Revelle!"

⌁⌁⌁

Many hours later, Vidarian pored over documents stacked high upon what had been Lirien's desk. It was strange to think that less than a year ago the emperor had granted him audience here and shown him what few knew: the dilapidated state of the imperial finances. Now Lirien was gone, and as he willed his tired eyes to focus on yet another ledger, Vidarian was all too familiar with Alorea's tenuous solvency.

The Alorean Import Company had laid a clever trap. The problem wasn't Alorea's fundamental value—its fertile bread-lands and sophisticated crafters still produced goods valued all across Andovar—but by goading the empire into war after costly war the Company had succeeded in indebting both Andovar and Qui to itself. A convoluted series of agreements that took an army of scholars to unravel revealed only how impossible it would be for either empire to fully settle those debts.

With the death of the emperor, the Imperial City itself would very nearly have fallen into chaos were it not for Thalnarra's pride, Calphille's own surprising governing acumen, and unexpected support from the West Sea Kingdom.

Marielle, a pair of silver wire-rimmed spectacles perched on the tip of her nose, traced down the rows of ledger lines with a fingertip. "Aye, sir," she said, tapping an entry, and showing her own fatigue in calling him "sir," a title that no Sea Queen ever need use. "Ferhian's right. The Weavers Guild is in arrears by nearly ten thousand lora."

"We'll have them pay it out in cloth or fibers, if they must—coin to the grainsmen if they can spare it. Proceeds to relieve Downbridge."

"I'll see it done," she said, marking the page with a bit of ribbon and collecting up the ledger, along with two others in which they'd found similar errors. "You should get some rest."

"I'd be lost without you, as usual," Vidarian sighed.

"It does appear to be our fate—Captain, sir." Marielle's eye twinkled as she stood and gave a jaunty half bow, this time exaggerating the old title. She draped a discarded coat across her arm and left the study.

Vidarian knew better than to interpret her ease as weakness. It was the first time in over a hundred years that the West Sea Kingdom was at peace with the Alorean Empire. There remained dissidents among the captains. Marielle kept a firm hand on them in part by observing caustically that, as the neighboring empires did not yet recognize Calphille and her daughter's claim to the Aslaire throne, they were all still technically pirates.

It was, at least, one less enemy to worry about. Though Calphille had rather miraculously retained her hold on the core of the court, the Alorean Import Company had withdrawn from the Imperial City following their defeat at Gryphonslair (the odd name for the remote desert encampment had stuck, rather to the amusement of the gryphons themselves), taking commerce with them. Several imperial cousins by now had made clear their intentions to recapture the throne, and the reprieve with Qui was precarious at best. When the gryphons had arrived in the city—without whom one of the cousins would certainly have seized the palace—more than half of the remaining citizenry had departed in fear, most of them merchants and craftspeople of means. Those who remained did so out of need, and the city crept by from day to day on the cusp of anarchic violence and poverty.

A tiny jeweled hummingbird buzzed into the room as soon as Marielle departed, arriving with a rattling whir of mechanical wings. It zoomed straight up to Vidarian and hovered an arm's length away from his face.

"Fairy-lights," the bird twittered, mimicking a high courtly accent. "I will have fairy-lights on all the fig trees." Khalesh, the Animator, had been unsurprised at the odd utterances of the tiny automata. They did have some memory, he'd explained, and before activated by their far-speaker would sometimes regurgitate fragments of messages they'd carried before. It was disorienting to think that the courtier the bird mimicked had probably been dead for a thousand years or more.

The bird's eyes, tiny gems that glowed green, changed color as its telepathic contact took over, darkening to blue and then lightening to lavender. It spoke then with a higher and even more metallic version of Iridan's cultured voice. *"I'm sorry to interrupt, lord regent."* Iridan was quite intelligent enough to realize that Vidarian was not actually "regent"—it was a kind of shorthand used to describe his function in Calphille's court—but the automaton's incredible politeness did not permit him to use a lesser title.

"I've told you there's no need to apologize," Vidarian said. "And not to call me 'lord regent.'"

"It's the delegation from Qui, Captain," the bird/Iridan said, flowing effortlessly into another now equally dubious title. *"I'm afraid they are quite insistent. I don't believe they can be put off again."* That would explain the "regent." He was likely communicating via relay sphere with the Qui imperial palace. Vidarian hoped they couldn't hear him.

"Convey my apologies," he said more carefully. "And arrange a council for tomorrow."

"They would like very much if you would speak with them now."

The wind-up toy rattle of the hummingbird's wings filled the silence while Vidarian's mind worked. The Qui had never been so insistent before. If anything, getting a definitive answer from them had been like trying to catch river eels with his hands. A demand for an immediate audience must have grated on their sensibilities, and couldn't be good. "Tell them I'm on my way to the relay chamber," he said at last.

The hummingbird's glowing eyes brightened and its wingbeats, already a blur of movement, picked up speed. While telepathically connected to Iridan—a feat theoretically possible for a human, but thus far only the automaton could manage it—the little bird also relayed his emotions automatically. This had the odd side effect of conveying emotion that Iridan's own body hid; as he had been built for diplomacy, his own eyes showed only what he deliberately told them to.

After a little midair pirouette—the bird's equivalent of a nod—it buzzed out the door, and Vidarian followed, flipping the book of accounts shut as he rose.

He followed the flash of the hummingbird's wings through the warren of hallways, chambers, and stone-tiled garden paths to the old palace. Vidarian marveled that these passages that had been dizzying less than a year ago had now become second nature. The brass hummingbird urged him on with its own speed, zipping around corners and finally disappearing down the long guard-flanked hall that led to the Relay Room.

Without its usual complement of nine telepathic relay officers, the octagonal chamber seemed empty enough to echo. Their blue-lensed glasses were tucked into protective cases; only Iridan maintained the relay sphere now. The great stone orb glowed in the center of the table, and Iridan's hand upon it had summoned illusion magic, an amazingly refined use of fire energy that relayed the visage of a Qui councilor into the air above the relay sphere.

"Fair greeting to you, Vidarian lord regent," the councilor said. "I am told by your golden attendant that today is the day of a most auspicious birth. I convey our fondest congratulations." It was unusual, but something of a relief, for one of the Qui representatives to come so close to what seemed like a point so early in a conversation. Indeed, the councilor looked flustered by this. A tiny strand of hair had pulled loose from beneath his silk hat. Vidarian had never seen one of the Qui councilors in anything other than immaculate condition.

"Thank you, councilor. I will deliver your congratulations to the Empress Dowager. Alorea has not had a crown princess in living memory."

This amplified the (still nameless, for they never introduced themselves individually) representative's discomfort. His hands came together at his waist, ever so subtly clenched.

It might be cruel to deliberately torture this high-ranking but ultimately powerless councilor, but Vidarian couldn't help himself. Qui had been playing both sides of the sand table for months, refusing to officially acknowledge Calphille but claiming to support peaceful relations with Alorea. And as always, Alorean Import Company "advisors" remained near at hand.

Iridan evidently did not condone Vidarian's plan to remind the councilor of his country's difficulty. He coughed. Vidarian turned toward the automaton in surprise. He hadn't known Iridan *could* cough, and wondered how it was accomplished. Iridan gave the slightest shake of his head, and Vidarian sighed. "I must apologize once more, councilor, for delaying our promised trip to your palace."

The councilor's hands relaxed with relief as he fled back onto safer verbal terrain. "Emperor Ziao is most anxious to make your acquaintance."

Out of the corner of his eye, Vidarian saw the hummingbird's tiny eyes brighten. It must still be picking up emotion from Iridan, and if the automaton thought this statement important, Vidarian was going to tread carefully. "I am of course most honored by the emperor's attention."

The slightest dip of Iridan's chin indicated this was at least an acceptable response. Knowing the Qui he probably should have made some sort of obeisance at the mere suggestion that their emperor might want to be physically in his presence.

"When might we expect you?"

The directness of the councilor's question raised the hair on the back of Vidarian's neck. Every other negotiation had been a dance of subtleties spread out over days. Now that Revelle was born, it appeared Qui patience was at an end. "It's a long journey—we'll need many weeks to prepare . . ."

A trace of a frown almost crossed the councilor's face. Another strand of hair slipped loose from his cap and he all but fidgeted. "We understand that you have the star passage technique."

Vidarian stared for a moment, then realized he must be talking about the gryphons' ability to open gates across large distances when working together. "Our gryphon allies can open such passages," he said. "But my understanding is that they require another gryphon at the destination that can communicate the location to them."

A wave of relief swept over the councilor's face. He had clearly been expecting an outburst when he revealed their knowledge of the gryphon's gates. Come to think of it, how *had* they known? "In this we can assist." He turned to the right and beckoned. A shadow approached, and when the councilor touched it, the relay sphere picked up its image with a burst of light.

It was a gryphon, but one unlike any Vidarian had seen. Its round face was ghostly white, its black eyes large and round. A slim beak almost disappeared into the soft, needle-thin feathers of its cheeks. When it bobbed its head in a greeting, its neck moved fluidly, its feathers merging at the edges, hairlike, where those of the gryphons he knew would have scissored like scales.

"This is Tephir. He is most curious about your star passage gryphons."

When Vidarian found his voice, he managed, "I am sure they will be quite pleased to speak with him. If they knew of gryphons in Qui, they have not spoken of them."

"Tephir and his people have lived here in secret for many centuries," the councilor explained. "They are the keepers of the Imperial Library." Now the white gryphon made a strange gesture with his foreclaw, and Vidarian saw that all but one of the talons on his long "fingers" had been removed in what appeared to be a deliberate and long-ago amputation.

// *It will take some hours to fluently join my mind to your gryphons' there,* // Tephir said, his voice delicate and cultured like fine water-pressed paper in Vidarian's mind. // *But I am confident the transfer can be made.* //

Again some several moments passed before Vidarian regained himself, realizing that the Qui councilor was staring at him. "We'll begin right away," he said at last.

∿∿∿

Ariadel was in the antechamber to Calphille's suite of rooms, supervising. Their daughter was in her arms, inquisitively watching the flow of attendants and visitors that passed through the doors bearing supplies or colorfully wrapped gifts. Rai, wolf-shaped, curled in the corner of the room. The shapeshifter—Vidarian still had difficulty thinking of him as a dragon—was larger than ever, and more elaborately spine-ruffed than he had been as a pup. His eyes rarely left Ailenne these days. Beside him lay Raven, cat-shaped; the smoke-grey kitten Ariadel had plucked from the Val Harlon dock long ago had become a scarlet-tipped adult, and a shapechanger as formidable as Rai.

"We'll come with you, of course," Ariadel said. Rai's ears perked toward them.

"Into Qui? You and Ailenne? You—can't," Vidarian finished lamely, caught between protectiveness and the realization that he was wading head first into treacherous reefs.

"I'm sorry," Ariadel said, with a dangerous honey sweetness. "At some point, without my knowledge, did you manage to learn spoken or written Qui? Will you be bringing anyone familiar with their customs?"

"Iridan—"

"You know as well as I do they'll never accept an automaton for truly delicate matters of negotiation. The Alorean court certainly wouldn't, and they at least are familiar with Iridan."

"*She is correct, sir,*" the bird chirped from Vidarian's shoulder. He jumped; it was so light in weight that he'd forgotten it had followed him to Calphille's rooms.

"None of this makes it remotely reasonable for me to bring my wife and infant daughter into the heart of an enemy empire," Vidarian said.

"By all means don't," Ariadel replied dryly. "Instead leave us in the heart of a besieged capital surrounded by assorted nobles all threatening to send assassins after the 'inhuman usurper' we protect." He must have looked stricken, for she gave him one more sardonic glance and then took pity, softening. She leaned toward him, balancing their daughter in one arm, and touched his arm. "We left 'safe' behind long ago, my love. This is the life we chose."

Vidarian clasped her hand in both of his. "You know your strength is the last I would doubt. If it weren't for the children—"

At that moment, one of the midwives pushed open the door from further inside the suite, bearing Revelle, who, though only hours old, squalled heartily. She was already strong.

Vidarian was glad to hear the power in her cries. "She has a winding path before her," he said. "Even if she were fully human—"

A dry chuckle behind them turned both their heads. It was another attendant, this one from Calphille's people, a far-distant cousin, she'd said. In ones and twos dryads had been arriving in the Imperial City, wakened from their long slumber by the opening of the Great Gate. This one was one of the most wizened old women Vidarian had ever seen. In her tree form she was a bizarre, tall plant from the deserts of the far southern continent, a pulpy tree covered with needle-like thorns as long as Vidarian's fingers.

"Centuries ago my people became one with the blood of Andovar and gained our shapechanging abilities. We do not borrow our magic from the land, or from your strange goddesses—our magic is our own." She smiled, and her small white teeth called to mind the thorns of that arid plant shape. "Perhaps it is we who are 'fully human.'"

CHAPTER TWO

THROUGH THE GATE

The Qui councilors might wish they could simply will Vidarian directly to their palace, but the fact was there was no rushing a gryphon. And especially, it turned out, there was no rushing a pair of gryphons who had each just discovered that the other existed.

Thalnarra's questions for Tephir began simply enough, but she sat on the floor, tail giving a telltale lash across the flagstones, when Tephir insisted that the detailed records kept by his people said that they had lived with the Qui for over two hundred years. Tephir, for his part, drew back, neck feathers a-fluff, when Thalnarra told him of the great diaspora of gryphon flights over the same period in Alorea—what they called the "northern continent."

// *Do you mean that there are now no gryphons at all in Kevali Sho'orna? But there must be in Arla'an?* //

This question from the owl-gryphon started a whole new branch of the conversation. The councilor beside Tephir looked ready to explode, but made no move. Vidarian moved to retreat from the room, claiming urgent business, after Thalnarra summoned another gryphon from her flight to exchange histories. The arriving gryphon, like Thalnarra, was a goshawk-type—and the talons of his right foreclaw were amputated, all but one, like Tephir's. It was the first time Vidarian had ever seen such a gryphon, and Thalnarra treated him with even more respect than she'd shown the pridemother gryphoness who ruled Gryphonslair.

// *They sacrifice much that our prides might have long memories,* // she said gruffly, her cedar-smoke mind's voice pitched for him alone. // *A gryphon who gives up his talons places his life in the claws of his pride. He cannot survive without them. It is the ultimate devotion.* //

Particularly after this explanation, Vidarian had trouble keeping his eyes away from the blunted talons of the gryphon's foreclaws. He endeavored to look away out of propriety, the way he would have avoided staring at a man with an amputated leg. It was not simply that the talons had been filed down or even cut off—it appeared that an entire segment of bone had been removed from each of three digits, permanently maiming them. The removal of three talons allowed the gryphon's "thumb," still equipped but with its talon blunted and intricately painted, to curve around the curled knuckles of those three claws, supporting the one intact "index" talon. He had never seen evidence of gryphon writing, but such an arrangement could only be for the purpose of marking some surface.

The two scholar-gryphons, true to their venerated status, made some token exchange of introducing themselves for the benefit of the non-scholars, but soon lapsed into a rapid private communication. All the while Iridan watched raptly, as he tended to with the gryphons; in his prior awakened time he had known nothing of their civilizations, and so absorbed all he could when they could be observed unobtrusively. It was the only thing Vidarian had ever seen truly distract the automaton from the still unresolved puzzle of his missing brother and sister.

But Vidarian's claim of business elsewhere was not purely pretense, and though his departure caused another strand of hair to slip loose from the Qui councilor's cap, he snuck out the door under cover of gryphon reminiscence.

Even as he made his way down the corridors, he did not relish the coming conversation. He was trying not to think about Ariadel and Ailenne coming with him into Qui to parley with the Alorean Empire's oldest enemies. But as monumental as that anxiety was, nearly equal to it was his distress at the thought of leaving the Alorean capital, and his erstwhile Dowager Empress.

It was a strange thing, having a new monarch—perhaps especially as he still felt some responsibility for bringing her into Alorea in the first place. No one had foreseen Emperor Lirien Aslaire falling in love with a newly-awakened dryad—nor she with him. In the back of his mind Vidarian still remembered Calphille as he had found her, wild and strong, cutting down attacking thorn-wolves as they struggled to rescue seridi driven mad by their time beyond the Great Gate. But once she had ascended the throne and declared the child she carried to be Lirien's true heir, she became his empress. Generations of Rulorat blood stirred in his veins, and she was no longer merely Vidarian's cherished friend, the love of his lost emperor, but now also Alorea's last and greatest hope for survival, and peace.

Worse, he knew what she was going to say.

∿∿∿

"Of course you must go," Calphille said.

The infant Revelle slept peacefully in Calphille's left arm. With her free right hand she perused correspondence, striking through suggestions she disliked and signing those she approved. A cup of steaming *kava* was kept fresh by an attentive steward.

Motherhood, like pregnancy, agreed with her. A flush of health lit her cheeks, and her steady gaze had a lively spark to it as bright as he had ever seen. Ariadel had not been quite so lucky. As she had put it during their long evenings spent recovering from the liberation of the Qui-Alorean prisoner camp, much of her leadership of the rebellion against the Alorean Import Company may have been dawn-sickness aftermath. The first months of her pregnancy had been hellish enough that she had emerged with the notion of either killing Vidarian or leading a civil revolt. Luckily for Vidarian the second phase of her pregnancy—and rebel leadership—had suited her quite well.

He cleared his throat, conscious of the stewards, who were ably protective of imperial protocol, and the two dryad guards who stood to either side of Calphille's chair. Like all of those who had turned up in Alorea, they were both female. Calphille insisted that there were male dryads, like her father, but they appeared not yet to have awakened. The sharp-thorned matron that he and Ariadel had seen earlier had vanished; these two were slender, young, and heavily armed. "I am much loath to leave the Imperial City when there is still so much unrest, your majesty."

"It is our wish that you represent us personally to the Qui, Vidarian," Calphille said, and Vidarian struggled once more with how adroitly and completely she had picked up Lirien's imperial mannerisms. He had to frequently remind himself that she was what amounted to a princess among her own kind. "Our royal guard is equal to the task of protecting us, and our allies the gryphons keep peace in the city."

All of this was true, and none of it reassured him. He regretted having promised the Qui that he would travel to their city—even though refusing would have re-ignited the war.

The audience chamber, a small one owing to the new imperial heir's need for privacy and quiet, was as full as it could comfortably be, but it managed to feel achingly empty. Vidarian had known that the audience with Calphille was a formality, really more informing her of his departure than truly attempting to avoid it. Still the acknowledgment of his mission fought against his throat.

Calphille couldn't move, lest she wake Revelle, but for a moment her shoulders tensed as if she meant to rise. Where her imperial demeanor had pierced, compassion now warmed. "We won't—I won't—forget your service, Vidarian. Nor what you have delivered to your people thus far. You are our champion and carry with you our fondest wishes and hopes."

Vidarian bowed. When he straightened, Calphille's eyes told him that she would be safe, that her confidence in her guardians, and in the gryphons, was true. He reminded himself of how strong she was, and found the reassurance he had been looking for. "Thank you, your majesty."

"Nazelle," Calphille said, and one of the dryad guards behind her straightened to attention. The woman was smaller than Calphille, and paler of skin, but possessed of the same delicate sharpness. "Gather your things and go with Vidarian, to guard his family as you would our person." The guard glanced between her empress and Vidarian, her face unreadable, and bowed.

Vidarian bowed in return to both of them, at a loss for words.

"You should see to your daughter," Calphille added, with a mirthful twinkle. "I am sure the Lady Ariadel can find a use for you."

∿∿∿

When he returned to the rooms allocated to his small family, he found, to his chagrin, a small crowd gathered outside their door. Ariadel was speaking to them, and Rai lay curled protectively across the threshold before her. The wolf's spines lay relaxed against his neck, but he gave a soft woof when he caught sight of Vidarian. Many heads turned toward him.

"They found us again," Vidarian murmured, mainly for Rai's benefit. They'd changed rooms three times now in what appeared to be a fruitless pursuit of privacy.

I am conspicuous, Rai said, his ears drooping with apology. A tiny spark of anxious blue energy crackled down his back. Raven, the cat-shapechanger, could take the form of a small golden spider, but Rai had no such unobtrusive option.

"It's not your fault," Vidarian said under his breath, sending a wave of reassurance to the wolf. He was right—there was no hiding him, especially in his dragon shape, but Vidarian had a feeling the petitioners would find them even if Rai remained closeted deep in the palace.

Summoning up a smile, Vidarian pushed his worries aside and approached the group. Leading them was a woman with a young boy in her arms. The boy was big to be carried—at least four years old—but weak and listless. There was something troubling about the distance in the child's gaze, the way his eyes seemed not to focus on the people around him.

"Please, Lord Tesseract," the woman said, "My son is grievous ill. They said your blessing might . . ." She trailed off into a hoarse whisper.

Vidarian exchanged a look with Ariadel. They had discussed this more than once. He knew that his refusal would be a rejection, the worst possible kind of omen. But he couldn't be comfortable reinforcing their faith in something he was fairly sure he wasn't. That didn't seem to stop the rumors from circulating, that "the Tesseract" had all manner of ridiculous and strange powers. He heard one story that said he could pickle vegetables with his mind.

The woman held the boy out to him, her face sunken with grief. It was something they'd seen far too much of these past months, as Val Imris emptied of its able-bodied citizenry, leaving those too poor or frail behind. Vidarian accepted the child from her outstretched arms, balancing him gently against his hip. With his free hand he caught the woman's hand, and then her eyes with his own when she started. "I believe in you," he said, and her widened eyes filled with water. "I believe in the strength of the people of Alorea."

The boy blinked up at Vidarian, then turned his head shyly toward his mother, who smiled, and dashed away tears with the heel of her hand. She met Vidarian's gaze bravely, though not without struggle, and finally nodded her understanding.

Vidarian handed the boy back to her. "Go to the Mindcrafter Academy and ask to see Grandmaster Anise. She may be able to help you. If they ask, have them send a messenger to the palace and I will make the request personally." A murmur went through the small crowd at his words, and fresh tears coursed down the mother's cheeks. She clutched her boy to her chest, bowed her thanks, and then retreated, surrounded by excitedly whispering companions.

Ariadel had a soft, thoughtful smile when he turned back toward their door. Rai had risen from the threshold and watched the Aloreans depart, his tail waving. "You've developed a way with them," Ariadel said.

"They need to know they hold their own fates," he replied, reaching to embrace her and trying to keep the gruffness from his voice. "And they need to trust the healers."

"I wasn't criticizing," she said, kissing him on the cheek and then moving away from the door. "Someone has been waiting for you."

At four months old, Ailenne already had her own language of sounds, and was gurgling away happily in her bassinet when Vidarian entered their rooms. Packs of supplies, clothing, and tools were already heaped by the door, and two maids bustled about, gathering up stray items and spreading sheets over the furniture. He wondered how long they'd been told the family would be gone.

When he leaned over the bassinet, Ailenne smiled and squeaked, reaching out with stubby fingers. Vidarian touched her lightly on the nose, and she laughed; he picked up a rounded wooden toy gryphon and placed it in her hands. She brought it immediately to her mouth and began gnawing on a wing.

The rush of emotion that poured through him at the sight of Ailenne's large dark eyes and porcelain-smooth face was familiar and complex: a kind of disbelief, elation, love of a fierce kind he had never known before—and a lingering fillip of sadness that his own family wasn't here to meet her. It seemed a cruel irony that one of the many effects of opening the Great Gate was the disappearance of Blood Plague, too late to have saved his brothers.

Rai nudged his hand with a wet nose, pulling him from moribund thoughts. He jumped, Ailenne's eyes widened, and the wolf nudged his chin over the rim of the bassinet. Seeing it, Ailenne squealed with delight and waved her arms. Vidarian picked her up, then set her on the floor in front of Rai, who crouched to bring his head level with hers. They proceeded to play Ailenne's latest favorite "game," which consisted of tiny hands grabbing Rai's nose until he licked her fingers.

Vidarian straightened just in time to see Ariadel approaching with Ailenne's traveling quilt. "Time to go," she said, and Vidarian's stomach sank.

"I'm still not sure about this," he began, as Ariadel bent to scoop up their daughter in the blanket. Ailenne reached for Rai with a squawk of protest. "We don't even know if gate travel will be safe for her."

"She passed through more gates before she was born than most adults ever will," Ariadel replied. "And every healer that's seen her can only marvel at her health." She smoothed Ailenne's hair, affectionately brushing the large birthmark behind the girl's left ear, which the gryphons counted as another sign of her strong future fire magic.

I will protect her, Rai offered. Vidarian frowned at him and his ears drooped.

Ariadel scratched between the wolf's ears and they perked back up again. "We'll have two of the most formidable creatures in the known world guarding us, not to mention gryphons and incredible layers of politics. We'll be safer in Shen Ti than in the imperial city."

"Don't remind me," Vidarian sighed. Ariadel took his admission for victory, patted him on the shoulder, and set about gathering up what remained of Ailenne's things.

∿∿

By the time they returned to the Relay Room, trailed by stewards bearing trunks and packs, the gate to Shen Ti had already been opened. It shimmered in the north wall, anchored by two gryphons on this side—harrier-types from Thalnarra's flight—and two owl-gryphons on the other side. Energy emanated from it, palpable on Vidarian's skin even across the large chamber, and ripples of colored light passed over its surface in random waves.

Thalnarra and Altair, arrayed in impressive formal armor, were passing through the gate one at a time. Iridan, with Khalesh beside him, already waited on the far side. Renard, Calphille's head steward, personally supervised the transfer of their supplies, which were efficiently tossed across from one team of hands to the Qui's. Nazelle, the dryad guardian, had also already crossed, and appeared to be sizing up the Qui guards on the far side, perhaps a little too obviously.

Ariadel followed her, striding across with Ailenne in her arms quite before Vidarian could summon up any worry. And before it mustered itself unbidden, he followed her.

⌇⌇⌇

Sunlight stained Vidarian's eyelids red as he steadied himself, eyes clenched shut. Nothing about gate travel required one's eyes to be closed, but it seemed to reduce the disturbing phantom images that had followed Vidarian into the outside world the one time he'd left them open. The momentary memory of that vast emptiness, ghost-touched darkness stretching beneath his feet into infinity, sent a shiver down his spine.

When he did reopen his eyes, that promised sunlight stung, blinding him in another way—as he blinked back reflexive tears, the room came into view.

The first sign that he wasn't where he was supposed to be was the large lead-framed window. It was heavy with blue velvet curtains, normal enough, but the twisting galaxy that hovered beyond, impossibly close, flipped his stomach.

"Hello, Vidarian!" the Starhunter said. "Long time no see!"

CHAPTER THREE
SHEN TI

She was sitting by the window in a red leather armchair, one leg slung over its right arm, an elbow propping her up on the other. Somehow she had glued tiny lights onto the tips of her eyelashes that twinkled when she blinked; she wore a red velvet smoking jacket edged with black ribbon, and a curved horn pipe issued fragrant smoke from between her teeth.

The Starhunter hadn't appeared to Vidarian since their return to the Imperial City. In the midst of the intrigue that had grown up like mold around Alorea with Lirien's death, it had been a welcome reprieve—but clearly whatever had amused her in the interim had now waned.

"Where are we?" he asked, looking around the room for hints.

It was a mistake. He'd gotten used to the Starhunter's strange appearance, and had accepted the window that looked out into space, but the rest of the room's contents made his stomach turn again. The giant celestial gryphon sleeping like an elephant-sized dog in front of the fireplace was the least unsettling. The animal trophies hung high on the walls were slightly worse—otherworldly things, one head that looked like a ram with six eyes each ringed with sea-urchin spines, another the face of a shark with human eyes and drooping wattles. A third head filled his gut with fear even though it was hardly recognizable as a face—one silver-toothed mouth inside another, black-carapaced, no eyes at all.

When he forced himself to turn away from that paralyzing eyeless gaze, the glowing spheres resting on several pedestals around the room drew him in. Before he realized he was moving, he'd come to stand in front of one of them, a glass orb as wide in diameter as his two spread hands, that generated its own light from within.

It was a terrarium of sorts, with a floor of soil and improbably tiny plants.

From the green rose a miniature city, its white spires and arcing bridges strangely familiar. Clouds drifted beneath the surface of the glass, and when they cleared he recognized the street-patterns, the shape of the hills. It was Val Harlon—but not as it currently stood. He was trying to make out the differences when a tiny dragon flew across the sphere, dove, and released a spear of fire that set fields ablaze and ant-sized farmers scattering. "What is this?" he breathed.

"You like my little room of curiosities?" the Starhunter puffed up proudly. "These are a few of my favorite things. How can you stack whiskers on kittens up against the severed head of a Milawan fear-beast, honestly?"

"Is that Val Harlon?" Gently, almost expecting an electric shock, he placed his hand on the sphere. Below, the dragon wheeled, blasting fire, and the tiny people screamed or shook their fists at the sky. He hastily withdrew his hand.

"I don't think they call it that. I can't remember, though. Too many worlds to keep track of."

Vidarian pulled his eyes away from the sphere to look at her. Asking questions was usually futile, but he couldn't seem to help it. "Why did you bring me here?"

The Starhunter gave a long pull on the horn pipe, then exhaled lavender smoke. "To check up on that little errand we talked about. Have you found them yet?"

He gestured at the spheres, the strange heads on the wall, the sleeping gryphon. "You have all this, why can't you find them yourself?"

She scowled. "You could just have said 'no,' you know, you don't have to be a jerk about it."

But he thought he knew why she couldn't find them. "Why do the other goddesses hate you so much?"

"You always fear people who know your secrets. Fear leads to anger, anger makes you eat . . . wait . . . that's not it . . ." She squinted, thinking, puffing again on the pipe.

"And how am I going to find them if I don't know their secrets?"

The Starhunter's eyes reopened, and now they were focused, vast. "Vidarian, you're my favorite, but you can be *so* tedious sometimes." She snapped her fingers.

◠◠◠

He was moving, completing his step through the gate. The sudden movement threw his head into vertigo and he stumbled. There were gasps all around him, demure ones, and he fell into someone—Ariadel, who gripped his arms and steadied him. Closing his eyes held the vertigo at bay, and when he felt safe opening them, he saw Ariadel's face full of worry and relief. Rai barked once, then flattened his ears when Ariadel and Vidarian both looked at him sternly.

"Where were you?" Ariadel asked quietly.

It appeared time had passed normally without him. He wasn't sure whether to be relieved or annoyed. "With the Starhunter," he murmured, and made a slight calming motion with one hand when Ariadel's eyes narrowed. She had a severe dislike for the chaos goddess, which may have had something to do with the Starhunter threatening her life in an attempt to control Vidarian. "She—caught me between the gates."

"I didn't know she could do that."

"Neither did I." Vidarian straightened, raising a hand in greeting to their hosts. During the excitement of his otherworldly abduction it had been easy to forget that they were now in the heart of the Qui Empire, an ancestral enemy that Rulorats had battled for generations.

Two of the nameless councilors who had arranged their visits were present, but with them was a much more elaborately garbed man—young to be wearing such heavily embroidered green robes and the tall, narrow hat of an imperial advisor. He stopped five paces from them and bowed from the waist, his hands clasped together in front of him. The two councilors bowed with him.

"I have the honor of conveying the welcome of his most august majesty, Emperor Ziao Fen Liang, most revered Son of Heaven, may he reign ten thousand years." The young man's High Alorean was flawless, if outdated, with an accent that had not been heard in Val Imris in a hundred years, Vidarian would have wagered. He stood there, eyes to the floor, unmoving.

"We are honored by the emperor's welcome," Vidarian said. "We look forward to discussing the future of our empires with him."

Now their host straightened. "I am Shao Ming, Grand Secretary to his majesty and our immortal Qui." He glanced to his left, where Thalnarra and Altair conferred with the two ghostly white-feathered owl-gryphons they had seen from the relay chamber. "If you will follow me, a special chamber has been prepared that may accommodate our friends for a meal to celebrate your arrival." Vidarian's stomach was still churning from the Starhunter's den of "curiosities," but he nodded in what he hoped was gracious thanks.

A stream of identically clad servants arrived to carry away the packs and supplies, and the gryphons closed the gate—the star passage, as the Qui and the owl-gryphons called it—behind them. As the Alorean imperial palace disappeared from view, Vidarian couldn't suppress the tiny roll of dismay that quivered through his heart, though he endeavored to mask it as they turned to follow Shao Ming.

Vidarian had known that the Qui relay sphere had resided in its Grand Library, but he'd had no idea how massive that library was. Alabaster hallways stretched before and behind them, so long that Vidarian was sure that the library itself must reside in the imperial palace. But as they passed room after room filled with clerks, honeycomb-style manuscript shelves, and quiet studies, he realized that all of this *was* the library and the library alone. Justinian's words echoed back to him: the Company had advisors everywhere. If Qui's library was, as it appeared, more than ten times the size of the largest such in Alorea, how much of the Company's "secret" knowledge had come from here? As they walked, he caught Khalesh's widened eyes—the Animator must be having the same thoughts.

Gradually they came to hallways more frequently populated by couriers and well-dressed servants, and exotic but tantalizing aromas promised kitchens nearby. Shao Ming turned at last through an arched entryway, then escorted them through a foyer and into a long—and, of course, gigantic—dining room.

The room and the long table that filled it went on and on—row after row of brocade-cushioned chairs gleaming with recently polished lacquer. Tall lacquered black columns added to the dizzying illusion of the room's infinite length. There were chairless spaces for the four gryphons, but the rest of the place settings—at least fifty, to Vidarian's rough count—were empty. Courtiers, councilors, and nobility of unrecognizable rank began to file in, bowing greetings, as soon as Vidarian and his company had entered.

It only took Shao Ming's easy bearing to confirm that the emperor would not be attending. The Grand Secretary seated them beside him at the head of the table, where they had an unsettlingly good view of the full assembly that had gathered for the meal. Once all stood before their chairs in an orderly, complete fashion, every Qui in the room performed one of those from-the-waist bows, this time in near-perfect synchronicity. Then, without another word, they took their seats.

Vidarian had been about to motion Ariadel, Khalesh, Iridan, and the gryphons to sit when a small group of elaborately costumed old women entered the room and headed straight for them. Each carried a wax tablet and a stylus, and there was one for every Alorean guest. The women divided up silently and bustled about, peering into eyes, gently touching arms, motioning for them to open their mouths or offer up their hands.

"Shamanesses, you would say," Shao Ming explained. "Food-healers. From our southern provinces. Their finesse with the art of medicinal meals is unsurpassed. It is the emperor's pleasure to welcome you with the gift of their art."

The woman who approached Vidarian was so old that her eyes, which must once have been brown, were now clear as glass. She looked into Vidarian's face, and when she focused on his eyes, he fell back half a step—her attention was like the Starhunter's, but rounder, deeper. It bore *into* him with such strength that it took him several moments to see her, to separate her physical presence from the powerful self that rose up in his mind and heart.

She made a shushing noise, smiling apology and murmuring words in Qui that he couldn't understand. When she took his hand, warmth shot through him as strikingly as had the cool energy of her regard, and he found himself relaxing. Now she was watching him with fascination, and the warmth continued to percolate beneath his skin, gently searching, observing. The faintest note of sadness crossed her features, and she patted his hand, still held between hers, before giving it a final surprisingly strong clasp and releasing him. When her presence withdrew, he realized he was breathing fast, almost gasping.

The other shamanesses by now had marked down notes on their tablets, instructions of some kind, in the spidery but beautiful Qui written language. One stopped in front of Vidarian and made a gesture of welcome. Shao Ming bowed to her, and she smiled, then withdrew back the way she came, followed by the others.

At a gesture from Shao Ming, they took their seats. This appeared to signal another stream of servants to enter, and they flowed through the room, placing tiny dishes of delicacies on the table, pouring glasses of wine and cups of tea. Cylindrical containers of lacquered wood painted with intricate floral designs were placed in the center of the table from end to end, one for every four diners.

More platters arrived, these of various vegetables and meat, their aromas strange but enticing. As they passed around the Aloreans and across the room, Vidarian's stomach rumbled, reminding him that he hadn't eaten all day. A new set of attendants appeared, these in black silk, opening the lacquered cylinders to reveal perfect spheres of rice and setting about serving the gathered Qui.

Vidarian was so caught up watching the procession that he didn't notice the approaching attendant until a dish was being set before him. The large porcelain plate was a work of art on its own, with its rim of gold leaf and meticulously painted black chrysanthemums, but the food atop it elevated its beauty. There was meat of some kind in a bright red sauce, leafy greens spotted with a fragrant black legume, and five purplish fruits the size of small plums, also cooked and sauced. The attendant added a bowl of rice to one side, and another bowl of light broth dotted with grass-like strands of some fibrous root.

Shao Ming's faint intake of breath drew his eyes away from the plate, and the Secretary looked abashed at having been caught off guard. Vidarian gave him a quizzical look, and the man made an uncertain motion with one hand. "They have given you *shen lo-tsing*." He hesitated, searching for words. "Plum of heaven. It is reserved for *mae kasuro*," Shao Ming said, scrutinizing Vidarian intensely. "Dragon spirits."

At this, Rai lifted his head. The wolf had quietly positioned himself behind Vidarian's chair, curling as close as he could to the lacquered legs. Now and then one of the platter-bearers would give him a startled glance, but he remained mostly unnoticed until his spine-fringed neck appeared above the table line.

Shao Ming, in a rare moment of undisguised emotion, paled as he looked from Rai to Vidarian and back to Rai again, visibly putting together figures in his mind. The diplomats had told Vidarian that rumors had reached even Qui of the dragon-riding Tesseract, but the shock in Shao Ming's eyes said he hadn't believed them. (And well he might not, considering the other bits about pickling vegetables and what-have-you.) Now that he did, the Secretary returned his eyes to his plate and resumed eating, lost in thought.

Beside them, Ariadel was regarding her plate with a mixture of fondness and consternation. She caught his eye and nudged some slices of a mottle-skinned melon whose pungent scent Vidarian could detect even from afar. "Cocoa-melon. My mother always wanted me to eat it." Ailenne slept soundly in a pillowed basket beside her. The shamanesses had ordered food for her, also—the milk of a pod-like vegetable sweetened with red berries, and rice cooked until it had turned to porridge, then scented with vanilla oil. Ariadel eyed the rice porridge enviously, but dutifully scooped up the melon slices—which, by her expression after eating, were extremely bitter.

Vidarian's own meal tasted strangely anticlimactic, after Ariadel's bitter melon rind and Shao Ming's reaction to the plum-like fruit. As he ate, a warmth grew in his chest, not unpleasant; the fruit had an assertive tang and a musky undertone that well contrasted the sharp and sweet flavors of the red meat sauce. By the meal's end, he felt rested and awake, alert as though he'd been sleeping for hours.

A soft chime sounded, and another servant approached, carrying a cylindrical etched steel cup on a green satin pillow. Vidarian looked around for others following, but there were none—and the servant came directly to Vidarian's side and set the cup before him with a deep bow. Like the cocoa-melon, the cup exuded a strong fragrance, but this one was sweet and faintly spicy.

When he picked up the cup, its surface ice cold and beading with condensation, Shao Ming was regarding him again with open astonishment. Vidarian tilted the cup toward him in askance, and the Secretary shook his head. "They honor you again. *Wei fa kasuro*: the eye of the dragon. The drink of great masters and the chosen of heaven. Also those who bear great burdens."

"It was a favored drink of Wen Ai Ko, the philosopher-king," Ariadel said, her tone turning upward in askance as she looked at Shao Ming.

The Secretary acted as if Ariadel hadn't spoken, turning instead again to Vidarian. Then he hesitated, which Vidarian took to mean that some of the boil in his blood had made it to his face.

When Shao Ming said nothing more, Vidarian took a long draw on his cup. The tang of metal rolled across his teeth and tongue first, the drink so cold that it took moments for its taste to register. It was effervescent, but gently so, and the fruit's tang opened up all his senses, so bright and pure as it was. No other fruit came close to its depth or roundness. Before he knew it, he'd closed his eyes, drawn inward by the powerful flavor. When he opened them, the cup was empty, and the Grand Secretary was standing.

"Show our honored guests to their rooms," he said, still regarding Vidarian thoughtfully, and still ignoring Ariadel. "Though quickly, they have traveled far."

CHAPTER FOUR

TWISTING PASSAGES

They were quartered in another wing of the Grand Library, and so still had not seen the palace proper. Whether this was practicality or containment Vidarian could not guess. His main focus at the moment was Ariadel, who remained silently fuming from the brief exchange with the Grand Secretary.

All of the rooms allocated to the Aloreans were at the end of a long corridor that opened up into a round salon of sorts. Heavy oak doors were spaced around it, with cushioned benches and chests of drawers between them. A sitting area with chairs and a small table filled the salon's center, and it was here that Vidarian and Ariadel retreated after settling Ailenne in the quiet bedchamber, Rai and Raven both curled at the foot of the cradle. By the time they had shut the door, Nazelle awaited, sitting cross-legged just to the right of the threshold, her eyes closed in meditation. As they emerged, she rose easily to her feet.

Nazelle was a few finger-widths shorter than Ariadel, and several shorter than Vidarian, so she looked up to read their expressions, quick as thought. "If you follow the corridor," she gestured with her chin back the way they'd come, "then turn right, there are night gardens. Quite beautiful, and fountains to make pretty music." She'd read in a glance that they had uncomfortable things to discuss, and had scouted a solution. Vidarian began to understand why Calphille had kept her close.

Ariadel was startled enough to forget her temper for a moment, but Vidarian thanked Nazelle and started down the hallway before it could assert itself again, or before Ariadel could refuse to leave Ailenne's guardianship to the dryad. Just as he stepped from the salon and into the hall, Ariadel hesitated, looking back at their closed door.

"I will protect her with my life," Nazelle said, almost diffident, as if her prowess were being questioned—and then she softened, making a shooing gesture with her hands. "I have borne three children myself, I know my way with them. Go." Ariadel blinked with the surprise that Vidarian felt, and they both peered at the dryad. It was so easy to forget that the tree-women were nowhere near as young as they appeared. Finally, Ariadel smiled her thanks and joined Vidarian.

They navigated the halls in silence, and met no one, for which Vidarian was grateful. This part of the Library was either sparsely occupied or populated by courtiers who spent most of their evenings in the palace. In reasonable time they came upon the courtyard gardens, and Vidarian was relieved that they were not far from their rooms—close enough, he thought, even to hear Ailenne should she wake and cry.

The promised fountains were particularly clever, and likely even designed for the purpose of covering conversations. Carp carved from white stone were frozen mid-leap, supported by stone waves that rose up from the polished slate floor. None of the fountains had rims, but the slate tiles were subtly sloped, guiding the water to drainage channels.

Vidarian took a seat on one of the stone benches out of reach of the spray, but Ariadel paced, at first approaching the fountain's edge and then turning back the way they'd come. For a moment he feared she would walk straight back to their room, but she turned again, an angry stiffness in the turn of her heel.

"He clearly means some sort of attack on you," Ariadel began, and Vidarian sat up with surprise. Before he could summon a reply, she brushed her hands together in frustration. "But it doesn't make any sense."

That was going to be his objection, and he was happier she'd voiced it, given that the contained energy of her current demeanor was not one he wanted to face head on.

But the fountains could be betrayers as well as protectors, as they discovered when a voice emerged from behind a large potted stand of bamboo:

"Shao Ming is a traditionalist. He does not approve of your mixed heritage, and feels conflicted over his assignment to you." The owner of the voice emerged, as wizened as he sounded: a tiny grandfather with what appeared to be a permanently affixed expression of peaceful bemusement. His near color-less eyes turned to Vidarian. "The Emperor, may he reign a thousand years, respects you, and so Shao Ming reveres you, but your, shall we say, *varie-gated* family repels him deeply." Was there irony in the honorific he gave the emperor? Vidarian wanted to bristle at the revulsion with which he described Ariadel—and by extension Ailenne!—but he may only have been imitating Shao Ming. The old man raised a cloud of questions with his tone alone, an impressive and surely practiced feat.

"Who are you?" Vidarian managed. Beside him, Ariadel looked stricken.

"I am Akeo Shisuno-mabari." He paused. "The Rikani ambassador in Qui."

"I had no idea there was such an office," Vidarian said, after very nearly saying something much less politic. "Your people, the Rikani court . . ." He trailed off, unable to find a courteous way of asking whether his assignment here was some sort of strange death sentence.

"Their assumption is that Qui cultural regard for elders will suppress any specific desire to kill me."

"Are they right?"

Akeo smiled, his face disappearing into wrinkles like the surface of a dried apricot. "We shall see." He moved forward, more graceful than his age should allow, and patted Ariadel on the hand. She looked down at him, eyes still wide with shock. "It will be well. I should leave you to discuss it. And ponder the properties of the whispering fountains." With that, he clasped her wrist affec-tionately, then turned to Vidarian, giving a bowing gesture with his hand, elegant out of proportion with the smallness of its movement. "We will see each other soon."

Vidarian emulated the hand gesture—poorly, by Akeo's friendly smile—and the old man retreated, humming a song in the strange-toned Rikani folk music style. The sound of his voice diminished quickly, assuring that he had left, or else that he had very good control over his vocal cords. Both seemed equally likely.

Ariadel settled onto the bench beside Vidarian, the looseness of her arms betraying a distant mind. When he touched her shoulder, she turned, a lostness in her expression. "In Alorea, I have only ever been Qui," she said, the words slow, disturbed. "Here, I am anything but. Not Qui. Not even Alorean." She gathered her hair in her hands and moved it across one shoulder, her hands clenched.

Vidarian brushed his hand across her shoulders, and she turned again. "You are you," he said. "And my partner, my family."

She smiled, then looked away. "I insisted on coming here, and now I am more burden than relief." He made it half a syllable into an objection before she shook her head, eyes still somewhere far away. "I'll just have to think of something they can't ignore."

Vidarian offered his hand and she accepted it, standing wearily. He endeavored to hide his trepidation, but for little; Ariadel's thoughts as they returned down the hall were pressed tightly within.

∿∿∿

When Vidarian woke the next morning, Ariadel, Raven, and Ailenne were gone.

Rai sat beside the bed, wolf-paws daintily together, his large blue eyes and quiet mind brushing Vidarian's own. He had been waiting, and with an intentness that could only come from specific instruction.

Vidarian stretched and rubbed his eyes. Shen Ti was in steppe country, among the gentlest of Qui's varied climes, but the air was much drier than nearly anywhere in Alorea. "Where did they go?" he asked, when his vision cleared.

Ariadel took Ailenne. Something about a morning meditation. Vidarian squinted at him, and his ears drooped apologetically. *I wanted to go, but she said to stay here, to tell you she was fine.*

Accustomed as he had become to speaking with intelligent non-humans, the increasing articulation in Rai's thoughts filled him with a kind of nervous admiration. Perhaps it was different because he had seen Rai grow from a pup, felt him gain language. It was like watching a child become an adolescent in the span of a single year.

A tap at the door interrupted his thoughts. Untangling himself from the sheets, he pulled on clothing and staggered to the door at the same time, earning a flick of an ear from Rai when he nearly careened into a side table. The wolf padded up behind him, delicate, feet almost soundless on the thick rug.

Vidarian opened the door and caught a single glimpse of dark eyes and hair before they dropped from view with a squeak and a dangerous rattle of porcelain on silver. The servant was on the floor, the green silk of her robe pooled around her, and Vidarian crouched and reached out, thinking she had lost her balance. But the tray with his steaming breakfast sat neatly on the floor, to which the servant had pressed her forehead, her palms flat on the ground.

Unsure of what to do, Vidarian redirected his hand to her shoulder. When he touched her, she looked up at him—then caught sight of Rai behind him, squeaked again, and returned her head to the floor.

She's afraid of me, Rai said, sadness and embarrassment rolling off him at startling strength. As his vocabulary had increased, so too had the strength of his telepathy, not just with Vidarian but with others.

The servant didn't lift her head, but spoke, muffled by the polished wood of the hallway but clear enough in tone, a reverence. Vidarian couldn't make out any of her words. She finally tilted her head to one side, enough to spot him with one eye, and said another, single word. When he shook his head, not understanding, she screwed up her face, then said, "dra-go-n."

It took him a moment to piece her word into "dragon," but then he nodded. "He is a dragon," he said carefully. "His name is Rai. He won't hurt you."

It was the only thing to say, but it was still wrong. She returned her forehead to the floor. Finally Vidarian stepped out into the salon, closed the door behind him, and picked up the tray. With the door closed, she peeked again, hurried to her feet, and then bowed, nearly bringing her head to her knees with the movement. Before he could try to reassure her, she'd shuffled backward, then turned, fleeing.

While he was wondering what to do about this, his stomach growled, drawing his attention back to the tray. It was covered with small dishes arranged around a large covered bowl and a porcelain teapot. The dishes were filled with a variety of minced delicacies both sweet and savory, along with more of the "plum of heaven" from the night before. Balancing the tray care-fully on one arm, Vidarian retreated back into the room, where Rai waited with worried eyes.

Vidarian set the tray on a small table in the foyer and lifted the cover from the large bowl, revealing a thick rice porridge. Just as he was realizing that there was nothing he could feed Rai—the small minced dishes seemed meant to mix into the porridge—there was another tap at the door. Stomach still complaining, he opened it again, this time taking care to block the wolf from view with his body.

Waiting outside was not one but at least seven servants all in a long line that wrapped around the hall. Each carried an object—a tray of meat, a painted urn, a sheaf of dried herbs, a thick quilted silk blanket—and the one in front, the one with the preponderance of very raw meat, bowed and began looking none too subtly over Vidarian's shoulder.

Taking the hint, Vidarian moved aside, and the parade of attendants streamed through, carrying their gifts straight to Rai, who first waved his tail in cautious greeting, then lifted his fur in alarm. One by one they set their gifts in an arc before him, then knelt, finally bowing, their hands and fore-heads pressed to the ground, as the first servant had done. In moments the room was full and still the line crowded through. Vidarian watched, dumb-founded, from his place by the table.

What do I do? Rai asked, his ears drooping.

"I have no idea," Vidarian said, sitting at the small table, more to get out of the way than anything else. His stomach growled again, and he appeased it by tipping the small plates of minced delicacies into the porridge and tucking into it with the large ceramic spoon. The porridge was thick and hot, punctuated by pungent attacks of flavor from the side dishes. "You can eat, I suppose," he told Rai, pointing at the tray of meat.

A thick red envelope bordered in gold leaf was pressed between the teapot and its cup. Now that some of the porridge had sated his hunger, etiquette tugged at Vidarian's attention. With a care for the paper's quality, he pulled the envelope free from its porcelain prop. As soon as it was separated from its confines, it opened in his hand like a flower unfolding, and indeed, when open, resembled a water lily with pointed petals edged in gold. Its center was inscribed in black, an invitation: first to an audience with Emperor Ziao Fen Liang (His Most High and August Majesty, Son of the Sky and Stars), and then to a formal banquet that, if Vidarian understood the markings correctly, would last three days!

He was still contemplating this when the servants began to look up from their bowing position, almost expectant.

Tell them I said thank you, Rai said, and cautiously bent his head to the tray of meat, keeping one eye on the kneeling servants. They did not move as he swallowed first one morsel and then another, though one watched avidly as Rai selected—without much consideration, Vidarian thought—chunks of meat.

"Rai wishes to say thank you," Vidarian said, pouring a cup of tea from the porcelain teapot and drinking it—eye-openingly bitter—before lifting it to the servants in a little salute. They looked at him blankly, and he was sure they understood none of his words when one of them, a young woman, moved to kneel before him, to his embarrassment.

"You speak with the dragon, my lord?" Though she bowed, this girl kept her eyes up, meeting Vidarian's with a sharpness that belied the deference of her "my lord."

"He is my companion," Vidarian agreed carefully. "What is your name? Why have all of these gifts . . . ?" He trailed off; the girl was watching his teacup avidly.

At his question, she bowed again, this time with her forehead low to—though not quite touching—the floor. "I am Mey, my lord. A humble maid in His Most August Majesty's palace." There her obeisance ended, however, and her eyes crept back up to his cup.

"Your Alorean is very good," Vidarian said—and it certainly was, forcing him to reassess his sense of what he should and should not allow servants to overhear. He finished the tea, then poured another cup, more to watch their reactions than out of thirst. "Is there something unusual about my tea?" he asked at last.

"It is only . . ." Mey trailed off, and her impression of a demure courtier was not a convincing one. Seeming to realize this, she cleared her throat, then said slowly: "To share tea with a dragon-speaker would be a fantastically great honor, my lord, and so of course one so low would never request such a thing."

Yet clearly, she was. His impulse was to offer her the tea, and he hesitated only to speculate on protocol. For all he knew, letting them drink his tea was some strange form of Qui sibling bond ritual. He wished Ariadel was here—

It can't hurt to give them tea, can it? Rai asked, and Vidarian started. The wolf had finished his tray of meat and was sniffing curiously at a small heap of preserved fruit. A subtle desire rolled off of him, brushing against Vidarian's thoughts—he badly wanted to thank the Qui for their generous gifts.

Vidarian sighed. "Regrettably, the kitchen has sent only one cup," he began.

Like magic, tiny cups materialized in the hands of the servants, who had lifted their heads and swiveled toward Vidarian. This only heightened his suspicion, but he could hardly refuse now, with so many hopeful faces turned toward him. Gamely, he took up the pot and reached out, met immediately by a clinking flurry of cups. He poured a tiny amount of tea in each, trying to distribute it evenly.

As each cup filled its owner brought it to their lips and sipped, eyebrows lifted as though they expected it to be whisked away at any moment. Mey took the longest draw on hers, then settled back onto the floor, sitting on her heels. "We have many questions about your Alorean empire," she began. "First, what is a 'guitar'?"

Just then, the door burst open—a bizarre spectacle at odds with the intensely quiet and careful Qui decorum—propelled by a broad-bodied matron with graying hair pulled back into a bun. "Mey!" she barked, both recognition and a command. "I have warned you about harassing imperial guests!"

The moment she erupted through the door, all the servants save Mey had scurried, as though their motion could protect them from the matron's eye. Even Vidarian felt an urge to minimize himself in her gaze. But it seemed unnecessary. She was focused wholly on the young girl before Vidarian, and strode toward her like a homing salmon, the other servants streaming around her toward the door.

"I saw the empress's kitchen empty and had to threaten Wo Tsing until he nearly wet himself before he would give up your location," the woman said, shaking Mey's arm and urging her to her feet. She took swings at the other servants as they passed, though Vidarian suspected she missed intentionally. Mey shuffled obstinately, her face a mask of rebellion waiting to happen. "Don't think your father will miss hearing of this!" At these words the matron actually shook her finger at Mey, and either the gesture or the sentiment seemed to break through; she gave one more stormy glance, first at the matron and then at Vidarian, then stalked out behind the rest of the servants.

The matron brushed her hands together, shaking her head and tsking at the trays that still littered the floor. "I do apologize, Lord Tesseract," she said. "I am Madame Wei, His Majesty's first chamberlain. I'll have someone up to clear this mess straightaway." Like Mey, her Alorean diction was without flaw, and unlike Mey, she seemed to know Vidarian's 'proper'—that is, Alorean-decreed—title.

"She has quite the fighting spirit," Vidarian observed.

"I should think so," Madame Wei said, her tone suddenly heavy with a you-don't-know-the-half-of-it weariness. "She's the emperor's youngest daughter."

Chapter Five
The Grand Library

fter the morning's excitement, Madame Wei's promised attendants had arrived, clearing out the plates but not Rai's gifts. For
his part, the wolf was content to remain, bemused, in the room,
a massive bone of mysterious origin clamped firmly between his paws.

At Vidarian's request, messengers had been sent to Khalesh, Iridan,
Thalnarra, and Altair, requesting that they meet the owl-gryphon Tephir at
the entrance to the Grand Library. The two gryphons, while attracting curious
glances—not as they would in Alorea, merely for existing, but for not being
owl-featured—were clearly eclipsed in oddity by both Khalesh and Iridan.
Massive man and automaton were quietly conferring when Vidarian arrived,
the former gesturing emphatically around the Library.

A blue-uniformed attendant met them and bowed, then gestured for
them to follow. The gryphons led the way, ignoring the stares of blue-robed
scholars with a regal air that, as far as Vidarian could tell, the creatures seemed
to be born with. At Vidarian's nod, Khalesh led Iridan behind them; although
the automaton was well equipped to acquit himself in a scuffle, his sheer value
was impossible to forget. Vidarian brought up the rear, glad for once to be
beneath scrutiny.

Whereas most structures spent their splendor on entryways, the opposite seemed to be true for Shen Ti's Grand Library. Though undeniably fine
with its brocade curtains and marble floors, the Library's colonnaded entry was
modest, its ceilings only a few arm's-lengths taller than Altair. Beyond the
single guarded hallway, the floor inexplicably sloped downward—and kept
sloping until it opened out into a chamber easily as grand as the imperial
receiving room in Val Imris.

The Library's lower chamber was not only grand in size, but accoutre-
ments: once the floor leveled out, they crossed a stone bridge beneath which

flowed a remarkable indoor river, complete with reed-lined banks and swimming carp. Sun-spheres twinkled overhead, feeding climbing plants that bloomed along the walls.

A colonnaded thoroughfare led straight ahead, and as he took in the columns' size—easily three times the height of those in the entry, and twice as wide, each individually carved with scenes of markets, battles, coronations—Vidarian realized that the entire external appearance of the Grand Library was a kind of mirage. The building appeared low and modest, surrounded by drab ornamental gardens, when in reality it was a vast underground labyrinth, clearly intended, by its single primary point of entry, to be vigorously defended if necessary.

"The columns tell a four-thousand year history of the Qui Empire," Khalesh murmured, and Vidarian fought to keep his eyes from widening. He'd known that the Qui claimed to a significantly longer history than Alorea, but four thousand years? It was near a gryphon's reckoning—

· // *Their calculations become a little muddy in the first 1,500 years,* // Thalnarra chuckled in his mind, her soft sage-smoke words pitched for him alone. // *But it is an excellent attempt; one of humanity's best.* // The faint silvery edge must have been amusement; of course a gryphon would be amused at a human civilization's quaint aspiration to ancient civilization . . .

High-ceilinged halls and more modest doorways branched off of the thoroughfare on both sides, but the attendant led them straight ahead, at last arriving at a wall that seemed to be covered entirely in gold leaf. Alternating textures created an impression of golden rays emanating from an oversized wooden door framed by carved panels that Vidarian assumed must contain more historical references. He wondered uneasily how often Alorea figured into the elaborate battlefields strewn with war-dead.

Beyond the door, which the attendant opened with a heavy golden key, waited Tephir at last, occupying what appeared to be a very strange librarian's office. It contained, among other things, a bamboo forest lining the back wall whose upper half disappeared into a gap in the ceiling; as well the carp-filled moat continued here, winding in a spiral pattern. Thick plates of glass covered the spiral, making the surface walkable, if one didn't mind fish beneath one's feet. The walls bore bookshelves of all kinds—not merely, as the entryway had contained, the hexagonal honeycomb scroll-cabinets favored by the Qui. There were shelves of western books here, stone and clay tablets lit by elemental lights, and, in a place of honor, some kind of device that looked like a relay sphere, but instead of emitting mere points of light, it emitted letters.

Tephir stood from his place behind a gigantic ebony desk—about half the furniture seemed sized for gryphons, albeit small ones. // *Welcome, friends, to the Grand Library, founded by Emperor Song Wen Huang in the year 2,153.* //

"This is why your people remained in Qui," Vidarian said, struck by realization and unable to keep to court niceties.

Tephir ducked his head in modest agreement. // *My family has kept the Grand Library for over a thousand years.* // Vidarian had not known the owl-gryphon long, but knew any imprecise expression of historical fact would be intentional. The owl-gryphons must have been in Qui for *much* longer than a "mere" thousand years. He was trying to wrap his mind around this when Tephir continued, // *When the other gryphons diminished from the eyes of humankind, my people came to an agreement with the Song Dynasty to keep the Library safe in exchange for our scholarship, protection, and secrecy.* //

// *That must explain my flight's lack of awareness of your existence here,* // Thalnarra said, her thoughts tinged with diffidence like thistle-milk. // *We knew of owl-gryphons, but only isolated populations very far to the south—far west of here.* //

Now Tephir's beak dipped even lower, a humanlike, and specifically Qui-like, motion of apology, embarrassment. // *The protection of the Library has been our sworn trust for thirty-six generations,* // he agreed. // *To keep its secrecy, we kept our own existence secret from all humans save those who have sworn their lives to the Library, and even from our own kind.* // His feathers lifted then, and he even twitched his wings partway open with excitement. // *But the time for secrecy is coming to an end. This is why it is such a great honor to have you here, where visitors, and especially Aloreans, have not tread since the time of my many-times great-forebears.* //

"There is much we're eager to exchange knowledge of," Vidarian began, recovering his composure and attempting to guide the conversation toward their ultimate mission in Qui.

Tephir seized on this as if it were a choice meal specimen. // *Indeed! We are most thrilled to have an Animator here, and of course Iridan—home after so many centuries.* //

"Home?" Vidarian repeated.

"Yes," Khalesh agreed, the upward lift of his baritone voice not quite admitting surprise at Vidarian's ignorance. "The art of Animation was born here in Qui, along with the very first of the Grand Artificers."

// *All driven from Qui generations ago, during the uprising that ended the Song Dynasty—which is surely to cast no aspersion on the great Liang lineage.* // This last Tephir added quickly, but if there was an audience for his caution, it was not among them. // *Emperor Ziao believes the time has come to return these lost techniques to Qui, that the empire may be adequately defended against the strange weapons now awakening from the past.* //

Vidarian seized on this, turning to Khalesh with a hand raised. "It is precisely this that interests us most." At his gesture, Khalesh pulled a large folded parchment from his sash and opened it onto Tephir's desk. They all approached, and Tephir tilted his head, inspecting the parchment avidly. "This is one such device, which we have evidence is in the possession of the Alorean Import Company." The gryphon's eyes darted toward him at this, but then returned to the parchment. "Have you ever seen anything like it?"

// *We have a record of a kind of watching device,* // Tephir said, tapping the parchment with his blunted talon. // *A map intended to show populated regions, to find the separated civilizations of Andovar and connect them back together again.* //

Khalesh was squinting at the figures etched into the paper, his expression grave. "Have you any record of a weapon being merged with this 'watching device'?"

The owl-gryphon reared back, his pebble-smooth facial plumage suddenly roused into a thousand fine hair-feathers. The effect was uncannily like watching his face split open. // *Who would do such a thing? Why? Its reach would be wildly uncontrolled . . .* //

Vidarian reached out to unfold the rest of the parchment, exposing the sketch of the weapon connected to what Tephir called the "finder." Upon seeing it again, Khalesh's mouth hardened, while Tephir glanced up and down the page, his eyes pinning furiously.

The small gryphon was silent for several long moments, his chest rising and falling with rapid breath, before he turned back to Vidarian.

// *Your pardon, but I must confess to a small misdirection on our part,* // Tephir apologized, his beak tipped down in an embarrassed bow, a thing Vidarian had never seen in an Alorean gryphon. // *I am not the senior archivist. I believe it is time you met her.* //

~~~

There was little time to wonder what other secrets the Library protected. Tephir turned toward the bamboo forest, pivoted just slightly, and, before their eyes, vanished as he strode between the towering green stalks.

Gryphons did not gasp, but the sudden sharpness of Thalnarra's attention was palpable in the air, as the presence of her mind oriented solely on the illusory patch of forest. It was not possible for Tephir to have simply passed between individual plants; some magic was creating the appearance of vegetation where none truly stood.

Altair, for his part, had turned toward Thalnarra, also in surprise, but of a different kind. // *It's fire magic,* // he explained. // *But—incredibly sophisticated, if neither of you could detect it?* // At this his eye roved over Vidarian as well, and he blinked, unaware that he should have expected to detect anything at all.

"There are devices," Khalesh said. "Rare, of course. This level of precision, exceedingly rare."

// *There should be an emanation of fire energy,* // Thalnarra offered grudgingly. // *I can detect none. It is exceptionally cleanly done.* //

Before she could continue scrutinizing, a subtle rumble echoed up from the floor, and the flagstones lining the edge of the bamboo forest began to sink, forming a stairway that led downward, bathed in golden light. Tephir reappeared, still ducking his head apologetically. This time, Vidarian watched closely, and could see exactly where his body emerged improbably from the stalks of bamboo.

Tephir lifted his blunt-taloned foreclaw in an invitation, and they descended the staircase one at a time. After following the line of the wall, the stairs spiraled—following, Vidarian guessed, the same spiral marked by the glass-topped moat. A pipe in the ceiling now above them issued forth a stream of water, a kind of cylindrical waterfall, that fell through the center of the staircase. As they descended, they wound around it, showered by a gentle mist as it reached a pyramid of rounded black river rocks at the base of the stairs.

The golden light was in fact white light reflecting off of pale golden marble walls. Vidarian was able to appreciate this a bit better than Thalnarra and Altair. Tephir might have made quick work of the staircase, but the two Alorean gryphons were still not at all accustomed to stairs, and in fact insisted that they were anti-gryphon inventions altogether, especially when traveled downward.

Here, as above, there was a strange and beautiful juxtaposition of stored knowledge and living decoration. There was another bamboo wall that Vidarian had to resist the urge to inspect for illusion, and numerous trees in cloisonné pots vivid with color. Tiny birds even flitted across the room, occasionally to dart up the staircase, and at first Vidarian wondered how they could be prevented from damaging the books. The answer revealed itself when one of them landed on a potted tree nearby and ran its tiny shining beak across its glittering feathers—an automaton messenger bird.

An ancient gryphon, larger than Tephir but more hollow-fleshed, lay opposite the bamboo wall, surrounded by brocade cushions. She put Vidarian immediately in mind of Meleaar, the oldest gryphon he had previously met, and who had sacrificed himself in the battle against the sorcerous automaton Veda. A similar patchiness affected her feathers, and her eyes were likewise far away, as if focused on some world other than this.

A massive book lay before her, and as they approached, she reached toward it with a gnarled and blunt-taloned foreclaw. The page lifted as if of its own accord, a subtle earth magic. Vidarian was so absorbed by the appearance of the old owless that at first he didn't notice the wiry and rough-clothed man who sat among the cushions to the old gryphon's side. As they approached, the man reached out to gently touch the gryphon on the shoulder, then gesture toward her visitors.

Tephir bowed, a strange crouching movement that lowered his beak and forelegs to the ground while his hind legs remained upright. // *Asalet, I bring you the travelers from Alorea. Vidarian Rulorat, called dragon-friend; Thalnarra and Altair of fire and wind flights respectively; the automaton Iridan and his attendant Khalesh vel'Itai, the Animator. Friends, I have the honor of introducing you to Asalet, the Librarian of Shen Ti.* //

Vidarian bowed, and the rest followed suit. "We are indeed honored to meet you, Asalet, and grateful for any advice you might have for us."

// *If Tephir brings you, you are welcome here,* // the owless said, and her voice had a resonance like the echo of a brass gong. Her eyes seemed not to focus when she turned her head toward them, and yet they pierced with vision. // *This is Eoin a'Rua-Choille, our companion.* //

"An honor to meet you also. We are far from the green isles of Ain Oilea," Vidarian ventured, and the man's slight smile told him he had guessed correctly at the origin of his surname. "You are pledged to the Library?" Vidarian asked, taking in the man's rugged attire uncertainly.

"No, not the Library as such," Eoin replied, then gave an odd shake of his head. At first Vidarian thought it was some sort of gesture, but then a slim white feather, its shaft tipped with beads, slipped loose from the man's hair, where it was braided.

Thalnarra and Altair's sharpened attention was bright as the scent of broken pine needles. As their awareness bore down on him Vidarian remembered where he had seen such a beaded feather before: in the hair of Thalnarra's former gryphon-ward, a man called Kormir. He lived with Thalnarra's pride, and she had called him "kinsman."

// *He is gryphon-kin,* // Tephir confirmed.

// *A most unusual young man, then,* // Thalnarra observed, and Vidarian worried that they might take offense, but both Eoin and Asalet chuckled with agreement.

"I am, and out of place in a city, as I'm sure you can see," Eoin said, and Vidarian liked the frankness of his clear blue gaze immediately. "But the Library is as close to a home as I have."

// *Eoin serves as our eyes to the outside world,* // Asalet said, and her voice was warm with fondness. // *His nature is to roam far in search of wonder.* //

"We have come far in search of knowledge, ourselves," Vidarian said, eager to discover why Tephir had brought them to the old gryphon, and well familiar with how long it could take to extract information from one. "The Alorean Import Company has designed, or discovered the design, for a terrible weapon."

// *Always in such a rush,* // the Archivist said. Amusement without malice crackled beneath her words, dry as week-old bread. // *You Aloreans always need a mark to hunt. You move from one to another, discarding the fresh kill to reach ever higher—dreaming one day of rest, of hunt's-end.* // Oddly, Vidarian had the distinct impression that she wrapped Thalnarra and Altair into her admonition when she said "Aloreans." Her attention drifted across each of them like the leaves of a tree dancing to unseen winds. // *If only you could dwell in the hunt itself, and not in the prey, which is always dead.* //

// *And you,* // the old owless said, turning toward Thalnarra, whose feathers immediately rose with surprise. // *You have such great potential.* // At this all presence radiating from Thalnarra ceased, dropping like wind falling from a sail. She was difficult to read at the best of times, but when her shock faded and thought returned, it was a low crackling flame that might have been disdain, curiosity—or rage. // *You know what I say to be true,* // the owl said gently, and her strange energy danced around them like a warm breeze. // *You have felt it in your quietest heart, which is also your bravest. That your teachings have been incomplete, and that you are capable of so much more.* //

Silence fell between them all, then, and the owless did not offer observations on any of the rest of them. Tephir's head tilted to one side, and he made a tiny gesture with his beak. Khalesh straightened, then bowed again, approaching Asalet with the parchment diagram of the Company's weapon.

Asalet's beak tipped downward, then from side to side, as she took in the diagram. She asked no questions, and no one dared speak. At last her eyes drifted shut, and remained that way for so long that Vidarian worried that she had fallen asleep. But then she heaved a great sigh, and when she opened her eyes again, they were brighter, less fogged, and more sad.

// *Toward the end of the Awakened Era during which this Library was built, there were those who felt that the creation of weapons such as these would act to secure peace,* // she said, and now the toll of her voice was quieter, darker. // *In truth, the very search for their creation sundered what tranquility Qui had achieved. The Artificers reached too far.* // She lifted her head, looking west, toward the bamboo wall, as though she could see through it. // *The empire was broken, and to prevent such terrible weapons from falling into the hands of volatile usurpers, the keys to their use were spirited far away. Legend said they were taken to the southern continent and placed in the hands of a peaceful, neutral people tasked solely with their protection.* // At this, she turned to Eoin, who startled, then nodded, slowly.

With a rattle of feathers and a discernible creak of bones, Asalet lifted herself to her feet, an action that, by Tephir's abruptly lifted ears, she did very rarely. Her wings and neck drooped with age as she walked, but there was a liveliness, an alertness, in her step. She went to the bamboo wall and dipped her beak within it. As Tephir's had above, her face seemed to disappear as she passed beyond the edge of the stalks. When she emerged, she carried a key hung from a golden chain. It was shaped for a gryphon's blunt-taloned fore-claw, rather than for a human hand; when she returned, she held the key out to Tephir, who took it and looped the chain around his neck.

// *This Library possesses an artifact that will lead you to these people. Your enemies doubtless race toward them also. They will be the first target of this weapon's wrath, should it be constructed.* // With this, she settled back onto the cushions, which Eoin arranged around her carefully.

"*Great lady,*" Iridan said, surprising them all by speaking after his long silence. "*In all your studying, have you read of others like me? Automata created by Parvidian, the Grand Artificer?*"

The ancient head swiveled toward Iridan, her opaque eyes taking him in.

// Parvidian journeyed here only once and in secret, // she said, and Khalesh's breath quickened beside Vidarian. *// He was searching for some of the oldest texts from the first Artificers, who preceded even the Animators. Tephir can direct you to the notes he left here. I wish you luck on the search for your family. //* Seeming fatigued, she lay her head on one of the cushions lowest to the floor, and closed her eyes.

Asalet said no more, and Iridan bowed, his eyes glowing with a fierce hope.

// The answers that you seek are on the southern continent, // Tephir said, facing the rest of them, *// and your urgency cannot be too great. I am sorry that we cannot decipher more with any certainty. //*

// Tephir, // the old owless said, without looking up. *// You shall accompany them. //*

Blood could not drain from a gryphon's face (at least not visibly), and Tephir's was already white, but the sudden slickness of his feathers enhanced an already ghostly appearance. *// As you wish, Librarian. //*

CHAPTER SIX
FIREBIRDS

When they emerged bleary-eyed from the Library, the sun had long since set. There had been time-pieces in the Library, luminous and mechanical, but between the subterranean location and the seemingly bottomless volume of knowledge there, time itself seemed to have little meaning. Only a growing desire to discover where Ariadel and Ailenne had gone drew Vidarian from its labyrinth.

The halls of the guest wing were eerily quiet as he threaded his way back toward his family's room. Iridan had, to no one's surprise, remained in the library along with Khalesh, and the gryphons had left Vidarian at the entryway to stretch their wings over the ornamental bamboo gardens.

As he drew closer to their rooms, another oddity solidified itself: of the few servants he did see, all were moving in the same direction, and seemed to be in a furtive kind of hurry. First unconsciously, and then consciously, he quickened his steps; the Qui seemed to be heading toward the water gardens just beyond the guest wing.

The hallway just before the courtyard where they had met Akeo was filled with servants, pressed as close as they could get to the entryway. When he forced himself to stop and breathe, he tried to imagine that it had nothing to do with Ariadel, but a thought-drowning dread had seized his stomach.

When he reached the crowd, he touched the nearest servant's shoulder, sure, with a sinking feeling, that he would not be able to press his way through—but as soon as the man turned, he shouted with surprise, then launched into a string of fast-spoken Qui. Heads turned toward them, and the man pushed his way through the crowd, dragging Vidarian behind him by the hand.

Shock and worry had dulled his senses, but as they drew closer to the garden, Vidarian became aware of a powerful emanation of fire energy, undirected and dormant but strong. Like sunlight but without warmth, it sank through him, strangely peaceful, taking the sting from his darkest fears on what they would find.

Qui pressed to the walls to either side, clearing the way and exposing a pale light that grew as they drew closer—

Raven was there, large and glowing, firebird-shaped, shining even more brightly than he remembered. Vidarian had only seen her this way once before, when Ariadel had nearly fallen to her death from a sky-ship, and only the shapechanger's newly revealed form had saved her. Thrice the size of a gryphon, the firebird curled around a seated human shape—Ariadel, who alone could withstand the bird's fiery aura. And in Ariadel's arms, to Vidarian's alarm, was Ailenne.

He was running before he realized it, leaving his companion behind, sure that some threat to their daughter had caused Ariadel to expose her to the firebird's magical flame. When he reached them, Ariadel looked up, smiling weakly, and Vidarian noticed for the first time that the angry redness of her skin was not a reflection of Raven's light. This, too, he had seen once before: when she had communed with Sharli, allowing the fire goddess into her body. Her smile further assuaged the fighting panic that surged through him, but still his heart hammered.

Wrapped in Ariadel's arms, Ailenne was sleeping—but there was a strange new mark on the baby's forehead: a single flame, its tip curled almost back upon itself, the skin around it raised and pink as if burned.

Getting as close as he could to the three of them without being burned by phoenix-fire, Vidarian knelt, reaching out by reflex before the bite of the flames forced him to withdraw. "What happened?"

Ariadel blinked, her eyes glazed with exhaustion and a kind of spent contentment. "I called upon Sharli, and she answered . . . beyond my wildest expectations. Ailenne—"

"Is she hurt?" Vidarian cut in, confusion now clouding his worry. Had Ariadel done this . . . on purpose?

"Of course not." Irritation furrowed Ariadel's brow before she winced with the movement.

His own ire, not a helpful one, rose up in Vidarian at her tone. When he spoke, he lowered his voice, aware of the audience behind them. "But you understand why I might think she would be, and why I'd wonder how you could do this without telling me?"

"She is marked by Sharli!" Ariadel said, astonishment and more annoyance sharpening her eyes. "The goddess herself confirmed the correctness of my commune. There hasn't been a marked priestess in centuries."

He looked at her, straining to understand how she could expose their daughter to one of the wild and volatile elemental goddesses without so much as suggesting the idea first, seeing her lack of comprehension and fighting back the anger that wanted to burn through him. The eyes of the Qui crowded in the hall behind them fueled his discomfiture; Ariadel seemed to feel the same, for neither of them spoke.

An imperial messenger broke their impasse, pushing his way through the crowded hallway. When he saw the firebird, he gasped, and nearly stumbled over his own feet.

The servant who had helped Vidarian through the crowd took the scroll from the messenger's numb hands and unfolded it, then approached and bowed. His Alorean was heavily accented, but clear. "The Lady Ariadel is summoned by the Empress to an audience, a—" he paused, searching for the word, "dawn-greeting."

"Dawn? That is when I am to meet the emperor," Vidarian said.

The man bowed again. "Their imperial majesties often hold audiences . . . at the same time."

"Together, you mean?" Vidarian asked, realizing he shouldn't, but unable to stop himself.

"Ah, no," the man bowed again, then apologized, which only made Vidarian feel guiltier.

His discomfort was palpable, and so Vidarian thanked him, standing and reaching out to take the scroll. He turned to the messenger and offered his own bow, hoping it wasn't as stilted as it felt. "If I could trouble you to carry another message," he began, and the messenger bowed quickly in return, agreeing. "I would greatly like to speak with Ambassador Akeo Shisuno-mabari."

"The ambassador breaks his fast in these gardens before dawn, also," the messenger said, still glancing over Vidarian's shoulder at Raven, but clearly glad for a distraction. "I will leave word with his apprentice that you wish to join him."

"Thank you," Vidarian said, then turned back to Ariadel, who was again studying Ailenne with intent, tired happiness. "Dawn is not far away. We should rest."

~~~

Rai nudged Vidarian's shoulder with his wet lupine nose well before dawn. Consciousness did not return willingly; it had to be dragged forth with considerable threat and cajoling. The night hadn't been an easy one. Few hours remained in it when they'd collapsed into bed, respectively exhausted—and then Ailenne, despite Ariadel's insistence that she had been blessed by Sharli, seemed to know only that her forehead was burned, waking often and unhappily.

It was blessedly quiet when Rai's cold nose bumped him, and so Vidarian pushed himself out from between the sheets in a state somewhere between misery and self-pity.

Ariadel's absence in the bed beside him startled him awake, and he directed a note of inarticulate inquiry at Rai.

Attendants from the empress came to wake her, Rai explained. *They said something about cleansing rituals. Nazelle is waiting in the anteroom to watch Ailenne while you're gone.* The wolf's ears drooped downward just slightly, half of a question.

"You can come with me, then," Vidarian said, rubbing his face.

Rai gave a little leap, for a moment the puppy he had been not so long ago. It was a quiet leap, thankfully, and Ailenne did not stir in her bassinet. Vidarian went to the water chamber and found a basin of steaming water waiting there, likely left by the attendants. He washed and dressed mechanically, then set out for the water garden, Rai roaming ahead with his tail held high.

Few traveled the halls in the pre-dawn darkness, but the occasional quiet-footed servant passed them by. Invariably they gave a small, hurried bow to Vidarian, then all but threw themselves in front of Rai. After the second such encounter, the wolf looked back at Vidarian sheepishly.

They keep bringing presents, too, Rai said, abashed and pleased at once. *Fewer now, though.* Vidarian grunted a wordless reply, unable to summon sufficient feeling about it at this hour.

A heavy, wet chill greeted them as they entered the gardens, palpable in the air. It was the only time of day that Qui could be said to be humid by Alorean standards; low, thick fog blanketed the stone courtyards and coiled around the feet of the bamboo. It would all evaporate within hours of sunrise.

Akeo was not where they'd first met him, to Vidarian's surprise and concern. An early morning dragging himself about the gardens before meeting the emperor was not his idea of effective diplomacy. But Rai caught a scent—toasted rice, he said—and threaded them through the warren of ponds and tall potted plants.

They found the ambassador at last beside the largest water-scape seen so far. He occupied one of two red brocade-cushioned chairs, between which sat a painted clay teapot, two handleless teacups in the Rikani style, and a tray filled with an assortment of toasted rice cake breakfast pastries. Akeo himself was staring into the water, studying the large white fish that swam there.

The Qui Imperial Palace seemed to be filled with fish, an odd thing for a city so close to one of Andovar's great deserts. The Qui themselves seemed to place great stock in the brightly-scaled carp of the kind that swam the tunnels of the Grand Library and occupied potted water-gardens throughout the palace. But these fish were cousins at best, strange pale beasts with tiny scales and long diaphanous fins that whirled and trailed behind them. Their eyes were a striking jewel-like blue, a shade Vidarian had never seen in fish or reptile.

As they drew closer to the water, the fish turned toward them, an eerily conscious movement—and when Vidarian had nearly reached the edge of the water, they began to thrash and leap. They surged up out of the water, writhing on top of one another, mustached mouths gasping air they could not breathe.

Akeo's rust-dry chuckle broke through his fixation on the thrashing fish. "They like you," he said, picking up a delicate painted clay teacup and sipping at its grassy contents.

"What are they?" Vidarian asked, still unable to completely remove his eyes from the fish. Rai was edging closer and closer to the water, his nose whuffling in the scent, though what particular scent fish could have Vidarian had no idea.

"They are called silver-eyes in the west; my people call them *riyun hikana*—dragon carp." He set his teacup back on the laden lacquered tray at his side.

At this, Rai's ears pricked upward, though he continued sniffing at the edge of the water, now and then earning a tiny splash that made him shake his head. "Odd," Vidarian said. "Their eyes aren't silver."

"Their eyes turn blue when excited," Akeo replied, drawing a handful of pressed yellow pellets out of a pocket and throwing them into the water. Most of the fish turned, but a stalwart few continued leaping up at the shore. "Some say, when in the presence of destiny." The old man brushed his palms against his blue linen robe, then turned back to Vidarian, a tranquil and faintly mischievous twinkle in his eye. "You are up before the dawn, and surely it is not to witness an old man's eccentric hobby."

"I was impressed, and grateful, for your advice on imperial politics," Vidarian said. "The Alorean ambassador traveled home upon Emperor Lirien's death, and so I lack an advisor here. I am to meet Emperor Ziao in her stead and negotiate for a lasting peace." Putting words to this errand made it abruptly loom in his mind, vying for prominence with his worries about the Company, their fearsome weapon, and, more sharply, his argument with Ariadel. He gave his head a tiny shake, and added, "I would be grateful for any of your advice. I am well out of my depth."

"One does not look directly at the emperor, much as one does not look directly at the stars," Akeo mused, once again regarding the carp. He shuffled his chair backwards, then motioned Vidarian to take a seat in the other. "You should stay away from the edge," he recommended, including Rai in his suggestion with a nudge of his chin. "The *riyun hikana* are not favored by today's court, but they are ludicrously expensive." Despite his clear affection for the fish, the ambassador seemed to be amused by their exhaustion; some of them had grown listless with spent energy, pushed aside by their still-hearty companions.

Vidarian first moved the little table with its burden of delicacies, then pulled the other chair back beside it and Akeo. He reached out with a thought, brushing against Rai's mind, and the wolf turned, circling behind their chairs and laying himself down on the stones, still watching the fish intently. He was mollified enough to give a brief wave of his tail when Vidarian took one of the rice pastries and, after a nod of permission from Akeo, placed it in front of Rai. The wolf sniffed it, then took it delicately between his teeth.

Akeo took his teacup again, and Vidarian took up the other as he sat. He had never been fond of the bitter grass tea of the Rikani, but could admit that as a pre-dawn aid to alertness it wasn't bad. The rice pastries, too, were surprisingly delicious, incredibly soft and complex in flavor.

"What would you like to know?" the ambassador asked, when they had both eaten a small handful of the cakes and refreshed their tea from the painted clay pot.

"I am curious about the Empress," Vidarian began, reaching for a suitably indirect beginning and managing to think only of Ariadel's unexpected summons. "She summoned Ariadel to a dawn-greeting also, and yet she and the Emperor do not hold court together."

"Ah, that," Akeo said, and chuckled without much humor. "It's simple, or as simple as these things can be. You have heard of the great Song Dynasty, and its last emperor, Fe-Lan Wey?"

"The dynasty that preceded this one," Vidarian said, not wanting to seem as ignorant as he felt of Qui history.

Akeo grunted agreement. "The Liang Dynasty, of which Emperor Ziao Feng is the latest inheritor—may he reign ten thousand years, and such—

achieved their precedence by brutally cutting down the Song Dynasty. Previously, the two families had historically been allies. And Shi Zhang Liang was an accomplished student of history. He knew that to secure his vision of an everlasting Liang Dynasty, he must either bind his family to the Song—or eradicate them completely."

"And the Empress . . . ?"

"Shi Zhang Liang was less prone to hubris than some of his predecessors. He knew that a complete eradication of such a long and established line was unlikely, that even if it were practically possible he would be dealing with pretenders for centuries. And so he married the second eldest daughter of the fallen Song emperor, and declared that the heir to the Liang dynasty would always marry a second Song daughter."

Vidarian blinked. "And they've managed to keep to that tradition?"

Akeo picked up another rice pastry, turning it between his fingers before biting into it. "Unless you believe certain wild theories about the fourth Liang Emperor, yes. For nearly two thousand years. Making Liang one of the longest-lived dynasties in the history of Qui—and making Song, if you are to believe their rhetoric, *the* longest contiguous imperial line in the history of the world."

Vidarian rubbed at his temple with his thumb, only afterward realizing it was coated with white powder from the pastry. He brushed the flecks from his brow, wondering how one was expected to be presentable at a pre-dawn ceremony. "And now the Empress has taken an interest in cultivating Ariadel."

The old man picked up another pastry, and Vidarian was about to be impressed with his appetite, but instead he handed it down to Rai, who twitched his tail appreciatively. "Gossip moves faster in Shen Ti than the scent of blood in water," he chuckled. "You two, and your daughter, have managed to personify an image that connects the imperial family itself: the dragon and phoenix."

Vidarian looked first at Rai, who was thoughtfully chewing the rice pastry, and then back to the ambassador. "Do you mean—Raven? The firebird?"

"'Firebird' is your word in the West, 'phoenix' we call her here, but yes, the great immortal bird who appears wreathed in flame has been sacred here for centuries. The word in Rikani is *kushiko*, and in both Qui and Rikan the symbol is reserved exclusively for the Empress."

The long-finned fish—*riyun hikana*, Akeo had called them—had calmed down by now, thankfully, and Vidarian regarded the water, feeling as though his mind was full of whirling mechanisms that could not arrive on a result. He gave a slight shake of his head, trying to put aside the "dragon and phoenix," as Akeo called them. The sky was beginning to lighten; little time remained. "None of this brings me closer to achieving the peace we sought between Alorea and Qui."

"Ah. Well, that, at least, is simple," Akeo began, refilling their teacups, and Vidarian watched him, trying not to cling desperately to what he might say. "You must convince the Emperor that Lirien Aslaire wed himself to Calphille, and that he designated their child as his heir." Vidarian's stomach sank, and Akeo lifted a withered hand. "This will not be as difficult as you think. Emperor Ziao's power rests on an assumption of the inherent nobility of imperial blood. If he believes that Lirien selected Calphille as his empress, he will never countermand that decision. It would become a matter of honor. You must merely make the Emperor understand why Lirien selected Calphille, in terms comprehensible to Qui culture."

"She is an 'original' Alorean, you might say," Vidarian said, suddenly remembering the old dryad's suggestion about her people being "fully human."

"Ah, that is excellent!" Akeo brightened, his dark eyes gleaming like a raptor on the hunt. He picked up one of the teacups and pressed it into Vidarian's hand. "The Qui greatly value the notion that the imperial family is directly connected to the land itself. If you can imply, as should be natural, that dryads like Calphille's people are an elemental manifestation of that land connection, Emperor Ziao will have great difficulty rejecting Calphille's claim to legitimacy, or her daughter's."

Vidarian looked up, meeting the old man's eyes, which were bright with interest. Perhaps all true diplomats required such fire for intrigue. "I have little stomach for these dancing webs of half-truth," he sighed at last.

"There are many kinds of truth," Akeo replied, with a softness that blunted chiding words. "There is the truth as we know it in our hearts, the deep truth . . . and there is what my people call *atemae*—the apparent truth, the truth that we agree to for the sake of others. The surface truth that a mirror shows us." The man's eyes disappeared into the wrinkled folds of his face as he smiled. "I believe this is something you must know much of, Vidarian."

CHAPTER SEVEN
ALLIANCES

Shao Ming was waiting at the edge of the water garden, subtly making himself more obvious as the sky continued to lighten. At last, to spare the man the indignity of clearing his throat, Vidarian bid Akeo farewell.

The Grand Secretary still eyed Vidarian with careful speculation, bowing to an imprecise angle as though to underscore the ambiguity of their relative status. His eyes darted every so often toward Rai in obvious contemplation of the relevance of a dragon companion. Like the gryphons, the Qui had insisted that such a shapechanger should not have been possible, that the few dragons known throughout Andovar's history had been distinctly their own beasts—perhaps, some records hinted, being travelers from another world. The thought reminded Vidarian of the Starhunter's partiality for Rai, and his for her; he had assumed her affinity was for all shapechangers, but perhaps it was not.

Once the greeting had been navigated, a cord of tension loosened across Shao Ming's shoulders, and he took in Vidarian's appearance with a more measuring eye. As he led them across the garden and through an archway on the opposite side, he clapped, and a pair of attendants emerged from around a corner, their footsteps softened by brocade slippers. One bore a thick embroidered jacket of black silk, the other a sort of knee-length vest, also silk, but lighter and vibrant red. The jacket went on first, and then the vest—both were surprisingly comfortable, keeping off the pre-dawn chill without stifling. Brocaded black slippers like the attendants' own replaced Vidarian's leather shoes; they tried to add a hat and jeweled necklace, but he declined, lifting his hands. Shao Ming almost frowned, but at last bowed acquiescence, probably because arguing would have taken too long.

As they bustled through a maze of corridors, Vidarian realized that for the first time he had been led into the palace proper. The differences at first came gradually: guards with their tasseled, symmetrical longswords were greater in evidence, and the archways grew increasingly ornamented with inset wooden filigree in geometric cloud designs.

The floors, too, grew richer, paved with some heavy black stone that seemed designed to swallow footsteps. Each hallway they passed through was separated by three or five (never four) steps upward, and after some time Vidarian realized they must now be at least two storeys above where they had started.

At last the archways changed again, now becoming entirely round, an interesting feat of architecture. And a final hallway led onto a terrace, also floored in the polished black stone and rimmed with low fountains of the "indoor river" type that had flowed through the Grand Library. The rush of moving water was louder here, and mist sprayed up from the edge of the terrace. There the fountains ended in a manmade waterfall that framed a spectacular vista, the sun a half disc of hammered gold rising over the sprawling clay-tiled roofs of Shen Ti.

The emperor stood at the waterfall's edge, shadowed by a stone column wreathed in climbing vines, a silhouette against the still twilit sky. Beside Vidarian, Shao Ming bowed low, his body bent nearly double; the attendants with him knelt and pressed their forearms and faces to the flagstones. They murmured blessings to the Empire, then withdrew, shuffling backward without lifting their heads.

Still looking out and over the city, Emperor Ziao Fen turned his head just slightly, then beckoned with the fingertips of one hand, a whisper of a gesture. Vidarian crossed the terrace and bowed, glad of his softened footsteps, and not of his suddenly hammering heart.

He held the bow for some time, staring at the edge of the water that cascaded down beneath them, fighting vertigo and trying not to think of the height of the drop. It wasn't easy; the waterfall sprayed into mist several marks below, and the treetops beneath were so distant as to seem like strands of moss on stone. Blood rushed to his face, and when at last it began to darken his vision he straightened, fearing rebuke, but less than he feared pitching over the edge of the terrace to certain death.

The emperor turned toward him, and some part of Vidarian shouted to look away, as he had been instructed. But some other part of him, a part that was still a Rulorat, descendant of men and women who recognized only the sea as their goddess, who had fought and died under a different banner—that part of him refused, seizing up his neck.

Slowly, gently, the emperor's eyebrows rose, elegant lines on a statue-perfect face. His dark gaze sharpened, a challenge—an offer of retreat. And then, just as slowly, he smiled.

"They told me you were different," the Liang emperor said, his voice cultured even in Alorean, educated to aristocratic shapes and tones. The voice was higher than Vidarian had imagined, almost soft. "That you are a man of power and directness. A man worthy to be called dragon-friend."

He was young. So young. He reminded Vidarian painfully of Lirien, whose youth had also startled him, unnerved him, filled his heart with a concoction of uncertainty and resentment at his own age. It was one thing to read a scroll of lineages and find that Lirien had had a mere twenty-four years, and his counterpart in Qui twenty-five; that unusual tragedies in both family lines brought the ascension of young rulers—it was another to look such evidence in the face. But it spurred Vidarian to remind himself that he had befriended an emperor before.

Vidarian summoned what he knew of charm, indeed a directness that had disarmed many a merchant, charmed contracts out of jaded purses, what seemed a lifetime ago. "My experiences have cut away what delicacy I might have had before, and that not much, your majesty."

"They say that only the virtuous may attract the attention of a dragon," the Emperor continued, giving a small bow of his head to Rai. The wolf, who had been sniffing the edge of the water (perhaps hoping for more carp), blinked back at him, then dipped his head in return, earning a chuckle. "It is right, then, that we should meet."

The way that he chose his words made Vidarian want to ask if he himself believed the folklore that his people did about dragons—and his omission of any guiding force (an Alorean might have said "the goddesses have brought us together") was significant. Did the Qui, as they were rumored, truly worship no god or goddess? None of these questions, however, were appropriate, and some might be significantly dangerous, so Vidarian smiled his agreement, and looked out over the city.

The emperor followed his gaze, looking directly into the sun that now rose above the horizon, casting the sky in the fire-streaked pastels of morning. "Beautiful, is it not?" he asked, and Vidarian nodded, for it was: the meticulously arrayed city with its winding roads perfectly curved like the stylized hair of an Ishmanti maiden. "And yet one day it must end, as all things end."

A surge of realization and panic coursed so strongly through Vidarian that Rai looked up and barked. Vidarian soothed him, then turned to the emperor, thinking quickly. "When must a dynasty end, your majesty?"

The twitch of the emperor's lips acknowledged that a dragon-friend's reputation for directness could perhaps—just barely—be forgiven for leaping beyond the more delicate language of diplomatic metaphor. "The Autumn Philosopher tells us that, like the sparrow or the birch, a ruling family must reach its natural end when it is no longer connected to the earth."

"Your majesty shows great patience explaining such a thing to a visitor not raised with the benefit of the Autumn Philosopher's teachings," Vidarian said, again treading carefully, watching the Emperor's eyes with each word. He longed to rush ahead into a more direct argument, but Akeo's advice and the diplomatic rolls from the Library all had been explicit. To rush would be a sign of weakness, and worse—ignobility. "The lion for which my friend and late Emperor was named—Lirien Aslaire—much upheld the Autumn Philosopher's admonition on this account. It was said that the roots of the Alorean imperial family should be woven around the sun-hot metal of the country's deepest heart. The lion must always hold close to that warmth, or indeed it would die."

The look that Emperor Ziao Fen gave him, a kind of quizzical amusement, said that watching an Alorean speak in the poetic style of the Qui diplomats was perhaps a bit like watching a monkey play the piano. He played along, but a feather's touch of flatness in his voice suggested he might not for much longer. "And would you say, then, that your friend and Emperor deliberately drew his line toward danger, away from this heart-stone?"

"Quite the opposite, your majesty," Vidarian said, changing tack to directness now that he had danced himself into trouble. "The Dowager Empress Calphille is in fact deeply Alorean." He watched the Emperor's face for any sign of over-directness. "Her people are an ancient lineage, hereditary masters of the southern territories. They are so deeply tied together that their bodies themselves have come to represent that august earth." It wasn't *precisely* true, given his understanding of how Calphille's people viewed their relationship to the land in which they lived, nor their shapeshifting abilities, but he hoped it was true enough.

"I see," the emperor said, his lips drawn downward in thought. Vidarian was relieved to see a thoughtful abstraction in his eyes, calculation outweighing courtly pretense. "Then it is likely Emperor Lirien sought to renew his tie to the land by marrying into this ancient line. This is admirable. An Emperor must achieve unity and harmony with the land, that balance be preserved." His eyes drifted down and across the city again, roving to a golden temple in the distance, whose roof seemed to be edged with stylized wings.

"This was exactly his intent," Vidarian pressed, hating the lie, but not the survival that it would buy for Calphille and the imperial princess. "He sought to return Alorea to its former greatness. And those who would seek to sever that tie themselves abhor all ancient tradition."

"The Company," Emperor Ziao Fen said, with a downward, less cultured turn to the word that reminded Vidarian again of his own lost emperor, whose sculptured mannerisms would betray a knifelike pragmatism on matters of finance. He seized on it, even while his mind whirled with the implications of Ziao Fen's casual disregard.

"The Company has no lineage nor dynasty as we would recognize it," Vidarian said. "They seek only their own gain, an individual dominance between themselves—an unceasing internal fight for power—and then that same dominance over all the world."

"It is a brutal, thoughtless thing," the Emperor sighed, the tiniest glance betraying his discomfort at giving voice to such doubts. That hesitation was like vinegar in Vidarian's gut; the Company's reach was far too great, to unsettle one of the oldest dynasties in all civilization. "Not only without tradition, which would be disturbing enough, but without even seeming to realize why those traditions might have formed. Without foresight. Without diligence."

The strange weight that the Emperor placed on these words would have escaped Vidarian if not for his coaching in the Library. The Autumn Philosopher, an ancient sage, had suffused her influence into the earliest years of the Qui Empire itself, and had laid down five virtues, of which diligence was one. "And without sincerity, your majesty," Vidarian replied, willing the ravaged spirit of his experiences into his words. "As I can personally attest. They place no value on truth nor history, nor even the present moment or far future. Only the next instant from this, wherein deceit is as good as honesty, and malice as good as kindness. All justified in the pursuit of power."

Ziao Fen's already long face drew downward, and for a moment Vidarian feared he had gone too far. But the Emperor—ruler of a country that had been Alorea's gravest enemy for generations far preceding their own—at last sighed again. "Your words confirm what has been in my heart. Their explanations were too ready, their faces too well-trained. It is my own detriment that I lacked the bravery to see clearly." He looked up at this, and again there was the faintest curious amusement: would Vidarian know the correct response?

To his relief, he did. "None could ever suggest that the most glorious Emperor embodied other than perfection," he said, and tried his hardest to mean it. "There was advantage in cultivating even the Company in ages past, but what decides the future is our present action."

"What do you suggest, then, dragon-friend?"

"Declare peace with Alorea, and recognize the Dowager Empress Calphille and the Princess Revelle. Allow myself and my companions to travel from here in pursuit of the world-devouring weapon that the Company now chases."

Ziao Fen's head tilted, his eyebrows drawn together. "The latter is easily done. The former I must meditate on. Its expression to my people, as you must know, will require great finesse. Is that all you advise?" He smiled at this last, inviting witticism.

Vidarian aimed for directness instead. "Consider also declaring peace with Rikan." The emperor's visage darkened instantly, and Vidarian rushed on. "Any resource spared battling another enemy increases the Company's chance of achieving their goal."

Emperor Ziao Fen shook his head, jaw set. "This is impossible. With Alorea we have held—one might say—sibling wars. Mutual respect. There have been times of peace. The cuts of Rikan go much deeper. If there were anything else you would ask, I would grant it."

Vidarian watched the emperor for any sign that he might relinquish his position on Rikan, and found none. It was not something he had ever even suggested to Akeo, but he felt compelled to try. The old man did not deserve to be suspended in the midst of this feud. At last, and mainly to divert the emperor to a lighter topic, he began, "There is the matter of your majesty's banquet . . ." He trailed off, knowing no inoffensive way of asking what manner of person could be expected to entertain for three days.

Ziao Fen chuckled. "I advise you and your party be gone by daybreak tomorrow, without explanation. Dragons are expected to be somewhat—unpredictable." The barest hint of a smile tugged at the corners of his eyes.

"I'll keep that in mind, your majesty."

∿∿∿

Shao Ming's attendants were just beyond the archway when Vidarian's audience ended, one of them bearing a message that Ariadel was waiting for him in the Grand Library. The attendant, who had offered the message on flattened palms, his head bowed, had also offered to take Vidarian there, and he had agreed with gratitude.

As they passed through the palace, Vidarian's thoughts spun between all that the Emperor had said—and not said—and what awaited him in the Grand

Library. For all that the machinations between Qui and Alorea twisted his gut with anxiety, they did not cut as did the memory of Ariadel, her face and skin burned, their daughter so close to that terrible power. It filled Vidarian with an inarticulate fury whose strength both wounded and disturbed him.

Rai's cold nose pressed into his palm, and he jumped, then relaxed, though not before he'd earned a startled glance from the attendant who led them through the halls. *I know she believes the fire goddess would never have harmed Ailenne,* Rai said, and Vidarian scratched the top of the wolf's head, careful to avoid his barbed spines.

It's one thing to believe that because you want it to be true, and another to be able to understand objectively that all of the goddesses are dangerous, Vidarian thought back, working to make his thoughts as clear as possible. It was much more difficult than simply speaking, and he had no real way of knowing whether Rai understood him, but it was not a sentiment he wanted overheard. For an instant he thought of how he would react to Ailenne being in the presence of the Starhunter, and suppressed the thought quickly. It was never possible to know when she would be listening.

Rai did not answer, but nudged himself closer as they walked.

At length—though more quickly than it seemed they had made the reverse journey—they arrived at the Library's main entrance, by way of the water gardens that connected the palace to the Library complex. There the attendant bowed them into the charge of one of the Library's many secretaries, who took them down into the main colonnaded thoroughfare, then quickly into a side passageway, and then a study chamber, where an elaborately costumed figure waited.

It took him several long moments to recognize her. Her face had been painted white, her lips a vivid red, but smaller than her natural features. Charcoal returned her eyebrows above the white powder, and tiny jewels had been fixed to her forehead in the shape of a pair of arced wings. Her hair, which he had rarely seen other than freely falling or practically knotted, had been elaborately braided into two crown-like shapes, each studded with pearls and fragrant white flowers. Silk swathed her body, red and black like his own, but several more layers and voluminous sleeves all atop a kind of white silk shift. Ailenne slept in a carrying basket that rested atop the large polished study table.

It was difficult even to think while taking all of this in, much less to remember their argument, but Ariadel was under no such impairment, herself.

"You're right," she admitted. "I should have talked to you about Sharli first." The words burst out of her, strange from her nobly painted lips, as if they'd been bubbling within her for hours. "I was so frustrated with—when we arrived—how they . . ." She trailed off, blinking, somewhere between heartache and rage.

Rai nudged his hand again, and Vidarian started, then took a step toward Ariadel. She closed the distance between them, answering his uncertainty about whether she could be touched in such elaborate costume. The layers of silk crushed between them, but she succeeded in laying her head against his chest, just below his chin.

"I don't know what I could have done if she'd been hurt," she said, then lost her voice again. "I just—I knew—"

"You knew that she would be safe with the same intuition that told you Sharli would receive your commune," he finished for her, and she nodded. Her sorrow had cut through his anger, evaporating it, leaving clearer thoughts behind. When she had communed with Sharli before, she had been similarly sure, and confirmed in her certainty; when Vidarian had spoken to the Starhunter, there had always been a palpable feeling that the goddess welcomed his contact, even demanded it. Sharli could be a violent goddess, but rarely to those so devoted to her as Ariadel.

"I'm sorry I've made this so difficult," he sighed, and she pulled away to look at him. The makeup was smudged but still otherworldly.

"You had rather a bit more on your mind," she said, with half of a smile that was relief, pain, and fatigue for them both all wrapped together. She blinked, reaching a hand to fuss with the makeup, then looked at him again, the liquid darkness of her eyes as arresting as it had ever been, slicing straight through him to a self he had never been completely sure he had. "We have so little time to be ourselves."

Ailenne stirred, and Ariadel turned toward her. Beside the basket on the polished table was another hamper heaped with scrolls, bottles, and what appeared to be tiny bags of herbs and preserved fruit. "They gave me all this," she said ruefully. "The Qui take childbearing very seriously. It is steeped in ritual and proscribed nutrition. For imperials especially."

"Is that all this is about?" He gestured to the costume, first hers and then his own. He was half surprised they hadn't given Rai some sort of drapery.

"I don't think they entirely know what to make of us," she said. "I came to the Library to find out what this makeup meant. It seems less important now."

He placed a hand on her shoulder, and she covered it with one of her own, while they watched Ailenne sleep. Rai pressed his head between them, sniffing at the table and the hamper of herbs.

"The Emperor advised that we quietly leave tonight, if we want to avoid the banquet and several more days here," he said at last.

Ariadel chuckled. "My uncle, long ago, had a silver toy, a long tube with glass at either end, and inside tiny mirrored chambers filled with sparkling bits. It was counterweighted, so once you turned it and looked inside, it never seemed to stop moving. The more you tried to make it stop, the more it would go." Ailenne stirred again, and Ariadel placed a hand on the basket, rocking it gently until she returned to sleep. "Part of me will be relieved to leave this place. But I wonder if that is just a desire to stop the glass again."

CHAPTER EIGHT
THE JADE PHOENIX

They spent the day in the Library, both to allay any suspicions and to allow Khalesh, who had broken into a sweat when he learned of their near departure, to glean as much as he could from the stacks in the little time they had left.

The big man had an uncanny endurance for research, and to Vidarian's knowledge had left the Library only to bathe, taking his meals in the study rooms and hardly appearing to sleep at all. Tephir had commented on his energy as well, adding privately that several of the under-secretaries had reported his ingestion of an herbal paste they feared the palace physicians would not have approved. The gryphon had decided not to act on these reports, which was a bit of a relief; Vidarian did not relish the idea of attempting to pry books away from the burly Animator, even when he wasn't herbally enhanced.

Thalnarra and Iridan had both spent their time closeted with Asalet, the ancient Librarian, and Eoin, her ward. When Ariadel and Vidarian joined them, they were in the middle of a complicated conversation about the nature of existence. By her expression, Ariadel seemed to be gathering some of their meaning, but Vidarian was at first quite sure they were speaking another language entirely.

At last, after a heated exchange (which was still no more comprehensible than what had preceded it, to Vidarian), they seemed to notice their guests and turned the conversation toward more practical matters: namely, where they were going and how they were going to get there. Eventually, Tephir and Khalesh joined them, and together they pored over a rather remarkable topographic map of the entire continent, formed out of the strange elementally "invisible" fire energy—the same that had created the illusions of bamboo that hid the entrance to the Librarian's lair. It was an ancient artifact, they said, older than the Qui Empire itself, and the making of its manner of device had been lost.

Thalnarra lay like a lion statue, reclining with her head raised and her foreclaws before her. Ailenne's basket rested between her formidable talons, positioned so that the baby could look up into the gryphon's face. Most infants would have cried at the sight of the massive beaked face, but Ailenne had loved Thalnarra from the moment she first set eyes on her. She was more ambivalent toward Altair, to the wind gryphon's dismay; this preference had led Ailenne's inevitable fire priestess attendants in Alorea to conclude that her already highly attuned fire sensitivity responded to Thalnarra's. For her part, Thalnarra seemed both pleased and amused by Ailenne's attention, and indulged it whenever she could; she insisted grandly to Altair that fire had nothing to do with it, and the little girl clearly could identify a superior personality when she encountered one.

At the moment, they were studying the southern continent, and the map, responding to their attention, had illustrated as much detail as any of them knew about that uncharted place. As far as the owl-gryphons could tell—and Iridan, who had some distant recollection of such objects—the map was telepathic in its function, responding primarily to the thoughts of those in its vicinity. It could show only what any of its immediate observers knew, in whatever conscious and subconscious corners of their minds.

An irregularly-shaped territory toward the center of the continent glowed with pale green light—the last known territory of these "neutral" people who had been entrusted, so long ago, with the key to the annihilation device the Company now sought. It was here they would have to go, and the formidable distance in between sank Vidarian's heart. The Company had still been eerily silent, which could only mean that they were winging in the correct direction with all the speed their technology could bring to bear.

The gates that the gryphons could create, this time, were of no use. In order to safely travel, at least one of those contributing energy to the opening of such a gate must have traveled to the target location before, in order to fix it in their minds and spirits. A blind gate-opening, Vidarian had discovered the hard way, was a suggestion that would elicit violent expressions of alarm from the creatures.

// *Only one portal has the strength to take us to a location not known by a gate-*

wielder, // Thalnarra said, her voice ringed with thoughtful speculation like roasting hickory. // *The Great Gate.* //

Asalet gave a soft *hrrr* noise, and nodded. // *Our star passage can take you from here as far as Jiquin,* // she said, then tilted her head. The map reacted to her voice, or perhaps her thought (they weren't quite sure), and a port town on Qui's far western border began to glow. // *From there . . .* //

Tephir tipped his beak downward, nervousness evident in his roused feathers. // *Our maps indicate that a Qui skyship from Jiquin could follow an Ishmanti sea route northwest by north to Maitri—* // Now the southern-most city in Ishmanti took on Jiquin's glow— // *and from there . . .* //

"The Ishmanti trade-routes are too dangerous," Ariadel said. "None but the Ishmanti themselves can travel them safely."

"I know them," Eoin said.

"Of course you do," Vidarian murmured, and Asalet chuckled.

Ariadel gave them a cool look that was not quite a glare. "We could return to Val Imris, or even Val Harlon, then fly south."

Vidarian sighed, staring at the map, then shook his head. "With Tephir's location device, we have a potential advantage over the Company. Carrying it across lands they control would be more dangerous than any unknown route. But if we stay far from their ships . . . from Jiquin . . . ?" He looked at Tephir.

// *From there,* // Tephir continued, his cheek-feathers fluffed in anticipation of another rebuke, // *the ship would travel overland, across Ishmanti and approaching the Great Gate from the south.* //

"The Company never made inroads into Ishmanti," Vidarian began, and both Eoin and Khalesh nodded agreement. He turned back to Ariadel. "It will be safer for us to remain as far away from any areas they control as we can." The next words tangled behind his tongue, but he forced them out. "But it may be safer for you to return to Val Imris, with Ailenne."

Ariadel's eyes widened, and she opened her mouth to object—then, to his relief, closed it and stopped. Her face said without words how much she loathed the notion of retreating to any suggested safety, but the risk to Ailenne was fresh on both their minds.

Finally it was Thalnarra who broke their impasse.

// *Gryphon hatchlings are not long sheltered from the ferocities of the world,* // Thalnarra said. // *And most have not a quarter of her gifts.* // She bent her head toward Ailenne, who cooed with delight.

"She's five months old," Vidarian said. "You're not suggesting she can defend herself?"

// *I am stating that no harm will come to her in our care,* // she replied, a wreath of pointed amusement hot as glowing coals around her words. // *And that I agree that she is safer with us than in the imperial palace. Her presence there would also make Calphille and Revelle greater targets.* //

None of it was near what Vidarian wanted to consider, and so he put it from his mind, the better to keep a grip on sanity. He glared hard at Thalnarra, daring her to show the slightest uncertainty. None surfaced; her unsettlingly red eyes were lambent with the opposite, and a subtle threat, not to him but to any who would attempt to harm Ailenne. When she grew older, Vidarian noted, he was going to have to keep an eye on that; Thalnarra had already beguiled one young human in Vidarian's presence into joining her flight as a gryphon-ward.

At length he gave in with an exasperated wave of his hands, though not without misgiving. But Thalnarra's logic was sound, and no small part of him would be relieved to have his family near him. He turned back to Asalet and Tephir. "You say that a skyship can await us in Jiquin?"

Asalet inclined her head. // *We can have one ready to sail by morning.* //

～～～

This time there were no servants, and they packed their own belongings— what they had brought in leather Alorean packs, and the few gifts they would take with them in wicker Qui baskets. More baskets contained provisions— primarily the leaf-wrapped rice-and-nutmeat sticky cakes that were far more nutritious than they looked—which the Library had ordered, ostensibly for a private research expedition.

Their arrival had been hosted in a formal antechamber of the Library, but their departure would be quite the opposite. At midnight, well after the Library was officially secured for the night (so as to spare Tephir's people any suspicion), a mute under-secretary came to escort them from their guest chambers. He led them down into the palace's subterranean grain storage—reserves of rice and preserved foods that could sustain not only the palace but all of Shen Ti for months in the event of a siege—and thence through a secret door into the Library itself, bypassing the thoroughfare entrance.

A round-walled chamber to one side of Tephir's receiving room appeared to have been built to support a gate—a star passage, as the Qui called them. Thin columns of grey stone topped with amplification spheres lay at the cardinal directions, each sphere colored according to its element. Already waiting upon their arrival were four owl-gryphons they had never met, along with Altair, who had been living among his nocturnal kin during their stay at the palace.

Nazelle quietly took their entrance into the chamber as an opportunity to say farewell. Calphille had ordered her to attend them in Qui, but not beyond. She embraced both of them in turn, then knelt to whisper a handful of words in a papery language to Ailenne. Vidarian was touched to see the warm sadness in the dryad's eyes as she withdrew.

Akeo, not entirely to Vidarian's surprise, was also in attendance. As the owl-gryphons took their positions and began the meditations that Vidarian had come to associate with gate preparation, the old ambassador approached them, bowing first and deepest to Ariadel, and then to Vidarian.

Upon seeing him, Ariadel shifted Ailenne's carrying basket gently to her left arm, then clasped Akeo's hand with her right. "We are so grateful for your counsel and assistance," she said, and Vidarian added his agreement. "We would have been long adrift without you."

"I'm not so certain of that," Akeo replied, bowing again over her hand. "But I could hardly turn down a clandestine excursion into the bowels of the Grand Library."

"We do apologize for the hour," Vidarian began.

Akeo chuckled. "Men my age rarely sleep. You shall see."

"The more time to scheme, yes?"

"Quite!" the ambassador smiled, guileless and wise at once as was his wont.

Tephir arrived last, equipped to within an inch of his life. He wore an elaborate harness covered with tiny pouches in various sizes; Vidarian hoped he would be able to fly in it. The question would have to come up later rather than sooner, though; Tephir bore Asalet's blessing of luck upon their journey, and once he had announced it, his fellow owl-gryphons opened up their gate.

The spectacular array of colors that opened in the center of the room always had a way of pulling Vidarian's stomach into his ankles. The disorienting display only lasted a few moments, though—and then a red lantern-lit cityscape opened before them.

This time Vidarian went first, attempting to keep a grip on his supper as he did so. When he emerged on the far side, merely feeling as though a strange lifetime had passed in the instant of his crossing—rather than truly being abducted by the chaos goddess—he let out a breath he hadn't realized he'd been holding. He remembered to clear out of the way of the next arrival just in time; Ariadel stepped through with Ailenne sitting up and cooing alertly in her basket.

The gate had placed them before a long pier, the city ranged behind them. It seemed that Asalet had been quite anxious to assist them in putting Qui to their rudder as fast as humanly—or superhumanly—possible. A man uniformed in black silk and an impressive emerald badge of office awaited them.

"I am Yuan Wan Hao, captain of the *Jade Phoenix*," he said, bowing adroitly, and not deep. "We are instructed to take you to your destination without question, and this we will do. You will find my sailors reticent to speak with you, and this is for the best; when they return home, this voyage will simply not have happened for them."

"I understand," Vidarian replied, taking in the man's anxiousness and trying to project an air of calm and comprehension. "We appreciate your service greatly, and will make it as easy as we can upon your crew."

Captain Hao bowed again, this time a little deeper, with gratitude, and then gestured for them to follow him down the pier. Vidarian spared one last glance for the gate behind them—Thalnarra and Altair were crossing, arrayed in their armor—wondering if he would ever see Qui, or Emperor Ziao, again.

The *Jade Phoenix* was sleek and beautiful, quite unlike the boxier batten-sailed vessels they had fought at Isrinvale. Its hull was polished pine, soft enough to allow seamless joins, and it seemed possessed of no straight lines whatever. Even the forecastle, which towered high over the main deck, seemed to slope up out of its planks, all curves and ornamented corners. Red silk pennants festooned its masts, so light that they snapped and billowed even in the faint breeze.

Its sail configuration was more similar to the Qui ships they'd seen in that battle and in both Alorean and Qui records—Qui ships favored a long and articulated rudder sail that now reminded Vidarian of the tail of a dragon carp. It explained some of their agility in the air, and he resolved to speak with a shipbuilder about it when they returned to Alorea. Also noticeably different were the ship's wing-sails, which—uniquely, Vidarian thought—were four instead of two, long and slender rather than voluminous.

At length all of their party had passed through the gate: Thalnarra, Altair, and Tephir; Khalesh, Eoin, and Iridan; and Vidarian, Ariadel, and Ailenne. Some of the Library's most trusted attendants had assisted in bundling across their supplies, but this they managed efficiently, and at last they stood on their respective sides of the gate. Akeo lifted his hands in farewell, and bowed; Vidarian did the same, and the gate winked out of being.

Captain Hao's sailors, as he had promised, were efficient and silent, seeming interested in witnessing the least they possibly could. In a short time they were all bundled into the *Jade Phoenix* and settled in their chambers; the holds of the *Phoenix* were honeycombed with compartments for all purposes. The gryphons were bunked in a chamber that did seem specifically intended to house large animals (though thankfully, by its fresh cedar and straw smell, it had been unused for some time), and the rest occupied smaller holds alongside precious cargo: crates of fine porcelain, apothecary bottles, and fragrant dried delicacies. It appeared that their journey would be couched as a mercantile one, and perhaps any observers would dismiss or not recognize the inappropriateness of sending such a fine ship on a merchant errand.

When the ship launched, it was not with the abrupt lift upward that accompanied what Vidarian knew of skyship embarkment. Rather there was a gentle outward push, as though the vessel were fond of the pier and reluctant to leave it. Then the upward motion engaged, all more smoothly than he had experienced on an Alorean ship. The captain eventually came to personally ask after their comfort, and Vidarian inquired; the hull, Captain Hao explained, was embedded not only with air crystals but earth ones, though they had to be carefully spaced. Earth had the ability to repel itself against other organic material, and so the launch was much gentler than an air-only vessel. He was justifiably proud of this attribute of the *Phoenix*, but admitted some disappointment in the failing earth crystals, which, according to his reading, had once been much stronger.

Eoin spent his time with the navigator, closeted in the tiny aftcastle when not standing abovedecks and gesturing at the stars. At first they seemed to argue, the navigator gesturing at his charts and Eoin pointing up at one constellation after another, both rattling off long and intense strings of Qui that Vidarian couldn't even come close to following. Captain Hao eventually had to intervene, and, after listening to more respectful explanations from both men, nodded to Eoin, and waved his hands at the navigator's charts. The slim officer was clearly not pleased, but bowed to his captain, and set about laying their course, murmuring questions to Eoin every now and then.

Ariadel, Ailenne in her arms and wrapped in quilted silk blankets that had been a gift from the empress, watched all of this from Vidarian's side with little comfort. As the *Phoenix* angled out over the wide, dark ocean, there was little upon which to fix their fears; the Ishmanti routes were entirely over water, and if they were to go astray, there would be little sign until they failed to see land when they should.

Nor, over the next three days of sail, was there an opportunity to be much concerned. The skies were sedate, streaked with high clouds, and far below the ocean—greener, Vidarian thought, than the West Sea—remained as it ever was, hardly fathomable. They navigated by the stars and sailed continuously, the crew working in shifts to keep the vessel moving; it would be six days altogether until they reached their destination.

On the third day the Ishmanti coast came into view, just as it should, and a ripple of unspoken tension lifted from the ship. Ariadel said that she had overheard the navigator expressing disbelief that Eoin's route had worked, but indeed it had, and the coastal city of Maitri hugged the cragged shore far below them. The Ishmanti had no skyships of their own, as far as anyone knew, and so they would sail above its country unchallenged.

Now that his navigational duties were done, Eoin himself became more sociable; a relief following days of quiet tension. The gryphons spent most of their time in flight, having been mostly land-bound during the stay in Qui, and Khalesh and Iridan remained closeted with the copied scrolls they had managed to wheedle from Asalet.

The Ain Oilean man had traveled far, and knew an astonishing amount of botany, herbology, and animal physics, but he had never seen the Windsmouth with his own eyes, and clearly relished the opportunity. It was unusual for any son or daughter of the tiny green island nation to be so adventurous—some of their sailors would venture as far as Alorea, but Eoin was the first Vidarian had met abroad. Vidarian found him at the bow two days after they had passed the coastline, shading his eyes with a hand and looking to the north.

"The Ishmanti have a legend about the Windsmouth," he said when Vidarian joined him. "As well they might, since its foothills would be on their horizon, and they could pass across it no more easily than could the Aloreans. It was said to be a great Ice Wall that blocked out the sky and marked the edge of the world."

"They thought it was an actual wall made out of ice?"

"Improbably enough, yes."

"Don't they know that such a thing is impossible, structurally? The ice would collapse on itself."

Eoin chuckled; impressed, by the lift of his eyebrows. "Well done. Yes.

Even the lower foothills of the Windsmouth are nearly half a mile tall. No structure of ice could sustain that weight without crushing itself."

"Makes a fine tale, though."

"It does."

As if their talk of ice had summoned it, a cold wind suddenly cut across the starboard bow, bringing lances of biting cold with it. At first Vidarian thought it was merely the shock of the cold air that stung his cheek, but when he raised his hand to ward it off, more knives struck: needles of frozen rain.

That was all the warning they had before the storm struck. A howling snowstorm materialized out of the morning fog that billowed below them, rising up to swallow the *Jade Phoenix*. Sails rattled, decks creaked, and in seconds none could see even a handspan in front of their faces for the snow.

Vidarian threw himself to the deck instinctively, throwing out an arm blindly to pull Eoin down beside him. As they clung to the deck, his one thought was of reaching Ariadel and ensuring she was safe below. A voice called out over the ringing of the alarm bell, muffled by the snow: *"All hands to lifelines!"*

Chapter Nine

Windsmouth

Vidarian kept his hand locked around Eoin's shirtsleeve and clung to the deck. When he'd thrown himself down, he'd landed hard against an iron cleat—not enough to break bone, but close. It was a painful bit of luck, and gave them something to hold onto as the ship pitched to port under a blast of storm wind.

He shook with the urge to get to the ladders, and down into the hold to find Ariadel—but knew that letting go of the cleat at this moment was likely suicide. Footsteps far away thudded, then slid across the deck as sailors scrambled for safety—punctuated by their cries as the wind, ice, or shuddering ship inevitably knocked them off their feet. There were as yet no screams, for they had lifelines; Vidarian and Eoin had none, and no one was likely to find them here at the bow.

For now, adrenaline kept them warm, but the temperature was plummeting, and soon the cold would set in. Vidarian shouted, trying to attract the attention of one of the sailors, knowing that with the wind spiraling around them no one would hear, much less gauge their location.

Eoin edged toward the rail, and Vidarian shook his sleeve; it was a noble idea, but a foolhardy one. The man hesitated, then edged back toward the cleat to lock his arm with Vidarian's.

He was about to shout, to at least yell about not having a plan, even if that would make one less likely to materialize, when a blanket of energy dropped around his mind, warm and uncanny. He knew that Eoin sensed it too, not from the man's suddenly stiffening arm, but because the proximity of his mind was almost physical, a presence clearer than his body.

His mind quested outward instinctively, and that shelter proved to contain all nine of their party. All of their thoughts thundered into him, drowning out his suddenly tenuous self.

Knowledge suffused his mind, blinding, burning—but three things most of all:

Ariadel was safe, surrounded by blankets and straw in the hold;

So was Ailenne, and Rai with her;

Thalnarra and Altair were still out there, in the storm.

The gryphons were being thrown by the blasting snow, their wings strained near to breaking. They alternated attempting to fight the storm and letting it carry them, but panic shot through their veins as the gusts took them further from the *Jade Phoenix*. Most disturbing of all was that the wind was not wind, not composed of air, but something else entirely. Neither had ever seen anything like this, nor heard of it, not in their own lifetimes or the melded experiences of their flight's memory-keepers—

He clawed at his forehead, wracked with pain as the barrage of thoughts grew more intense, each concept radiating out into a thousand more, and then a thousand thousand, memories connecting to memories. He was an osprey, a fire priestess, an Animator, a naturalist—

"Apologies," came Iridan's voice, and Vidarian felt himself mouthing the word, so close was the connection still. The cascading thoughts stopped their relentless advance, dimming into moth wings that battered at his skull, but with muffled strikes. *"The contact can be overwhelming at first."*

"Iridan?" Vidarian asked, and heard his words echo again and again—he closed his eyes against a wave of dizziness. In that moment Rai sensed where he was, and lurched—Vidarian sharpened his thoughts. "Stay there! Protect Ailenne!" Reluctantly, Rai acquiesced.

"I reached out to you, Captain," Iridan said, and as before Vidarian's lips moved to shape the words of their own volition. *"As you observed —we must help the gryphons."*

Thalnarra and Altair were strong, but were fast growing exhausted against the storm. The dimming of their minds sent a panicked wave of adrenaline sizzling through Vidarian's veins again. "How?"

"A sphere of fire energy will protect you from the storm's assault."

Vidarian wanted to argue, but speaking this way with the automaton was more draining than summoning fire. He pulled it from himself like a thread, reaching into the ever-present furnace that seemed to live just below his heart and drawing coals of energy from it. Clutching the deck closely for balance, he coaxed the fire outward, willing it to expand.

To his surprise, as the corona of energy widened, it pushed back the snow-storm in its path. The flakes of ice danced outward, avoiding the fire, not melting or resisting it as water would have, but making way for it as though conscious.

"Very good, Captain. Now you must reach Ariadel, and pool your energies."

The automaton's voice nearly made him lose his grip on the fire, but he held it close, even when it lashed back out at him painfully. With his free hand, he pulled at Eoin, whom, now that the snow had receded, he could now see. The man nodded, and, holding his breath, Vidarian inched across the deck. He left the cleat and pulled himself with his newly freed hand across the slick planks, sticking close to the rail in case the wind could sweep up and knock them back.

But the wind, too, danced away from their growing hemisphere of fire energy, raging and howling but never within the fire's touch.

Handspan by handspan they crossed the deck, pressed to the wet pine, their guts lurching when the storm winds pulled the *Phoenix* sharply to port or starboard. But it never threw them, and finally they reached the forecastle ladder.

They fell, more than climbed, down into the hold, quaking with reaction, hands and arms numb. Vidarian's head swam as sudden heat enshrouded his head after the wind's icy onslaught.

"You must move quickly!" The voice, half his own and half in his mind, jolted him out of his congealed thoughts, and he stumbled toward the next ladder, and the next, working toward the cabin where a throbbing in his mind told him Ariadel and Ailenne sheltered. Eoin was still with him, and they staggered together, careening into bulkheads when the ship pitched.

By the time they reached the cabin, Vidarian's mind and body had adjusted to the temperature, and strength was returning to his limbs. Ariadel met him at the hatch, stumbling herself as the ship rocked. Over her shoulder, Vidarian could see Ailenne, inexplicably sleeping peacefully in her nest of silk blankets.

"Iridan wants us to——" he began, then stopped when she nodded, taking his hands with her own.

Fire energy roared into him, stronger than anything he'd felt since Thalnarra confronted him before the opening of the Great Gate. He nearly lost his balance, and then——

"Expand the shield!"

This time Iridan's words (spoken also by Eoin and Ariadel) held a command, and Vidarian was feeding Ariadel's energy into the shield he'd created nearly before he realized what he was doing. He had never channeled or shaped another person's energy before——save perhaps Ruby's, and that had been altogether strange and different——nor had he built a shield this large, but Iridan's demand showed him the way.

Eerie calm descended upon the ship as his shield reached outward, pushing the storm back wherever it passed. A hot sweat broke out on his forehead as he continued to expand the circle, reaching outward into the sky as fast as he could make the energy move. Ariadel, too, had clenched her teeth, and was sweating with the effort of pulling as much fire energy into herself and then into his hands as she could.

Just when he thought he would falter, unable to keep extending himself into nothingness, the shield found Altair, who desperately angled his wings toward the ship, near collapse. The sudden flare of Altair's presence, not just projected through Iridan but within Vidarian's elemental grasp, gave him a surge of hope and renewed determination.

He pushed onward, reaching, stretching——and she was there, falling now, her wings caving inward beneath the wind and exhaustion.

As she plummeted Vidarian reached out frantically with the shield, stretching himself, stretching the energy so quickly that he now pulled energy from Ariadel rather than being fed it.

He reached again, a flailing grasp——and surrounded her, shouting with victory.

But though the shield had spread around her, it could not repair her collapsed wings, and she fell again, passing beyond its reach.

Stunned, Vidarian stretched again—but there was nothing. He was at the end of his reserves, and only tremblingly held the shield as open and wide as it was.

There was a thud from above, almost a distant crash, made even more distant by the expansion of his awareness into the shield, which now encapsulated the entire warship and far beyond. A muffled cry, aquiline, a gryphon's—angry, defiant.

It was Altair, and as soon as he'd landed on the deck above, he threw his energy into Vidarian's, a torrent of pure wind.

Vidarian would have blacked out, he was sure, but Iridan's mind was there, still connecting and sustaining them all. It held him into consciousness, would not let him acquiesce. His legs faltered, but Ariadel was still there, grimly leaning against his weight, steadying him.

The shield grew again, faster this time, its melded energies accelerating it far beyond what Vidarian could ever have hoped to do alone. Fire was stubborn, volatile—air knew only motion. So Altair's energy catapulted them onward, and when they found Thalnarra again, it enveloped her, lifted her—seemed to use the storm's energy itself to direct her back up and toward the ship.

There was a creak of deck plank, but it was their telepathic closeness that made Vidarian aware of the moment when Altair pushed his aching body back into the sky, pumping wings that screamed with exhaustion and clawing his way back into the air. He dipped sideways in a controlled fall that took him below the ship to where he could see Thalnarra, and there directed his own energy, taking it from Vidarian, to lift her back onto the deck of the *Jade Phoenix*.

Once Altair took his energy from Vidarian, the shield began to collapse, but now that the gryphons were safely on board Vidarian allowed it to do so, stopping it only when it was close to the tips of the sails above and below.

The crisis past, Iridan gently released their minds, and physical sensation rushed back into Vidarian's awareness. He nearly stumbled with its sudden force, but it came with a welcome renewal of strength in his limbs. Together he and Ariadel shared a glance, then closed the cabin hatch and scrambled for the ladders, leaving a dazed Eoin to slump by the bulkhead and attend Ailenne if need be.

They rushed up to the topdeck, passing dazed sailors who still clung to their lifelines, and found the gryphons strewn between the forecastle and mainmast. Thalnarra was very still, and the sight of her prone form caught in Vidarian's throat—but as Altair lifted his head to look at her, she stirred, and Vidarian breathed again.

He started toward them, calling for help from the sailors, when a muffled cry of surprise set him spinning back toward Ariadel. She held a hand raised to the horizon, pointing, her other hand raised unconsciously to her face.

"It's the Windsmouth," Ariadel said, incredulous. "We're south of it!"

ᔓᔔᔓ

The storm had indeed carried them the remainder of the distance toward the mountain range. With the help of the fire shield, Captain Hao and his men were able to guide the ship toward the mountains and down, angling to reach land as quickly as they could. Only once they could see birds passing between the boughs of the trees below did Vidarian dare release the shield, afraid that the storm could descend again as quickly and undetectably as it had the first time.

His head spun and he dropped to his knees on the deck once the energy was released, taking the last of his adrenaline with it. Ariadel managed to keep her feet, and was calling out in Qui for something—tea, it turned out. In moments a hot cup in the handleless Qui style was being pressed between his hands.

"What *was* that?" Vidarian asked Altair, who groaned as he raised his head. It was an unsettlingly odd sound from a gryphon, his long-throated voice somewhere between a horse and a tiger. "If it was a storm, why didn't you sense it coming?"

// *It wasn't air,* // Altair said, shaken as Vidarian had never heard him. // *It was—a foreign energy, tremendously dangerous, almost a consciousness unto itself. I think it was a fragment of the Everstorm. //*

Thalnarra lifted her head with the heaviness of a much older creature, and turned a glassy eye on Vidarian. *// How did your fire repel it? Mine was consumed instantly. //*

"I—don't know," Vidarian said, blinking at Ariadel, who also shook her head as they both realized that something should have seemed amiss when Thalnarra couldn't return to the ship with her own energy. "Iridan?" he asked the air, then waited for the automaton's voice. But there was none; he had left their minds, and was now "only" wherever in the hold his body was.

Thalnarra sighed, her chest heaving like a bursting barrel. *// You have always seemed intent on proving every elemental principle wrong, why not this one, I suppose? //* Her crossness should have been chastening, but Vidarian could only be relieved that it seemed she had not been seriously injured.

Altair, however, remained in a kind of shock, his facial feathers roused and trembling. He tilted his head at Thalnarra, one eye pinning. *// There were always stories about the Everstorm . . . especially among air wielders. That it was no element touchable by gryphonkind, and so not even the strongest wind magicians could traverse it. That it was made of Ice. //* The peculiar way he emphasized the word flickered a memory in the back of Vidarian's mind—he had heard another gryphon speak it that way, once . . .

Thalnarra's eyes opened fully now, though she did not raise her head. Her presence expanded itself as if she was about to speak, but then receded, banked like the embers of an old fire.

"It might explain why his elemental nature would repel it, and ours alone would not," Ariadel said, a muted note in her voice that echoed Altair's distress.

// I'm going to sleep, // Thalnarra announced, and closed her eyes again.

"Are you sure—" Vidarian began.

// She'll be all right, // Altair murmured, his juniper-sharp voice pitched for the humans alone. *// She's unhurt, but sleep is best for now. //*

Meanwhile, their ears crackled with the ship's swift descent, which had now brought them below the tops of the towering trees that bordered the southern edge of the Windsmouth. Here Captain Hao held its altitude, assured that they were out of range of the storm, or as close to as they could expect.

The captain had been occupied with the marshaling of the ship and seeing to his sailors, but now he approached them, the stiffness in his bow a reach for protocol in the kind of situation that burned officer's manuals to cinders.

"Your sailors acquitted themselves well, Captain," Vidarian greeted him, returning the bow with what he hoped was a bit less stiffness. He was gratified to see a line of tension dissipate from Hao's shoulders.

"They did," the Qui captain replied, "and your observation is high praise. We owe you our lives."

"Your *Phoenix* has carried us safely to our destination," Vidarian replied. "It is all we could have asked for."

Hao nodded, then cleared his throat. "There is, then, the matter of where the *Phoenix* flies next," he said. "We cannot return the way we came, and risk sailing into the teeth of that same storm."

Vidarian's heart sank as he realized that the man was right. They could hardly retrace their course, not for months with any certainty. "You could sail north," he suggested, "and return to follow the overland trade routes back to Shen Ti."

"And venture across Alorea, with its marauding small lords and their shapechanger steeds? I think not, Captain."

His mingled concern and disdain for what remained of the Alorean Sky Knights gave Vidarian a pang, even though he had no love for those Knights who had refused or ignored the call to return to Val Imris and protect their Empress-Dowager. He had grown up idolizing the knights and could not easily relinquish the notion of their heroism. Rather than argue, "There is another option," he said, hesitant to suggest it, but the sharp interest in the captain's face compelled him to continue. "With a fresh peace accord between Alorea and Qui, you will also have, by extension, a peace with the West Sea Kingdom."

"Pirates?" Captain Hao drew up, on the edge of affront.

Vidarian lifted a calming hand. "Their queen was once an Alorean captain, and before that, my first mate." Hao's eyebrows lifted. "She is utterly trustworthy, and if we were able to make contact with her in Val Imris—as I believe Iridan should be able to do, with the use of your relay-sphere—I know that she would welcome you in their West Sea stronghold. It is a sight to behold, and would be a benefit to Emperor Ziao to secure their alliance besides."

Captain Hao thought on this for a moment, then bowed. "I must of course contact Shen Ti regarding this. But I thank you for the suggestion. My crew will help you disembark."

Hao's crew, some of them still wrapped in protective head-scarves from the snow, unloaded the party's supplies when the *Phoenix* briefly landed. The imperial palace had included a small train of three verali to carry them. The Qui, it seemed, had discovered and appreciated the long-necked beasts' usefulness in carrying supplies. These were a longer-coated variant, black in body with white faces and feet, but they smelled as badly as Vidarian remembered. At his request, they picketed the beasts along the tree line, far on the edge of the mountain meadow where the *Jade Phoenix* had touched down.

When the Qui crew had returned aboard, Captain Hao descended the ramp to bid them farewell. He bowed deeply to Vidarian, a different air about him, a kind of energy in his eyes when he lifted his head. "Your advice was most prescient," he said. "The West Sea Kingdom had already begun overtures to Shen Ti, and they do indeed find it convenient that we should journey there." The Captain hesitated, then bowed again, very slightly, seeming not to know the proper protocol. "This will mean much to my family. I thank you for the suggestion."

"Fly safely, Captain," Vidarian said, first giving a small bow and then reaching out to clasp the man's forearm. "Please convey my fond greetings to Queen Marielle."

"I shall," Captain Hao bowed again, then returned up the ramp to his ship, a lightness in his step. His gratitude seemed sincere, but once on the gangplank he did not look back.

Together—three gryphons, six humans, and three disinterested verali—

they watched the *Jade Phoenix* ascend, finally drifting west over the treetops and out of sight. As they watched, Vidarian felt his eye continually drawn to the tree line itself. He realized that he knew this clearing, or one very like it, here in the Windsmouth's southern shadow.

Just then, a scarf-wrapped crewman from the *Jade Phoenix* came hurtling out of the forest, running recklessly fast. They only had a moment to take in what this meant before the scarf fell away, revealing a young and fine-boned face.

"Mey?" Vidarian gasped. Dread soaked through him, and he ran to the center of the clearing, hoping to find the *Phoenix* still in sight. She was not. "Thalnarra?" he shouted, but the three gryphons were already taking off, silently agreeing.

// *We'll bring them back,* // Thalnarra said, circling low around the clearing and then angling herself upward.

"You don't understand!" Mey cried, hauling on Vidarian's arm. He looked down at her, aghast—having no idea how one responded to being manhandled by an imperial princess.

The gryphons, with their eagle-sharp eyes, spotted them before Vidarian did, and screamed warnings, diving back down from their brief ascent. Beneath their cries, a particular unnerving howl echoed through the forest behind them.

"No," Vidarian said, shocked into speech at no one in particular. "It can't be . . ."

But it was.

He shoved Mey behind him, looking wildly around for Ariadel and Ailenne. "Sightwolves! Protect Ailenne, and the princess!"

CHAPTER TEN
SIANE

*// T*he princess? // Thalnarra bellowed. // *What fresh idiocy is this? //*

"I'll explain later!" Vidarian called, drawing his sword. He whispered energy into the blade, weaving water and fire the way old Meleaar had shown him. Tracing an eye around the tree line, he ran for the verali before he could decide on a more prudent tack. Without them, if the *Jade Phoenix* could not be summoned, they would starve.

The beasts were trembling with fear when he reached them. The call of the sightwolves echoed through the forest: an eerily intelligent overlapping cry, one wolf after another in a heart-stopping rhythm. He grabbed their lead ropes and hauled, snapping the knotted ends at their hindquarters when they leaned back in stiff-legged terror. At last the lead animal brayed and bolted, followed by the others, and Vidarian struggled to keep them pointed at the center of the clearing.

The verali wanted to circle, and he let them, keeping Ailenne and Mey in the center. The princess, for her part, seemed to have bent to reason, and held Ailenne's basket tight to her chest.

Ariadel stood just outside the circle, her face pointed toward the two girls, but her eyes focused somewhere distant, an expression that Vidarian recognized from past action. The energy that began to well up in her sent a chill down his spine. At the same time, Khalesh was pushing Iridan toward the circle of verali. Vidarian turned to them as they drew closer. "Iridan, can you contact the *Jade Phoenix*? They have a relay sphere!"

But the automaton seemed to be asleep while standing. He would move if guided by Khalesh's hand, then grow still again, his eyes dim.

"He's been like this since the storm," Khalesh grunted, but turned from his charge, focused, to Vidarian's relief, on assisting in their defense. From his pockets the big man drew several small brass spheres which, when tossed into the air, unfolded themselves into winged automata. They loosely resembled the hummingbird automata that had awakened in Val Imris, but those tiny birds were not dressed beak and claw in tiny glinting needles.

Khalesh gave them a command in a language Vidarian didn't recognize, and the birds each gave a tiny flute-like tweet, then buzzed away in three directions. The Animator was not done; to Vidarian's surprise, he went to the parrot cage that he had always insisted they haul everywhere, and opened it. The bird's eyes whirled into an awakeness of bright colors, and it hopped out onto his offered arm. He said more words in the archaic language, actually seeming to have a conversation this time, and as he did the parrot's eyes whirled red. When he finished speaking, the bird spread its wings—much wider than Vidarian had expected, the spread wingtips nearly as wide as he was tall—and launched itself, screeching a deafening repeating cry that cut beneath breastbone in its intensity, disorienting. At last, Khalesh drew on his glowing Animator's gloves and reached for a tube-shaped object at his side—a weapon of some sort.

"Can you wake Iridan?" Vidarian asked, and Khalesh's hand stopped. "We need to call back the *Jade Phoenix* if they can at all be reached."

Khalesh glanced at the tree line, then at Vidarian, clearly skeptical that they could defend the clearing alone, but nodded at last. He went to one of the verali, soothing it with a palm over its nose before rummaging through its packs.

The gryphons dove back into the clearing just as three wolves broke the tree line. Eoin shouted a warning when he sighted them, lifting and pointing a polished staff as long as he was tall.

They were smaller than Vidarian remembered, but his first reaction was a ripple of shock and unease—from Rai.

He stood in front of them all, growling, his formidable spines mantled, but recognition and uncertainty radiated from him in waves, dropping his lip in a moment of weakness that wolves knew only too well. Rai had never seen wolves before, except his own pack, in his dimmest and earliest memories.

The sightwolves, for their part, howled with recognition, calling him a name that had no human language counterpart. They echoed it between themselves with the same madness Vidarian remembered from his first excursion past the Windsmouth.

The clearing was too small for Rai to safely assume his dragon shape, barely large enough for the gryphons to have circled tightly into the air. Not only did the sightwolves recognize their larger thornwolf cousin, but they seemed to know how to attack him, circling him just beyond his reach, forcing him to turn or lose sight of them.

An arc of white light sizzled to Vidarian's left, immediately followed by a lupine howl of pain. One of the sightwolves cowered backwards, stumbling on numb feet.

Poised to one side of the gathered verali was Tephir, his foreclaws raised and gauntleted in elaborate worked silver studded with glowing blue elemental stones. He traced a symbol in the air with a talon blunted in nature but sharpened by metal, and where his claw-tip passed, blue light burned in the air. When he traced the symbol a second time, the elemental stones flashed and released another blast of white energy that struck the stunned sightwolf a second time, knocking it to the ground. It did not rise again. Vidarian resolved not to further underestimate the shy gryphon scholar.

The distraction freed Rai to leap for the throat of the middle wolf, overcoming his hesitancy, while Altair closed on the third. They dispatched the wolves quickly, and verified that the one Tephir had shocked was indeed dead, its heart given out under the repeated shocks.

More howls echoed from the forest beyond the fallen wolves.

Are you all right? Vidarian thought at Rai. He could never tell if his thoughts "carried," but this one must have, for Rai lifted his head from the wolf he'd just killed.

They are attacking my family, Rai said, a cold resolution in his voice that overlaid a complexity of thought that surprised Vidarian, though by now he was becoming accustomed to being surprised, if such a thing were possible, when it came to Rai. *That's all that matters.*

There was more beneath it, a discomfort, a kind of loneliness, but the sightwolves howled again, and there was no time.

The forest ahead was alive with yips and barks, howls and menacing thoughts that drifted toward them like waves of mist. It was an incoherent malice threaded with promises of vengeance, at its peak so fierce and disorienting that it made Vidarian's eyes water. Behind him, Ailenne started to cry, high and angry; he did not turn, for fear of taking his eyes off of the forest, but heard Ariadel running to her.

Eoin's second shout drew all of their attention to the right half of the clearing, and that was when a dozen wolves attacked from the left.

Thalnarra, still circling, dove into the center of the pack, screaming a challenge and flaring out her wings in a breathtaking display. It was meant to intimidate, and it did, drawing the wary attention of every wolf near her. She landed on one, claws and talons rending it apart before it could so much as howl, and lashed out at others, catching one across the throat and knocking another aside with a flaring wing. Then she mantled again, releasing a concentrated blast of fire energy that blew five wolves at once off their feet, crying out as their fur and skin sizzled. She was capable of much more, Vidarian knew, even as he marveled at the precision and texture of the fire attack—a weaving of energy calculated to blast in one direction with no backdraft—but, like Rai, was limited in her attack lest she sear the rest of the clearing.

Eoin, too, showed himself equally brave, running to attack two wolves that snarled behind Thalnarra. His staff was more effective than Vidarian would have guessed, fast for its lightness, and able to sweep his enemies off balance.

A sparkle darted through the air, and Khalesh's metal hummingbirds descended, spiraling toward the wolves that remained. Their attacks were too fast to witness, but they fell upon two wolves, glints of dark brass gathered on furred necks, and where they passed, their targets slumped to the ground and did not rise again.

// *The pack shouldn't be this large,* // Altair murmured, worry in his voice like slow-forming ice on an unexpected wind. // *Nor expending its warrior wolves over an empty clearing.* //

More wolves had lurked where Eoin had previously been, and now advanced—not to defend their fallen kin or attack those who had brought them down, but toward the center. Toward the verali—and Ailenne.

Now Vidarian cursed himself for positioning the pack animals near his daughter, even though they created a kind of shield—surely they must be drawing the wolves. In a rush of fury and panic he almost lashed out with uncontrolled energy, but just managed to withhold it, channeling his rage into a running charge at the stalking line of creatures.

Rai barked, a larger and more menacing sound than Vidarian last remembered, and charged with him, bellowing a challenge. The gryphons, too, both still on the ground, gouged furrows in the soil with the force of their leaps toward the verali, whose feet drummed the ground while they wheezed out a bizarre, high-pitched alarm call.

As they all drew near the circled verali, the advancing wolves turned to one side, falling back. Vidarian dared to hope that this was the last of them, and that, despite the calls that still echoed through the outer forest, the pack would withdraw.

But the wolves surged again, and too late Vidarian realized their trap. While they had drawn in toward the verali, more wolves poured out of the trees to overwhelm their concentrated position. There were at least twenty now, closing from three sides.

// *It isn't possible . . .* // Altair objected, and Vidarian was inclined to agree.

It wasn't merely that the pack was never-ending, or showed human intelligence—it showed *more* than human intelligence. It had known exactly what they were going to do and moved to outmaneuver them, calculated how to draw them into wasting what advantages they had before the real attack began.

"Ariadel," Vidarian yelled, while releasing a sear of braided water and fire energy that tore toward the wolves, consuming one where it stood. "Can Raven carry you, Mey, and Ailenne into the mountains?"

"Not here," she shouted back, having left Mey to harry another side of the pack with lances of fire. "Even if she wouldn't burn them—" she meant but did not say Mey, as Raven's firebird aura had no harmful effect on Ailenne— "there isn't enough room for her to take off." Panic tightened her voice.

"Altair, you're going to have to go after the *Phoenix*—they're our only hope now." Even as he spoke, he continued to unleash elemental energy on the wolves, taking out one at a time only to see it immediately replaced by another.

// *They could be leagues away by now,* // Altair began, but charged bodily at the wolves nearest him, raking at them with his talons even as he launched into the air.

Another wolf emerged from the forest, this time to the east where the trees met the cliff wall that began the Windsmouth. It drew Vidarian's eye, and after a moment he realized why: a band of color around its neck wasn't just marred fur, but a kind of decorative band hung with feathers.

Four younger wolves ranged behind this one, also marked with pheasant plumes. Just when Vidarian was beginning to accept that unsettlingly intelligent wolves might also have begun to decorate themselves, a human woman crept into the clearing behind them, a crude bow and arrow at the ready. Her clothes were so motley, her hair so woven with bark and leaves, that she seemed ill or mad. Despite this she proved skillful; she loosed one arrow after another, sinking their flint tips into wolf flesh, chest and neck and soft lower belly. Likewise, the wolves marked by the feathers moved with her, attacking their wild brethren.

"This way!" the woman shouted, unaccented Alorean at odds with her mad hermit appearance. When they continued battling the wolves, "You cannot defeat them," she added, punctuating the statement by planting an arrowhead neatly between the eyes of another wolf. "The pack is thousands upon thousands strong. They will never stop."

// *There is no sightwolf pack so large,* // Thalnarra argued, acrid disbelief like lightning-struck stone lacing her words, even as more wolves poured out of the forest. // *They would go—* //

"Mad, yes indeed," the woman snapped, turning her head and spitting into the dirt. "The cave!" she shouted, pointing to the rock wall behind her. "There's an entrance! Go, or die here!"

Another eerie series of howls echoed through the forest, taken up by voice

after lupine voice. It went on and on, lending credence to her outlandish statement about the pack's size.

Whether the pack numbered hundreds or thousands was of little import.
If the woman was crazy, at least they would deal with only her and her feather-
garlanded pets. "Follow her!" Vidarian shouted.

Eoin rapped his staff on the rump of the nearest verali, which squealed
and danced away from him. Together he and Khalesh herded the animals
toward the woman and her wolves, which made way for the verali and thankfully refrained from making meals of them.

Vidarian and Thalnarra remained behind, still picking off the enemy
wolves, trying to slow them down. But for every sightwolf that fell, those
that remained seemed to move a little quicker, fed by rage at the fall of their
comrades.

As the woman promised, there was a cave entrance behind her obscured
by thick brush. She began to pull it aside, and Thalnarra sped their retreat by
searing it away from the cliff face with a controlled blast of fire energy.

The narrow gap in the cliff wall was just barely wide enough to accommodate Thalnarra, if she arced her wings nearly vertical. Altair landed behind her
just as she squeezed into the rock, preceded by Tephir, who entered without
issue.

// *The* Phoenix *is nowhere in sight,* // Altair said, his beak parted with
exertion. // *Three bars and nothing.* // Thalnarra added her frustrated assent.
Vidarian had heard the gryphons speak before about height measurements,
but had little idea how they translated. The essence was clear: with Iridan still
asleep, there was no way of contacting the *Jade Phoenix* for rescue.

When the entire party, including the verali, had been hustled into the
rock, the woman who had led them there used a stave of wood set by the
entrance to knock a hidden support free. A cascade of rocks each the size of
Vidarian's head barreled down, filling the entrance.

With a whisper of thought, Thalnarra summoned a ball of fire energy over
her head, illuminating the pale red rock that surrounded them. The tunnel
remained barely wide enough for her to pass, but roughly three times as tall

beyond the entrance. Despite the height, Vidarian fought against an instinctive sense of suffocation.

"How will we get out?" he asked their rescuer—or abductor, perhaps.

The woman turned, her grey eyes tired and unfriendly. Vidarian realized that she was much older than he had initially thought, the lines on her face not just forest grime, but age. "Elsewhere. You wouldn't get out that way anyway. The pack will wait for weeks, now that they've been blooded."

Vidarian had assumed that, at worst, they could have found a way for Rai and Raven to take their dragon and phoenix shapes. But there was a deadness in this woman's eyes that made him realize it wouldn't have been that simple. Was it possible? *Thousands* of wolves? "You saved our lives," he said.

She snorted, and the large wolf to her left lolled his tongue, the faintest whisper of laughter rolling off of him. "Don't thank me yet." The wolf started down the passageway, and she followed him.

"My name is—"

"You're the Tesseract," she said over her shoulder, and gestured at the wolves when he stopped short. "They know. The pack remembers you. They started howling about you as soon as your ship drew near. It's how we found you."

"Who are you?" Vidarian asked, disarmed into bluntness by the barrage of questions he longed to ask.

"Daelwyn Crossgar, not that it will mean anything to you. These are Rue, Yarrow, Bael, Tamtu, and Foxglove." She turned her head as she spoke, pointing down the line—first at the big wolf that preceded her, then the four smaller behind, which seemed to be his offspring—but did not stop moving. The verali pawed at the ground anxiously as the wolves passed, and one of them wheezed half of an alarm call, but Khalesh hauled on its lead.

Rai followed the line of young wolves, and at first Vidarian assumed it was out of curiosity toward these sane-seeming new relatives. He still burned to know why these wolves seemed tame and not susceptible to the madness that infected the rest, but there were many questions and little time. Thalnarra's pinning eye as she stared at Mey indicated that she would need an explanation as to how a Qui imperial princess had joined their company—an explanation Vidarian himself still did not have.

But all this dropped away when Rai did not merely follow the wolves, but passed them, the hackles on his neck lifted. The urgency that billowed off of him through their bond—an unthinking fixation—sent a chill trickling down Vidarian's spine.

The chill bloomed into full-fledged alarm when Rai gave a soft *whuff* and launched himself down the corridor, quickly disappearing into the darkness beyond the reach of Thalnarra's light.

Vidarian managed a "Stay here!" to the rest before he ran after the wolf, soon engulfed in shadow himself. Ahead, Rai's eyes glowed, bouncing sparks of blue light that were all that prevented both of them from careening into sheer rock walls. A metallic hum followed them, accompanied by pale light— Khalesh had sent one of his needle-beaked hummingbirds, and it carried a small amount of white light with it.

Not once looking back, Rai wove through a downward spiraling laby- rinth of tunnels, loping easily as though he knew exactly where was going. They seemed to run forever, but at last the thornwolf stopped, and Vidarian fetched up beside him, out of breath and totally lost.

The brass hummingbird buzzed ahead, illuminating a heavy stone door inlaid with swirling veins of cobalt and silver.

Siane, Rai said, his eyes fixed on the door. *Siane is in there.*

Part Two
Shadows of Infinity

CHAPTER ELEVEN
GODDESS IN CRYSTAL

"S iane," Vidarian said, sharper than he meant to. Rai was oblivious.
"The air goddess?"

The wolf looked at him, large blue eyes still flickering with light but able to suggest Vidarian was stupid nonetheless. He managed the look for only a moment before returning his attention to the door.

A rhythmic clink of glass and metal accompanied by heavy footfalls came ahead of Khalesh, first to ignore Vidarian's instruction to stay behind.

The second was Altair, drawing close on soft feet. A ball of pale lavender light was suspended ahead of him, perpetually whirling. The gryphon's hackles were a-fluff, his head held slightly down as if ready for battle. When he saw Rai sitting in front of the door, his neck straightened, the feathers slicking down.

"Rai says that Siane is beyond this door," Vidarian said.

Altair's head twitched to one side, his near eye sharpening. A moment passed before he spoke. // *Some significant artifact, perhaps . . .* // Altair had once urged Vidarian to kill Rai, when he thought him a mere thornwolf; since his shapechanging, and the development of his intelligence, he seemed to go out of his way to treat him respectfully. The air gryphon's reaction was oddly comforting; surely if his own goddess lay trapped nearby, he would sense her.

Rai did not reply. He still stared at the door, the slightest twitch of his tail and the quickness of his breath all that belied his excitation.

Not wanting to provoke an argument, Vidarian gestured to the door that blocked their way. "Can you make anything of this?"

Altair drew close to the door, which was not much larger than his body. Rai stood and backed away, a hopeful wave of his tail nearly banging into Vidarian's leg as he watched the gryphon.

// *It's an elemental lock,* // Altair concluded, a lively interest threading his words like the scent of fresh-crushed rosemary.

Khalesh murmured a wordless agreement, now equally fascinated with the door. He passed his hands in front of it, but did not touch the stone.

Distantly Vidarian sensed Altair reaching out with an arm of elemental energy; he could detect the air only as the slightest vibration of his fire and water senses, as if they knew something moved that was missing between them.

As soon as Altair touched the door with his magic, it bloomed with light.

The dark stone was indeed threaded with silver and cobalt, but invisible between them was a transparent smoky quartz that now glowed a brilliant pale blue. Silver and cobalt spirals that had appeared randomly placed now revealed themselves to be arranged around a sigil formed by the glowing quartz.

Both Khalesh and Altair seemed taken aback by the sigil, and Vidarian coughed to recapture their attention. "What does it mean?" he asked.

Altair flicked his ear at Khalesh, the gryphon equivalent of a shrug, and Khalesh rubbed a hand through his hair. While Altair returned his attention to the door, threading it with yet more air energy, Khalesh said, "It is a very ancient language. At the dawn of the first Age of Light—some two thousand years before the Alorean Ascendancy—these symbols were used as motifs, decorative elements, if you will . . . calling cards. The markings themselves were said to be even older."

// *It's gryphon language,* // Altair said, a distracted aside as he wreathed yet more energy into the door.

"What does this one mean?" Vidarian asked.

" 'Forbidden.' "

"*Forbidden?* Should we be opening it, then?" The challenge in Vidarian's voice earned him a displeased noise from Rai.

// *Wait . . .* // Altair said, and Vidarian let out his breath in agreement. // *No, it's . . .* // But the tall gryphon's voice was far away, his mind somewhere deep inside the lock. Vidarian had seen him preoccupied before, but never like this. It called to mind the mad seridi, or the water priestess who guarded the tower at the far foothills of the Windsmouth.

Just when Vidarian was about to let his apprehension get the better of him—

// *There,* // Altair said, a richness in his voice as if wakened from a year of sleep.

The door . . . *sighed* . . . letting out its breath, and something deep inside the lock clicked open. Altair raised a foreclaw, and the passageway opened before them, each of the door's four quarters rotating into hidden pockets in the stone around them. Vidarian took an involuntary step back, spooked by the strange movement.

Khalesh was grinning from ear to ear in a way that often meant something very dangerous had just happened. "A labyrinth door," he said, and thumped Altair on the shoulder. The gryphon flicked a bemused ear at him. "My old instructor loved these doors. I never thought to see one in the flesh."

Vidarian, for his part, was very much not amused at all, and was peering into the darkness that lay before them. His body tensed in anticipation of whatever horrifying manner of monster might guard a door upon which someone had written "forbidden" in gryphon-sized letters.

No monster appeared, nor any movement.

The labyrinth door still exuded a pale blue glow, but the chamber beyond it was far too large for that light to be remotely adequate. Cold air drifted from inside, not strong enough to be a breeze, but chilling nonetheless.

"There's nothing," Vidarian said, more to jolt his companions into movement than anything else. Khalesh was still inspecting the doorframe with avid zeal, and Altair seemed to be scenting the air, his feathers roused. "What could be 'forbidden'?"

Altair made a thoughtful rolling sound in the back of his throat, a kind of birdcall rattle. // *The sigil is more warning than command. It implies that anything within can protect itself.* //

This was little comfort, but Rai stood, stretched, and strolled through the doorway, leaving them to follow or be left behind.

Altair followed first, his lavender light bobbing ahead of him. Vidarian crossed the threshold next, pulling Khalesh by the arm as he did so.

As they entered the chamber, light from the labyrinth door shot across parallel channels in the floor—more of the translucent quartz—and streamed upward into branching arms that engulfed the chamber's western wall. There the blue light dimmed, almost diminishing; each branch bounced between a handful of points, and then most winked out entirely. Three positions held their light, which pulsed.

Fix her, Rai said. The wolf had trotted right up to the wall and now nudged it with his nose, then sat back on his haunches, radiating self-satisfaction.

"Her," Vidarian said flatly, earning another bored look from Rai.

// *This is what he thinks is Siane?* // Altair asked, with a dull tone that said his words were pitched for Vidarian alone.

Wordlessly, Vidarian thought back agreement, both with the statement and the concern that underlay it. Rai had always been privy to strange knowledge, an artifact of being a shapechanger that, against conventional wisdom, had genuine intelligence. His mind was aware of spaces between the elements, and more than once he had known things without being able to explain why.

They drew closer to the wall, and as they approached, Khalesh picked up speed, nearly running by the time he reached the glowing rock.

Only it wasn't rock at all. It was crystal.

There was something familiar about the luster of the stone, the way that the energy-light passed through it.

Khalesh lifted his hands, passing them over the crystal without touching it. "This—" he began, pointing at a pattern in the stone, "is a larger form of a memory device, a prism key, and this—" his hand swept across to indicate another pattern, "is a locking device, distantly related to the labyrinth door. But this . . ." He trailed off, eyes moving faster the more he saw.

The words *prism key* closed the distance in Vidarian's mind.

The wall's crystal looked exactly like a prism key—a sun emerald or ruby of the kind that had housed Ruby's mind, or the storm sapphire that had opened the tunnel beneath the Windsmouth.

But the entire *wall* was made out of it. And not just one gem, but thousands, all of varying sizes, laid together and connected by the luminous quartz.

"This is a master-work," Khalesh said, his eyes darting across the glowing wall. "An artifact of tremendous genius. Not only have I never seen its like, I have never read a single reference even *suggesting* its like." His hands lifted to comb through his already tortured hair. "Taken all together, the implications . . . the size . . ." The Animator stepped away from the wall, taking it in with a sweeping glance. He pulled a small device of glass beads and wire from the heavy belt at his waist and rolled his thumb across it dozens of times in succession. Periodically he would frown, shake it, and begin again.

"What is it?" Vidarian asked at last.

"Holiest mothers," Khalesh whispered. He turned to Vidarian, the color washed from his face. "Rai is right. These devices together—it's—*she's*—an automaton, only much more than an automaton could possibly be. *Much* more. And all arranged with gems aligned with wind energy. This—the only explanation—is that this is Siane."

// *What you suggest is blasphemy,* // Altair said softly. Vidarian stiffened slightly; he had never heard Altair use that particular word, nor did he ever expect to.

Khalesh raised his hands, which trembled. "You of all of us are best equipped to pass judgment. You should be able to speak with . . . her." The pinning of Altair's pupils caused Khalesh to make more soothing motions with his hands. "Just—touch one of the active areas with your air sense, the way you did with the door, and we will know."

Altair stared at Khalesh for a long moment, then turned to the wall, a dark heaviness radiating from him. Vidarian felt the vibration of his air magic, and then—

Altair, the wall said. Lightning arcs of energy leapt across its surface. *Malitar Aliesen Riis.* And one of the spots of light went dim.

Altair did the most frightening thing Vidarian had ever seen him do— beyond *twice* plummeting from astronomical heights with no way of landing: he collapsed onto the floor.

The gryphon's legs went out from under him for all the world like a swooning bride's. It would have been comical if not for the wild chaos of disbelief and anguish that rolled off of him in waves. Not for the first time Vidarian wished that they had brought Isri with them, but she had had her capable hands more than filled rebuilding the demoralized mindcrafter hospital in Val Imris.

// *It's her,* // Altair whispered, and would say no more.

~~~

"He said she called him by his wind name," Vidarian said, in the latest of over a dozen attempts to explain what had happened to Thalnarra and Ariadel. When Altair had collapsed, Thalnarra had felt his discomfiture, and the remainder of the party had rushed toward the chamber that contained Siane.

// *It could be a telepathic device,* // Thalnarra said. // *It would not be impossible for one of sufficient strength to pull that name from his mind.* //

For an answer, Vidarian turned toward Altair, who still lay stretched in front of the crystal wall where he had fallen. The gryphon was listless, unresponsive, even to Thalnarra.

"There were stories of a kind of master-pattern," Khalesh said, his voice still hoarse. "Parables, I thought. We all thought. It wasn't *possible* that they described something real, something that had actually at one time been made."

They had made a rudimentary camp in the crystal chamber, rather than abandoning Altair to it. Thalnarra had created a kind of self-feeding elemental fire at the cavern's far side, allowing the humans to prepare food. Khalesh stared into the flames, leaning against one of the verali. The beasts were skittish underground, but seemed reassured by the campfire, log-less as it was.

Rai and the young sightwolves, in defiance or perhaps obliviousness toward the solemnity of the humans and gryphons, played a puppy game in the center of the chamber. In spite of the mysteries of their discovery, or possibly because of them, the cavorting wolves were a welcome distraction.

Daelwyn Crossgar watched the wolves also, sitting cross-legged by the fire and repairing a seam in her tunic with borrowed thread and bone needle. One of the wolves yipped, its tongue lolling, and she chuckled.

Vidarian caught her eye and raised his eyebrows.

She gestured at the young wolves with the needle. "They say he does not smell like a thornwolf, and it puzzles them."

"This amuses you," Vidarian said, without aggression.

"They are not themselves entirely sightwolves, either—not anymore."

"Because of you?"

The woman shook her head, turning the fabric in her hands. "They were on their way before I happened along. Sightwolves that don't run with a pack are—different."

"The pack that attacked us was—impossible," Vidarian said, struggling for any other descriptor and finding none. "How is it that sightwolves can run together in the thousands? Why would they drive themselves mad?"

Daelwyn's whole face darkened and her hands grew still on the tunic and thread.

"I apologize—"

She shook her head, interrupting him, her teeth set together. "I was once as ignorant of their ways as you are. Humans everywhere have forgotten that it was our war that did this to them."

"*Our* war?"

Daelwyn sighed, finishing her seam with a chain of precise stitches that raised more questions than they answered—how did a wild woman sew so adeptly? "The War of the Ascendancy."

"Sixteen centuries years ago?"

Daelwyn nodded, knotting off the thread and pulling the needle free. "Alorea and the southern packs were allies, or at least had common cause. The Qui killed them indiscriminately. And some enterprising young Aloreans decided that the wolves could be a nigh unstoppable southern defense force and messenger relay network, if only they could all band together in one pack." Vidarian was silent, holding back his disbelief, and she continued. "They summoned all the pack leaders and used telepathic devices to break down their minds." She turned her head and spat, and Vidarian worked to keep his eyes on her. "They got their unified pack—but the connection of so many minds drove them insane."

"And—" Vidarian gestured toward the romping wolves. Three of them together had managed to pin Rai's shoulders to the ground, though even they weren't large enough to keep him there.

"Escapees," Daelwyn said. "Their father," she tilted her head to indicate the large black wolf behind her, "is a lone. It happens, usually through blood. A diminished telepathic connection to the pack."

"Fortunate in this case."

She shrugged. "He is outcast. Not insane, but forever feeling the absence of the pack. Sightwolves don't just share companionship, a pack shares intelligence. He is forever diminished for having only his cubs."

The natural question was after what had happened to the cubs' mother, but Vidarian shied away from it for fear of dredging up another hurtful story. "Can the pack be broken apart again?"

Daelwyn spun the bone needle between her fingers absently as she watched the wolves play, a distant look in her eyes. Behind them, the father wolf yawned. "It is possible. But I suspect you'll have more on your hands." She pointed her chin at Thalnarra, who was accepting the box containing Asalet's artifact from Khalesh. While they watched, Thalnarra left the chamber, passing through an archway that led east, away from the glowing wall.

"If you'll excuse me," Vidarian apologized, and levered himself to his feet. Daelwyn smiled without warmth, and he wasn't sure if it was deliberate or just her natural way.

He followed Thalnarra into the adjacent chamber, where she had already found herself a place on the stone tiles. The floors in both chambers were covered with thumb-sized mosaic chips, but whatever pattern their subtle color variations had made out was lost to time.

The sandalwood box containing Asalet's artifact was open in front of Thalnarra. She stared into it, but her large eyes, russet in the dim light of the antechamber, were far away. The crystal wall had obliterated her interest in Mey's stowing away; the princess herself had the wisdom for the moment to lie low.

The artifact itself was tiny, a strange shape like two pyramids joined at the base. Smooth as polished glass, it was a pale celadon green in color, opaque toward its center. Vidarian couldn't help but wonder if there were dozens of others like it embedded into the great crystal wall that Rai called the air goddess. *Fix her*, he'd said—as if it were a matter of tar and caulk!

Altair's malaise disturbed Vidarian more than the crystal wall, which, if it was somehow alive, a kind of massive automaton, at least it wasn't embedded with the fragmented soul of one of his oldest friends turned enemy.

He settled himself on the tiles beside Thalnarra, taking a raw child's comfort from the warmth of her large body, the forest musk of her feathers.

"Can he be consoled?" he asked at last.

// *Not if what you say is true,* // Thalnarra replied, a heat in her words like burning walnut shells. // *You rarely seem to know what you suggest, but we should be accustomed to that by now.* // The acrid bite dulled to a gentler hickory. But despite her fiery words, Thalnarra's attention was still somewhere more distant, and Vidarian thought he knew where.

"Asalet . . ." he began, unsure how to continue. He braced himself for a storm, the lash that had lain beneath Thalnarra's strange silence at the Librarian's suggestion of her untapped potential.

// *She was right. I have been the master so long that I'd forgotten the exalted state of the student mind.* //

Vidarian didn't know whether to feel relieved. "You'll always be a master to me."

Thalnarra chuckled, a crackling fire in winter. Delicately she reached out to touch the artifact with the rounded edge of a talon. It flared to life in response to her energy, then dimmed. // *And you will always be a student.* //

Chapter Twelve

Great Artifice

"It can't be Siane," Ariadel said. She spoke quietly, restraining herself to avoid waking Ailenne, who slept on her shoulder. For once Vidarian was thankful of the need for quiet.

The denial that flattened Ariadel's tone was identical to Thalnarra's, and unspoken beneath both was that if this was true of Siane, so must it also be true of Sharli, Nistra, and Anake.

"I have hosted Sharli in my body," Ariadel said slowly.

"And I have met her," Vidarian said. "I have called to Nistra on the ocean and felt her reply. But we've seen what Iridan can do. We've seen what *Ruby* can do."

Despite his words, Vidarian wasn't sure what to believe. He felt numb, stricken; he couldn't yet reach the part of him that remembered Sharli on the mountain beneath Sher'azar, or Nistra's face in the maelstrom off Maladar's Horn.

But some deeper part of him knew that Rai was right. The strange distance of the priestesses guarding Siane's Eye, the emptiness exuding from its windwell—things he hadn't the knowledge to apprehend then, but saw now through the lens of memory. The Living Flames of Sharli had filled him with a sense of life, but the windwell at Siane's Eye had drawn life into itself, a perpetual void. And even the priestesses there had felt, more than the fire priestesses or even the mad Vkortha, the weakening of their element. This fractured crystal wall that spoke Altair's secret name to him fit that melancholy puzzle.

He saw in Ariadel's eyes the pieces coming together as well. When they filled with tears that she blinked away, his heart rent. Her life had been for Sharli.

To his surprise, she smiled and shook her head. "It's not what you think," she managed, and laid a hand on his arm, pushing him toward Altair and Thalnarra. "They need you."

Torn between his family and the obvious distress of Thalnarra and Altair—a distress he had little idea how to assuage—he hesitated until Ailenne twitched herself awake, making the small squawking noises that would soon lead to cries if not soothed. Ariadel rocked her, murmuring, and turned toward the eastern antechamber, which Thalnarra had vacated.

"I should have found a safer place for you," Vidarian said, and she stopped, turning. The attack of the sightwolves, and the many ways that things could have gone poorly in Qui, weighed on him, eroding sleep and will.

"Safe," Ariadel chuckled, giving him a wry smile that was without barb. Her expression softened further before she added, "There is nowhere we would be truly safe from the Company. We're underneath a formidable mountain and in the house of a lost goddess. Few other places could be more safe from them than here."

She was right again, and it was little comfort. The Alorean Import Company had remained ominously silent, which could only mean they were closing fast upon the weapon they both chased. He wondered whether they had found Ruby, or Veda, after Ariadel and her gryphon allies had dropped them through an untargeted gate. Briefly he wondered where those gryphons were now, and if they were well. He wondered if Val Imris was holding. There were so many he couldn't keep safe.

Ailenne struggled again, and Ariadel gave him another quick smile—meant to be reassuring, and it was—before turning toward the antechamber again, humming a soft song to their daughter.

Behind him, Khalesh had guided Iridan up to the crystal wall, where two patches of light still glowed. He held the automaton's right hand out toward one of them, and Vidarian caught the flash of light that resulted just as he turned.

Iridan stirred and moved on his own for the first time since their passage through the fragmented everstorm. A low hum emerged from deep inside the automaton's chest, but as he straightened, it diminished and finally disappeared. His lavender eyes, dim but glowing, spun their lenses, focusing.

"Are you all right, my friend?" Khalesh asked.

Iridan moved his right arm haltingly: shoulder followed by elbow followed by wrist. *"It will take some time,"* he said, *"but I will recover. I did not expect to see you all again."*

"You knew that you would . . . fall asleep like that?" Vidarian asked.

The automaton's eyes dimmed and then brightened again, a kind of non-committal reply. *"I knew that to connect your minds the way I did would expend almost all of my energy, but it was necessary."* He offered no other explanation, but continued, *"Thank you for waking me. How did you manage it?"*

Khalesh and Vidarian exchanged a glance, and the animator gestured at the crystal wall. Iridan's gem eyes rotated with curiosity, and then he turned.

The automaton stood looking at the wall for several moments, and the hum returned from within his chest, a whir of fast-moving gears. *"My goodness,"* he said at last.

"Have you ever seen its like?" Khalesh asked, quick with urgency, even desperation, as he had been since he first set eyes on the wall.

Iridan turned back toward them slowly. *"She is magnificent,"* he said, and beside Vidarian Khalesh virtually inflated with hope. Then, *"I have never even heard of anything like her."*

Khalesh's shoulders slumped, but he rallied enough to ask, "Could Parvidian have known about . . . her?" How automatons assigned gender was a mystery, but it must have seemed impolite to ask even to an Animator.

"My creator kept many secrets," Iridan said. *"Most especially from his creations."* There was a ruefulness in his voice, so human; Iridan's emotionality seemed only to have increased since he first woke. It was easy to forget that, although he might be thousands of years old, he had spent most of that time inert. *"I am sorry to be of so little help."*

"You certainly weren't when we needed you," Vidarian said. It was hard to put aside the memory of the Everstorm, and the easy way in which Iridan had connected their minds, though it cost him greatly.

Iridan was listing slightly, his eyes dimming and glowing by turns. "You should rest," Khalesh said, placing a hand on the automaton's shoulder. "That jolt was enough to wake you, but you'll need more than that to recover." He bent and rummaged through a pack of tools sitting beside the wall, withdrawing a wooden case and passing it to Iridan. The brass hands hummed softly as they accepted the box, mechanisms moving slow enough to be heard in another betrayal of fatigue, and Iridan nodded over the box, then moved to a quiet corner of the chamber to use the artifacts within.

Vidarian watched him go, then looked from the automaton to Khalesh and then to the wall. "Have you uncovered anything that might wake her?" he asked.

Khalesh shook his head, thick brows lowered together to darken an already intimidating face. "It was theory that suggested her energy might wake Iridan. You saw what it took to bring him back. It will take much, much more to revive her. More than I can honestly imagine."

They turned together back toward the wall and watched it for some time in silence. It appeared fractured, but it was an artifact of the energy that passed across the wall's surface, and through its many channels. One remaining area of light coiled sinuously through threadlike rivers in the crystal, while deeper dividing lines cut off one region from another.

"There are so many patterns here that I recognize only from ancient diagrams, their artifacts lost to time—still more that I studied and worked with directly—and last, some handful that I can't recognize at all, not even in relation to other known structures," Khalesh said. The big man had never been so talkative in Vidarian's presence, not even in the Grand Library. "But this—" he drew a thick fingertip beneath a lozenge-shaped formation in the crystal wall, "is . . . extraordinary." Vidarian had to admit that he had only known the Animator a short time, but doubted he had ever been like this even before, his eyes so wide with a reach for comprehension. "It's a . . . net, you might say, a gathering structure. It passively absorbs telepathic activity from a particular kind of mind, even at great distance."

Something like that sounded ominous. "You've seen its like before?" Vidarian asked carefully, wondering which "class" of object it was, and how many more existed like it.

"Only as a theoretical structure, a diagram," Khalesh said, impossibly warming even further to the subject. "I've seen pieces of it, lesser artifacts that attempted related feats, but never one structured to actually achieve it. It's related, in its way, to the very device we all seek to keep away from the Alorean Import Company. The energy and craftsmanship needed to create even this piece alone . . ."

"What does it do? For—the wall?" he asked, trying to head off another long interlude of awe.

"If my understanding of its structure is correct, it gathers thoughts from great distances and—sorts them. It leads to this—" he pointed to another section of the wall, an area separated by grooves that held the last pool of light left. ". . . which structurally resembles the sections of automata that control behavior—personality, even."

"Personality," Vidarian repeated, not for the first time feeling like a dullard in matters of animation and automata.

"It's as though you and I and every other Alorean were connected together telepathically, without our knowing it, and were fed into an artifact that could then create an automaton that *was* Alorea."

Thinking about this was enough to give Vidarian a headache, but he struggled to understand. "So this," he took in the entire wall in an expansive gesture, "creates a kind of projection of Siane, anywhere in the world, the way that Iridan can create pictures out of light near him, and that projection is made out of pieces of every . . . what? . . . air elementalist in the world?"

"That's just it," Khalesh agreed, a fervor lighting his eyes. "I believe that's exactly what it does. The artifact—Siane—is an aggregate personality."

Vidarian was thinking, as he had done since they first entered this chamber, of Nistra, of Sharli. The goddesses that his family had spent so many generations devoted to or dancing around. When he didn't answer immediately, Khalesh grew slightly agitated.

"Don't you see? It's remarkable—breathtaking, even." His hands shook as he held them up to the wall. "It's an answer to some of the most ancient questions of our culture. A magnificent answer."

"But one that raises so many more questions," Vidarian murmured.

While speaking to Khalesh and Iridan he had grown increasingly aware of the attention of the gryphons, whose ears had swiveled toward Khalesh and there remained tilted at a suspicious angle. "Who—do you think—built this?"

Khalesh caught onto his divided attention and turned toward the gryphons. "I know it was no Grand Artificer. They could not have been capable of this, and refrained from taking credit for it in our archives."

Altair still lay with his head resting on the stone, one of the most despondent sights Vidarian had ever seen. It clawed at his heart. Thalnarra reclined, lion-like, her talons crossed together and her tail coiling and uncoiling. She stared at Vidarian for some time, her large scarlet eyes unreadable.

// *Gryphons recall a history that predates the elemental goddesses,* // Thalnarra said at last. // *But certainly not that the goddesses were* created. //

And if this were truly Siane, not only had she been created, but she had been so during a time of remarkable elemental technology eclipsing even what was recorded in the Shen Ti annals of the Grand Artificers. Could it possibly have been that the Grand Artificers themselves were mere mimickers, copying and creating smaller iterations of much more ancient work?

// *It is gryphon-made,* // Altair said miserably, not lifting his head. // *I would stake my life on it.* // He wouldn't yet call the glowing wall "Siane"—or, as the gryphons called her, Sia'Kalia.

It was the first he had spoken since the wall had addressed him, and Vidarian turned toward him with a start. But Thalnarra drew his attention back again.

// *We have been lied to all this time,* // Thalnarra said, simmering with anger.

Imagine that, Vidarian itched to say, but restrained himself.

// *The rightful action is to destroy the artifact,* // Altair said. Across the room, Iridan grew very still, but neither gryphon noticed. // *Even if this . . .* is *Sia'Kalia as we have known her, she was created through deception for a purpose that could only entail controlling the minds of gryphonkind.* //

"You don't know that," Vidarian said.

// *What other explanation can there be?* // Fury rattled beneath Altair's words, bottomless. At last he raised his head, blue eyes searing. Vidarian had encoun-

Your receipt
Albuquerque/Bernalillo County Library

Customer ID: **********0382

Items that you checked out

Title:
 Sword of fire and sea / Erin Hoffman.
ID: 39075047360273
Due: Tuesday, November 22, 2016

Title:
 Lance of earth and sky / Erin Hoffman.
ID: 39075051640263
Due: Tuesday, November 22, 2016

Title:
 Shield of sea and space / Erin Hoffman.
ID: 39075051644752
Due: Tuesday, November 22, 2016

Total items: 3
Account balance. $0.00
11/1/2016 1:04 PM
Checked out: 18
Overdue: 0
Hold requests: 2
Ready for pickup: 0

Thank you for using the Tony Hillerman
Library http://abclibrary.org

tered this in the gryphons before, but rarely: a sense that there was far more beneath their words than they could communicate. It could only be unnerving, a reminder that they might speak the same language, but the essence of their species would forever separate them. Altair, unusual among gryphons, had always been better able to bridge that separation than Thalnarra or her wilder fire kin. // *You ask us, in believing this, to unwind everything we know about ourselves*—and *to accept a terrible betrayal on the part of our ancestors, who did this and hid it from us.* //

And there was the center of it. No gryphon that Vidarian had met could countenance the notion of betrayal. It reached so deeply into the very sinews of their souls that it made them nearly mindless with rage.

Vidarian knew that he walked a very thin edge, that Altair even now struggled against a wild beast in his own mind, a creature created by a nightmare become real. And worse, the burn behind his eyes said that he had made it his own responsibility to undo the betrayal committed against his people.

None of it was fair.

It took fighting against every physical instinct he had, but Vidarian walked up to Altair and knelt beside him, his hands loose at his sides. The white gryphon's feathers were still roused with his anger, making him seem three times as broad-shouldered as he was—and his neck bent downward to keep Vidarian in view, positioning a massive grey beak two handspans' above his head.

"You once called me brother," Vidarian said, now looking up to meet Altair's flashing eye. "And if you decide that—the artifact—must be destroyed, you have my word that I'll help you." He left out that he had no idea how one would go about destroying so massive a crystal, with or without a goddess inside.

Slowly, Altair's feathers slicked back down, and his head leveled. Then he moved again, dipping his head to brush the side of his beak against Vidarian's cheek. The sudden bone coldness of that touch, smooth as a river stone, barely gave him time to flinch before Altair lowered his head again to the floor and shut his eyes.

"They need time," Ariadel said.

The passageways away from Siane's chamber led deeper underground, eventually opening up into a network of natural caverns. Nearest was a massive egg-shaped grotto remarkable for what filled it: a vibrant tropical subterranean forest.

A sunsphere suspended from the ceiling—hundreds of feet away—must have awakened with the opening of the gate, and in the intervening year filled the chamber with lush vegetation. There were even birds, implying that somewhere the underground city—a ruin more ancient than those that surrounded the Great Gate—opened to the outside air.

It was not enough to banish the specter of their discovery, but it was not far. Raven had come with them, and now capered, cat-shaped, through the low vegetation. Like Rai, she seemed able to speak only with her partner, and, from Ariadel's descriptions, seemed just as intelligent. Discovering the cat as a smoke-grey kitten scavenging the docks of Val Harlon seemed many lifetimes away.

"You're taking this remarkably well," Vidarian said.

Ariadel half smiled, stroking Ailenne's back as the baby shifted in her sleep against Ariadel's shoulder. Then her eyes grew distant, thoughtful. "I—think somehow I always knew," she said, now vulnerable, almost guilty. "When I hosted Sharli—it was as though thousands of voices filled me, millions of points of light . . . I always thought it was the ecstasy of her presence. And maybe it was."

In that moment, breathing in the tropical air of the hidden forest, Vidarian was grateful for his life, strange as it was and would be. He reached out to touch Ariadel's arm, careful not to wake their daughter, and she leaned into him, her warmth and the wonder of her filling his senses.

It seemed impossible, here, to think about the nature of the goddesses. It was as though the world spun twice as fast as it should—but that, too, was an occasion for gratitude. It meant that they were alive.

When they returned to Siane's chamber, little had changed. Khalesh now sat in front of the wall, his eyebrows knit together with fatigue and frustration. Thalnarra was silent and unresponsive, even to Mey, who had turned her attention to Daelwyn and the sightwolves. Part of Vidarian still wanted to shake the girl, demand why she would place not only her life but the peace of empires in such jeopardy, but more immediate was Altair's collapse, to say nothing of waking a goddess.

Something that Ariadel had said had hit home, and Vidarian resolved to try once more to explain it.

"Altair, my friend," Vidarian said, kneeling again in front of the gryphon. Slowly, one blue eye opened to regard him, heavy-lidded. "Everything you were and are remains, with or without the goddess as you knew her. I know I can't speak this to you and have you understand it, but I also know that the strength of Siane is in your heart, and remains there regardless of her origin. A goddess does not even have to be . . . divine—" he stopped himself from saying *real,* "to give you that. The strength was always in you."

The large white head tilted, looking at him more closely now. There was no belief there, no agreement—but something had changed. It was as subtle as the lifting of a breeze, a moment of fragrance quickly forgotten. // *How would you wake a broken goddess?* // Altair asked.

For that, Vidarian turned to Khalesh, who rubbed at his forehead. Arduously the big man levered himself to his feet, then snatched up a bit of parchment that rested on the stone beside him. He brought it to Vidarian.

Scrawled across the parchment were sketches and numbers, a kind of accounting. It was energy, Vidarian realized. At one end, and with a small number beside it, was the sketch of a prism key. In the middle, an automaton like Iridan, and further down, one like Ruby. The difference in figures between the two was already astronomical, nearly unimaginable. And then, at the furthest end of the scrap of parchment, a sketch of the crystal wall, and a number larger than all the previous ones combined. Below each figure were calculations and smaller numbers—distillations, Vidarian thought, of how much energy it would take just to start each of the devices on the path to waking, the way that the crystal wall had awakened Iridan.

Even those numbers were impossible. The only time Vidarian could remember seeing that kind of energy was—

"Rai," he said. The wolf's ears swiveled and he lifted his head. "I think you're the one who has to wake her."

CHAPTER THIRTEEN

AWAKE

Siane's chamber was just barely large enough to hold Rai in his dragon shape.

Rai stood facing the crystal wall, his head low and the tip of his tail swaying. Even as a dragon, he retained many wolf behaviors, and now he looked back over his shoulder at Vidarian for reassurance.

Vidarian, Khalesh, Thalnarra, and Altair huddled in the antechamber behind Rai. Daelwyn, Tephir, and the sightwolves protected Ariadel, the baby, and Princess Mey in the underground forest. Iridan had gone with them in case the blast of energy intended for Siane could disrupt his still fragile construction; he'd taken Khalesh's various mechanical birds with him for the same reason.

They hoped the wall would indeed absorb Rai's energy the way that Iridan had absorbed it. There was no way of conducting a smaller test—they would have to wait days for Rai's natural electricity to regenerate itself from any discharge.

You're sure you don't want to wait in the forest? Rai asked, his small ears drooping with worry.

"We won't leave you to do this alone," Vidarian called, trying to fill his voice with reassurance. "Take your time." He knew that he could hide little from Rai, part of whom seemed to live close inside his mind. Thus he left himself bare, showing everything: no, he was not sure; yes, he feared being struck by the dragon's lightning; yes, he insisted on being there so that Rai would not face the air goddess alone, if it came to that.

As all of this sank in, Rai's bone-plated face turned back toward the wall, and he inhaled deeply, the tiny scales on his massive chest glittering like diamond dust in the wall's pale blue light. His wings fanned outward, brushing the rock walls, a protective shield; he *thought* that, should the wall fail to absorb the lightning, his wings would catch it, but none of them could be sure.

Rai's eyes began to glow an electric blue that matched the wall's light, and so did each of the strange flat-topped spines that ran down his back from neck to tailtip. As he drew in another breath, he snarled, igniting whatever internal fire called the lightning to him. Arcs of electricity crackled between his fangs and danced down his spine, more and more spiderwebbing fingers of light, so many that some leapt off of his body to sputter on the stone floor.

He reared, balancing on his hind legs, horned head nearly touching the ceiling, and the lightning in his maw grew brighter, so frequent now that it appeared to be a blinding ball of light. Even in their battle against the Alorean Import Company's fireships, he had never released a single bolt containing all of his energy. As a pup, he had been unable to restrain himself—a time Vidarian remembered both fondly and painfully, punctuated by nasty shocks—but no longer.

The dragon's wings arched, two clawed 'fingertips' touching above his head, and the bolt loosed.

The *CRACK* was phenomenal, deafening—it knocked Vidarian off of his feet. His vision blurred, sound obliterated, as he struggled on the stone floor to regain his balance.

A tearing sensation from his own chest, burning—then sound, all at once, a high-pitched whine followed by a roar like the ocean against the cliffs in a storm—then his own body, a choking sound to match the fire in his chest. He was coughing up dust, his lungs laboring to clear enough to breathe.

Beside him, Thalnarra and Altair had thrown out their wings in instinctive defensive postures; they hadn't fallen, but gripped the floor with talons and claws. Dust covered them, tossed into the air by the concussive blast, and they too choked and sneezed to clear their throats of it.

But before Vidarian could wet his dust-coated mouth enough to ask if they were unhurt, Altair was shouldering by him, shaking—and not to dispel dust.

Rai's wings had drooped toward the ground, along with his head, bowed low on his arched neck with fatigue—baring the crystal wall to their sight.

As the dust drifted down, the first suggestion was light—vibrant blue light everywhere, not in one or even three places but across the entire wall. Only one section remained dim, a triangular area that now revealed itself to have been damaged, perhaps even removed.

But the presence was clearest of all. There was another mind among theirs, roving, stretching—waking.

Altair came to a stop in front of the wall, his wings half mantled. His beak stretched upward and he made a series of sounds, incomprehensible clicks and rattles punctuated by sharp throat noises. Then, thoughts, a wash of them, too fast and complex for Vidarian to understand.

"I . . . hear you," the wall said.

// Sia'Kalia, // Thalnarra breathed beside him, her voice hushed and quick, hardly believing.

// I felt you, once, // Altair said. His neck was stretched upward to its fullest height, his beak slightly parted. He did not gasp or even quicken his breathing, but his talons were splayed on feet set at bracing distance from each other. His eyes shone, all pupil with shock.

"You were but a hatchling," the wall—Siane—agreed. There was a fondness, bright like spring sunlight, and then a shadow. "One of my last memories, before the Dwindling took me. I had such high hopes for you."

// How can you be . . . like this? // Altair asked, and Vidarian's heart convulsed for the pain in the question, so much layered within it.

"How could I be anything else?" Siane replied. "You are the first of my true children in a hundred generations to see me for what I am."

There was a rustle, and beside Vidarian Khalesh was picking himself up off the ground. Tears streamed openly down his face.

// What happened to you? // Altair asked. His voice had faded from the bright sear of shock, and his talons seemed to have relaxed as well. The blue of his irises overtook pupil; he seemed to be accepting Siane for what she was. It must have helped to realize that gryphons many generations ago had known her true nature. And there was—a boldness in him. He spoke to her with something more than the pure reverence gryphons reserved for their goddess. Siane, too, seemed to be reflecting this; she did not speak in riddles or with the authority Vidarian remembered from Sharli.

"When the Dwindling tipped the elemental energy in the world and extinguished the light of so many elemental devices, our constructed nature had been forgotten by humans and gryphons for a thousand years. We retained our powers and thought that we would be safe, so great were our internal reserves of elemental energy. And we were: diminished, weakened, but neither destroyed nor slumbering.

"Fifty years ago, men came into my chamber, the first in thousands of years. They broke the crystal configuration that stored my reserves of energy, and I gradually fell asleep over the following decade. I have been asleep since."

// *It would explain why Sharli could appear to us, but Siane—and Anake— seemed to refuse to manifest to their temples,* // Thalnarra said. The bite in her tone—pungent like fish oil over a smoking fire—said that she did not like this truth. But if Thalnarra could be distilled into a single virtue in Vidarian's eyes, it would be her ability to reshape her mind around truths she did not wish to accept. It was an agility he envied.

"I still will not be able to project myself," the wall said. When Siane spoke, light played across her crystalline surface in mesmerizing patterns. *"Only in the direst circumstance could I afford that much loss of energy. But my windwells will recover, and I hope that this will reassure my children."*

Vidarian found his thoughts blurring with her every word. Was it Siane who thought of her wind followers as children, or was it the followers who wished to be so considered? Where did one begin and the other end?

As if sensing his thoughts, Siane turned her attention toward him. *"This discomfits you. You do not belong to any of us,"* she said, *"but we will all owe you our thanks."*

It seemed that she would draw a circle around the Starhunter with her words, but without full acknowledgment. Sharli had done the same. What did it mean for the nature of the chaos goddess? It was more than his mind could contain for now.

// Without Rai, will you . . . Dwindle again? // Altair asked, and Vidarian's back twitched with surprise. It was a good question. She couldn't expect Rai to stay here, underground? The thought of it clenched Vidarian's ribs.

"*This energy will keep me for some time, but not forever,*" she said. "*Only by replacing the missing pieces can I truly be made whole again.*" Despondency settled on him like a cloak; surely those pieces had been lost, or even destroyed. Was Siane tasking them with finding them again? If she asked it, must they answer? "*But you must first find and awaken Anake,*" she said.

"The earth goddess?" Vidarian asked. Did Siane know where she was? And why would she ask for Anake's return above her own restoration?

"*Her shrine, too, was in a known location, and no longer guarded,*" Siane explained. "*I fear that she is in an even deeper sleep than I was, and will be more difficult to revive. But she must return.*"

"If we can find her, we will wake her as we did you," Vidarian said. He'd learned to be careful when speaking to a goddess. It was always better to use conditional phrases.

"*The objects that you seek will bring you to her,*" Siane replied, sending a chill down Vidarian's spine again. Of course she would know what they sought, if she was constructed to reach inside the mind of every air wielder—including Altair. With such knowledge it was easy to believe she was a goddess in the truest sense.

// I should stay here with you, // Altair said. The scent of his words was blackberry thicket and honey, sharp and sweet and careful. *// My life is yours. //*

The wall—chuckled, a play of light in dancing whorls that could be nothing else. "*Air does not stay.*"

Altair drew back at this, his wings almost mantling. *// Of course, //* he said at last.

"*If you wish to perform my will, you must wake Anake. I fear that the longer she sleeps, the more she falls away from us, and to lose her entirely would be catastrophic.*"

～～～

They left Siane to rest, or to go into a kind of half-aware state that Khalesh said was an automaton's equivalent of meditation. Before they departed, Siane showed them a map of the underground city, drawn in lights on her polished surface. Khalesh produced a small prism-key he'd risked keeping with him and captured the map inside it through some arcane Animator's trick. The city, Siane explained, would indeed take them all the way to the Great Gate without the need to resurface, if they followed the aqueducts, which led all the way to the sea.

When they rejoined Ariadel, Mey, Daelwyn, and the wolves at the tropical forest, Ariadel came quietly and swiftly to Vidarian. Ailenne was awake and playing with one of the young wolves under Daelwyn's surprisingly tender eye. Tephir, Eoin, and Iridan also turned toward them as they arrived.

"She is awake," Vidarian said, and Ariadel embraced him, half in wonder and half in relief.

"We felt—something," she said, her eyes wide, though not quite with fear. "The walls trembled, only for a moment."

"Rai's doing," Vidarian said, and dropped his hand—though not far—to the wolf's head. Rai's tongue lolled, and then he went to Ailenne, sniffing her for any damage. She laughed, a high squeaking sound that always sent a sharp pulse of pure delight through Vidarian's heart. Rai whuffed out a breath into her wispy hair, and she laughed again.

"*Would you mind,*" Iridan began, startling Vidarian, "*if I went and spoke with her?*"

There was only one "her" he could mean. Vidarian exchanged a glance with Khalesh. "Of course not," Vidarian said.

"I can accompany you, if you'd like, my friend," Khalesh offered.

"*Thank you, it is a kind offer,*" Iridan answered, "*but I would prefer to go alone.*"

"Of course," Khalesh said, and if he was hurt by it, he did a good job of pretending otherwise.

Iridan departed up the corridor, and they all watched in silence until he disappeared around a corner. No one spoke, but the thought hung between them: what must it be like to be an automaton? Lonely, Vidarian imagined. The one desire Iridan had ever expressed for himself was to find the few others like him.

Tephir watched Thalnarra and Altair surreptitiously, but his owlish eyes were far too large to carry this off successfully. He had volunteered a bit too quickly to remain with Ariadel and the rest—peculiar in particular since his scholarly curiosity about Siane's nature was at least equal to Khalesh's. But he'd spoken hardly a word since they'd entered her chamber, and now regarded Thalnarra and Altair as though he were a different species altogether.

// *Your curiosity speaks though you will not, friend owl,* // Altair addressed him at last, and Tephir's round-edged feathers ruffled with consternation. There was only exhaustion in Altair's voice, and no accusation.

// *There are records of owl-gryphons who worshipped one of the elemental goddesses,* // Tephir said, delicate as new ice. // *Anake, the earth goddess. But Qui does not recognize the elemental goddesses, and I am afraid the culture proved contagious. But even if she were not a remarkable artifact, my curiosity regarding Siane would be great.* //

// *It would appear your people were not incorrect to move away from them,* // Altair said, with a heaviness Vidarian had never known in him. // *But I find my appreciation of our goddess renewed for knowing her true nature.* // His blue eyes found Vidarian's then, and a wisp of wind touched his face.

Vidarian gave a tiny nod, wishing that he could share his thoughts as easily as gryphons did between themselves.

Thalnarra had had enough of her world disrupted to have forgotten temporarily about Princess Mey, but now seemed to have recovered herself. Mey, for her part, stuck close to Ailenne since the sightwolf attack, and seemed much less brazen than when first they met.

Gryphons could loom with great effectiveness when they put their minds to it. Mey, to her credit, did not cringe beneath Thalnarra's gaze, but set her jaw stubbornly.

"I skipped formal introductions," Vidarian interposed himself between huge gryphon beak and small girl, "as Iridan will surely be able to bring the *Jade Phoenix* back to recover the princess as soon as we exit the mountains."

// *And being that we were attacked by wolves,* // Thalnarra agreed dryly—the kind of dry that was ready to become kindling. // *I'm sure Emperor Ziao will be thrilled to hear about that.* //

"Not to mention the Empress," Ariadel added, looking a little pale.

Vidarian glared at Thalnarra, but had little reply. As if he himself had personally arranged for Mey to hide aboard the *Phoenix*!

"It is my fault," Mey said, blinking a little as their heads all turned toward her. She bowed, a sudden movement, and behind them, Tephir and Eoin immediately returned the bow, stooping deeper than she had. The rest of them stood awkwardly, not knowing what to do. Still bent, she said, "I apologize for stowing away." When she straightened, her face was a mix of emotion, far too complex for so young a girl—regret and determination, defiance and fear. "It was the only way I would see the world. I have never been allowed to leave the Imperial Palace."

The burning grass scent that flickered through their minds from Thalnarra's said all that the gryphoness could without words, and Vidarian couldn't help but agree. He took a long breath before he replied. "Our aim will be to return you to the *Jade Phoenix* as soon as we can. This is no pleasure tour, Princess. Your life is in danger."

"What life?" Mey snapped. "I am the youngest of three sons and four daughters. I matter not to my parents nor my empire and I never will."

// *That is surely untrue,* // Thalnarra said. Her ferocity aside, Thalnarra had a remarkable acuity for the pain of young people. // *Your family surely grieves your absence. Likely they will raise their entire might to find you.* //

Mey didn't answer, but neither did she argue, and that was enough. It was an impasse, of sorts; even had Mey wanted to return home that instant, none of them presently could manage it.

When Iridan reappeared, he would not speak of his conversation with Siane, if there had been one. He skirted questions without outright refusal, but even Khalesh gave up hope of a clear answer. Instead, they gathered themselves for the journey to the gate.

Daelwyn and her wolves rested beneath a great tree, too large to have grown since the gate's opening. Indeed the tree itself seemed to be dead, but was festooned with green vines. Daelwyn leaned against it, throwing sticks for the young wolves to chase and wrestle over. Nearby, the verali grazed, seeming accustomed to the wolves' presence, even glad of it.

Khalesh showed the map to Daelwyn, and she muttered as she studied it, nodding intermittently. The city was long, clinging to the edge of the Windsmouth like a lichen. She pointed at the grooves that ran through it, and they glowed where her fingertip passed. "These are the aqueducts," she said. The large black wolf came to rest his head on her shoulder, also watching the map. "We can take you to the nearest opening, and follow the channel from there. We've explored parts of the city on this side, but never the whole way through."

Vidarian nodded as Khalesh accepted the map back from her. "We'll rest here, and start in the morning."

CHAPTER FOURTEEN
CITY IN THE MOUNTAIN

Vidarian had worried that they would have no sense of night or day in the warren of underground passageways, but the sunsphere in the forest seemed to have its own such sense. It dimmed, traversing a gentle arc of sunset pastels before settling into moonlight, and they slept.

The twitter of birds responding to the artificial dawn woke them gradually; Iridan had kept watch through the night, accompanied by some of Khalesh's tiny mechanical assistants. They made a morning meal of bamboo leaf-wrapped rice cakes for the humans and dried spiced venison for the gryphons (save Tephir, who had his own supply of what appeared to be fermented beans of some sort). The verali by now were restive and more than happy to be urged onto the mosaic-tiled "road" of Daelwyn's promised aqueduct entrance.

The underground city was seridi-built, improbably enough—or perhaps it had been built by gryphons and seridi together, and populated by the latter. If Thalnarra, Altair, or Tephir knew why winged creatures would build a city with no access to the sky, they did not say. The aqueduct passed beneath market squares and tall-columned halls, elaborate bathhouses and theatre rounds. Often the channel they followed—a wide one that formed a sort of central artery through the city—remained at ground level, but periodically it became a high bridge suspended above chambers dug deep beneath them, inverting their sense of altitude. But it wound inexorably northwest, following the granite foothills, taking them ever closer to the sea.

As they walked, Daelwyn's wolves ranged ahead, loping easily back and forth along the channel and roving through adjacent rooms and corridors. Their living, undulating wall of attention was comforting; if anything had made a home in the city, it would not catch them unawares.

Vidarian was especially grateful for their guardian presence as he took his turn carrying Ailenne, asleep against his chest and nestled in a kind of quilted silk hammock given them by the Empress of Qui. In spite of the gravity of their journey—the prospect of venturing into uncharted regions of the southern continent, the constant specter of the Alorean Import Company, the concern for Calphille and Val Imris, the thought of finding and waking another goddess . . . all of it faded when he breathed in the peculiarly sweet fragrance of Ailenne's dove-soft hair, listened to and felt the subtle rhythm of her breathing.

Never would he have guessed that so small a person could so totally consume his attention. He found himself wondering what she would look like as a young woman, whether she would want to travel to Kara'zul to study at the fire temple as her mother had done, what it might be like for her to be aboard an ocean-sailing ship for the first time. The mere notion alone that Ariadel was a mother—the mother of his daughter—was still enough to send his thoughts reeling with wonder.

Rai ranged at his side, never seeming to want to be far from Ailenne. Vidarian wasn't sure if it was the wolf's sensitivity to his own thoughts and feelings that caused this, or some more primal protectiveness over what he perceived to be a family cub. But he was enjoying himself, his tongue lolling as he flickered inarticulate happy thoughts into Vidarian's awareness. He was happy, too, for the companionship of the sightwolves, which added both sadness and gratitude to the strange cocktail of Vidarian's thoughts.

Together they came upon Iridan, who was walking alone ahead of the group. When Vidarian looked askance at him, wondering if he was intruding on some private thought, the automaton beckoned in greeting.

"In the furor around Siane, I never thanked you," Vidarian began, speaking softly so as not to wake Ailenne. Despite his caution, the baby was oblivious, deeply asleep and curled like a tiny pink nautilus shell. "It was terribly remiss."

Had he been human, Iridan might have blinked or drew back. Instead he grew still, without nervousness. *"What for, Captain?"*

"You saved our lives, on the *Phoenix*," he said.

"*It was the only rational action*," Iridan replied. "*Had the* Phoenix *gone down, I too would have been destroyed.*"

"Rational or not, it was well done, and brave. We owe you our gratitude and more." He hesitated, then said, "I haven't forgotten about your siblings. Arian and Modrian?"

Iridan turned toward him, and for a moment Vidarian was afraid he'd given offense. But the brass fittings that served as Iridan's eyebrows tilted. "*That is well remembered, Captain. It honors me greatly.*" He turned forward again, and one of the large gears in his chest rotated slowly, a kind of sigh. "*But I must admit I retain little hope of finding them now.*"

"And yet," Vidarian began delicately, "you haven't a human's mortality to limit you. You can search a very long time."

"*The search will be long,*" Iridan agreed. "*But I will not abandon it.*"

"And you have my word that if there is anything I can do to help you, I will gladly give it."

"*My appreciation is too great for words, Captain.*"

They walked in silence for a time, and then:

"*Would you really have destroyed Siane?*" Iridan asked quietly.

Vidarian walked in silence for a few moments, trying to imagine it. He had promised Altair that he would have, if the gryphon had asked, but the thought of fulfilling this pledge raised the gorge in his throat with its wrongness. Finally, he said, "The honest answer is that I don't know," hoping that his sincerity would come through. "I don't even know if I could compare the thought to ending another person's life, but that is how it feels. Greater, even."

His answer seemed not to offend Iridan, to Vidarian's relief; the automaton bent his head slightly, his eyes rotating. "*It's peculiar,*" he said. "*I was created by a human, and so it seems not unfair that I could be destroyed by one. You are as gods over us.*"

"And yet we have made you into gods," Vidarian replied, still uncertain if he had even fully accepted what they had seen of Siane. Who could possibly have created such an artifact?

But Iridan, to his surprise, was shaking his head. "*Siane and I are quite* different," he said. "*We might be formed of similar components, but she is ultimately human. Her mind is all of your minds, her strengths your combined elemental strengths. We are different, that way.*"

The thought that Siane—that all of the elemental goddesses—were in some way human was both shocking and somehow obvious. Perhaps it wavered in that space his mind could not grasp still. Was a city human, if all of its residents were? Did it have an opinion, a heart? That answer, too, was obvious—it did. And like a human a city could be unpredictable, wild, or strange.

The aqueduct was lined with lights, elemental artifacts somehow kin to the sunspheres in that they made exceptionally clever use of very small amounts of fire energy—mere wisps of it to Vidarian's senses—to glow beneath frosted white glass. And like the sunsphere outside Siane's chamber, they tracked the phases of the day, dimming by afternoon before warming into sunset colors. Against the arched white ceilings of stone high above them the effect was enchanting, otherworldly.

Just as the sunspheres had completed their quiet journey into moonlight, two of Daelwyn's wolves returned from a scouting foray with their tails high in excitement. One of them barked as she drew near, and they all turned to Daelwyn for a translation.

She closed her eyes, listening, and when she opened them again it was with a smile, slightly sardonic as always. It was very near impossible to imagine the woman in a state of total happiness. "They've found books," she declared, kneeling to knit her fingers through the neck ruff of the wolf that had barked.

"They like books?" Vidarian asked, puzzled, and Daelwyn chuckled.

"They know that I like books," she said. "We've come in here before searching for them. Yarrow says they've found a *lot* of books."

"She . . . speaks in your mind, does she?" Vidarian asked. There hadn't been time, before, to interrogate Daelwyn on her relationship with the sight-wolves, but he'd burned with curiosity about it. Other than the Alorean Sky Knights and Ariadel, he'd never met another person who had the kind of bond with an animal that he had with Rai.

Daelwyn gave him an oblique glance, first measuring and then curious. "Sightwolves share pack intelligence," she said. "This little band is just a family. They took me in . . . after I was banished from Astralar." This last she offered simply, defying judgment. When Vidarian gave none, she continued, "They don't speak in words, really—not while they're awake. When we sleep, they speak, even appear to me as children—the pups, that is. When they're awake, it's images, impressions, scents." Her eyes fell on Rai and she smiled again, this time with guarded amusement. "They say this one's far too smart for a thornwolf, if you cared to know."

"Sometimes I think he's far too smart for any of us," Vidarian said, and Daelwyn chuckled, as he hoped she would. The smile she gave him then was genuine, if still appraising.

The library reminded him of the famous City Library in Val Harlon, which, he'd only recently learned, was also seridi-built. Even had Daelwyn not been partial to books herself, there would have been no living with Khalesh if they'd passed the library by, and Tephir was no better. It was no use telling them to sleep; they'd only wait until they were unguarded and begin rummaging in the stacks anyway.

This collection was only a fraction the size of Qui's Grand Library, but it was filled primarily with Alorean-style books, their covers made of leather and hide and paper pages sandwiched between. Tephir, Eoin, and Khalesh disappeared into the shelves as soon as they'd established a camp in the central chamber. There was even a dormant hearth of sorts, artifact-built, that received a whisper of Ariadel's fire energy and expanded it into a warm, bright, but safely contained dome of fire.

The sightwolves, all except the father, were still young enough to collapse into a heap shortly after arriving. Rai was not tired, by the alertness of his thoughts, but he, too, lay down near the younger wolves, content with their companionship and the warmth of the fire. Ariadel had fed Ailenne and was settling her in a basket beside Rai when Vidarian finished hauling water for the verali. He'd feared they would find no water in the empty city, but as with the hearth, a pump near the library's entrance needed only the lightest touch of water energy to summon a thin spigot of spring water up through the stone. What must it have been like to live during the heyday of such devices?

With Rai and Daelwyn keeping watch over the hearth and Ailenne's basket, Ariadel crept away, beckoning for Vidarian to follow. He did so, thinking that she had some request for the camp and wanted to avoid waking Ailenne, but she kept moving, eventually weaving through the tall shelves of books.

Dust coated the floor and was slowly making headway into the books, but they hummed with the faintest traces of air energy—repellant spells bound to the shelves themselves. Even Sher'azar had not had such casual and refined use of elemental energy. Admiring it caused Vidarian not to notice that they'd passed into a section filled with brightly-covered folk tales until Ariadel stopped in front of a shelf.

"This was one of my favorites," Ariadel said, gently touching the book's spine, but not daring to pull it from the shelf. The inscribed title was vaguely familiar.

"My mother spoke of that book," he said, for a moment lost in a memory. "I tried to read it once. Couldn't make much sense of it."

"It's a complicated story," she admitted. "If you're not paying attention, you'll miss half a dozen things."

"I didn't like that it thought it was smarter than me," he chuckled. "Maybe I didn't like thinking that she was."

"It's not so much about intelligence," she said, nudging him. "That can be as much the book's fault as anything else. The problem is, you don't want the answers handed to you. That would ruin it. It's not a mystery unless you puzzle it out yourself."

"That seems a terrible lot of work for a book."

"It's a bit like magic. The answers can't be given to you. You realize them or you don't. They can't just be told." She looked at him, and must have caught that he wasn't quite convinced. "Think of it like a game. If someone was playing it for you, it wouldn't be nearly as fun."

"Do games always have to be fun?" He was thinking of several—such as those played by Justinian Veritas, Senior Partner of the Alorean Import Company, or his Second, Oneira—that were anything but. Ariadel herself had once played a very serious game of Archtower with Ruby.

"Not always. Sometimes they're about realizing something. Like books, or like magic."

"I have a long way to go in all of them, still, it seems," he said, smiling to remove any sting. But as he realized the truth of it, a hint of regret crept in. "But never enough time. I could use a lifetime with you in a library."

She smiled, touching his arm. "The philosophers say that this is the human condition," she said, a gentleness in her voice that was not quite teasing, also touched with sadness. "That there is never enough time."

"I am no philosopher," Vidarian said, taking her hands in his own and turning them over, tracing the smooth skin between her thumb and palm with his, "but I would be happy with an eternity with you, in a place like this."

She clasped his hands, smiling, with the barest hint of sadness. "That's what a book is, isn't it?" She turned, gesturing at one of the shelves with its rows of leather-bound tomes. "It's grasping for more time. Trying to reach out beyond the limits of your own life and into the future, into the lives of other people who might understand you."

"But how much do we ever understand?" His question was actually agreement, and she smiled again, shaking her head. "This feeling that it all flies by, too fast to understand—that's all I know of life, the slip of the sea past a wooden hull, unknowing."

"Ship captains and fire priestesses are alike, that way," Ariadel said, reaching up to lightly touch his nose with her fingertip, almost catlike. "We're made to seek truth."

"Fire priestesses, perhaps," he allowed. "A ship captain knows it can never be found."

She did the right thing then, which was to kiss him, all mischief. It was an argument of a kiss, a kind of rebellion that could not be countered—which made it cheating, of course, but he had no objection.

They managed to pry Khalesh and Tephir from the seridi library only because they had found no book that was unrepresented in the Great Library at Qui. It was, in and of itself, an impressive statement of the Great Library's collection, but Tephir in particular couldn't help but radiate disappointment. This one seemed to be a recreational library of sorts, filled with familiar titles; Khalesh postulated that elsewhere in the underground city there might be a research library with rarer works, but even Tephir reluctantly agreed that they hadn't the time to go book-hunting.

After two more days of walking they emerged at last on the far side of the city, through a grand archway carved into the stone—here no longer granite foothills, but limestone, the Windsmouth itself. The wolves ran first, Rai with them, sniffing for any hint of the sightwolf pack, but there was none, and so the rest of them stepped gratefully into the gentle morning sunlight there. After days underground the evergreen-spiced air was rejuvenating and welcome. It was a jarringly familiar sight, seen from a different angle: they were at the threshold of the Great Gate, now abandoned by the gryphons who had congregated there upon its opening.

The sightwolf pack's absence was an odd one, and when he asked Daelwyn about it, she shook her head. "They avoid the city, and these ruins—we don't know why. The answer is down there, for certain, but it won't be we who ferret it out."

As Mey emerged from the arch, Vidarian also recalled his first objective upon their reaching the surface.

"Iridan, can you attempt to reach the *Jade Phoenix*?"

The automaton had been gazing at the tree line, and the nearby ruined arch of the Great Gate, but now turned back, his eyes glowing. He nodded, then brass eyelids closed over the glow of his eyes, still for a moment. Finally they reopened.

"*I apologize,*" Iridan said. "*I am unable to make contact with any relay sphere within the space I can reach.*"

Vidarian let out a breath. Part of him had known they would be out of range, but he'd held out hope. "It looks like you'll be staying with us a while longer, Princess," he said to Mey.

"It is my destiny to travel with you," Mey said, with simple surety that held neither import nor levity. Vidarian squinted at her, nonplussed; he cast an eye on Tephir and Eoin, but neither offered up a convenient answer.

"And this is where we part ways," Daelwyn said, saving them, and Vidarian found himself grateful for the rueful note in her voice. He'd enjoyed her company, too, far more than he would have expected when they first met.

"You would be welcome to come with us," he said, after hesitating— it would complicate their rations in the unknown terrain that would soon follow. "We might be able to uncover some way of breaking apart the sight-wolf pack that hunted us, of healing them."

But Daelwyn was shaking her head, chuckling. "You can't save all of us," Daelwyn said, an uncanny echo of Vidarian's earlier thoughts. She must have seen his face fall, for she swatted him on the arm, a playful strike that none-theless sent him staggering a step. "And we can take care of ourselves," she continued. "This is our fight."

One by one the humans embraced Daelwyn—even Eoin, who of all of them had spent the most time with her by the fire, deep in discussion of the natural world—and Rai capered with the young wolves, playing. When she and her lupine entourage left at last for the distant tree line, Rai looked out after them, his thoughts opaque to Vidarian.

∿∿∿

The Great Gate, once opened by the storm sapphires, now served as a kind of powerful extender of gate energies. Ordinarily it would have still required at least four elementalists to open it, one of each element—but the artifact that Asalet had given them was its own key, containing not only the energy to open the gate by itself, but the knowledge to direct it to a specific location.

Vidarian had thought, upon looking at the small pyramid-shaped crystal, that they would have to spend some time learning how to integrate it with the Gate—but it was as simple as placing it in a pyramid-shaped indentation still carved precisely in the strange stone of the gate's arch, and touching it with elemental magic.

The gate responded so quickly that they all jumped back from it in surprise, fearing a backlash of energy—but there was none, only a wash of light.

The door punched through the world's fabric opened, shimmering, and beyond its threshold lay a rolling grassland. It reminded Vidarian of the great prairies of central Alorea, but something about its horizon told him this was much more vast. There were riders, so distant as to be thumbnail-sized, slipping through the tall grass—human populations?

"The southern continent," Iridan murmured, and Vidarian nodded without turning to him, transfixed.

CHAPTER FIFTEEN

OLD FRIENDS

Thalnarra and Altair passed through the Great Gate first, insisting on landing on the far side as a vanguard against any possible unfriendly greeting. They arrived beyond without incident, their bodies blurring in the heat haze of the gate's shimmer, but unharmed.

By silent consensus Iridan passed through next, with Khalesh and Tephir, leading the verali behind them. Eoin escorted Mey, Ariadel, and Ailenne after, leaving Vidarian to follow. Carefully, he extracted Asalet's artifact from the pyramid-shaped indentation—and exhaled a breath he hadn't known he was holding when the portal itself did not wink out of existence. It only dimmed, flickering, and he stepped through it before its energy could expire.

The gate seized him, a now familiar wrench that washed sensation into starlight, infinite motion, and then—darkness.

∿∿∿

She had small white animals strapped to her feet.

Vidarian was bent double, kneeling on a black and white tiled floor. Asalet's artifact was still clenched in his right fist, and he slipped it into a pocket with quaking hands.

At first it looked like the Starhunter had gutted two fluffy rabbits and wrapped their bodies around her feet, but upon closer inspection, the rabbits in question weren't real. Their heads were decorated with mouths of pink thread and eyes of black glass, and the fur itself had a stiffness to it as if it, too, wasn't real, at least from any rabbit he knew.

She was looking down at him, wrapped in a wide-sleeved silk robe and holding an ornate porcelain cup of tea with both hands. The robe was black, peppered with tiny pink flowers, and she was pouting.

"The longer you lie there, the longer you make them wait, you know," she said, quite as if it were his plan to have appeared here, confronted with her strange foot coverings.

Carefully, he levered himself first to his elbows and then his hands, standing when he could be reasonably sure the world wasn't going to fall out from under him. The floor was cold and hard as polished stone, but smooth as glass.

The room was like a fine lady's parlor, if the lady were excessively strange. The walls were striped pink and white, decorated alternately with silver filigree shelves and varnished display cases. Both shelves and cabinets were crammed with knick-knacks, only about a third of which he could recognize as fanciful salt cellars, display plates, cutlery. One held a small portrait of a gryphon, a horse, and a child that appeared to be half of each.

Curled up on the rug was a small gryphon whose appearance tugged at Vidarian. He levered himself upward and looked at the creature, which turned a gap-beaked grin at him, the first time he'd seen a gryphon do such a thing. The easy expression seemed permission to look more closely, however, and the distracting difference leapt out: the gryphon had four leonine paws, no fore-claws at all! His wings—normal enough—had an iridescent rooster-tail sheen to the tips of their feathers.

"That's Snerl," the Starhunter said. "He's visiting for tea." As she spoke, the gryphon raised a hind foot and gave a good long scratch behind his ears, wolf-like. And indeed he did have a steaming cup of tea on the floor in front of him.

"What is this place?" Vidarian asked.

"You reacted so poorly to my nicer curio room," she said. "Don't think I didn't notice! I just thought you might need some comforting, now that you've seen Siane for what she really is." There was a downward turn to her voice, as if "what Siane was" was something unclean, preposterous as that was coming from a creature who had once appeared to him in a dream as a tower of beetles, and worse. She pointed her forefinger at him, then made a kind of exploding noise with her lips and teeth, as though firing a tiny cannon. Tea poured out of her fingertip, followed by sugar, cream, and a spoon, all of which landed in another garish porcelain cup that appeared and floated toward him.

"Strangely, this is not that comforting," he said, flattening his hand when the cup bumped into it like an insistent dog. Thus invited, the cup settled on his palm and gave a tiny sigh of contentment. The Starhunter glared at him until he sipped the tea. It was shockingly good, fit for the fussiest fire priestess, a dimensional richness that spoke of alpine mountaintops and autumn rain.

"You like it," she said, blushing like a nursemaid in what would have been a pretty effect had she stopped at pink and not gone on to purple and then lavender blue. "It's special, you know. Very rare. To congratulate you for doing as I asked. We'll make a champion of you yet."

There were no windows in the room, nor doors, and yet the tea still managed to exaggerate the slowness of the passage of time. In his mind, ages passed before he harnessed his thoughts back together enough to ask a question:

"Are you—like they are?"

The Starhunter laughed, a sound like cracking glass, or bones splintering. "Me? Don't be ridiculous." He was about to ask again when she tilted her head to one side—too far, exaggerated, and his neck twinged in sympathy. "But then," she tapped a sparkling fingernail to her lips, "would I think I was, if I was? You'll have to chew on that for a while."

She chewed on the fingernail, ruining its glittered pattern, then dipped it into her tea and flicked her fingertips at him, splattering droplets.

"Ta, dah-ling!"

∿∿∿

He stumbled through the far side of the gate, into sky, into sun.

Ariadel was waiting beside the gate, Ailenne in her arms and Rai at her side. Her look of worry lifted into a kind of resigned relief that cut at Vidarian deeper than anger would have.

"Are you all right?" she asked, glancing down the hill onto which they'd arrived. Behind him, the gate sputtered shut, folding in upon itself infinitely.

Below, the gryphons were speaking with a pair of riders. Their steeds were not the horses they'd seen at a distance from the gate, but giant long-necked birds with stubby wings, hair-like plumage, and formidable taloned feet not unlike a gryphon's. One bird was mottled brown and black, the other a ghostly white.

Vidarian pulled his eyes away from the riders—their hosts?—and back to Ariadel. "I don't know how to stop her from doing that," he said, hoping that just enough frustration had crept into his voice.

Ailenne squirmed and fussed, complaining, and Ariadel offered her to Vidarian. He tucked her against his chest and she settled, still burbling to herself, but not struggling. The warmth of her small body and the alertness of her eyes grounded him, reassured him that he was here and not still trapped between two worlds.

"What did she want?" Ariadel asked, watching the conversation below them from the corner of her eye, poised to catch any sign of concern from the gryphons' body language.

"She wanted to talk about Siane."

Ariadel turned toward him more fully, sharper. "What did she say about her?"

Translating the Starhunter had never become easier, in part because Vidarian still understood so little of her behavior. Explaining that she'd wanted to make him a cup of tea would raise more questions than it answered. And that strange gryphon . . . "She wanted to know what we thought about Siane's nature," he finally managed, then added, "and wanted me to wake Anake the same way we woke Siane."

"Is the Starhunter . . . like them?" Ariadel asked, and a wash of dissonant comfort and worry coursed through him that she had immediately come to the same question. But there was something else in her face—a deeper worry.

"I asked her that," he said, aiming to reassure, "but she didn't answer."

"What does it mean if she isn't?" Ariadel asked quietly, but turned down the hill, folding her arms tightly around her chest. Her discontent was clear enough, but Vidarian could not answer it, for he shared it. Much of the Starhunter's disregard for the other elemental goddesses now seemed rational—not a word he was accustomed to applying to her. But she seemed as adamant as Siane, if not more so, that they should all be awakened.

And in spite of her dismissiveness—which it occurred to Vidarian was no greater than that which she applied to most entities not directly in thrall to her—she had always respected the goddesses and their wills. If the goddesses themselves were the unified and amplified will of their respective magic-wielders, did it follow that the Starhunter would extend that respect to the magic-wielders themselves? Perhaps not all individually—she had destroyed more people before Vidarian's eyes than he cared to think about—but if she knew the nature of the goddesses, and respected them still, she respected the will of humans and gryphons. The thought was staggering.

In realizing the nature of Siane—and therefore Sharli—Ariadel had in effect lost a goddess who had been much more to her than Nistra had been to Vidarian's family. He had prayed to Nistra on every sail of his life, but Ariadel had *known* Sharli, had hosted her in her own body. If Sharli was somehow unreal—was this composite—and the Starhunter wasn't . . . it was little wonder she walked as though chilled even under a sun that cast these plains into perpetual summer.

He could think of nothing that would comfort her, and so he followed in silence, navigating the slope foot by careful foot. Ailenne was staring fixedly at him in a way that she sometimes did, her eyes like great dark pools of infant mystery. He smiled at her, and she smiled back, waving her arms. Beside them, Rai tipped his head toward her, tongue lolling.

The great birds belonging to the two riders appeared even larger as they drew closer, their feathered shoulders at Vidarian's nose level and their small heads carried high above them. Far from the indifference of horses, their eyes turned toward Ariadel and Vidarian as they approached, bright with inquisitive intelligence.

The riders, too, stopped in their conversation. Both were large, broadshouldered and tall. The first, a man clad in soft hides trimmed with fur, bore a large hooked staff. His was the dark mottled bird, which in addition to a saddle wore a wild array of red and blue beads strung from its harness. It was leaner, cannier of eye, and more predatory than the white bird, whose leather harness was also white, and devoid of beads or decoration. The other rider, a woman, wore an abundance of white feathers tied into her hair in a kind of second mane, and her calfskin clothing was bleached pale, though not as white as the bird.

But there was a third human as well. The large bodies of the gryphons and the riders' avian steeds had blocked another face from view: a familiar one.

"Luc Medicka," Vidarian said, shifting Ailenne and extending his right hand.

The *kava* merchant clasped his arm warmly with both hands, his sun-dark face split with a broad smile. "I had not thought to see you again, my friend," he said, "especially this far south!"

"New needs, and new methods of travel," Vidarian said.

"Yes!" Luc brightened, clapping once. "Sky ships, your companions say—and elemental gates." He gestured to Khalesh and Iridan, who stood nearby. The bird riders seemed to be not too subtly keeping their distance from him.

"Isn't it late in the year for you to be this far from Alorea?" Vidarian asked, hoping to avoid discussing the gate before they must.

Luc's expression wavered into gravity. "The word from the north is not a comforting one," he said. "Those of us who travel widely pass information across the trade routes. They speak of war, and worse." He looked closely at Vidarian, and seemed to find, if only in a lack of denial, what he was looking for; he let out a breath. "I thought it safest to remain here, among friends."

The two riders inclined their heads when Luc held his hand out to them. The male rider—a warrior, it was now apparent, by the glittering black lava-stone knives at either end of his hooked staff—spoke a long sentence in a lilting, almost musical language that Vidarian had never heard before.

"He says that much has changed since the Breaking, some good and some bad," Luc translated. "They were explaining to the gryphons—he calls them chosen of the gods or some such, quite a long phrase—that they have called a gathering with the Plainsrunner khans to discuss the rumors caught by their seers, and the songs of the ocean brethren."

"Ocean brethren?" Vidarian repeated, developing a suspicion. "Are they—shapechangers?"

Luc drew back, looking at Vidarian with new respect, and curiosity. "Why would you say that?"

Vidarian paused, trying to think of how to describe An'du's people. "You know the legend of the An'durin?"

"You mean the green whale?"

Vidarian nodded. "I've met her. On several occasions now. With the gate opened, she resumed her ability to shapechange into . . . a kind of human. Her people have roamed the oceans for thousands of years."

"Well, I'll be," Luc said, and spoke to the bird riders in their own language. Whatever he said caused the warrior rider to laugh and retort a few words. Luc shook his head. "He says I'm a fool for not knowing of the ocean folk. But this gate . . ." he trailed off, squinting. "You wouldn't mean the Great Gate, beneath the Windsmouth, would you? And that wouldn't have anything to do with how you got here?"

Vidarian sighed inwardly. But there would be no avoiding it. "The Great Gate," he agreed. "We last saw you before the Windsmouth. Before I opened the Gate."

Luc's eyes widened and sharpened simultaneously, an impressive trick. "You . . . were the one who opened the Great Gate. That was where you were going."

Ariadel shifted, and Vidarian silently agreed with her tension. But hiding the truth would be more than simply dishonest. "I did," he said, hoping it wasn't a mistake.

Luc turned toward the riders and spoke quickly and for some time. Both riders gasped early into the exchange, and Vidarian took a subtle half step away from Luc, preparing to defend himself if necessary. Beside him, Rai's neck ruff crackled, and Vidarian sensed his wariness, and readiness also.

The woman in white calfskin came up to Vidarian, her hands held palms forward in a gesture of goodwill, even reverence. Her eyes were wide and startlingly green against her dark skin.

"If true, you have restored balance to the plains," she said, her Alorean simple but clear. "Our brothers and sisters return to us, wearing their human skins once more." She turned to Luc. "Is there proof it is he?"

// *This is Vidarian Rulorat, the Tesseract,* // Thalnarra said, her voice tight and thin like tomato skin. // *I witnessed him open the Great Gate with my own eyes.* // Vidarian thanked her with a look, feeling the pain in her diffidence.

"The word of a gryphon is beyond question." The woman turned back to Vidarian. "If you are this man, if you are He Who Wakes, it is our honor to welcome you into our circle."

CHAPTER SIXTEEN
BEAR TRIBE

The two bird riders led them south over the rolling hills. Gradually they began to sight sentries mounted on birds like the warrior's, dark of plumage and sharp of eye. But there was no "circle," or village as Vidarian expected. He was about to ask their guide if they must ride for days— when suddenly they were surrounded by riders, male and female, young and old.

They seemed to materialize from the hills themselves, and upon closer inspection this was not far from true: these hills had doors, and were not hills at all, but fantastically camouflaged earthen mounds dug out like lairs or wolf dens. When he could cast a surreptitious glance behind them, Vidarian could not make out where the mounds ended and the true hills began.

An old woman—at first difficult to distinguish from a moving pile of bearskins trimmed with beads—shuffled out from one of the hill-houses. She was given a great berth of respect by the other villagers, one that, once she drew near, Vidarian understood more viscerally: she radiated earth energy.

As she drew nearer to him, that aura of energy pressed upon him like a repellent magnetism, a force that was as discomfiting as it was odd. It was half completion and half opposition—and as he felt it, Vidarian realized that part of what Justinian Veritas projected was a low-level earth energy. In Anake's absence, there were few if any earth-wielders left in Alorea, but if he understood correctly, the shapechanger civilizations were not so much wielders of earth as they were part of the earth itself.

The warrior bird rider bowed to the woman, his hands together, when she reached them. She smiled, nodding, and gestured for him to rise, revealing long pointed fingernails painted a gleaming black. When he straightened, she asked a question in their flowing language.

Cautious, the warrior translated for Vidarian: "She asks if this is the one who calls himself He Who Wakes?"

Vidarian imitated the warrior's bow as best he could, then glanced over his shoulder to Luc Medicka, who gave an uncertain shake of his head. "I am called so by your people, I am told," he replied carefully.

The warrior translated again, and the old woman smiled more broadly, nodding. She spoke again to the other rider, whose head jerked upward slightly at her words. He repeated them back to her, followed by another question, a quickness in his tone that raised the hair on the back of Vidarian's neck. The old woman said something then, more sternly, and the warrior bowed quickly. When he spoke again to Vidarian, his throat was dry. "She says— defend yourself."

And then the warrior shuffled backward rapidly, clearing away from Vidarian.

The old woman's hands thrust outward, palms flat, and the ground cracked beneath Vidarian's feet. He spun, wheeling his arms, turning to wave the others back behind him—Thalnarra and Altair both uttered piercing challenges, their wings flaring.

"No!" the warrior shouted, throwing himself between the gryphons and Vidarian, showing surprisingly little hesitation in doing so. "He must prove himself, if Watiwa demands!"

Now the earth woman—Watiwa—steepled her fingers, long fingernails crossing like scissor-blades. She slid one hand downward, nail slicing against nail, and Vidarian's gut twisted: she was pulling on the very earth-matter of his body!

Lifting his hand, Vidarian summoned a shield of water energy around himself, pushing back her touch—matching his substantive energy to her own. She smiled again at his resistance, and he expanded the shield, using water's quickness to envelop her before she could react. Once the shield passed over her, he reached out behind it with a swirl of fire energy, carefully withholding its heat, aiming to restrain rather than harm.

Watiwa dropped her hands, balled into fists, and the ground fell out beneath Vidarian's feet again. He redirected the shield beneath his feet, pushing away her energy—but in the process lost his hold on the restraining fire.

Below, the ground stabilized, but now Watiwa lifted her hands again, this time the fingernails curling inward like claws. The earth rose up around Vidarian, circling his shield, mounding upward in spears that matched the curve of her fingers. The arcs continued to curl, and in moments gravity would bring them crashing down, unresisted by the shield.

Gritting his teeth, Vidarian twisted his energies together, forming the blended strike that fused water and fire, revealing the chaos at its core. This spiraled knife he sliced upward in an arc, and it cut through the earth without resistance. Around him, the spears fell one after another, opening like the petals of a flower.

Dropping to a knee, Vidarian brought the energy around, lifting it in front of him like a sword. The air boiled where it passed, rippling like the perimeter of a gate.

Watiwa, who throughout had never broken her calm demeanor, smiled yet again. She brought her hands together, fingertips touching, and bowed to him. Before she rose, she spoke again, a long sentence.

"She says there is much you do not yet know," the warrior rider said, shaken. "But you are He Who Wakes."

The white rider, who all the while had watched with unreadable interest, now also spoke: "Welcome to the home of the Chatika people."

ᘓᘓᘓ

All were quiet as they continued through the village—contemplating, Vidarian thought, what had just occurred. The Chatika, as they were called, seemed friendly—but their interpretation of what that meant seemed somewhat unique.

Luc ranged beside Vidarian, his sandaled feet clearly accustomed to long walks. The riders were leading them to the center of the earthen village, and the Ishmanti at last leaned in to ask a question Vidarian that had been dreading.

"I would not have thought to see you without Ruby guarding your back,"

Luc said. The lightness in his voice said that, however wide-ranged the traders' communication lines, they had not carried word of the death of the West Sea Queen.

"She's . . ." He stopped. How did one describe what Ruby had become? Much less to one who had admired her? "She has—taken up a personal alliance with the Alorean Import Company."

"That can't be," Luc said, disbelief so strong that it was emotionless. "Every free trader despises the Company, to say nothing of the West Sea Kingdom."

Vidarian regretted then not just claiming she was dead; he realized that, despite everything, he didn't want to believe that she was. "My fear is that she is not herself," he said, hating the half-truth, but Luc's face darkened with recognition.

"Have they some hold over her? It must pain you greatly to see a friend so bound, especially such an honorable one."

The man's sympathy was acid in the wound of his lie, and Vidarian only managed: "It does, greatly."

To his relief, they were drawing upon their destination, a massive hill twice as tall as the rest and four times as wide. This hill was decorated with hooked lances tied with cloth streamers in a rainbow of colors, but primarily red and blue.

Outside the hill were two horsemen, and at first Vidarian was relieved to see that they must be the riders whose silhouettes had marked the horizon from the gate's other side. "Plainsrunners," the bird riders had said. But as they drew closer, a chill crept down Vidarian's back, and it took several moments to pick out the wrongness.

These riders' horses had no heads, and the riders themselves had no legs. Rather, the bodies of the men—their chests and arms covered by quilted brocade jackets, vibrant yellow sashes at their waists—continued into the bodies of horses, one black and one chestnut. They were not two men and their horses, but two creatures total—"horse men" like those that decorated Malu pottery, and were commonly known, in Alorea at least, not to exist.

"Tolui and Altan, messengers for Khan Zhenjin," the white rider murmured, when she saw Vidarian staring. Vidarian only managed to keep himself from jumping; the distraction hardly helped, but their guide could move with unnerving silence. Her presence was oddly—absent, and suddenly he realized why it troubled him so: the last such "blank" person he'd met had been an assassin sent by the Alorean Import Company, long ago on Ruby's ship. Ariadel had called him a "null." This woman was not so invisible, but she was close.

She led them through the banner-strung door built into the hill's face. The entry was not tall enough for the gryphons to pass, and she practically fell to the ground in the course of apologizing to them for this shortcoming; surely, she said, the Atira would promptly come out to greet the gryphons, which would be a great honor. Khalesh, Eoin, and Mey elected to remain with the gryphons and Iridan, leaving Ariadel and Luc to follow the white rider at Vidarian's side. Riders, some with their birds and some without, were gathering to marvel at the gryphons, Iridan, and the verali. Rai remained with them—unsure at first, but convinced when the children came bearing tidbits of dried meat.

Vidarian expected the mound to smell of fresh dirt, and it did, but stronger still was the fragrance of dried plains grass that both lined the floor and was woven into wall-coverings. Savory food aromas, also: bright pumpkin, toasted corn, pungent onions, among others.

The hill house boasted multiple round rooms branching off of the main hall that cut straight through it—pointing east, if his bearings remained true. At the end of the hall—a tunnel, really—was a large chamber, also round, with holes cut in the ceiling to direct sunlight down upon the massive pelt-covered chair where an ancient woman sat.

"Atira, I bring you travelers," the white rider said, and Vidarian was startled that she spoke to her leader in Alorean. But then she spoke a stream of words in the musical tongue they had heard before. The old woman's eyes were clear and bright, and she took them in with a measuring gaze; she seemed to understand both the Alorean and the musical language.

She wore a necklace of polished black bear claws, each separated by a carved bone bead. At her side, its long legs folded beneath it, sat an ancient bird. Nearly all of its feathers were painted, and when its head moved it rattled with red and blue beads; mostly, it rested its head in the Atira's lap, its great eyes closed.

"If you are He Who Wakes," the Atira said, her voice low and clear, a voice meant to be obeyed, "you are welcome in our circle, as our saman says. Share our harvest, and allow us to display our gratitude for the reuniting of our people."

"Your hospitality is a great gift, Atira," Vidarian replied, looking to Luc and the white rider for approval. They gave tiny nods, but both seemed to be avoiding looking at either Vidarian or the old woman. "We look forward to knowing more of your home. But I must ask you, with some urgency, if you have had other visitors recently, men or women from the north."

The Atira stroked the feathers of her bird's crest thoughtfully, putting Vidarian in mind of his mother and her favorite cat. She seemed to be weighing whether to answer, or how. At last, she said, "We have had riders from the north—three times in the past year, once since the Waking." She paused then, a hardness that worried Vidarian, but her anger seemed not directed at him. "They claimed that they were responsible for the Waking, but they lied easily, and must also have lied in this. They came on strange animals with the body of a Plainsrunner and the head of an antelope, but they were stupid animals, unable to speak." At this, the bird made a rumbling sound in is throat, and Vidarian nearly jumped—it had clearly reacted to the woman's words, not by coincidence.

It seemed that the birds possessed some intelligence, but the Atira's other proclamation dominated Vidarian's thoughts: the Company had been here, and recently. They knew about these people, likely knew far more than Vidarian or his companions did.

"They wanted to open trade relations," Luc murmured, still oddly keeping his attention away from the Atira. "Made my skin crawl. I never for a moment thought them sincere. They think of the southern tribes as savages, no better than animals."

The flatness in Luc's words, the barely restrained passion, brought another memory unbidden to Vidarian's mind, and his hands clenched at his sides. Justinian Veritas, that rarest of Company Partners who had survived the opening of the Great Gate, had all but admitted to a murderous plan of near unimaginable scale: the death of entire peoples, entire species, to cull the world down to his own ideal. In his attempt to win Vidarian to the Company's side, to convince him of the inevitability of the Company's victory, he had insinuated that the Company intended to wipe out entire populations—gryphons and seridi among them, but also *humanoid shapechanger* populations. And the strange energy of the riders became clear: it was the same energy, beyond elemental magic, that he had felt from Calphille: they were shapechangers. And these were the people that Justinian and the Company intended to extinguish. *No better than animals* . . .

Vidarian's mouth was dry, and he fought to remain still, and again to speak. At last, he said, "Forgive me, Atira—we have traveled far. But we thank you for the welcome, and look forward to knowing your people."

"Come," the white rider said, touching Vidarian's arm. Her hand shot lightning through his veins, and he almost drew away. Instead, he forced himself to understand that energy, and slowly it became more familiar: not quite human, but something more, a humanity threaded with chaos. A shapechanger.

∿∿∿

The sun was descending when they emerged from the great hill—the *atira aktarus*, the white rider said, home of the Atira—staining the sky pink and lighting the hills in deep gilded bronze; the magic hour.

Just as they emerged, a silhouette appeared atop the nearest hill to the west, surrounded by lances of falling sunlight. One of the tall birds walked beside him, and at first Vidarian assumed it was the white rider's, but her bird—almost identical, slim and white—was patiently awaiting her return, standing next to Iridan. Rai, beside them, wolf-shaped, waved his tail when he saw Vidarian, brushing his mind with his thoughts. He liked this place.

The new visitor, also dressed in white, was a willowy young man, pale of hair and radiating an almost otherworldly gentleness, as if he belonged in a place that had never known shadow.

Khalesh was staring at him. It must have been the light, Vidarian thought—Khalesh is blinded; the angling rays still hit him.

But they didn't. The young man had descended the hill and now enjoyed the same twilit definition that they did. When Vidarian recognized Khalesh's expression, it startled him; the Animator had never so much as lingered an eye on an attractive companion, male or female, before.

The second white rider noticed Khalesh's attention and immediately blushed. He looked away, turning to their escort, and Khalesh forced his eyes downward also, discomfited. "I come from Donama to welcome you to the Chatika Home," the young man said. His voice was soft, almost dulcet, exactly suiting his sculptured face and large eyes. Like the other white rider, his Alorean was clipped, but clear. He took a bundle of grass and herbs from a pouch at his side and scattered it on the ground, then held his hands, palms downward, over them, saying: "I, Tirus, welcome you. *Tihakka washista titiri kaa Chatika aktarus.*"

A quiet came over the young man then, and he tilted his head upward. At first it was just that, a lifting of his chin—but his face kept stretching, and his shoulders followed it, rising and thickening until he was twice his former height. In moments, a massive white bear towered above them, his long-clawed paws hung downward toward the ground, his black eyes focused with an un-bear-like intelligence.

The bear lifted its head and roared, a low trumpeting sound, and around them other Chatika lifted their hands and shouted back at him, a high welcoming call. Some of them whooped and whistled; beside Vidarian, the other white rider was smiling broadly, and in a moment her eyes were bright with water.

It took effort to remove his gaze from the white bear, but he looked askance at her.

"Tirus's great-great-grandfathers slept in bear shapes for eight hundred years. We wake into our true selves, we become the Chatika people once more." She reached out to clasp Vidarian's arm, and said, "I, Shiriki, welcome you. *Tihakka washista.*" And before him she, too, stretched, grew, reshaped; the hand on his arm widened and grew coarse with scaly footpad, soft with plush fur. Shiriki was brown as pine bark, her ears and paws tipped in white.

She roared, and the Chatika roared with her.

∼∽∼

Shiriki and Tirus took them to the saman's circle, where a great fire was being built. They sat around it on the trampled grass, and dark-haired children brought food on woven grass platters while Shiriki told of the emergence of the bear people from sleep. Her palms swept across the stars as she described the wild bears converging on the Chatika home, and how they had become men and women again, the two halves of the clan become one once more.

The children and adults alike displayed a clear reverence for the gryphons, and were surprisingly accepting of Iridan. There were legends, Shiriki said, when she settled beside Vidarian on the grass to partake of the sweet corn cakes and stuffed squash passed around the circle, of beings like Iridan within the story-memory of the Chatika.

Vidarian shook his head with awe. "We have libraries," he said, "Qui and Alorea alike, Velin and Malu and beyond—and yet so few knew that creatures like Iridan could possibly exist."

"I have seen your books," Shiriki said, "brought by the few northern traders who come here," she gave a little nod to Luc. "They are beautiful, but for the carrying of stories . . ." She paused, careful. "A book can be written and its contents forgot," she said, miming the writing and then pushing the "book" away from her. "The two hundred and eight tales of the Chatika are told—all by saman, most by all. The story-memory of the Chatika spans three thousand years."

Thalnarra watched Shiriki closely as she spoke, her expression—feathers slicked down and eyes sharp—tense and thoughtful. The more Shiriki spoke, the more that tension slipped away, until eventually she shook out her feathers.

Vidarian resolved to ask her what the bear woman's description had meant.

In the meantime, Ariadel, equally fascinated with Shiriki's words, was asking her about the earliest memories of the Chatika.

"Our people came first from the ocean," Shiriki said. "We did not always separate ourselves by the shape of our spirits. At one time there were clans where wolf and eagle and bear ran together. Some say that time will come once more. The clans gather, and begin to speak to each other for the first time since the beginning of the Great Sleep." She nodded across the circle to where a pale-skinned woman shared a bowl of toasted hazelnuts with two bear warriors. Her beads were striped and black, her hair held aloft with polished porcupine quills.

Vidarian tried three times to ask Shiriki about the artifact they sought, but some hesitation stopped him. Perhaps it was as simple as a reverence for the invitation the Chatika had so freely given—how easily they had welcomed foreign visitors into their home, given them food and story. He couldn't bring himself to ask more of them just yet.

That philosophy seemed tacitly shared, for no one suggested the artifact or its finding, and nor did any of the Chatika demand their purpose in arriving. There was only the fine meal, whole and true, and long after the food was gone they sat by the crackling fire, revering its heat in the night. At length, the Chatika themselves retired, seeming to sense that their guests might desire privacy of their own.

They sat some time in silence, and then: "It's as if in a single day the world is remade anew," Khalesh said. Vidarian thought he wasn't speaking only of the nature of the gods, of how Siane had transformed him. He was looking across the fire, but then marshaled himself, giving a tiny shake of his head. "I wrestle with these . . . ultimate artifacts," he said, and the calculating intelligence of focus was back in his eyes. "If . . . your elemental goddesses . . . connect their respective elementalists, are they also responsible for, or connected to, telepathy itself? We have known for centuries that great telepathic skill is almost always accompanied by powerful elemental presence, if not powerful elemental capability."

// *These distinctions between the elements are unique to Western imperial thinking,* // Tephir offered, his mind's voice quiet as he, too, looked out over the flames. // *In Qui, powerful telepathic ability is likewise revered, but young elementalists are trained to attune themselves to multiple elements.* //

"Could this be why the elemental goddesses have so little sway in Qui, though?" Vidarian asked. "The Eastern thinking does not commit to any one goddess or elemental training."

Beside them, Eoin chuckled, and Vidarian looked askance at him. The man looked faintly abashed; he'd spoken only rarely during their journey, seeming consumed by the study of his surroundings. He had a scholar's mind, and an adventurer's, and was no doubt cataloging unimaginable details. But when prompted, he cleared his throat.

"For centuries the illusion of 'east' and 'west' has held sway in the two empires," Eoin said. "But it's just that—an illusion. East disappears the further east you go—the same for all directions, west, east, north, and south."

// *This is very much the Qui way of thinking,* // Tephir agreed.

"Perhaps there is no such thing as 'Qui thinking' and 'Alorean thinking,'" Eoin pressed, a sharpness in his voice that belied depths of emotion. "Perhaps there is only knowledge."

CHAPTER SEVENTEEN

KEY

Morning on the plains dawned bright and chill, a fine coat of dew dressing the grasses in a sparkling gown. They had slept under the sky, wrapped in dark blankets given them by the Chatika, buckskin on one side and fur on the other. This was a romantic notion, and indeed the nighttime vault of the stars—different stars than Vidarian had ever seen—had been spectacular beyond imagining. But the reality following the romance was a unique kind of bone-deep pain that accompanied the ornamental dew, and a body complaining bitterly of the stiff cold. It occurred to Vidarian that at some point he was going to be too damned old for this kind of thing.

When he managed to rise, Vidarian found that he'd been abandoned. The gryphons were nowhere to be seen—likely hunting, save for Tephir, who seemed not to hunt even given the opportunity—and Ariadel and Ailenne were also gone. This, too, was not so surprising; their daughter woke early always, and Ariadel, given her many-years habit of dawn meditation, was the better suited of the two of them to take care of her. Only Rai remained, and he stretched sleepily as Vidarian worked the cold from his limbs.

With only a little exploration—crossing behind the saman house beside which the great bonfire had burned last night—he found Mey and Eoin sitting beside a morning cook fire with the black-garbed woman they had seen across the circle the night before. Then, Vidarian had thought her pale-skinned, and this was half true: she had skin unlike any he'd seen before, both light *and* dark, in streaks along her chin. Her forehead was pale, and what he'd taken for shadows on her cheeks were symmetrical curves of darker skin that continued down her neck, which bore thin stripes of white. Beside her, settled on the ground with its feet folded beneath it, was a white saman bird, smaller and more delicate than those belonging to Tirus and Shiriki.

Mey was watching the woman avidly, and seeing the two of them together, one young and one grown, revealed a surprising similarity in facial structure, pushing Vidarian to look past the oddness of the older woman's skin color. There was a distinctive flatness of nose, a height of cheekbone, that was unmistakably shared. Yet how could that be? Qui was thousands and thousands of miles from here, and its Grand Library had contained no maps of the southern continent.

The woman stood as Vidarian puzzled over this, and Mey and Eoin stood with her. She gave a small bowing motion with her hands together, another almost Qui-like mannerism.

"This is Matpri," Mey said, and Eoin gave her a startled look.

The woman—Matpri—also lifted her eyebrows, but her smile said she was unoffended. "We do not give the names of others unasked, *lek syha*," she said. "This is *kahw*, forbidden. A person's name is theirs to give only."

Mey's hands covered her mouth, all contrition. When Matpri waved them down, Mey said, "My parents gave me my name. I hardly feel it's mine."

Vidarian looked at Mey, startled not for the first time by the philosophical expressions that bloomed in her mischievous mind.

He wouldn't have known how to answer, but Matpri turned to her, taking her narrow shoulders in her hands. The striped coloration of her face amplified the solemnity with which she said, "Your name is yours, *lek syha*. You must never allow another to treat it unkindly. Our names connect us to *phi-khwan*, the great all. Your parents may have given your name, but you have given your name life."

Mey's eyes were large, and Eoin too had watched this exchange with alertness. They were all saved from having to answer her by the arrival of Shiriki. The bear saman bowed to Matpri, bidding her good morning, and then to Eoin, Vidarian, and Mey.

"You have slept within our circle, and are therefore most welcome guests," Shiriki said. "You may tell us now what you sought in crossing the world to find us."

Vidarian wanted to ask if by "crossing the world" she meant that they knew of gate travel, but stopped himself. They might have only one opportunity to ask clearly after what they sought. "We're searching for a key," Vidarian said, pulling from his pouch the carved wooden box that contained Asalet's pyramid-shaped artifact. He opened it before them. "It may look something like this."

"This I have seen," the woman said. She turned to Shiriki. "It is atop the *phi-klehn*."

Shiriki audibly drew in her breath and stared at Matpri for a long moment. The two women locked eyes, and Shiriki's sudden stillness spoke louder than a shout would have. If they had been gryphons, Vidarian would have been sure they were communicating telepathically—but neither the Chatika nor the Kala, nor any of the shapechanging tribes according to Tirus, had the ability to speak mind-to-mind.

"It is *kahw* to speak of the spirit stone to *suun-wat*," Shiriki said at last, though her tone was a demurring one, not fighting. Vidarian did not know what to make of her use of the Kala words—perhaps reminding Matpri of her own taboos.

"They are not outsiders," Matpri said, kneeling. She held her hand out to Rai, who amenably lowered his nose to her fingers. "You feel the energy from this one. The companion of He Who Wakes is *winjan*. He must see the *phi-klehn*, and therefore his brother also."

"You are sure of this?" Shiriki said carefully.

"I am," Matpri said. "His fire woman, also, whose companion is *winjan*."

With that, Matpri pressed her palms together, fingertips upward, and departed, leaving in the direction of the Atira's hall.

When she had passed beyond hearing range, Vidarian asked, "Have we offended?"

Shiriki shook her head. "Matpri has declared you to be *winjan*," she said. "One of the people. But for this to be, you must stand in the light of the *phi-klehn*, the spirit stone, that which binds all *winjan*." Her face tightened with concern. "You must go, also, He Who Wakes. And you must go today, this hour."

"Right now?" Vidarian blinked, too startled to speak more carefully.

"When one is *winjan*, one is recognized by the spirit stone before one's twelfth year," she said, almost diffident. "In those cases where one is raised far away from the stone, one must stand before its light immediately upon returning. We must leave at once."

~~~

Before the sun reached its zenith, they were following an honor guard of two bird riders over the hills to the south.

Mey, Eoin, and Luc Medicka had been permitted to join them, but Shiriki had respectfully asked—in a tone that was not a request—for Khalesh, Iridan, and the gryphons to remain behind. Of the three, Khalesh was the most discomfited, and extracted multiple promises for Vidarian to assiduously report on anything he should see. They shared the same suspicion, and Vidarian was discouraged not to have the Animator along: the way in which Shiriki and Matpri described the spirit stone—the *phi-klehn*—suggested a crystal elemental artifact, perhaps even an intelligent one.

Vidarian found himself walking beside Matpri. Just ahead, Ariadel was deep in conversation with Shiriki, Ailenne perched in her arms.

"You recognized Rai as *winjan*," Vidarian said to the striped saman, wrapping his mouth carefully around the unfamiliar word. "You said you felt it in his energy. What did that mean?"

Matpri smiled at Rai, who ranged back and forth along their trail as was his wont. Rai paused on his circuit and waved his tail at her before continuing. Matpri, as well as the Chatika, had treated Rai as they would a human from the first moment they saw him—another little puzzle. "He radiates the energy of the changing people," Matpri said. Behind her, her bird dipped its head over her shoulder, and she reached up to stroke its crest as she walked. "Surely you must know this?"

"I—" he began, then paused. He had been about to explain that the Starhunter had described this, but he was loath to believe her. Yet he hesitated to mention the chaos goddess, given the reaction that her name usually evoked. Was she *kahw*, as they would say? "One of the goddesses claimed that his energy was hers, once."

"Dara. The Evening Star. You speak with her?"

Vidarian looked at Matpri, wary, but her face was open and unafraid. "The elemental priestesshoods refer to her as a goddess of chaos," he said, now feeling as though he had trapped himself in the subject.

But Matpri smiled, turning her eyes to the horizon thoughtfully. Her bird, complaining that she had ceased scratching its head, made a kind of hollow honking noise and nudged her shoulder. She batted it on the beak and it ducked its head playfully. *Run!* it said, hopping—a sudden and springing movement for so large a creature.

Vidarian jumped. The bird's voice was simple and clear, a feminine note to it that was more human than the gryphons' voices.

"No, silly beast," Matpri told it, and it settled back down. She chuckled, then looked at Vidarian. The way she had of looking *into* people reminded him of Isri. "You are nervous to speak of Dara. Why? It is a great honor that she speaks to you."

"Most people I've met who have known her have feared her," Vidarian said. "Many told me that she would bring destruction, an evil force in the world."

The saman tilted her head to one side, again taking this in. "The Evening Star is neither good nor bad," she said, and Vidarian heard the echo of Luc Medicka's Ishmanti sentiment from a journey that seemed a world away. "She cannot be contained to such human ideas. But she is feared by those who reach too far, who do not recognize *tula*, the balance of all things. The Evening Star will always return the world to *tula*—though the path to this may be through the gate of death."

"You worship the—Evening Star, then?"

Matpri laughed. "It is an odd northern word, 'worship,' isn't it? To give of ourselves while also asking. It is dangerous to ask anything of the great powers of the world. More dangerous still to give oneself to them."

Given all he had seen, Vidarian could only agree.

Matpri's levity diminished then as she caught the angle of the sun. "If you will excuse," she said, and Vidarian nodded quickly. She tapped the shoulder of her white bird, which dropped immediately to the ground, allowing her to vault onto its back. It rose and trotted ahead, an easy ground-eating stride that carried her far ahead of him in moments.

The beast's pace took it swiftly ahead of Ariadel and Shiriki, who turned back to look at him. Rai bounded, eager to release some of his own energy, once he could avoid spooking Matpri's bird. But the birds showed no fear of him; Shiriki's bent its head to greet him as he approached.

"She seems uncomfortable," Vidarian said, motioning ahead to Matpri. "I hope I did not offend her."

Shiriki shook her head. "She intended to leave Chatika Home this morning. She does not like to be here on the *sikasi* of the Kala," she explained, frowning thoughtfully when she saw that they did not understand. She held up her hands. "Chatika are a people of one-time-moon," she said, holding up one finger. "Kala are people of two-time-moon." She held up a second finger. "To the Kala, six *dian*—month, you say—there are in the year. To the Chatika, twelve." Shiriki looked to make sure they were following, then added, "In Kala month, one day is the day-of-death, the *sikasi*. Tomorrow."

"Ominous," Vidarian said, though he wasn't at all sure he understood. If one day in every month — was devoted to death, there must be six every year, by the "two-time-moon" count.

Shiriki lowered her hands. "Death is a part of life. *Sikasi* day is for hunting, for blood hunger; the ending of one thing old and the beginning of one thing new. It is a day when spirits cross the world."

"Why does she dread it, then?" Mey asked. It seemed the Qui also did not share the idea of *sikasi*.

Shiriki blinked as though surprised that they hadn't understood her explanation. "Chatika hold one-time-moon," she said again. "*Sikasi* for Chatika—we say *katit*—passed ten days ago. Tomorrow is Chatika day of *eyrit*—day of seeing." And so Matpri's people accounted for the days and their significance differently.

"You seem to defer to her," Vidarian said, encouraged by Shiriki's openness about their two people. It had been something he'd wanted to ask since Matpri had declared they should visit the spirit stone.

"The Kala are *khwan-saman*," Shiriki said, and he was relieved that she seemed unoffended by his question. "You might say—saman-to-saman, highest saman. It was a Kala saman that brought the people together to create the *phi-klehn*, before the Great Sleep came upon us. Without them, we might have lost our selves." She chuckled softly, patting Vidarian on the arm. "If Matpri declares that you will stand before the spirit stone there can be no argument. In this only may the antelope rule the bear. And she risks death-day among the Chatika to witness it."

∼∼∼

The sun was tilting toward the horizon by the time they reached the sacred cave. They had passed many sentries along the way, to which Shiriki and Matpri had vouched for the passage of what appeared to be two foreigners. The guards seemed to be arranged in rings, increasing in frequency the closer they drew. Many were bear people, but others were clearly not, and Vidarian could only identify one as Kala, antelope clan.

"You must enter the cave," Shiriki said to Ariadel and Vidarian, including Rai and Raven with a gesture. "And under no circumstance should you touch the *phi-klehn*, for it brings instant madness. I can instruct you no further."

Ariadel lifted Ailenne hesitantly. "Will she—"

"It is better that she remain with us, if you would permit it," Shiriki said.

With some relief, Vidarian watched Ariadel hand their daughter to Matpri. His heart wrung when she struggled, complaining, but Ariadel caught his eye and nodded. Better for her to remain here if they could know nothing of what the cave would contain.

Ariadel took his hand, squeezing it, and they entered the cave.

The light within was immediately dim, but not black; a subtle glow emanated from further within. Vidarian expected to hear voices, but there were none; the silence drew them further.

The spirit stone—the *phi-klehn* as Matpri called it—was massive, as tall as Thalnarra and as wide as her outstretched wings. It did exude its own light, and seemed to be a strange kind of granite, many-faceted and formed from thousands of smaller stones fused into one great shape. And not all had fused: carpeting the ground around the single great stone were thousands of rock chips in every color imaginable, some translucent and some opaque. More chips were heaped atop the stone in a pile.

All of the stones exuded chaos magic, so strange and pure that Vidarian's stomach flipped within him. He expected to see the Starhunter emerge from within the quilted stone, or manifest herself out of its light. Until that moment he had never been completely sure there *was* such a thing as chaos magic, but the way the *phi-klehn* seemed half in this world and half outside it, ready to become something else—or nothing at all—in any moment . . . only one other presence exuded that kind of energy.

But as he calmed himself, accepting that it did emanate from the stone and from no other source, he felt its resonance with Rai and Raven. They, too, were drawn to the stone as if by compulsion or magnetism. Rai's neck-ruff was roused, his tail high with excitement, and Raven, cat-shaped, purred with contentment.

"Do you feel—any presence?" Vidarian asked Rai.

The wolf sat back on his haunches, reaching out toward the stone with his mind. Vidarian was startled to notice him doing this; the wolf had never reached out beyond the two of them, and so it had been natural to assume that he couldn't. But he projected his mind now, feeling the surface of the spirit stone the way a blind man would find the edges of a door-frame with his hands.

There is nothing, Rai thought at last. *Only the stone, and its great energy.*

"You like it, though," Vidarian pointed out.

The wolf's large blue eyes turned toward him. *It feels like home.*

Vidarian knew what he meant.

Rai took a step toward the stone, and both Vidarian and Ariadel made wordless objections.

She didn't tell us *not to touch it,* Rai argued. *She told* you.

Raven, who had passed the journey as a spider on Ariadel's shoulder, as was her custom, sat cat-shaped at Ariadel's feet. Her tail twitched agreement.

They stood at an impasse, then jumped when a scrabbling sound behind them indicated another visitor.

Mey trotted into the light of the spirit stone, and now Vidarian and Ariadel said her name, a yelp of surprise.

The princess held up her hands, an unsettlingly Chatika-like gesture of appeal. "Matpri sent me in here," she said. Vidarian stared hard at her, remembering her many deceptions, thinking that he should march her back out of the cave and see for himself.

He was about to do just that when Ariadel laid a hand on his arm. "There's only one entrance to the cave, and they're in front of it," she said.

Mey approached the stone, and none of them moved to stop her. She held her hands up to its light, entranced. Then, just as abruptly as she'd appeared, she knelt, picking up one of the stone chips that littered the ground. It was pale green and translucent, a little like jade.

"We weren't to touch the stone—" Vidarian began.

Without looking up, still cradling the chip between her hands, Mey said, "We weren't to touch the *phi-klehn*, and I didn't." There was the slightest edge of defiance, dulled by her transfixion on the stone in her hands. She stared into it, her eyes seeming to find a world there, and Vidarian remembered what it was like to gaze into one of the sun emeralds for the first time. Yet before that moment he would not have compared the stone chips to this—they instead repelled him, somehow.

A fluttering streaked by Vidarian's head, and before he could dodge away from it, it had landed on Mey's raised hand, and she laughed with delight. It was a bird, a finch of some sort, small and bright yellow, its face and wings streaked with black and white. It hopped, and Mey petted its head, whispering to it.

The bird flew to the top of the *phi-klehn*, landing atop it brazenly. Rock chips flew out from beneath its feet, rattling down the sides of the great stone.

It bent down and dug around in the chips as if they were a dust bath, scattering them everywhere. Ariadel and Vidarian watched, open-mouthed, unsure what to disbelieve more: the bird's behavior, or that Mey had summoned it.

The pale light of the spirit stone gleamed off of a larger faceted crystal beneath the chips at its top, and the little bird shoved against it, pushing with all its weight. The crystal was almost as tall as it was, but it tipped, then fell, bouncing down the side of the *phi-klehn* and coming to rest in the chips beneath.

Mey bent to pick it up. It was identical to Asalet's artifact, but larger, and pale rose in color. She walked to Vidarian and held it out to him.

He accepted the artifact from her, more concerned for the glazed look in her eyes, and what she had done, than for the key they had sought. Mey trembled as though cold, and Ariadel put an arm around her shoulders. Raven wove around her feet, and the little golden bird flew to her shoulder, perching and chirping there.

The chill that had taken her was not subsiding, and so they led her from the cave. As they emerged, Matpri rushed up to Mey, shouting something in her own language and embracing her. Mey, still stunned, smiled.

"It is as you said," Shiriki murmured, watching them, bowing with her hands together toward Matpri. "We are one people."

CHAPTER EIGHTEEN

SILENCE

Vidarian did not know what Matpri had expected of sending himself and Ariadel into the cave, but the celebration of what had happened to Mey—a rite performed by all of the changing people for thousands of years—eclipsed any expectation they might have had. They were received back into the Chatika home with wild celebration that lasted into the night, as the people shouted the return of one of their own into the stars.

The celebration came with the opening of many clay pots of some kind of grain alcohol so strong Vidarian was convinced it was actually intended for the Chatika's bear shapes. Indeed many of them drank it that way, making for an interesting night of staggering, bellowing beasts. The Atira's minders had shooed all of them away from the hill houses and into the surrounding grassland, where new fire pits were dug and celebration lights raised, rare foods brought out for cooking on the fragrant wood fires.

Now that they had seen the cave with its spirit stone and gem fragments, they noticed more such carried by the Chatika, some on necklaces and others strung into their hair. None seemed to have more than five, and those most frequently saman. Small animals, too, everywhere, that Vidarian had previously taken for wildlife or "mere" pets: spotted grass cats, striped finches, curl-tailed dogs, slender snakes: all subtly responding to the calls of their *sou-khlen*, their stone spirit brothers.

Under the heady influence of the Chatika's brew, which over time developed a flavor depth that suggested wild grasses, medicinal herbs, bonfire smoke, the boundless vault of the heavens—it was as though all life here were connected, as if there were no boundary between man and animal, spirit and stone, sky and plain. The great stone merely activated this connection, pulled back the human-made veil to reveal what had been true beneath for all existence.

He did not remember when they slept, or where, for these distinctions, too, had long since melted away.

~~~

In dreams, Vidarian explored the night sky—only that wasn't quite right, because there was no "night," such a silly relative concept, and come to think of it there was no "Vidarian" either. He breathed, they breathed, and galaxies smashed together, suns burst, coronas of light spread across the heavens, which were the foreheads of the universe.

The Starhunter was there as he had never seen her before. She turned toward him, all glittering raiment and silver eyes, a ring of blue stardust her ethereal coronet, beautiful beyond mortal comprehension, a radiance achievable only by the calculation of infinite planets. She seemed startled to see him there, a sentiment expressed in a rippling of asteroid field, a pulse of solar flares.

You have to go back now, she said, and there was something more astonishing, sadness! A quake of cosmic ocean, a sigh of diminishing comets. She touched his forehead, an explosion of light, an event horizon, there was something she was about to say—

~~~

A bird call woke him. It was thin and high, not close, but cutting. Mist shrouded the hills, muffling sound, but the call echoed. As moments passed, it did not stop, but continued to warble, strange enough to draw him out of sleep. One call was joined by others from other places across the village.

Beside him, Ariadel was stirring also, her furrowed brow saying that she, too, was trying to make sense of the sounds, almost familiar but subtly unnerving. Ailenne rolled over in her basket, murmuring monosyllabic Ailenne sounds, and Rai, curled protectively around the basket as was his nightly habit, lifted his head sleepily.

Another call sounded, this one closer, inside the saman circle of hill-houses. Vidarian bolted upright, the unease that had been growing in the pit of his stomach burst into full dread.

It wasn't a bird.

Ailenne stirred again, and Ariadel moved to soothe her. Vidarian stood, and Rai stood with him, his fur on end, his eyes intent. Ariadel picked up their daughter, holding her close, and nodded for Vidarian to go. He was loath to leave her, but the call—a human one—was one of grief, not attack or fear, and the three gryphons lay nearby, now also stirring out of sleep, more than capable of protection.

Rai whined low in his throat, a worried sound, and they set off through the mist.

The call—a high, thin wail of grief—led them to Shiriki's hill house. Two saman birds were outside; one, Shiriki's, bent its head over the smaller one beside it, which lay with its feet sprawled beneath it on the ground.

Matpri's bird was making a low, hollow sound that traveled upward from its chest and echoed along its throat. It was stirring, unearthly; unlike any noise Vidarian had heard from the many birds in the village. As they approached, Shiriki's bird tilted its head toward them without moving. *She grieves*, it said, and both Rai and Vidarian stopped in their tracks, startled. The bird's voice was feminine, human- and bird-like both.

Another wail—sharper, louder, its voice half familiar—drew them inside Shiriki's house.

Within, Matpri lay in her blankets beside Shiriki's small cast iron brazier, too still. Shiriki knelt nearby, pulling Mey away from her. Tears were streaming down Shiriki's face, and Mey was wailing, not the high bird sound they had heard from around the camp, but full and anguished. Above them, her little striped finch flew back and forth between root twigs in the ceiling, chirping with distress.

A black grass snake raced into the house, sliding so quickly past Vidarian's feet that it was coiled before Shiriki by the time he'd flinched away from it. The saman bent, one hand still clenched tightly around Mey's, and the snake jumped onto her wrist, then slithered to her shoulder and pressed its head against her chin.

Shiriki, still kneeling, fell to one side, catching herself with an out-flung palm before crumpling to the floor. Her chest shuddered with a single silent sob, but when she spoke, it was with a clear, low voice: "Many are struck down as Matpri—Chatika, Kala, Tenger. More, we fear. Like Matpri, they did not wake from sleep."

Outside, the two birds lifted their eerie, mournful voices again, low flute notes like an owl's hoot, but sustained. With it, and Shiriki's words, a creeping dread eeled through Vidarian's soul. They had not been fast enough in countering the Company's weapon.

"Did I do this?" Mey asked softly, and Vidarian flinched, as though she had unconsciously voiced his own looming guilt.

"No, no, no, *lek syha*," Shiriki said, turning and taking the girl in her arms. Mey clung to her, sobbing upon hearing the name Matpri had given her.

Their grief wrung his heart, and a matching urgency roiled up inside him: he wanted to run, to find Khalesh, to ask him what this use of the weapon meant—and to wreak vengeance upon whomever had unleashed it. The cut of Shiriki's pain, fire-bright, made him want to be in a dozen places, doing these things, and yet it anchored him there also, helpless.

"You must go," Shiriki said, her voice harsh with grief but high with worry. Vidarian almost jumped again, wondering if she had somehow heard his thoughts. But then she continued: "The Chatika will look for war on this. The grief will drive them mad."

Mey made a soft sound, a murmur like a child caught in a frightening dream. The striped finch fluttered down to land on her shoulder. Rai went to where she knelt with Shiriki and lay down next to her. Vidarian followed him, settling onto the floor at the wolf's side.

"Surely they will see that we grieve with you," Vidarian began, his own throat tight around his voice.

"They are men and women," Shiriki said, with simple sadness. "Their stricken hearts will crave blame, and they will settle on you as a convenient target."

He thought of Ariadel and Ailenne, of departing the way they'd come. With the key in hand, they could return to Alorea, seek what protection there might be in the imperial city.

But the thought of leaving the Chatika in the face of their grief, of sneaking away from the village as though guilty—he knew he could never live with that memory.

"We will not leave you to face this alone," Vidarian said. When Shiriki's chin firmed to argue, he placed a hand on her shoulder. "I appreciate your care for us more than I can say," he said, "but your people would ride after us if we fled, and there could be no stronger admission of our guilt in their minds."

At this, Shiriki turned her head toward him, thoughtful even through the opaque wall of her anguish. It was such an honest and unselfconscious expression that it pulled the confession from him, unwilling.

"There is more," Vidarian said. "We may know who has done this."

Shiriki's honesty of a moment ago vanished now behind a curtain of disbelief that was almost anger. She almost turned away, and the tenacity that kept her eyes on his was beyond human. Vidarian wanted to turn away himself, to flee from the intensity of those dark eyes, but was transfixed as by the gaze of a predator.

"We came here searching for the key that would stop this weapon from being created," he said. "Our enemies have used it, unfinished. My people and yours are in terrible danger."

Now Shiriki's eyes turned inward, and she did not speak.

"I must try to tell them, if they will hear me," Vidarian said.

Shiriki stared at the floor and did not answer, her thoughts somewhere far within.

"They will answer for this," Mey said, speaking to none of them, her head bent and her hands clenched tight around Shiriki's vest. "I swear that whoever did this will pay in blood and fire."

⌒⌒⌒

The Atira sent the Chatika's swiftest messengers in every direction known to lead to a clan territory. Already some of the closest clans had done the same, bringing news of their losses. The Kala, though they were closest to Chatika home, had not yet arrived. For the Tepda, the fox people of the south, and the Kamui, a northern white bear people considered cousins by the Chatika, it had been as it was for the Chatika: one in fifteen had not awakened from sleep this morning.

In the saman's circle there was an air of helplessness underlaid with worry. As if in agreement with their loss, the sky clouded over into a roof of towering prairie thunderheads. Luc and Eoin had gone to gather leaves for Shiriki, who would create a chalky blue paste to mark the dead for their journey. As outsiders they could not participate in the ceremony, but were allowed to help with the preparations. Khalesh and Iridan likewise tried to find solace in industry: they had been given an old summoning stone, a *sou-klehn*, that had belonged to a saman who had recently departed the world. Her stones would be returned to the *phi-klehn* in a ceremony, but Shiriki had allowed their study in the interim. Iridan believed that the strange chaotic stones had some relationship to the relay stones of the Aloreans, enough that they might, with modification, be able to communicate across the distances between shapeshifter clans.

The gryphons spoke little, but declared their opinions with their bodies: they lay in a loose ring around Ailenne, instinctively moving to protect the most vulnerable among them. Part of Vidarian wanted to insist to them, as he had to Shiriki, that they would prove their innocence, but mostly he was grateful for their protection. He tried not to imagine it being required.

"This is the Company's doing," Vidarian said. The thought had hung between them, and the camp's silence seemed to demand he voice it. "I should have killed Justinian the moment I met him." It was a wild and violent sentiment, the kind that launched him back to his childhood, his father reprimanding his lack of control—but the thought that he had been in the same room as the man who had orchestrated this, had shared meals with him, filled Vidarian's gut with a molten sickness. In a world that threatened to drown with pain, the thought of ending the life of the man responsible afforded a single moment of control, and his heart seized on it. He had never so deeply desired the death of another before. If Vidarian had stopped him, if they had succeeded faster, Matpri might still be alive. "I worry that our very presence here endangers Shiriki's people."

"They couldn't have known we were here . . ." Ariadel said, her voice distant with shock. She held Ailenne close to her chest, as if she could keep away another attack through sheer strength of her arms and force of will.

"This was no calculated attack," Khalesh said, looking up from the summoning stone in Iridan's hands and rubbing his thumbs against his temples. "It was reckless. Desperate."

Vidarian turned toward the Animator, willing a calm he did not feel into his voice. "How can you be sure it isn't functioning as they intended?"

"Well, in the first place, we'd be dead," Khalesh grunted, then visibly mastered himself. "They used the device unkeyed. Many have died this day, I promise you—even their own people. It is the only thing that can explain the lack of pattern in the deaths."

None of them spoke for a long moment as his words sank in. Had it been luck only that spared their lives? Was the grief and disbelief felt here also being felt across the world, in Alorea, Qui, far Malu?

"What need would they have for such desperation?" Vidarian whispered. "Such terrible waste?"

Thalnarra's large red eye turned toward him, thoughtful. // *You,* // she said only.

// *They know that the longer they wait, the closer you come to devising a counterattack,* // Altair said. // *They fear you.* // The softness of his thoughts, with a bright cast like spring blooms, was meant to gentle the words. It did not work. Guilt settled on Vidarian like a heavy cloak.

A steady rain began to fall, drops large and cold. In moments they were all soaked, save Ailenne, whom Ariadel returned to her basket and covered in a protective evaporating shield of fire energy.

The beat of a drum echoed from the Atira's circle, and across the village voices lowered to listen to it. Shortly it was joined by a high rattling sound—

from the distance of the saman's circle, a high hiss that melted into the patter of the falling rain.

Shiriki emerged from her house, Mey close behind her. The saman was arrayed in multicolored bear skins, black and cream and brown and spotted, and bright red paint streaked across her cheeks, forehead, and hands. In her arms she held a bundle of objects tied together with leather—small instruments of aged wood, frayed feathers, porcupine quills, beads of horn and bone. When she saw them, she managed a sad smile, becoming herself again beneath the costume, and gestured for them to follow.

More white-clothed saman emerged from the houses, a dozen in all, including Tirus, the young man who assisted Shiriki. They formed a kind of procession to the Atira's circle, where the rest of the Chatika were gathering.

Beside the Atira's large house, a banner had been erected, a round emblem painted in red upon a copper-furred bearskin. The rattling sound they'd heard came from two young women to either side of the house, shaking the instruments in their hands: leather strips sewn with hundreds of black bear claws.

"It is as I feared," Shiriki murmured. "They are declaring an attack upon the people."

"They are right to," Vidarian answered quietly, and she gave him a single inscrutable look, then went to take her place at the Atira's side.

The Atira emerged from her house, also garbed in ceremonial dress, many layers of bearskins covering her shoulders in a long mantle, and a heavy necklace made of discs of polished bone. Her hair had been woven with feathers, and a large white raven—one of her *sou-klehn*—perched on her shoulder, eyeing those assembled cannily.

She lifted her hands, and the drumming and rattling ceased, leaving a palpable silence. She spoke several words in Chatika, her tone measured and ceremonial; when she paused, the Chatika repeated the words back to her. At first Vidarian feared that they would understand none of the gathering, but Tirus had stolen up beside them, and began quietly translating.

"She says that they gather to discuss the great tragedy that has befallen the people, Chatika and our brothers and sisters—Kamui, Lin, Tepda . . ."

The young saman gasped then, along with the rest of the Chatika—some wailed with grief or astonishment—before hurriedly translating: "—and the Kala people, who fell heaviest of all, fewer than fifty survive." The Atira lifted her voice above the cries, and Tirus continued translating, "It is an attack on the people, and the Chatika would know their enemy."

One of the warriors shouted something. Vidarian could only catch the words *suun-wat* and *phi-klehn*. Another warrior shouted agreement, and a third cried out, translated by Tirus:

"It is the *phi-klehn*'s rejection of the *suun-wat* that has brought this upon us! A lesson to keep clean the land of the people!"

Vidarian could not see the young man who spoke, but Shiriki swiveled toward him like a stooping eagle. The warriors to either side of him parted as though to evade her gaze. Her words rattled out, and Tirus translated them: "Do you speak for your ancestor spirits, Abeytu? Did some greater magic steal upon you in your sleep and turn your bird *miakonda* white? Please tell us at once of this miracle that has been visited upon you in our time of great grief."

With each of Shiriki's words the young warrior withdrew into himself, and those surrounding him seemed to lose their nerve as well. Even as he translated, Tirus had grown tense, eyeing the group as Vidarian did for signs of violence. Behind them, the gryphons' feathers were slightly lifted, and he hoped the Chatika would not recognize their battle-readiness for what it was.

Another voice called out from across the gathering, and there was a strange note to it, a kind of hoarseness. As the speaker drew closer, the Chatika parted before her and her two tall companions. The three of them towered over the Chatika, who were not small—when they reached the center of the circle, it was obvious why.

The two companions were Tolui and Atlan, the Zhenjin centaurs they had seen upon their arrival. The centaur woman who accompanied them was significantly stranger. At first Vidarian thought that she was wearing some kind of ceremonial garb, but the large, black shapes at her side were feathered wings. The small black feathers that framed her face were not decorative, either, but natural.

The Atira greeted the centaurs, and Tirus translated: "Chatika home welcomes Qinde of the Kaitan people, and Tolui and Atlan of the Zhenjin. The Atira asks after the occasion of Qinde's visit, when Chatika home has never hosted a Kaitan visitor, much less the daughter of the Kaitan Khan."

Qinde's wings lifted slightly from her sides and she stretched even taller. What she said sent murmurs throughout the gathered Chatika, an eruption that Tirus had to shout his translation above:

"The Tenger people have called *parika pau*. The Kaitan invoke their right to gather all the clans."

CHAPTER NINETEEN

PARIKA PAU

I t took only moments for Shiriki and her circle to confer with the Atira and affirm that the Kaitan and Zhenjin people did have the authority to call a *parika pau*—a great gathering of all the clans. There was some discussion over whether Qinde could speak for the Tenger—the name used by all the centaurs collectively—but it was quickly decided that it did not matter, as any clan authority could invoke the great gathering.

Chatika scattered across the hills, given purpose that, for the moment, overcame their grief, or allowed them to escape it: provisions were to be gathered, grasses cleared, and roads made to the cave of the spirit stone, where the great gathering would take place. Together, the white-clad saman prepared the bodies of the dead with blue *batu* paste, and gathered their spirit stones, from which the summoned animal spirits had departed. Matpri and the other fallen saman were not so prepared, but taken to a separate cave deep underground to await further ceremony. When the bodies of those remaining had been lain on funeral pyres, the saman carried their stones in a solemn procession all the way to the cave of the *phi-klehn*, where the smaller stones rejoined the larger. Shiriki, as mother-saman, led the procession, her bark-brown bear form streaked with paste that turned to pale blue streamers in the soft but steady rain. As they passed, grieving Chatika cast fragrant branches and flowers at their feet, many weeping openly in human or bear shapes.

By the time they had returned, the sun was advancing toward the horizon, the sky a riot of fiery gold just turning to orange through the lingering thunderheads. Vidarian was looking for Altair—the gryphon had not been seen since the Chatika had begun their preparations. He had circled the village, careful to avoid intrusion, and had made it back to Shiriki's hill-house when the saman procession returned.

Shiriki, her bear-shape dark and washed of *batu* from the steady rain, lumbered toward him, her large jaw parted with weariness. He moved to clear out of her way, but her massive head swung toward him, eyes alert as though she had expected to find him there. When she drew close enough for him to smell the fresh mud on her paws, she opened her mouth wider, and a polished stone dropped to the ground. Shiriki watched him, her eyes small beneath the broad and furred forehead, until he bent to pick it up.

The stone fit perfectly in the hollow of his cupped palm, and he held it up to let the rain wash away traces of mud from its black iridescent surface. It was something like an opal, but heavier—and like all the summoning stones, like the *phi-klehn*, it glowed with adularescent chaos energy. The effect was distracting now as it had been in the cave; it was still the only time he had seen such energy manifesting naturally in the world.

By the time he pulled his attention up from the stone, Shiriki had returned to her human shape. Her white bird bent its head over her shoulder, watching him also. "This stone belonged to Matpri," Shiriki said. She reached to steady Vidarian's hands with her own when he flinched, nearly dropping the stone.

Vidarian turned his palm to slide the stone into Shiriki's hands, but she wrapped his fingers back around it with her own, then released him.

"It does not wish to return to the *phi-klehn*," she explained. "Because she annulled it, it has no grief, and does not seek the parent stone. I believe it was meant for you."

"I don't understand," Vidarian said, careful to keep his voice neutral. He wanted to keep the stone, an odd desire that troubled him with its strength, one he had trouble trusting.

"Matpri, like our Atira, was bound to a white raven she called Inoke. But she released Inoke from the *klehn*, before she slept." Droplets of water beaded on Shiriki's eyelashes, not all from the rain.

Vidarian's hands went numb, and he clenched his fingers around the stone against the risk of dropping it again. "She—knew?"

Shiriki shook her head, tears now standing clear in her eyes, but she smiled, the kind of smile that is the thinnest veil against a cascade of grief. "I do not believe she knew," she said, her voice suddenly hoarse. "I believe she followed some saman instinct—which I follow now, too."

"Will it . . . ?" Vidarian began, both awed and repulsed.

Shiriki smiled. "No. You are not of the people. It will not summon for you." When he looked at her, hesitant, missing the right answer, "Your sword," she said.

Vidarian jerked, reflexively dropping his hand to the sword's hilt at his side. He had been careful to draw as little attention to it as possible since the trial in which he'd displayed his abilities. Shiriki clearly had not forgotten it. He looked at her, searching for some sign of suspicion or testing—but there was none. She pointed impatiently to the scabbard.

Carefully he drew the blade from its sheath, turning his left forearm to rest the flat against it. The metal was cool, but alive; rain beaded immediately on its oiled surface. Once, what seemed a lifetime ago, the fire priestess Endera had explained to him the fire that lived in forged steel that was properly maintained. He could sense it now, though dimly; the deep fire that dwelt in its heart. It was an odd side effect of fire sensitivity, the ability to instinctively tell the quality and care of a blade.

And there was something more in the Rulorat steel now, something that had grown as he mastered the unruly elements that named him Tesseract. There was *water* in the blade, a phenomenon he knew that Thalnarra's teachings would call impossible.

Shiriki took Matpri's stone from him then and pressed it to the sword, just above the rain guard.

And the sword—*took* the stone.

The elements that warred within Vidarian were accustomed by now to being coaxed, or forced, into the longsword blade; channels of habit carried them there. But they had never moved on their own. Now both leapt together, unified in hunger, before Vidarian could even ask them to go. They surged through the metal, rushing into its familiar embrace, and *seized* Matpri's stone, drawing it into themselves.

Before his eyes, the stone brightened, its iridescence becoming a thousand lances of starlight that bent, refracted, wrapped the hilt of the sword in a spiral of strange radiance. Where there had been strife, where water and fire had bickered, there was a bridge, a void forever separating them: the dark energy called chaos.

"An instinct," Shiriki murmured. "A saman instinct." She turned to him. "You are meant to come among us. There is much that we must yet do."

<center>~~~</center>

The sword—*hummed*.

"Irritating" was not the right word. The sword's vibration in his mind was somewhere between euphoria and anxiety; it occupied a space beyond the world, persistently suggesting everything that existed beyond his awareness. It was a small piece of the nothing that connected all things.

When holding Ariadel's life flame had kindled Vidarian's own magic—adding fire to the water awakened in him by Sharli—the two elements seemed to find every piece of dissonance within him to use in their battle against each other. Matpri's stone, a whisper of chaos that spoke to him through the very torch of his family's lineage, did not so much bring peace among them as dwarf their contentious concerns. *You are small*, the stone said, and they listened. It was the strangest, most unsettling peace Vidarian could imagine.

He returned to the hearth circle, still disoriented and developing a steady headache. Eoin, Thalnarra, Ariadel—all had returned to the erstwhile camp, drawn like roosting birds beneath the now scarlet sunset.

All but Altair.

Vidarian found the gryphon at last sitting atop a tall hill, watching the fiery horizon. He seemed to have deliberately faced away from the Chatika's preparations, and from here looked across a series of rolling valleys where the storm alternately raised and flattened the prairie grasses like wind ruffling a wolf's mane.

Altair's feathers were drab with rain and compressed into points, giving him a mottled and spiked appearance. He seemed not to notice, his eyes somewhere far away, or turned deep within. Vidarian realized he knew little detail about Altair's people. He had met members of Thalnarra's flight, knew something of how they related to each other and saw the world. Altair seemed to be different not just from his fire kin but from his own. He was like Eoin, like Luc, seeking a truth that was solely his own in the world.

"You're thinking about Siane," Vidarian said.

The gryphon's blue eye cocked down at him. He neither argued nor agreed, eventually turning his face back toward the setting sun.

Vidarian was about to speak again when Altair answered: // *I cannot say who Siane is anymore, or if I think of her.* //

Evening insect song, a whir almost metallic, filled the air in the silence that followed.

"I want to help, my friend," Vidarian said. "But I'm not sure I understand."

// *I have felt from the day that I was hatched that Siane was with me,* // Altair said. He continued to watch the skyline, and his voice was distant, spring flowers from miles away.

When he didn't speak again, Vidarian said, "She would take care of you—"

The gryphon shook his head. Droplets of rain flew from his beak, and Vidarian wasn't sure whether the gesture was negation or reflex. // *Siane was never like that to me. She was—a calling. She was purpose.* //

A sadness settled on Vidarian, deeper and more dark than before. "I feel I have had some part in taking purpose from you," he said, partly because it was easier to say than to think.

The gryphon chuckled, startling Vidarian. // *Your reach in this world is wide, but you give yourself too much credit in this. Your part was in the revealing of knowledge, of truth. It would be a weak mind that could resent this.* //

Altair's reserves were there then, the vastness of a sky through parting clouds. A "weak mind" he would never be.

// *I am afraid,* // Altair said. The words were bright, simple, sharp like broken juniper. Vidarian was struck in that moment by how different the two gryphons he knew best were: Thalnarra would never have admitted fear, or at least not easily.

Is that what the gods were for, Vidarian suddenly wondered? A shield against fear? But if that shield were false—the implications spun into too many possibilities for his tired mind to grasp.

Instead, he sat down on the grass, surrendering to the chill rain that coated it without complaint, and without answer. Worlds away, the falling sun, too, had no reply.

∿∿∿

Parika pau came with a heartbeat of drums at dawn.

When Vidarian woke from mercifully dreamless sleep, Ariadel, Ailenne, and the gryphons were once again gone from the hearthside. Rai was beside him, and gave an apologetic wave of his tail when Vidarian wondered why he'd been left to sleep.

They thought you needed rest, the wolf said, the tips of his ears drooping. Though groggy, Vidarian regretted his irritation immediately—it was so easy to forget that Rai seemed to pick up on any strong emotion he had. This also meant that he felt the regret, too, and pushed his nose to Vidarian's palm, forgiving.

"They weren't wrong," he mumbled, levering himself to his feet. In short order he had cleaned himself up in an iron cauldron of rainwater left for that purpose, and followed Rai toward Shiriki's hill-house.

The mother-saman was arrayed for ceremony—and so were the gryphons.

Vidarian's first thought was to wonder who they had convinced to paint their feathers—but bits of gold and silver speckling Eoin's sleeves gave away the answer. And although a gryphon in ceremonial array—albeit without armor—was a breathtaking sight, Tephir, smallest of them, shone brightest. Eoin might have managed the silver air spirals and leaping golden flames for Altair and Thalnarra, but the delicate silver edging on even the tiniest of Tephir's soft owl feathers, causing him to shimmer like the scales of a dragon carp, spoke of prior practice.

Shiriki held in her arms three gryphon feathers, painted: silver, gold, silver. One from each gryphon, and none of them simple covert feathers, as Vidarian had seen them gift before, but primaries. Altair and Thalnarra held their wings resolutely closed, but Tephir's were parted slightly, going lightly on the pain his left wing must still hold with its feather prematurely removed. As Vidarian arrived, Shiriki was handing the feathers—each more than half as long as she was tall—with the greatest reverence into another shaman's arms: Tirus, the young man who, since they had arrived, had rarely been far from Khalesh's sight.

As Tirus accepted the feathers, he wrapped their hollow shafts with leather, preparing to add them to the Chatika's bundled artifacts. At his side, his white saman bird gave an odd little whoop.

"His bird does not speak," Shiriki murmured. "It is a great shame. He is a gifted saman. The first to regain his true form after the Waking." She gave Vidarian a long look, and he blinked, wondering what he was missing.

With the feathers prepared, Tirus set off toward the cave of the spirit stone, the site of the *parika pau*. Another saman followed him bearing an earthen bowl of burning bone and herbs.

The going was slow, for the road to the spirit stone, newly widened, was nonetheless filled with *winjan*, the gathering changing people. Some were indistinguishable from the Chatika, others notably paler of skin, still more wilder and harder, bearing weapons as their ceremonial objects.

When they came at last to the cave mouth, the sea of faces that extended out over the plains to the west was dizzying. Thousands at least, more that could not be seen, and still they were gathering. At the cave itself sat a ring of elders, three each from every clan—including six centaurs, three with wings and three without. The ground in front of the cave had been painted in a colorful ring made of triangles, and tall wooden poles painted with patterns and fixed with sacred objects were spaced throughout the gathered clanspeople, each placed opposite the tip of a triangle.

The three centaurs without wings were among the most ferocious looking part-humans Vidarian had ever seen. The largest was clearly the one that Tolui and Altan had called the "Great Khan": his human half looked about a decade older than Vidarian, but he was massive, his equine body nearly the size of a Sky Knight royal. The thick layers of ceremonial fur draping his body, and the red banners streaming from his mane and tail, only made him look larger. At his side was a younger female centaur so similar in appearance that she could only be his daughter—a counterpart, Vidarian realized, to Qinde, daughter of the Khan Kaitan.

Shiriki and Tirus joined the Atira at the circle, while another of the Chatika saman led the gryphons to another position, near but not within. Vidarian was about to follow them when one of the centaurs called out to Shiriki.

At the right hand of the Great Khan's retinue were Qinde and her people, the only winged centaurs present. One of them had called to Shiriki. If Vidarian had seen Qinde before as she appeared now, with black makeup transforming her face into the illusion of a beaked countenance, he would not have thought her even partly human. The makeup, and the long clawed gauntlets her people wore—not just on their human hands but almost mechanically cuffing their front two hooves—suggested nightmare chimera, distorted hippogryph.

Qinde and her father, the Khan Kaitan, stood out not only for their ornate headpieces, but their black wings; the elder Khan's were faded with age, but uniformly dark throughout, contrasting with the mottles, stripes, and banding that marked the others' wings. As Vidarian watched, Qinde exchanged some words in the Chatika tongue with Shiriki—who turned to Vidarian and beckoned.

Vidarian turned to Ariadel, who was following Eoin, Mey, and the gryphons. She gave a nervous look around her, but motioned for him to join Shiriki. Whatever the gathering intended, it was too late to avoid it now.

With a reluctance that he tried to mask as demure respect, Vidarian joined Shiriki, Tirus, and the Atira at their place in the circle. Rai trailed after him, his head low, but none objected to him.

And with that, the *parika pau* had begun.

Vidarian had expected ceremony, but beyond the costume and positioning, there was none. Qinde walked to the center of the circle, her metal claws clinking against her hooves and the ground, and called a greeting. The word was immediately echoed from each of the decorated poles, first in her language and then in others; in this way were the words at the circle relayed in arcs of sound even to those furthest.

"Khan Kaitan has called *parika pau* to discuss the great loss of our people," Qinde began.

A cry rippled through the gathered clans as her words were translated, punctuated by shouts. Vidarian was surprised, having expected greater preamble; he instinctively edged away from the circle, closer to Ariadel and Ailenne. Near them, Thalnarra and Altair were doing the same, subtly extending their wings to create distance between Ariadel and the gathered clanspeople.

Several shouts continued even after Qinde raised her hands for silence. Only a few could Vidarian understand—one of them the ubiquitous shout of "*suun-wat!*"

"I agree," Qinde shouted, stomping a forehoof for emphasis until the crowd quieted. "Khan Kaitan would hear, too, from these visitors, upon whose footsteps death visits us so quickly."

A chill shot down Vidarian's spine as he realized what she was saying. He only just managed to keep his hands from trembling as hundreds of faces, human and otherwise, turned toward him.

"Is this wise?" Shiriki murmured, mouthing the words to Qinde.

"Better now," Qinde said, too quietly for the gathering poles to echo, "than when they have worked themselves up."

This was not reassuring. But Vidarian kept his back straight, and went to join Qinde in the center of the circle.

"I was born far from here," Vidarian began, "And I understand your shock, your rage." He stopped himself from saying despair. "I have lost friends to this enemy—friends whom I intend to avenge."

Shouts began almost immediately after his first words were translated, and he raised his voice above them:

"But most of all, I intend to safeguard the future of my home, and your home—for my family, and all who have as much right to sky and land as anyone across these five continents. The enemy that has struck you has struck my family also, and I can tell you that they intend not to stop until every creature beyond their narrow circle is dead."

An eerie quiet rippled across the gathered clanspeople then, and Vidarian knew that, whatever they had expected him to say, it had not been so incomprehensibly terrible.

"Why should we believe him?" one of the Chatika cried, in heavily accented trade-tongue, an ancient dialect, Vidarian thought.

"This man has proven himself to be a speaker of Dara," Shiriki answered, and Vidarian eyed her with surprise. "He was so marked by Matpri of the Kala."

More murmurs answered her, and she pointed to the sheath at Vidarian's side. He drew his sword, summoning his magic through it in what, by now, was instinct. The stone that had belonged to Matpri flared like an aurora, iridescent colors playing about the edges of its white light. The murmurs of the crowd turned to shouts of surprise, pointing hands, and he knew he had to press the advantage while he had it.

"If you'll go with me," Vidarian said, hardly believing what he was about to suggest, "I can take you to the humans that have begun this. If you help me, we can end it."

Now a cacophony:

"The northern humans are cunning, this is surely a trap—"

"They have angered the king of heaven—"

"He says himself that these humans are bloodthirsty and treacherous—"

"The changeless cannot be trusted—"

Qinde reared then, and Vidarian nearly threw himself out of the path of her claw-shod hooves. Her broad wings flared out from her sides, then arced upward, a fearsome black mantle. Those who were near the circle gasped and fell silent, and the silence slowly spread through the gathered crowd.

"I am shamed that none will answer this human's call," she said. "Khan Kaitan is shamed."

From the centaurs there came a restless shuffling of hooves, a rattling of the bone-ringed spears. They were ready for violence, but Vidarian wasn't sure whether it was against their unseen enemy, the winged centaur, or himself.

"The humans make war on each other, it is not our concern—" one of the Khan's advisors began.

"Our people swore a kinship oath with all *winjan*," the Great Khan's daughter said. She did not shout, and the low note of her voice was dangerous. "It pains me to be forced to remind you of this, Yisun."

Qinde did not have the restraint of the other Khan's daughter. She advanced on the advisor, the feathers along her wings and spine lifting with agitation. "Those struck down are our brothers and sisters, Yisun Tenger, and you find them insufficient. Give me the number of brethren dead that you require to become brave!"

The one called Yisun was standing his ground, but his eyes widened the nearer Qinde drew to him, and he clutched his long lance in a splintering grip. At length he dropped his eyes, not answering, and Qinde turned triumphantly back to the Great Khan and his daughter.

"We make no oath," the Great Khan said, meeting Qinde's stubborn gaze with one of his own. "Kinship or not, this is a human war—"

A startled chirp, not human, interrupted the Khan, and he paused. Hundreds of heads turned toward the sound—toward Iridan.

The automaton radiated a wave of embarrassment, but chirped again, seeming unable to help himself.

"*I'm receiving a message, Captain,*" Iridan said. His words, laced as always with emotion, were especially powerful: surprise, carrying directly through him, unsettlingly as though Vidarian were experiencing it himself. "*It comes from Rivenwake.*"

At Rivenwake was one of the five most powerful relay spheres known to exist—strong enough, it appeared, to contact Iridan's automaton mind outside of his natural range.

A piece of Iridan's copper chest plate shifted to one side, propelled by the gears beneath, exposing the relay sphere where his heart would have been were he human. Words poured out immediately, repeating:

"*Rivenwake is under attack,*"—the voice was Marielle's—"*This is a distress call. Rivenwake is under attack—*"

CHAPTER TWENTY
RIVENWAKE

"**H**ow can we get there?" Ariadel asked.

In what must have been a breach of custom, Ariadel and the gryphons had left their places to approach Vidarian with Iridan in tow when the automaton began repeating the message from Rivenwake. He still seemed unable to silence it.

Vidarian searched Ariadel's face for any sign of uncertainty, and found none. A strange mixture of dread, gratitude, and pride washed through him as he took in the calm determination in her eyes. Ailenne, for her part, seemed mostly amused at the gathering, and at Iridan; she babbled back at the voice in the metal man's chest. Vidarian knew that he would protect them with his life—but he was haunted daily by the potential insufficiency of that dedication. That all he had might not be enough.

"Come with me," Qinde said, startling them.

Her advisors, and the Great Khan with his retinue, were surprised as well, frowning.

Qinde glowered back at them. "You know my position on this. I have no desire to remain through pointless deliberations that will tarnish my family's honor. Let history know that others hesitated, and Qinde did not." And she stalked off toward the Chatika home, tossing over her shoulder: "I leave my proxy with Katalun."

The Great Khan's daughter straightened, first in surprise, but she was quick to turn it to assertion. She called the *parika pau* back to order, and began what promised to be a long speech in the strident language of the Plainsrunners.

Those gathered seemed thankful for the distraction, and so Vidarian and the rest were able to quietly follow Qinde up the road toward the Chatika home.

"They will natter for *days*," the centaur muttered, her artificially clawed hooves tearing at the flattened grass of the road. She seemed not to intend the damage, but neither did she stop it.

Before they reached the hill houses of the Chatika, however, Qinde took a sharp right turn, weaving through a narrow trace marked by the passage of many hooves.

The smell assaulted them first, distinct and unforgettable: the crazed not-saman who had helped Vidarian prove himself to Shiriki. It seemed so long ago that he had used their earth energy to prove he was the Tesseract—by opening a gate. The handful of pitiful Chatika who could not change their shape or summon spirits using the *klehn* stones—driven mad, it seemed, by their deficiencies—were being tended by centaurs from the Great Khan's tribe. By their odd radiance to Vidarian's mind, a presence of energy his ability could not directly sense or grasp as it could fire and water, the centaurs, too, were earth-wielders.

The complex crystal that powered Iridan remembered the peculiar energy signatures of the most powerful artifacts it encountered. Thus, through him, Vidarian could channel his own energies, and those of an earth wielder, to open a gate to the Grand Library at Qui, to the Animator's Vault in Val Imris—or to the great cloaking device in Rivenwake.

Mey, trailing beside Thalnarra, recognized the significance of the earth-shapers. "I don't want to go," she said, planting her feet. She looked back toward Shiriki's hill house. "I'm staying here."

"I'm sorry, Mey," Vidarian said, deliberately avoiding the use of her imperial title. "The *Jade Phoenix* is likely to be at Rivenwake. When we repel the attack, they'll be able to take you home." The dark glower she directed at him was the full-force assault of a young imperial much accustomed to getting her way. "From the gate in Shen Ti you should be able to return here someday."

He was expecting an argument, but Mey grew very quiet, thoughtful. Considering, he hoped, what she could do for Shiriki's people if she could successfully be the bridge between Shen Ti and the Chatika.

At her shoulder, Khalesh, too, wore a conflicted expression. He was not so overt as to look back toward Shiriki's house, but his concern was obvious.

"You know what we face," Vidarian said to him. "I need you with me, my friend. But the choice is yours."

Khalesh jerked upward a little, surprised, and Vidarian realized he had misread the man's hesitancy. "Tirus offered to come with us, whenever we departed," the Animator said quietly.

Vidarian searched the man's eyes, questing also for the right words that could answer the agony there. Tirus might be a formidable saman among the Chatika, but nothing in his life would have prepared him for flying ships, automata, the murderous monsters the company would set against him. What would his flightless white bird do atop the deck of a skyship? Khalesh, by his expression, knew all this, but was loath to leave him behind, perhaps to be struck down by the silent attack of the weapon they had failed to prevent.

"If it were Ariadel," Khalesh said at last.

Vidarian looked at the Animator for a long moment. He knew his answer, but owed it to the man to look harder inside himself to make sure it was true. "I would protect her," he said.

Khalesh looked at him, misery laying bare his heart, but only for a moment. The famed walls of his people, a small city-state further from here than Alorea, closed around him, and he was the Animator Vidarian had known once more. He did not look back again.

The distress chime continued to sound from Iridan's chest, and Vidarian drew his sword. He felt the lightest brush of Thalnarra's disapproval—it was a sign of weakness to use an artifact as a crutch to channel one's energy—and he had a single tiny instant of satisfaction; she did not know about Matpri's stone.

Vidarian called water and fire through the blade, and that satisfaction vanished: the elements surged through him, stronger, brighter, as difficult to control now as they had been when he had known nothing of taming them. He struggled, sweat breaking out above his eyes, and he wrestled them back. All the while Matpri's stone continued its dissonant little song in his head, whispering that his every action was trivial.

Both gryphons noticed his struggle, but neither had time to react. Qinde had been speaking to one of the centaur earth-shapers in the language of her wingless kin, and he—a wizened creature with a dusty coat and withered limbs, nodded. He lifted a kind of saman's stick, and a wave of earth energy joined Vidarian's, rising beneath it like an island emerging from the sea.

They hung that way for several long moments, waiting, every instant a battle. Vidarian first glanced at Altair, then said his name—too absorbed by controlling the elements to see at first that the air gryphon was struggling.

// I . . . I can't . . . // The words were all he could manage, accompanied by a tide of fear, doubt, self-loathing.

Matpri's stone chose that moment to act.

The dissonant melody in his mind *reached*, breaking the boundaries of the stone, and knocked Vidarian off his feet. He barely managed to land on his knees, swaying for balance. The light was blinding, terrible—but of an elemental kind that Vidarian knew only he could see. It touched the merged elemental energies, which writhed away from it—and opened the world before them.

By the stiffening of their neck-feathers, both gryphons knew what had happened, or had some sense of it, but there was no time to object. The gate was opening. Vidarian clenched his every thought on the visceral memory of the docks at Rivenwake—the wood beneath his feet, the vaulting sky with its shimmer of the floating city's protective spell.

The field beyond the gate was blurred, distorted—partly from towers of black smoke that rose from fallen ships in the harbor, partly from something else, a distortion in the magic of the gate itself.

"*The camouflage device,*" Iridan said, recognizing the energy. "*It is safe—but we must go quickly.*"

"Go," Vidarian whispered, not yet trusting himself to rise. He looked at Thalnarra, asking, and she nodded, then leapt decisively through the gate. Through the blur on the far side they could see her large wings lift, but she looked back over her shoulder, dipping her head. The landing place, at least, was safe.

"Call and we will come," Qinde said, as the gate's energies twisted. She shot a defiant look up the road toward the *phi-klehn*, as if her father could receive it.

ᕙᕗᕙ

They emerged onto the east docks of Rivenwake, and into chaos.

Fire and smoke filled the sky, but merciful luck had landed them far from the major engagement on the west side docks, where a flotilla of skyships rained fire onto the city. Rivenwake had no defensive lines; it had been protected by a camouflage spell and its location deep inside the West Sea kept secret by penalty of death. Someone, or something, had betrayed it.

When Vidarian had last been to the floating city, it had been a tropical wonder, its farm-barges dotted with fruit trees in pots that filled the air with exotic perfumes. Now: smoke; screaming; death.

Overwhelmed by what he saw, Vidarian lost his concentration, and the gate flickered shut behind him. They needed to find Rivenwake's commander—if she still remained to be found.

"Can you contact Marielle's relay sphere?" Vidarian asked Iridan, his eyes still fixed on the western battle line.

By way of answer, Iridan's lavender eyes cooled into blue, and he barked in a deep, almost-familiar voice: "*Who is this?*"

Vidarian jumped, startled, then turned toward Iridan, knowing that the automaton's vision would be reproduced in the relay chamber of the *Viere d'Inar*, Marielle's flagship. "This is Captain Vidarian Rulorat, responding to Queen Marielle's distress call."

"*The Tesseract,*" the voice replied, now a little less curt. "*Nistra knows we could use you.*"

"We have no ships, but—"

Thin laughter, hard and brittle, issued from Iridan's chest. "*Just as well. Every ship of ours to challenge them has been destroyed.*"

The brittleness of the man's voice was a too-familiar ring of shock and disbelief, and it leached into Vidarian's heart like freezing rain. "We are at your command," he said, willing his own confidence into the man, channeling the leadership voice his father had used on many a shaken crew.

"*You have our gratitude, and my admiration for your composure.*"

"My what?" Vidarian asked, startled again.

There was a pause. "*Have you seen what we're fighting?*"

The man's words sent another chill down Vidarian's spine, and he realized that, beyond the assumption that the assault from the sky was an armada of skyships, he had not actually seen the enemy. He squinted at the horizon, searching through the smoke for what the relay officer might be referring to.

Fire poured from the sky, terrifying but familiar: the Alorean Import Company's skyships had borne fire weapons when he'd engaged them before. Steam boiled up from the sea, occluding the air, interspersed with the black clouds of soot that billowed up from the burning city below.

Gradually, through the clouds of unnatural smoke, fragments of armament could be seen that raised more questions than they answered: ships with metal plate armor that must have been incredibly heavy to lift.

As the wind shifted, more of those hulls revealed themselves.

Not ships. A ship.

What Vidarian had at first assumed to be several huge skyships—a formidable armada—was one structure, a single massive platform suspended high in the air by metal cables attached to—

Wings. Golden wings, easily eight times the span of a gryphon's. Mechanical talons, riveted beaks.

They were eagles. Six giant golden automata inscribed with Targuli spiral patterns, their wings and bodies studded with glowing blue elemental crystals like those that powered the skyships. Their wings rose and fell in eerie synchrony, mesmerizing and terrible.

More terrible still was the golden figure that towered atop the platform, five times the height of a man, its feet planted and arms folded in study of the destruction wreaked beneath it. Like the eagles, its body was coated with elemental gems, including two large amethysts set beneath a scarlet prism key in its forehead.

Ruby.

Despite her automaton body, there was some trace of the woman Vidarian had known in her stance. It was there in the sharpness with which she regarded the battle below, a commander trained at the heels of her long-dead mother, the West Sea Queen Rhiannon. But there was no humanity, no hint that she mourned or even felt the ravaging of her former kingdom's greatest stronghold and secret heart.

Vidarian had last seen Ruby disappearing through a portal he and the gryphons had opened to an unknown target. It should have destroyed her, and Veda, Iridan's sister. The Company had succeeded in locating her, wherever that gate had sent her—and she must have remembered Rivenwake's hidden location.

"We can't even get near the damned thing," the relay officer's voice echoed through Iridan's body. *"None of our ships are fast enough."*

Vidarian turned to Thalnarra and Altair. "Can you get close enough to search it for weaknesses without risking yourselves?" he asked them. Both gryphons nodded—Altair was shaken by his failure with the gate, but determined—and took off from the dock, winging low over the water.

Tephir, Khalesh, Eoin, and Ariadel remained, Ailenne in her arms.

"We can fight," Ariadel said, a flash of gold emerging from her hair and leaping into the air. As she fell, spider-Raven became the ash-colored cat, then ran down the dock, gaining enough distance to change again into the firebird. Ariadel turned to Iridan, then looked significantly at Vidarian. He knew what she was suggesting, and the problem was she was right. Of all who remained, only he and Ariadel, with their formidable shapechanger companions, were remotely equipped to face the Company's attack-ship.

"Where is Mey?" he asked abruptly, realizing she was nowhere to be seen.

They looked at each other, chagrined, and Vidarian swore. She must have snuck away in the confusion around opening the gate. He could only hope that she was safe with Shiriki.

Ariadel cleared her throat, and Vidarian turned to Tephir, Khalesh, and Eoin. "Will you protect my daughter?" he asked. "And try to find some of the Rivenwake captains, if they aren't in the thick of things?"

"With our lives," Khalesh said, and Ariadel carefully handed Ailenne to him. There was a shimmer of water in her eyes as she relinquished their daughter, but it faded quickly to determination.

"*And with mine,*" Iridan added, this time in his own voice. Vidarian turned to him gratefully. "*I believe I can lead us safely to the relay sphere in the* Viere d'Inar."

Rai had trotted up the pier, moving opposite Raven so as to avoid sinking it with his weight and hers. He took his dragon shape, and the floating structure sagged beneath him, but held. Vidarian went to him, climbing up his shoulder and settling himself between the formidable neck-spines before he could think of a reason not to. As he did so, Ariadel took her place on Raven's back; both shapechangers seemed to have "absorbed" the harnesses made for them with long wear, a strange process that had been as unsettling as it was convenient.

A boom of fire striking another dock reminded them of their purpose, and both dragon and firebird took to the air, as the others ran up the pier toward one of the main floating "roads." It wrenched Vidarian's heart to be moving further from Ailenne, but as he ran, Khalesh was already pulling tiny automata from his pockets and loosing them into the air, some shooting off to scout and others forming a protective pattern around them.

"We need to get away from them quickly!" Ariadel shouted, and Vidarian called out agreement. The two huge shapechangers would be a sure target. Raven gave an odd screech, half audible as a high-pitched ringing, and shot off to the south in a shower of elemental sparks.

Rai tipped a wing downward and slid north in the air, skewing the world crazily sideways beneath them. The spines of his neck lifted upward, tensing; Vidarian could feel him working to summon up his lightning for an attack at need.

They circled toward the flying platform, whipping through and around pillars of smoke that grew more frequent as they drew west. When they came upon the platform itself, Vidarian braced himself for an attack, but the giant ship continued resolutely pouring fire down upon the city. Now that he was close enough, he could see the sailors running back and forth along its surface, and along narrow railed corridors carved into its sides; as they passed, one of the fire-spigots halfheartedly fired upon them, but Rai dipped easily out of its way.

In moments it became clear that the structure would not be baited, but remain inexorably consuming Rivenwake. At a loss, Vidarian directed Rai up toward the top of the platform—toward Ruby. Rai rumbled, nervous that this would bring them within easy reach of Ruby's own devastating water magic, but Vidarian urged him again.

In her automaton body, Ruby radiated emotion the way Iridan did, but with less control. Iridan had some ability to mask his feelings, but Ruby seemed not yet to have developed it. The coldness with which she watched the explosion of the docks below them, the market stalls where she must surely have played as a child, rocked him.

"Ruby, what are you doing?" Vidarian called, hoping to at least distract her, but the automaton head did not turn. He forced himself back in time, imagining when Ruby had been his closest friend, before they'd decided to kill each other. "This was your home, the pride of your mothers before you!" At the word mothers, there was the tiniest flicker in her resolution, but it dimmed quickly.

"I've gone so far beyond you, Vidarian."

At Ruby's side was Veda, the steel-clad automaton, whose head did turn toward Vidarian and Rai. She chuckled at Vidarian's surprise.

"I did not endure the crucible of existence for two thousand years to fall before you, human," Veda said. Despite her bravado, she had not emerged unscathed—the right side of her body was scored with abrasions and melted in hand-sized spots, souvenirs of her encounter with Malinai, the ancient fire gryphon.

Ariadel wants us to attack them, Rai said, startling Vidarian. Rai met his disbelief with a wave of agreement, but continued, *She thinks that they may be able to disable one of the eagles if Veda and Ruby are distracted.*

What do you think? Vidarian asked.

This time Rai was startled, but rumbled thoughtfully. *Worth a shot?*

Do it.

Rai dropped his left wing and they plummeted toward Ruby and Veda. Vidarian clung to his seat with both legs and hands, squinting as the wind of their movement lashed his face and trying not to imagine what would happen if they crashed into all of that metal.

Ruby and Veda turned toward them, hands raised in humanlike astonishment. Rai released a crackling bolt of electricity directly into their faces, then folded both wings and *rolled* in midair. The world spun, righting itself only half a breath before Vidarian was sure he would be sick.

He braced himself for retribution; there was no imagining that they could escape the automatons' counterattack at this range.

Instead there was an explosion, then a high deafening squeal too bright to be animal in origin.

Above them—for Rai had rolled to one side and beneath the surface of the flying platform—the metal structure shuddered before listing violently toward the sea on one side. The flat deck tilted up and away from Vidarian and Rai as the far hull dropped, with one of the huge golden eagles spiraling toward the sea beneath it, one wing sheared nearly off its body and trailing smoke and fire.

For one long moment the craft was silent. Then, from the far side of the platform, a thud of feathered wings, and Ruby's voice:

"If you expect mercy—"

"I do not," came Ariadel's reply, and the flicker of elemental energy that meant she was summoning another attack. "I expect you to fail."

Vidarian's blood turned to ice just before a pulse of energy emanated from the platform: Veda, summoning fire and water in a fused form that she had learned from Vidarian.

Raven screeched her strange above-sound call, and dove, appearing beak-first beneath the platform. But rather than remaining in that shelter, the firebird immediately started angling back upward, screaming for retaliation.

"Fall back!" Vidarian cried, and Rai roared agreement. The dragon charged toward Raven and Ariadel, bodily interposing himself between the firebird's rage and the flying platform. Raven was forced to backwing madly to avoid a collision, and it was all that saved them from a full-force blast of searing fire from Veda.

The platform had stabilized, though tilted—and their distraction tactic would not work a second time. Rai dove back beneath the platform, and this time Raven and Ariadel followed.

A dark streak passed beneath them, then banked and rose: Thalnarra. She radiated displeasure.

"Where should we strike?" Vidarian called.

// *You are looking at one of the most elaborate pieces of elemental technology ever imagined, much less created,* // Thalnarra snapped, her voice like blackening charcoal. // *Would* you *leave an obvious and externally identifiable weakness?* //

Altair, too, arrowed beneath the shelter of the platform, exuding frustrated agreement. Above them, the mechanical monster resumed pouring fire down upon Rivenwake, eating dock after dock. It had progressed halfway to the heart of the city, and the *Viere*, its movement slow but inexorable.

Of the few hundred ships the West Sea Kingdom possessed, perhaps half had been at harbor—and even now, many were making a full-sailed retreat from the city in all directions. At least thirty ships had sailed in to challenge the automaton vessel and wrecked themselves in the process; who knew how many more lay unseen beneath the waves.

Only Vidarian and Ariadel had succeeded in disabling any of the eagle automata, and any similar attack was sure to be met with Ruby and Veda's wizened and attentive rage.

Vidarian looked across the shadowed sky at Ariadel, and then down to the *Viere d'Inar*.

They realized it in the same moment. There would be no repelling the attack.

"We have to get everyone we can out of here," Vidarian shouted. "Rai," he looked down the dragon's neck, and two ears swiveled back toward him. "Back to the east dock."

Together the two gryphons and two shapechangers shot out from beneath the platform, flying east. Two blasts of fire and water respectively tore toward them, but poorly aimed and easily evaded. In moments they were circling over the east dock again, and Vidarian looked to Altair and Thalnarra.

"Bring Khalesh and the rest back here—and anyone else you find along the way. Spread the word that we are opening a way to Val Imris."

Raven banked in front of them, and even against the smoke and fire Vidarian was struck by the firebird's beauty, feathers seemingly made of sun and starlight, of infinite color.

"I'll bring Khalesh and Ailenne," Ariadel said, and tapped Raven's shoulder. The bird dove, and was soon winging toward the *Viere d'Inar*.

Vidarian took a deep breath, signaling Rai to land. As the dragon's claws touched the dock, he closed his eyes, searching for focus. He had no idea if what he was about to try would work, or what danger it presented.

Before he could dwell on it too long, he touched Matpri's stone with his mind, then quested outward with his water and fire sense, weaving them into the pattern that prepared the gate.

As it had before, the chaos stone awakened and reached, scattering the elemental magic before it and slicing open the world where it passed. Vidarian drew its energy back into him forcefully, rocking back in his seat with the effort—terrified of what it would mean to loose that chaos energy upon the world.

The stone did not want to be contained, and fought, but quickly relented, muttering at him in a dark and wordless language. Sweat had coated his forehead again, but he rallied, directing the tear in front of him to connect itself to the Relay Room at Val Imris. The memory stung: Lirien, his friend and emperor, now dead, but alive in memory, the blue glow of the relay glasses a halo around his head.

There were relay officers there, and they jumped to their feet with surprise, but raised hands in greeting when they recognized Rai and Vidarian. By now, footsteps were thudding against the pier, sailors from Rivenwake who had thought themselves trapped. Vidarian swayed in his seat, but directed them through the gate, and they wasted no time in passing through.

More and more came, first handfuls and then dozens: old men and children and mothers who had refused to leave them. There were ships, too: small ones, skyship-rigged, and Vidarian laboriously widened the gate to allow them to pass through with their sails furled. Some elder had arranged for the evacuation of artifacts, and a parade of treasure and elemental devices—including a series of ancient automata—passed through also.

Ariadel and Raven returned, carrying Khalesh and Ailenne with them. The firebird's claws were locked around Iridan's outstretched arms; carrying the automaton had slowed them, but they arrived. Raven released him, then landed, and Ariadel slipped down to the dock. The firebird dwindled into the cat, and Ariadel pressed a hand against Rai's side, then hurried through the gate.

At last the evacuees began to dwindle—and none too soon. The advancing platform's shadow was just passing over the *Viere d'Inar*.

Thalnarra and Altair arrived, winded from intense flying, but satisfied that they had rounded up any who remained alive in Rivenwake.

"Where is Marielle?" Vidarian asked. They had not seen Rivenwake's Queen.

// *On her ship,* // Thalnarra said simply. Vidarian stared at her, and she gave the tiniest nod of her beak.

Rai, he thought, and the dragon bent, then sprang into the air. Neither of them spoke as they flew toward the heart of the city—into fire and ash.

As the smoke grew thicker, Vidarian used a thin line of fire energy at the tip of his finger to sear off a section of his shirt. He called water to his hands after, soaking the fabric, then wrapped it around his nose and mouth, tying it behind his head. He touched Rai's neck, offering to do the same for him, but the dragon shook his head.

The *Viere d'Inar* emerged from the smoke beneath them. They had minutes before it would be overtaken by the fire from the Company's ship.

"Drop me on the quarterdeck," Vidarian called. Rai growled a protest, but Vidarian pressed him, and reluctantly the dragon descended, hovering just above the deck. Vidarian slid down the huge scaled shoulder, gripping the harness as his feet found empty air, then dropping. His feet hit the deck, and he swayed, gathering himself—then called up: "Stay close!" Rai snorted, blue lightning flickering from his snout, and began to circle.

Marielle was at the wheel, where he knew she would be. Smoke poured from the fore and aft holds of the venerable flagship, the pride of the West Sea.

"Marielle, we need to go," he said, trying to keep his voice as steady as he could in the face of the crumbling deck.

"The nine hells I will." Marielle stood transfixed, refusing to move, or to take her eyes off of the burning wreckage of the *Viere d'Inar*, or the platform that inched toward them. The sight of her tore through Vidarian's heart; superimposed across his memory were the flaming masts of the *Empress Quest*, his family's ship, which Marielle, too, had witnessed burning.

Her hand moved, drawing across a panel in front of the wheel.

The *Viere d'Inar* came to life, elemental crystals lighting up one after another along her hull.

The ship began to rise, and then to accelerate.

They were hurtling toward the platform, but Marielle's hand on the wheel was steady. She brought the ship higher, pitched its bowsprit untenably high. Rope, sail, and rigging tilted crazily, barrels tipped and rolled down the deck.

Then, just as the ship's nose tilted above the edge of the platform, Marielle wrenched the wheel sideways, spinning it to starboard. The great ship rolled in the air—directly at Ruby, whose golden body had just hoved into view.

Vidarian threw his arm around the shoulder of his former first mate and dragged her toward the quarterdeck. She fought him for a moment, then her arms lost their tension. "A friend did this for me, once," he shouted over the roar of the blaze.

"A friend," Marielle repeated, her head turned back toward the impossible sight. Behind them, Ruby's massive metal arm tore downward, shearing through one of the once-proud rails of her mother's ship. It had been Ruby who dragged Vidarian away from the crumbling decks of his *Empress Quest*, but not this creature of metal and madness.

Rai, his mind a wave of panic, nearly slammed into the deck in his urgency to get to Vidarian. They ran toward the dragon's claws, leaping, and his huge talons closed, lifting them off the ground. A tremendous roaring crash filled the air, uncannily slow, as the *Viere d'Inar* collided into Ruby's body, her arms still raking at the hull, crunching through prized wood and metal.

The dragon's claws shifted for a surer grip, and then he tilted sideways in the air, winging through a hellish miasma of burning smoke toward the gate.

PART THREE

SONG OF LIGHT

Chapter Twenty-One

Hall of the Emperor

The Relay Room was cluttered with artifacts, only a narrow passage available between them. Despite their surprise, it must not have taken long for the palace's minders to master the situation: when Vidarian staggered through, there were healers waiting.

Marielle collapsed as soon as her feet touched the stone floor, pure will being all that had prevented her from succumbing to the smoke that filled her lungs. Her face was blackened with soot beyond recognition. The healers—one of them in the badge of the Mindcrafters—rushed forward and took her from Vidarian, freeing him to drop the gate behind him.

Relief and exhaustion staggered him, and as he, too, dropped to the floor, Rai pushed close, his wolf nose nudging at Vidarian's shoulder. He managed to drape his arm carefully around Rai's spine-ruffed neck, not liking the way the breath rattled in the shapechanger's chest. They all had been far too long in the smoke; he only hoped that Ailenne had not been harmed by it.

Marielle was carried away, and when Vidarian lifted a hand after her, one of the healers hurried up to him with a poultice. She pressed it to his face, and he jerked back, but she made a soothing noise, and he closed his eyes, allowing it to be pressed against his mouth and nose. Beside him, another healer was treating Rai as well.

Cool air crept down his lungs, thick and smooth as water—sweet and sharp. His breath eased so swiftly his eyes started to tear, dripping from the corners of his eyes. He moved to brush them away, blinking, but the healer touched his shoulder.

"Let them flow," she said, and he nodded, mute. "Your body rids itself of poison."

The burning in his lungs did not totally subside, but the longer he breathed in the grassy, pungent herbs, the less he strained for air. Exhaustion slowly crept in, encouraged by his lack of movement, and it became a struggle to keep his eyes open.

At first, the pale blue glow that trickled through the evacuated artifacts stacked on the Relay Room's massive stone table seemed a mirage, a trick of his exhausted mind. But even his darkest imagination would have spared him the voice that accompanied it:

"Vidarian. So nice to see you again."

"Justinian," he answered, moving his face away from the poultice. The healer started to object, but Vidarian shook his head, mouthing an apology. She frowned, but withdrew. "I wish I could say the same."

"It would be difficult, with all of that rubble."

So he could see into the room somehow. Vidarian was going to have to ask Iridan how that was accomplished. He levered himself to his feet and worked his way to the door, holding it open for the two remaining healers. They each gave him a worried look, but filed out.

When he shut the door, Justinian spoke again:

"Let me ask you this: do all of these people have to die?"

He knew that the Senior Partner was goading him, trying to push him to rashness as he had from the first moment they met, but the rage that flushed his face was near blinding nonetheless. *"You* killed Lirien. Nistra knows how many sailors, how many Qui and Aloreans. You killed the Kala People."

"Of course we did. We had to."

Vidarian had known that the Company was behind the deaths, but it was altogether different to hear Justinian so casually admit it.

"We have Tepeki, and we promised not to kill his people." He made it sound as though he were discussing a birthday present for a cherished nephew.

So Justinian had kept his promise: in exchange for the young otter boy's murder of the Alorean emperor, his own people had been spared.

"But we could hardly refuse the sample of blood that the boy agreed to give us."

Vidarian went to the great table, shifting two crates enough to pull free one of the chairs and collapse onto it. "You used it to find a people related to Tepeki's."

"Why, yes. The Velshi are, you might say, the Kala of the sea."

A mystical folk, rare and mysterious even among the larger clans around them, secretive and capricious—it described both the otter and the antelope folk. Small wonder that they shared a common ancestor.

"He was right to protect them. An inordinately talented strain of humanity that would have been unfortunate to lose. They will fit well into the new Andovar, Tepeki proved that. It is a shame about the Kala, but they lacked the Velshi's warrior spirit."

Vidarian's hands clenched atop the table, his thoughts swimming through a haze of weariness.

"Rivenwake did not need to fall, you know. It was a wonder, much admired in fact, and could have been a key trade anchor in a Rulorat principality. But my colleagues believed that you would use it against us."

"What would have led them to believe such a thing?" Though exhausted, Vidarian raised defenses within himself around the still-raw injury of Rivenwake's destruction.

"A rather expensive little automata hidden on a certain Qui ship notified us that an alliance was in the works between Qui and the West Sea Kingdom. An alliance you introduced."

The *Jade Phoenix*. It was the *Phoenix* that led the Company to Rivenwake—not Ruby. There was no knowing if what remained of Ruby's mind and heart even recalled that she had been born there.

But who in Shen Ti would have known Vidarian was leaving? Even the imperial family had not known the name of the ship—

Akeo. The Rikani ambassador had been present at the launch. There long enough to sneak a small object aboard and leave none the wiser. Who knew what he had even bought with the action—or whether he'd been owned by the Company all along.

Through his anguish, a tiny realization managed to crack through the simmering wrath that filled Vidarian's heart: the listening device that Akeo planted had gone to Rivenwake. It had hidden in such a place as to overhear secret conversations. It could easily have also secreted itself in the evacuated materials.

His arms tensed with the thought, but he forced himself not to move. If Justinian could see the Relay Room, he would know if Vidarian began searching for the device. He would have to wait—and perhaps keep Justinian talking.

"It isn't just the Kala that you mean to kill," Vidarian said. "They're just the beginning. But your device is ill-tuned. Incomplete."

The accusation of failure struck true, as Vidarian hoped it might, a reaction revealed in the silence that followed.

"*Certain events forced our hand,*" Justinian agreed, the silkiness of his diction betraying a sentiment that was anything but. While he prevaricated, Vidarian concentrated intently on his voice, trying to uncover whether it emanated from a specific location.

Justinian's "certain events" were Vidarian's retrieval of the rose-colored crystal key from the Chatika. When they knew that Vidarian would be drawing near it, the Company must have panicked, releasing their weapon before it could be sufficiently focused by this last artifact. "How many did you kill?" he asked, through a tight throat. Part of him did not want to know—the part of him that admitted he had his own contribution in all this.

"*The nature of these things is that we do not know,*" Justinian replied, again all breezy, as if he were discussing grain prices. "*I am sure you will be relieved to hear that very few of the Partners were killed.*"

But some of them had been. It was slim comfort, and in his discomfiture Justinian had revealed just how little control they had over the device. Enough, Vidarian hoped, to stay their hand from using it again.

Rai came up to the table, his tail still low with exhaustion, but drawn to Vidarian's tension. His presence sparked an idea.

Can you find where that voice is coming from, without looking like that's what you're doing? Vidarian asked.

One of Rai's ears twitched at the oddness of the request, but he yawned in response, eyes drooping—and began sniffing around the room, for all the world like a bored terrier.

"*You still haven't answered my question,*" Justinian said, agitation still laying beneath his words—perhaps he thought that Vidarian had ignored him out of aggression.

"It is impossible for me to answer as to whether you will continue to murder and destroy in the pursuit of your own selfish goals." Let the man think that he was growing aggressive.

"*And if I said they could be spared?*"

"I would know you were lying."

"*Such a pity. But that doesn't explain your disposal of many thousands more lives in a futile and arrogant exercise of resistance. Especially when you now know yourself to be out-armed.*"

"The resistance is hardly mine alone."

"*Ah, but it is. You asked them to fight for you.*"

He had. Greater numbers were the only advantage that the distant and varied peoples of Andovar had against the Alorean Import Company. A united resistance was their only chance.

"*How many? How many innocents is your cause against us worth? And would your followers agree if they knew we had offered you a seat at our table, one you could have used to protect them?*"

Justinian was full on the attack now, and Vidarian was not going to stop him. Rai continued to slowly sniff around the room, and a sudden tilt of his ear showed that, though initially unsure, he had developed some idea as to where Justinian's device was hidden.

It would be so easy to acquiesce to the Company. To take Justinian's offer, and force his people to keep their promise. A deep, cold part of Vidarian wondered if they had killed enough people already for their scheme—to re-concentrate the available magic in the world into a new generation, their oligarchy. He could protect Ailenne, Ariadel, his friends. By fighting, was Vidarian merely bringing about more unnecessary death? Had they already lost?

Rai sat, tucking his paws close together, his nose pointed at a crate.

"*Destroying Val Imris is not what I want.*"

Dread prickled Vidarian's neck. "But?"

"*I extended my hand to you. Remember that.*"

As soon as he could stand, Vidarian started toward Calphille's audience chamber, pushing open the Relay Room's door and leaning upon it as the blood fled from his head, leaving darkness. He faltered, and Rai whined beside him, a high sound accompanied immediately by shuffling feet on the flagstones.

The two healers had remained, a young man and woman, rightly suspecting that their skills would be needed. One of them pressed a clay cup of water into Vidarian's hand, and he drained it, then requested *kava* and whatever they could find for a fast meal. Then he set off again for the audience chamber, determined not to wobble.

Ariadel was there with Calphille, as he hoped she'd be, a bassinet with a sleeping Ailenne tended by nursemaids just to one side of the imperial princess's cradle. Khalesh, too, was there, with Iridan, and Vidarian motioned to the Animator as he entered the room.

"There's a crate in the Relay Chamber. Rai will show you which one," he said. "It has a device that the Company is using to listen from afar."

"I will eliminate it," the Animator said.

"*I'd like to accompany you,*" Iridan said, and they turned toward him. "*I may be able to discern information from it.*"

Vidarian regarded the automaton for a moment, then nodded. Iridan had more than a reason to resent Justinian's involvement.

Rai gave a soft whuff and started back toward the Relay Room, and Animator and automaton followed.

Calphille came to take Vidarian's hands, followed by her captain of the guard and two dryad warrioresses. Ariadel lingered behind them. The Empress Dowager was exactly as she seemed always to have been in Vidarian's memory: a creature not of their world, but somewhere older and more true. It was what Lirien had seen in her from the moment they met, what stole his soul in a mere glance.

"That bad, is it?" Calphille said, a teasing smile stretched across worry— fear for her people.

"They're coming," he said, the words thick with apology. He looked to Ariadel, and she nodded—she had explained the fall of Rivenwake to Calphille.

"How long?" Calphille asked.

"Hours," Vidarian replied, "if we're lucky."

"We will not trust to luck." She turned to the guard captain. "The people, those left in the city. Bring them all within the old wall," she said, raising her hand when the man began to object. "Have the Sky Knights send scouts for those unable to move quickly.

"I'll go with you," Vidarian added, and the man looked at him, startled. "To rally the Knights, as best I can."

One of the healer's apprentices arrived then with the promised *kava* and cold meat rolls from the kitchen. Vidarian drank down the former while it was still hot enough to scald, and took the latter along with the cloth napkin.

He went to Ariadel, and she embraced him tightly, fierce enough to press the still labored breath from his lungs. When she released him, she touched his face with a warm hand. "I'll meet you out there," she said, and he nodded.

Calphille waved them off, and he followed the guard captain out and through the warren of passageways toward the Sky Knights' field. The meat rolls were cold and doughy but satisfying, and he swallowed one after the other until they were gone.

By the time they reached the training field, the first explosions had begun on the far eastern side of the city.

CHAPTER TWENTY-TWO

CHILDREN OF CHAOS

It was a surreal sight, the bursts of lurid green light on the eastern horizon, an ominous false dawn. Only Veda had ever produced that strange green glow, some ancient fusion of fire and air magics that was as terrifying for what it implied—her grasp of multiple elements—as the damage it wreaked. By attacking just after sundown, the Company was making it clear that it intended to use every advantage, to break the minds of those loyal to Val Imris if it could.

The Sky Knights' training field was transformed from when Vidarian had seen it last: a motley array of tents filled the space, varied but pitched in precise lines. Beyond the field were skyship anchorages cleared of tall grass where Vidarian had once ridden with the Emperor. The anchorages were painfully empty, so bereft of skyships that the Sky Knights had reclaimed one of the large clearings for a replacement training field.

It was there that Calphille's guard led Vidarian, and there that they found Caladan, Knight-Captain of the Empress Regent's Sky Knights.

When Vidarian first came to Val Imris at the behest of Emperor Lirien Aslaire, Sir Caladan Orrin-Smyth had met them at the gates, then only a Master Handler of a single Sky Knight wing. He had since led knights in battle against the Company's skyships numerous times, and for his loyalty had been raised to Knight-Captain, commander of those few knights who both remained loyal to the imperial family and had retained their steeds after the gate's opening unleashed in them a long-lost ability to shapechange into formidable—and difficult to control—forms.

The Knight-Captain was mounted, his lance ready and his steed armored. Rai changed into his winged cat shape—one he had learned from an attacking Sky Knight steed—and went to sniff noses with the tall armored horse, whose wings and ears twitched in recognition.

"We came to support you in the city's defense, sir knight," Vidarian began, but couldn't keep his eyes from straying to the empty anchorages.

"The Empress Dowager has most of the armada dispatched to the borders, protecting villages from the Company's mercenaries," Caladan said, answering his unasked questions. "So we're glad to have you."

A young man in what appeared to be a makeshift uniform of some kind hurried up to Caladan then, bearing tubes of rolled message paper. He took in Rai with a glance, doubtless thinking him one of the Sky Knight steeds, but froze when he caught sight of Vidarian. "It . . . it's an honor to meet you, sir," he stammered.

"Lukas is one of the infantrymen who arrived from the border cities to defend Val Imris," Caladan supplied, and Vidarian nodded his thanks to the boy, reminding himself that he had fought pirates at sea when he'd been that young. The thought of him in pitched battle was nonetheless disconcerting. His uniform was clearly homemade, bearing an inelegantly embroidered black imperial eagle, and a second charge, a red flame ringed with curls of blue.

"What is that insignia?" Vidarian asked, indicating the mark.

The young man drew back, discomfited, and struggled to answer, finally looking to Caladan for help.

The Knight-Captain cleared his throat. "Why, it's the mark of the Tesseract, of course."

Vidarian's head swam. It was not the first time he'd seen the device, he realized; it flew on flags around the makeshift camp that filled the training field, and had even been pinned to the shoulders of the healers in the Relay Room. Without knowing its significance, he had assumed it to be a house insignia of some sort.

But the young soldier was looking at him, openly desperate for some kind of acknowledgment. "Thank you for your service," Vidarian finally managed. "Defend your Empress bravely—and stay safe."

The boy bowed, then saluted Caladan as he rose. The knight nodded, and accepted the pouch of messages. "I imagine it must be strange," Caladan said, looking into the pouch and thumbing through the rolled notes, "having them act like that all the time."

"You have no idea." He poured as much sentiment as he could into the words, intending them without sting: how could he measure the effect this would have on so many lives? How could he have asked them to follow him? And did even his own uncertainty render him unworthy of such loyalty? The abyss of doubt threatened daily beneath his feet.

"I suppose I don't," Caladan said. Then: "The Knights," by his tone about to suggest something Vidarian wouldn't like. "They'd rally at a word from you."

That was the rub of it. Women and men needed leadership at a moment like this, not doubt. And he had asked it of them. "I came to assist in any way I can," he said.

Caladan swung astride his steed, which pawed the ground as another distant explosion trembled the dirt beneath them. Need would dictate brevity, for which Vidarian tried not to be grateful—every moment not spent at the engagement's front seemed an eternity.

Rai swelled into his dragon form, and Vidarian accepted the offer of his outstretched claw. It had taken some practice, but he could now easily vault from Rai's folded arm to his seat between the shoulder-spines even as it was moving.

Before them, Caladan rested his hand on his steed's shoulder, concentrating; Vidarian was just barely aware of the brush of thought between them. So Rai and Raven were not unique; many of the shapechangers, it appeared, had evidenced some telepathic ability, though it must not be strong if it needed touch.

Word passed quickly, relayed silently from the mind of one steed to another, and within moments a crowd had gathered: some three dozen Knights that were all that remained of the Alorean loyal, and a handful of gryphons, to Vidarian's surprise. Most of those who remained from Thalnarra's flight were seeing to the evacuation, but it seemed they had made the Sky Knight camp their base of operations.

Rai's head dipped on his sinuous neck and he sat back on his haunches, raising Vidarian high into view. A murmur passed through the gathered knights—most of whom he'd never met. But Linnea was there with her yearling royal—a creature Rai had saved from death as it hatched. Brannon, Linnea's brother, had been assigned to Thalnarra when they first came to Val Imris, and later became her ward, a kind of bonded apprentice.

The murmurs died down, and Vidarian cleared his throat. "What you will face I cannot promise to describe," he began, looking from knight to knight. "The Company has awakened mystery after mystery from our past—devices long forgotten and ill-understood. They are cavalier with the lives of their own people, and indeed even themselves.

"But I have looked into the searing eye of the unknown, and I promise you that you possess the fortitude to do the same. I promise you that you fight for the greatest treasure that I know—for Alorea, for her people. And that this rightness will carry you wherever you need it to. Against tyranny and terror, against a force whose highest values are greed, deception, and viciousness, the greatest challenge is to stand in defiance. But that is what we will do. And to so stand is victory itself."

Vidarian drew his sword and lifted the blade in a salute to the gathering knights. Part of him, the boy of his childhood who had idolized such tall and seeming mythical figures as paragons, was still in awe of them, fabled Sky Knights of Alorea. "Remember that you defend a mythic legacy. You have my greatest respect—it is an honor to fight at your side!"

They cheered then, heartily as he had hoped they would, their spirits raised in a shield against what may lay before them. Some would have leapt into the air right then, but Caladan quickly interceded, shouting orders, forming them into combat wings.

"Ready?" Vidarian murmured, and Rai stretched his wings by way of answer. As the knights cleared from their vicinity, Rai crouched, then leapt, launching them into the air with gut-abandoning force.

The training field with its swarming trainees dropped away beneath them. Shreds of errant cloudstuff swirled around Rai's wings as they rose, whipped to froth by their passage. At evenly spaced distances and altitudes, the Sky Knight wings were beginning to form up under Caladan's command. From all quarters of the city, individual gryphons were arrowing upward to join them.

As the horizon tilted before them, height revealed a sickening sight: a dark army marching on the imperial city. The Company had not sent its automaton eagle platform this time, perhaps leery of how Ariadel and Vidarian had managed to damage it. Instead, they had sent Ruby, Veda, and an occupying army of some two thousand mercenary pikemen and cavalry. This number had been reported by Sky Knight scouts, but in the way of such things, seeing it spread in a dark moving cloud at the edge of the city illustrated more than a report ever could.

A strange feeling welled up in Vidarian's chest, piercing through the thick layers of hardness that the last year had built around his heart. He could not have imagined his life leading to this point, and yet, looking out over Val Imris, a dragon's wings spread to port and starboard, his will to stop the Company's assault took on a ferocity that burned. A rumbling growl shuddered up from Rai's ribs as he shared it, and a brief crackle of lightning flickered between the dragon's jaws.

Caladan approached then, the spotted wings of his steed rising beneath them. He drew up just above Rai's right shoulder, his mount tossing its head, tail flagged, eager for action. "Our wings will sweep the city first," he called. "Half will search for stragglers in the outer city. The rest will form up to attack."

It was crude, but should prove effective. Below, another figure was rising from the training field, red and gold despite the falling light—Ariadel and Raven. "Leave the automata to us," Vidarian answered, and was close enough to see a line of worry relax across the Knight-Commander's forehead. "Stay clear of them, out of range if you can."

Caladan drew his horse closer, its wings fanning in an arc to keep them in one place. "Good luck to you, then," he said, touching his visor first in salute, then closing it.

"This is it," Vidarian said, looking out over the city.

The helmeted head turned toward him, voice muffled. "This is what?"

"This is the moment when you know who you are," he said. "When everything falls around you."

"What a fantastically bleak notion," the knight replied, freeing his lance and hefting it. "The kind that comes with a gallant death. I plan to live."

"Good plan."

The knight tipped up his lance in a final salute, then directed his mount downward, bellowing a summons and a rally to his knights. As one, the knights answered him, lifting their own lances, their horses joining the echoing call. Rai roared, his otherworldly voice cutting the sky, and loosed a bolt of lightning that tore through the clouds. The knights shouted back in even bolder answer.

The Sky Knights descended over Val Imris like an arrowing flight of armored angels, their plating catching the final rays of the fast-disappearing sun. Their feathered wings slipped over the city like so many flying clouds, and at the rim of the old city wall they parted, half spreading out in wings of five and seven to rescue citizenry. Those remaining advanced, Caladan at their vanguard, toward the enemy host.

Ruby was another matter. The gryphons and the Sky Knights had a fighting chance against the infantry, despite being outnumbered—but Ruby, left unchecked, could level the entire city by herself. Her golden body, too, glowed in the sunset, lit by its elemental gems and the poisonous glow of Veda's green energy beside her.

Ariadel—helmed, somehow, assumedly from the Val Imris armory—was drawing close on firebird wings.

She wants to know what you are going to do about Ruby, Rai thought, and Vidarian looked across at the pair. The strange indirect telepathy through the shapechangers was jarring but practical. He showed Rai his plan, knowing that the dragon would echo it to Raven.

I don't want to ask her to challenge Veda, he began.

The firebird banked, then dropped one silver-edged wing, dipping down and to the north.

At Vidarian's flush of surprise and alarm, Rai said quickly: *I didn't tell them. She saw it immediately when she saw what you planned to do.*

It was a struggle to put it out of his mind, but he made the attempt. Veda was deadly, but a single moment spent worrying about Ariadel could give Ruby the fatal advantage she would need.

Without being asked, Rai folded his left wing, dropping them in a shallow arc toward the east, and Ruby. He straightened out just above the tallest roofs, close enough that the wind of his wingbeats scattered dust on the cobblestone streets below. They followed the main artery known as Celadon Row, a famed avenue that was once home to the most talented potters on the continent. The sand packed between the cobblestones glinted with glazed chips of clay, as did the columns surrounding dozens of storefronts, the priceless displays of generations of Alorean artists.

The clay ovens at length gave way to the bakers' district, over which Ruby's golden body towered. As they drew near, the breath pressed out of Vidarian's chest—she was drawing the water energy out of the air, preparing to bring down a massive blow on a grain store.

Rai snarled, and a *crack* of lightning arced from his open throat, exploding the water energy just as it left Ruby's hands. Boiling, electrified water sizzled against her metal body, then ran in harmless rivulets to the ground.

Ruby turned toward them.

His months with Iridan had taught Vidarian to read an automaton's subtle emotional cues—and to know that Ruby was expressing none of them. Her three gemstone eyes—one the sun ruby through which she had first spoken to him, a ruby given as payment by the now High Priestess Endera—would have chilled the most battle-hardened warrior, but it was more than that. It was impossible to extract Ruby's fate from his own; every part of her current existence he had a hand in creating. And so her pain was his, her destruction.

Her choices were her own, Rai said, jolting him. The dragon's neck arched, turning one of his large blue eyes back on Vidarian, even as he kept the other on Ruby. There was fury there, and no time to determine whether it was battle-readiness or something more.

Ruby's eyes passed over them without reaction, turning down toward the buildings at her feet.

"Justinian wanted me to tell you that this was your choice," Ruby said, then

lashed downward through the roof of a bakery with a sharpened spear of water energy. *"But I want to tell you that it isn't."*

"Isn't," Vidarian repeated, stunned by her refusal of Justinian's claim, knowing that it must be a ploy, but stumbling in that surprised moment into the lurking morass of his own guilt.

"No. It's mine." Her metal hands came together and energy leaped out from them, coursing down toward the grain store.

Vidarian reached outward with his own energy, surprised when it leaped forth obediently. He redirected Ruby's assault, turning her force along the edge of his own, directing it into harmless impact with the street below.

"I don't know what's left of you, Ruby," Vidarian began, and the truth of the statement tightened his throat. "But if any of you remembers your family—your mother—surely that part of you must see how wrong it is to stand with the Alorean Import Company."

"I am more myself than I have ever been," Ruby replied, directing another lash of water through the roof of a pastry stall. *"If you think that my mother wouldn't have wanted me to kill thousands of landers in a bid to seize immortality, and destroy any who stood in my way, whether friend or foe—then you didn't know her very well at all."* She continued the rampage, steadily working west up the street, leaving wreckage in her wake.

He needed her to keep talking in order to gather his thoughts for what he must do. And he wasn't entirely sure it was going to work. Ruby could not know that Matpri's stone now allowed him to summon gate energy without other elementalists—but *he* wasn't sure he could open a gate large enough for her. "Immortality—is that what this is about?" Slowly, he drew his sword.

Ruby turned a motionless eye on him, almost as if amused by the weapon, then continued, this time cracking open a flour mill with a sweep of one massive metal arm. *"Even my mother could not evade death,"* she said, and this time the mechanical buzz to her voice was low, ominous, but full of pain. *"I plan not to die."*

The eerie inversion of Caladan's earlier words nearly broke Vidarian's concentration, but he held fast. Still wielding the water energy he had earlier summoned, he wreathed it again with fire—and fed both energies to the *sou-klehn* stone in his sword.

Chaos answered. The crippling starfire energy burst forth into the world, coalescing from that place of unmaking, the nothing between all things. He stretched it wider, feeding it energy from deep within himself; it fought to collapse, but he willed its existence.

"*Your parlor trick,*" Ruby hissed. "*Indulge yourself, but know that I will outlive you—and I will see the Rulorat line end.*"

The chaos opened a void beneath Ruby's feet, and swallowed her.

Even as the void's maw spread open, it demanded an answer of Vidarian— threatened his mind, pulling at him, promising to devour him as well if he did not redirect it. He pushed Ruby's threat from his mind and had half a second to wonder what would happen if he refused to answer. Would it consume him as well? All of Val Imris?

The risk was too great. He thought of Rivenwake. Broken Rivenwake, and the shipwrecks that now lay far beneath the water's surface. Let Ruby stay there a while, and find a way to summon her friends without their automaton assistance. With luck, the city's camouflage shield would disrupt her.

It took the remainder of his energy to convince the gate to close again, and he realized that the exhaustion he'd felt before was not merely due to smoke. The chaos energy drained him as only the touch of the elemental god-desses had done before, absorbing some ephemeral life energy as the cost for its summoning.

He deeply wanted to collapse, to fall against Rai's saddle and allow the dragon to carry him wherever he would, but he clung to consciousness, thinking of the battling Sky Knights, and of Ariadel. *Take us to her,* he thought at Rai, and the memory of Veda and her fluorescent energy stirred a wakening adrenaline in his veins again.

As Rai's muscles bunched beneath him, wings lifting to gain altitude once more, Vidarian did slump against the saddle. The next thing he knew, Rai's mind was brushing with his, gently, and without alarm.

They were still; the dragon must have landed. Distant sounds of battle from the city still raged, but here the streets were eerily calm. When Vidarian lifted his head, he saw Raven, firebird-shaped, her long neck bent downward, beak pointed toward the automaton called Veda. Ariadel rode between her shoulders, carrying a long lance whose point seemed to be a broad blade, almost sword-like.

The first time Vidarian had seen Veda, she was training Ruby to her new automaton body by way of attacking the resistance camp nicknamed Gryphonslair. Now, up close, her arms bent in an attitude of surrender before Raven, she was only slightly less terrifying. The plates of dark grey armor that covered her body were pointed and inscribed, intended to intimidate where Iridan's evoked elegance; the circlet of twisted steel and wild striped feathers suggested metal's brute power over the organic.

"She's asked to speak with you," Ariadel said. "She surrendered as soon as she saw us." At the same moment, Rai relayed a question: *Should we destroy her?*

An explosion to the north drew all of their attention; the Company's ground troops had some kind of weapon. Vidarian cursed, and Ariadel turned to him again, torn.

"You should go to them," he said.

"She's dangerous," Ariadel replied.

"If I had wanted to fight, I would have done so before now," Veda said.

"They need one of us. Rai and I can contain her if necessary," Vidarian said, hoping it was true. Rai rumbled unhappily, but did not contradict him. Every moment cost the citizens of Val Imris.

Raven hissed a warning at Veda, a chilling raptorial sound. Then, reluctantly, she and Ariadel took back to the air, flying toward the battle line.

When they were gone, *"We could be brother and sister, you and I,"* Veda said. *"We are children of chaos. No other in this world hears the song you hear the way I do."*

"That doesn't strike me as a strong argument for allowing you to live," he said.

"To know chaos is to be limitless," she said. *"And how can those with no limits constrain themselves to those that labor within them?"*

Vidarian looked at her, struggling to discern her motivation. In this, automata seemed not all that different from humans, or gryphons, for that matter. At least mechanical creatures advertised their machinations openly.

It was the thought of Iridan that stayed his hand. The automaton might not be human—but neither were some of Vidarian's closest friends. Iridan might be endowed with mysterious and even terrifying abilities, but this was through no fault of his own. And indeed he had been dealt a raw hand by the humans that had thus far been entrusted with his care. The only thing he had ever cared about for himself was locating his missing siblings, the automata Arian and Modrian. Veda, despite the geis that prevented Iridan from thinking of her when she was not present before him, was the third sibling.

And yet.

"Parvidian, knowing my nature, did not destroy me," Veda continued, leaping on his hesitation. *"I can be a powerful ally, and I have no allegiance to Justinian beyond his convenience to me."*

"How could we possibly trust you?" Vidarian asked, knowing that he was stalling, knowing that Veda was sure to seize upon it as weakness.

But by way of answer, the glittering gray automaton reached up to her throat, pressing a series of indentations there. A section of metal below her ribcage hinged open, revealing a familiar blue glow.

Within was the triangular piece that had been missing from Siane. As she drew it from her body, the energy wreathing her lessened, dimming. She held it upward as if in supplication.

It was not an answer for trust, but neither was it an offer Vidarian felt he could refuse.

"Come with me, then," Vidarian said.

"Gladly."

CHAPTER TWENTY-THREE
ALLEGIANCE

Caladan, Ariadel, and Vidarian reported to the Empress Regent at dawn. Few had slept that night, and by the dim white light of early morning the candles in the sconces guttered in tiny seas of melted wax.

A steady stream of attendants filled porcelain cups with steaming *kava*, and presented trays laden with cream biscuits and thick buttered bread. The kitchens had set to distributing the most perishable items with abandon both inside and outside the palace, as the ice route running north to Eagle Bay was now blocked. The rich food was a strange reminder that the imperial city was now under siege.

"Thanks to our friends," Caladan nodded across the hall to Thalnarra, who stood beside a ceremonially armored member of her flight, a tall gryphon named Arishak, "we were able to sweep the city in time. We know of no Alorean citizens left beyond the wall. Our casualties were few—thirteen knights injured, two lost." He paused, and Vidarian thought he was mourning his comrades, but he continued, "The civilian militia I fear fared rougher, despite their defensive position. Some two dozen injured, and eleven killed."

A ripple of surprise and sorrow passed around the room, and Vidarian felt it in his heart. Beside him, Ariadel pressed a hand to his shoulder. His mind knew that the casualty rate was remarkable, for a force repelling two thousand mercenaries—they had the advantage of the wall's defenses, and the demoralization of Ruby's loss, but nonetheless it was a well-executed defense. But he could not be other than haunted by the notion of men dying under a banner named for him.

"Summon the families of the fallen knights, if they can be found, to stay in the palace," Calphille said gently, "And the militia. We will provide for them as best we can."

Caladan bowed, his hands clenched with emotion. When he rose, it was with calm purpose. "For now, we're holding the line at the old wall. My knights have spent the last several weeks shoring up the stone—a precaution, we thought, but vital now."

"You have done well, Captain," Calphille said, and Caladan bowed again. "Alorea thanks you, and I thank you." It was a humble audience chamber that the Empress Dowager kept, but there was nonetheless an air of ceremony as she rose, went to Caladan, and took his hands in hers. He bowed again, and this time his eyes shone as he straightened.

When Calphille returned to her seat, she sipped delicately from the peppery tea she favored over *kava*, then folded her hands. "How long can the wall hold?" she asked, and around the room a soft exhalation answered her.

Vidarian cleared his throat, and Caladan nodded to him. When Calphille's amber eyes turned toward him, he felt a chill, not unpleasant: it seemed only days ago that she'd transformed from tree to human before his eyes, only hours since he had brought her to Val Imris, there to love and be loved by an emperor. But it was worlds ago, and her eyes carried that distance, far from unkind, but changed. "The wall may hold," he said, grasping at his thoughts, "but the greater fear is when Ruby may return."

Now those in the chamber stirred, murmuring unhappy agreement.

"The difficult truth is that we have no way of knowing when that may be," he continued, swallowing a sigh. "It could be weeks. Months. Or hours."

A moment's silence passed, and then Calphille nodded. "We must resolve the siege quickly, then, if we can."

None would argue with her, even if she were no empress, but silence fell again as any other answer seemed similarly impossible. There simply were no forces that could be spared to truly break the siege.

"These men and women, they're paid soldiers," Calphille said, her dark eyes thoughtful, inscrutable. "Send a message to the mercenary captains, and construct a safe meeting ground at the borderline. We will offer them amnesty and land holdings if they will swear allegiance to my daughter."

Now the stewards in attendance jumped, startled; one even lifted a hand to his throat in surprise. "Your majesty," one ventured, steeled by anxious looks from the rest, "there is little unclaimed land, save far from the imperial city, so far they would scarcely believe a grant."

"My sympathies for those who have abandoned Val Imris in her hour of need are thin," she said. "They will be granted land within the city. The empire will validate the new land claims should the original owners return. If they will not act to defend their city, they will have paid the price of her defense with their holdings here." There was a hardness in her, and this was little surprise—she had been a warrior as formidable as any of her guardian handmaidens when Vidarian first met her. But this was deeper, and borne of pain: she would fight for Val Imris as Lirien had, and could no longer. Vidarian's heart ached for her even as he admired her political will.

"I will deliver the message myself," Caladan said, when the stewards did not answer.

Calphille smiled, calling to mind birdsong, sunlight through branches. "You must value yourself more dearly, sir knight," she said, fondness blunting any sting, "Particularly as I intend to elevate you to Commander of the City."

The Knight-Captain—now Commander—bowed, and Vidarian wondered if he would become dizzy from so many such movements.

// *We will carry the message, if it please your majesty,* // the gryphon Arishak offered, his voice bright and lively like greenwood flame. Mostly, the gryphons seemed amused at human conventions of rulership, but this young fire gryphon seemed to earnestly enjoy them. Doubtless he had been assigned to the court for that very reason.

"I would be most grateful," Calphille replied, and Arishak touched his beak to his foreleg in a deep and rather dramatic bow. She turned then to Vidarian. "Before the attack, you were bringing news of the southern continent."

"I was, your majesty," Vidarian agreed, searching a memory dull with fatigue. "The Chatika people—and more perhaps, the clans Kaitan and Zhenjin—stand with you and await your call."

"The Plainsrunners," Calphille said, sounding surprised, and Vidarian could only echo her expression. "They have not gone to war together in generations."

Calphille, he realized, being of the forest near the southern continent herself—and being a shapechanger, would of course have known of the half-horse Plainsrunner clans as no Alorean would. And, perhaps, the force that they represented. "The clans of the southern continent took a terrible loss from the use of the Company's weapon," Vidarian said, grateful for the grave look that came across Calphille's features. She knew, somehow, that he yet blamed himself for the weapon's use. "They will go to war with us, if we call."

"How can they be summoned?" she asked, ginger again, but determined.

"By Iridan, I believe."

∿∿∿

But there was something else Vidarian needed to show to Iridan before requesting the summons. Upon returning to the palace, he had asked Thalnarra to appoint a gryphon guard on the sorcerous automaton called Veda. Only the gryphons, outside of himself and Ariadel, had elemental energy sufficient to even hope to restrain her if she should decide to turn violent.

They guarded her in the very chamber where Justinian had first awakened Iridan: an underground alchemical lab of sorts beneath the Arboretum, an astonishing sunsphere-lit indoor garden in the heart of the palace. Iridan and Khalesh had set up their workshop beneath the sunsphere, doubtless unaware that Iridan's "sister" dwelt beneath them.

When he arrived at the Arboretum, Iridan greeted him with an enthusiasm that pulled at his heart.

"*Greetings, Captain,*" the automaton said, moving quickly to a table that held the device he and Khalesh had found in the Relay Room. "*The hidden device contained a wealth of information. Not only was I able to disarm it, but I believe I may be able to learn the location of their next target.*"

Khalesh was watching the automaton with a reticence that troubled Vidarian. "I am advising caution," the big man rumbled, and Vidarian breathed a little easier upon realizing it was not Iridan he mistrusted, but the action proposed. "We may be able to invert the device, but it promises to be dangerous."

"Gentlemen," Vidarian said, partly by way of returning Iridan's greeting, and two sets of eyes—one glowing and one not—turned toward him. "I'm afraid I came on other business, though we will surely discuss the advice soon. If you'll follow me?"

Curious, but silent, the Animator and the automaton followed Vidarian as he led them through the Arboretum, navigating its labyrinthine paths of tangled greenery by memory. At last they came to an alabaster courtyard and a pair of fire gryphons: by the gold paint tipping their feathers, they were high-ranking fire elementalists. Thalnarra had taken no chances in her choice of guardians. The gryphons nodded to Vidarian as he lifted the heavy iron-handled trapdoor set in the courtyard's center; behind him, Khalesh and Iridan exchanged a very human glance of surprise before following him down the winding stairs.

The door that Justinian had once unlocked with a glowing cube-shaped key was open, and beyond it, sitting at a stone table and manipulating a handful of glowing elemental gems, sat Veda.

Iridan stiffened behind him so abruptly that Khalesh grunted with surprise, nearly running into the automaton, who had halted on the stairs with one foot poised to descend.

"She surrendered to Ariadel at the battle yesterday," Vidarian said, forestalling their questions. "And although she is dangerous," an understatement if there ever was one, "she is your sister, Iridan, and I do not forget a promise."

Veda watched them silently, her metallic face as ever unreadable. Her hands were stretched over the table, turning the elemental artifacts this way and that; a heavy set of manacles linked her hands together, inhibiting much greater movement. Vidarian had little idea if such fetters would serve to restrain such a creature as she, but dared not take any risk with her.

"*You took a great risk,*" Iridan said, his already odd voice hollow with shock and hesitancy. "*But I thank you for it.*"

Vidarian let out a breath he had not known he was holding. There had been no way to predict Iridan's reaction; he would have sympathized with virtually any.

Khalesh and Iridan filed down into the chamber, more to busy their feet than anything else, Vidarian suspected. The three of them stood in a kind of half arc, leaving the darker automaton a wide berth.

"*Iridan,*" Veda said at last, her voice a grating slide of iron files compared to Iridan's smooth music. "*You look well.*"

"*You needn't waste pleasantries,*" Iridan said, startling Vidarian. The automaton was making no attempt to mask his dislike of Veda. Again, it was hard to fault him. But having heard her surrender, Vidarian found himself with more questions than he had answers about this created artifact that could summon and learn elemental magic faster than any human or gryphon he had ever seen. "*You know already the only questions I have for you,*" Iridan was continuing, and this time his tone was flatter, absent even animosity. "*Where are Modrian and Arian?*"

"*Modrian was destroyed to create Ruby's body,*" Veda said simply. "*I do not know where Arian is.*"

There was a soft click as Iridan's arms slackened at her words, and the ever-present light of his eyes dimmed and strengthened by turns. "*Modrian—destroyed?*"

"*It was the moment when I knew I could stand with them no longer,*" Veda said softly. "*I will carry his dying protest in my mind for eternity.*"

Iridan stood, still as the alabaster walls, for several long moments, while Khalesh and Vidarian watched him anxiously. At last, he turned and retreated up the stone steps, offering not another word to Veda. Almost, Vidarian could pity her, locked there beneath the earth and scorned by her only kin.

They followed Iridan to the surface, and Vidarian replaced the heavy door. Khalesh rested a hand on Iridan's shoulder and the automaton turned to him, touching the man's fingertips with his own.

"*I must find Arian,*" was all he would say.

Together the three of them walked in silence through the strange garden, until at last they came to the archway that led into the outer palace.

"I am sorry, my friend," Vidarian said, knowing Iridan would be able to sense that he meant every word. "And sorrier still to have to ask you . . ." He drew the prism key tuned to the Chatika's location from a pocket.

Iridan was subdued as he accepted the prism key from Vidarian. Without comment, he lifted it to the level of his eyes, which closed, then reopened blue with contact. There was something like relief in the blue light, as if Iridan could retreat there from his thoughts. Vidarian hoped that he could.

"*We hear you,*" Iridan said, in Qinde's voice.

"Qinde," Vidarian greeted her. "It is good to hear you again. We have returned to the palace at Val Imris, and call to you now, as promised. The imperial city is under siege by the Alorean Import Company."

There was a pause of scarcely half a breath.

"*Open the way,*" Qinde said, "*and we will come, as I have sworn.*"

CHAPTER TWENTY-FOUR

ABSENCE

The Relay Room was nowhere near large enough to accommodate an arriving army, especially one made of centaurs and horse-sized birds. After a brief debate, an old stone archway leading from the rose garden kept by the late Dowager Empress—Lirien's mother, Revelle's grandmother—was deemed large enough, and situated adjacent to an old parkland that could contain an arriving clan. In truth, Vidarian had no idea how many warriors to expect; a cautious side of him wondered how much of Qinde's claim was bravado. But they would be ready for thousands, if necessary.

While the preparations were made, he felt the urge to return to the wall, but recalled Calphille's amnesty plan. Such things were far better handled by diplomats. Calphille's representatives would be guarded by gryphons from Thalnarra's tribe, more than sufficient to protect against even heavily armed mercenaries, and far more impressive than Vidarian himself could be.

He longed, then, with burning responsibilities momentarily fulfilled, to find Ailenne and Ariadel. The imagined sound of his daughter crying for an absent father was enough to guide his feet directly to their old quarters, but another lingering responsibility stopped him. With reluctance, he turned instead toward the hospital established deep within the palace for fallen officers and guests of the imperial throne.

Marielle was easy to find, and sat in her bed demurely enough, propped up by pillows and drinking broth with a sour expression that indicated she would prefer perhaps to crack raw marrow bones with her teeth. One of the healers murmured an entreaty to avoid upsetting her just before he entered the room, and he bowed an earnest agreement.

"I'm glad to see you upright," he greeted her, looking closely for lingering signs of injury. Her skin was scrubbed smooth and pink, all trace of ash and soot gone, but the treatment left rawness behind it. A loose robe discreetly covered the poultice of pungent herbs applied to her chest, its trailing bandage wrapped scarf-like around her neck.

"I yearn for a boar steak," she replied, voice barely above a whisper, looking mournfully at her soup. "I think this watery stuff is intended as motivation to clear out and make way for the next poor soul."

"I'll see that you get one, as soon as the healers will allow it," he said.

A near companionable silence stretched between them as she continued to eat, making faces all the while—mainly for his benefit, Vidarian thought. He stretched after what to say to her.

"Spit it out, Captain-sir," she said at last, setting aside her final spoonful of broth. As was her wont, now that she was royal, she succeeded in bending the title halfway toward an epithet.

"I fear that I've failed you again," Vidarian said.

Marielle managed to glare at him. "We welcomed the *Jade Phoenix*. The alliance would have been a powerful one. There was no way of knowing . . ."

"I should have known. The failure is mine."

"Speak of it again," Marielle said lightly, "and I will inform Master Anglar that an agent of the Empress Dowager questions the leadership of the Queen of the West Sea." Her voice gained a bit of strength at that, and he peered at her, wondering if she were serious. Studiously she took her spoon back up and levered the last bit of broth to her lips. "I advise against it, personally. Anglar is sixth-generation free-sail. He takes that manner of thing rather seriously."

Grudgingly, and with ill manner, Vidarian abandoned the point, taking the exit she offered. "Where are the other captains?" he asked, still ginger.

"I have summoned them, but it will take time for them to get here, even those with skyships." She paused then, looking out her window to the palace walls. "And I don't know if they will come," she admitted finally, then looked at him, the slightest sparkle back in her eye. "You know how pirates are."

They talked of ships then, and crews long past—of Vidarian's family, and Marielle's, who had also struggled boldly to attain their rank. It had been Marielle's father's dream that a Solandt might one day captain an imperial ship. Vidarian wondered what he would have thought had he lived to see all that his daughter achieved.

Years as his own first mate had given Marielle a finely honed sense for when Vidarian was fighting wandering thoughts. "Off with you," she muttered at last, far from unkindly, and yawned. "They'll be in to ply me with poppy if you don't leave off. And you've done your duty. You'll be wanting to check on that wee daughter'f yourn." The lilt into her father's brogue spoke to her fading energy—an accent she had seemed to leave behind when she became queen.

"More than duty, as you know," he said, and gently rested a hand on her shoulder. Settling back against the pillows, her eyes drifting shut, she clasped it with her own by way of answer.

～～～

By the time he made it back to their sleeping quarters, Ailenne and Ariadel were both fast asleep. He whispered an automatic thanks—only in time to wonder to whom it could now be directed. Nistra? The Starhunter? All options now seemed absurd. But the image of his family, secure and sleeping, filled any void in his heart, and then some.

He was about to join them, as quietly as he could, when Khalesh tapped softly on the doorjamb.

The Animator was too large to effectively retreat, which he did attempt to do when he saw that Ariadel and her daughter were sleeping. But if he was determined enough to track them across the palace, Vidarian knew he was not going to be able to rest until he knew why. With the softest sigh under his breath, he returned to the hallway.

Khalesh immediately gestured the beginnings of an apology, but Vidarian waved him off. Then, when the Animator began to speak again, it was Vidarian's turn to apologize—he forestalled him with a raised hand, pointed back toward the room where his family slept, then motioned him further down the hallway.

They continued in companionable silence until the low wall that surrounded this section of the guest quarters opened up into a neglected rose garden. Weeds crawled up from beneath the large flagstones, and flowers poured wantonly out of their sculpted containers, but the overgrowth had not progressed to the white marble benches. They each took seats, and Vidarian looked at Khalesh expectantly.

"Something about—the nature of Siane troubles me still," Khalesh began. Vidarian was about to agree that indeed a great deal still bothered him, but the Animator's mind was already elsewhere, his eyes turned inward. It was a challenge not to remind the man of certain pressing needs, such as sleep, or the disengagement of an attacking mercenary army. "From my understanding of the working of such great artifacts, and from what Siane is so clearly capable of doing . . . if you had . . . destroyed her . . ." The words came haltingly, and Vidarian felt a chill creeping through him that drove away any remaining thoughts of rest. Khalesh, whom Vidarian had witnessed fighting for his life on multiple occasions now without the slightest loss of nerve, was nearly quaking at what he was about to say. "If she were destroyed," he continued, a fine sheen of sweat slicking his forehead, "the effect, by my calculation, would be catastrophic."

"Well, it must be," Vidarian began, thinking that Khalesh was speaking as a scholar would, of loss of knowledge.

But Khalesh shook his head. "You misunderstand. Imagine that not only have you lived your whole life bonded to this other mind, but your mothers and your mother's mothers have lived that way," the Animator said, watching Vidarian closely, willing understanding with his eyes. "Then, suddenly subtract that bonded life."

Silence fell, broken only by the soft afternoon chirp of a confused songbird.

"It could ravage a person's mind," Vidarian said at last.

"It is not unlike what the seridi must have experienced behind the Great Gate," Khalesh said quietly. "They were not harmed—their bodies were in fact perfectly preserved—but their minds were collectively severed from that which bound them all together, and to all life in Andovar: the goddesses."

"Some seridi fared worse than others," Vidarian said, beginning to catch on to Khalesh's theory.

The Animator's curled beard bounced with the vehemence of his nod. "Yes. Yes! Those seridi connected to the goddesses that were already fading would have been the most impacted, and those belonging to border elements."

"Lightning," Vidarian ventured.

"Exactly. Those that remained sane—"

"Water seridi," Vidarian said, feeling his own legs growing weak with realization. "Treune. Isri is Treune seridi. Ocean clan."

"The water and fire clans would have retained the most of their minds. Earth and air . . ." He trailed off.

"It might not only be the seridi," Vidarian realized, looking up, a fist of unease clenching in his stomach. "The gryphons, too—rarely have I met an earth-wielding gryphon, and air . . ."

Khalesh nodded mutely, his eyes tight. Vidarian knew they were both thinking of Altair, and how the white gryphon had grown more distant over time. Almost, he had seemed to awaken when he learned the truth about Siane, but it was a dark awakening. The air gryphons had long been described by their outer-element brethren as being highly distractible, absent-minded—Vidarian wondered if that reputation was older than fifty years, the fracturing age of Siane.

"Siane said that she had limited herself from manifesting so that she could still serve some of her purpose," Vidarian said.

Khalesh nodded, grim. "But if she were completely destroyed—"

"Is it possible that elementalists—humans and gryphons—would go mad the way the seridi did?"

"That is my fear."

"And you're afraid that the Company aims to destroy Anake, and perhaps even Siane," he ventured further—and, by the whitening of Khalesh's face, struck true. Again, the Animator nodded without speaking.

Vidarian let his head tip into his hands. He had no answer. But if the Animator were true—and he had yet to be wrong when it came to elemental devices—then the mercenaries, and even Ruby, were the least of their concerns.

When Vidarian returned to the Empress's audience chamber, he found her, too, in what seemed a rare moment of introspection. She was alone with Renard, the steward who had first clothed her upon her arrival to the palace as a wild dryad from the southern forests. When Vidarian moved to retreat, not wanting to interrupt their converse, she waved him in, and murmured something to Renard that Vidarian could not hear.

"Our Lirien loved you," Renard said, brushing her cheek with his fingertips. "And your daughter has his eyes."

"I plan to see that she has his heart, as well," Calphille replied, her voice hoarse. It strengthened when she turned to Vidarian. "Are we prepared, Captain?"

"We are, your majesty," Vidarian said, clearing his throat against the grip of emotion that swayed him against Calphille's hoarse voice. She carried so much, and little of it fair.

The Empress Dowager was in ceremonial dress, no doubt provided by Renard and explained by his presence. A long gown of imperial black worked with silver eagles made her dark skin seem warmer than it usually did, her pine-sap eyes brighter. Her own heritage was acknowledged in an elaborate golden hairpiece made of tiny leaves and seed pearl flowers. Vidarian could not help but wonder what the tribes would think of one of their shapechanger brethren in such disguise, and framed by the marble and alabaster of the imperial palace.

Such curiosities would be soon answered. Renard led the way to the old Dowager Empress's garden, and as they passed, they were joined by a retinue of curious nobles—those few who had remained with the palace and not fled the city—and attendants, all in what finery they could manage under the circumstances.

Thalnarra and Altair waited beside the gate with two other gryphons—but neither were earth nor water. Vidarian almost asked after this, but a look from Thalnarra suggested that she, at least, considered it wiser not to reveal the nature of his new gate ability unless it were necessary.

After a token platitude and pleasantry, the Empress waved them to begin the opening of the gate. Vidarian produced the prism key that had been tuned to the Chatika Home and placed it on the wall beside the stone archway.

The gryphons' attention on the prism key was palpable as sunlight or wind. It flowed through the prism key, amplifying its energies—pointing them at the stone archway.

The space beyond the stone began to waver, and, very slowly, Vidarian transferred his right hand to his longsword, and reached his mind toward the *sou-klehn* embedded there.

Guided now by the prism key, the chaos energies were eager, even obedient. They *wanted* to be joined with the crystal, embrace it: and so they did, opening in the archway a door leading to familiar golden grasses, endless hills.

And centaurs.

Beyond the centaurs were arrayed the shapechanger clans: Chatika and Lin, Kala and Kamui. And more. More than Vidarian knew or had names for.

They came through the gate, centaurs first, row after row bearing lances, banners, and strange tall poles topped with totems of bleached horsehair. Qinde led the way, her face and forelegs painted with symbols, her expression triumphant. Behind her filed the rest of her winged centaur kin, and behind them, the centaurs of Khan Kaitan, led by the khan himself, and his daughter, Katalun.

As the Chatika began to follow, led by the red-clad Atira, and Shiriki, in white, Vidarian was very glad that they had moved to the larger courtyard. Tirus followed them, and it was all Vidarian could do to avoid looking for Khalesh. When more clans passed through, he began to wonder if even the parkland would be large enough.

When all the clans had emerged, and not one but two adjacent fields were full of gathered shapechangers, Calphille filled her lungs to address them—

And the gate began to shimmer of its own will.

Hundreds of battle-ready warriors turned toward it, prepared for an attack. Vidarian reached out toward the gate with his mind, demanding its obedience—but it slipped through his fingers like rain.

When the gate's image resolved, it showed red-lacquered columns, black marble—and a woman, opulently dressed in brilliant yellow. Beside her stood a smaller figure more simply attired:

It was Mey—and her mother, the Empress of Qui.

CHAPTER TWENTY-FIVE

SONG EMPRESS

Vidarian had not known that a gate's origin point could be disrupted. He made a small note in his mind to take up that subject with one of the gryphons when there was a moment less ripe for instigating continental war.

When he recognized Mey and the Empress, he immediately threw up his hands in a gesture of resistance, striding in front of the gate and interposing his body between the raised weapons of the shapechanger tribes and the gate. A cacophony of words and languages had broken out, as those further from the gate shouted demands for details they could not see, and those in front whispered explanations backward.

Shiriki came to him, also lifting her hands, and shouted to her people, first in her own tongue and then in her thick Alorean: "We come here in trust, and this girl—" she gestured behind her, to Mey—"is *winjan*, so named by Matpri of the Kala."

More surprised exclamations rippled through the gathered tribes then, but weapons were lowered with them, and Vidarian turned back to the gate.

Beyond it was the relay chamber adjacent to the Grand Library of Shen Ti. As they watched, Empress Cetian Song turned and bowed deeply to a figure shadowed by the doorway. The other bowed back, careful and stiff—a narrow beak, feathers pale with age. It was Asalet, wielding in her stunted foreclaw a device shaped like a curved rod.

The Qui Empress crossed the gate threshold, followed closely by Mey. Both were darkly garbed, but in rich clothing, complete with long hooded capes. Vidarian expected guards, warriors—but there were none. The two women crossed, and the Empress turned back to the gate, raised a hand in farewell, and Asalet closed the way behind them.

Mey ran immediately to Shiriki and embraced her. As they touched, the goldfinch Mey had bonded before the *phi-klehn* darted out of her hood, its striped wings flaring. A murmur of recognition passed through the gathered tribes as they grasped the bird's significance—followed by surprised exclamations, even from among the Chatika, and hands pointing back toward the archway. The girl was young—Vidarian realized he did not even know how young—and yet what she had accomplished was nothing short of remarkable: the unification of a people none had known were separated.

The Empress had turned toward those gathered, revealing the companion she carried as well. At their exclamations, she lifted a fine-boned hand, and the animal—a glittering green viper—slithered down her arm to wreath itself fondly around her wrist. And lest any of them mistake it for a pet, she delicately lifted her other hand, around which curled a sinuous bracelet of bright new silver with a large amber *sou-klehn* balanced in its spiral setting.

"This is magnificent," Shiriki said softly, and Mey beamed. It took Vidarian a moment in his weary state to appreciate what she must have seen immediately: as Mey had shown herself to share some distant blood with the southern shapechanger tribes, so now she had shown that the same blood passed through the line of the Song Dynasty.

A strange thing occurred to him then—a hazy memory of Ariadel on the docks at Val Harlon, so long ago. How she had picked up the grimy kitten hiding in the crate there and insisted it come with them—how its eyes had flashed when first it saw her. Was it was perhaps Ariadel's Qui blood that gave her a resonance with shapechangers? Could she be some long descendant of the Song Dynasty herself . . . and had it been her life-flame that transferred that resonance to Vidarian?

The complex network of connections was too dizzying for him to grasp and remain standing. And Mey's mother was approaching Calphille, and Shiriki beside her.

The two most powerful women on the continent stood at arm's length and took each other in. The green viper, upon close inspection patterned in stripes and diamonds of brighter and darker greens, slithered back up the Empress's arm to drape around her neck like a jeweled torque. Calphille held out her hands to the Song Empress, who responded in kind.

A cheer went up, beginning with the Chatika and quickly carried by the centaurs and other tribes. Vidarian found himself smiling at their gaiety, even while he could only wonder what this would mean for Alorea, Qui, and even beyond.

∿∿∿

Qinde and her centaurs proved as good as their word and more. However she had navigated the *parika pau*, the centaurs themselves showed nothing other than total conviction to their strange world-bridging assignment. They set up camp in the old pastureland beyond the park—pastoral gardens set up by some long-departed Alorean empress to be just this side of wild. The low hills reminded the tribes of their homeland, and they took to them readily. Such isolation also helped preserve them from the constant trickle of Alorean observers who were bold enough to come and witness the strange and unbelievable army that had come to the aid of the Empress Dowager.

Repelling the last of the mercenaries, it turned out, involved very little glory whatsoever. When those few who had not already accepted the Alorean amnesty—less than half of those that had attacked on the Company's behalf—caught sight of Khan Zhenjin's approaching warriors, accompanied by a contingent of Sky Knights and war-painted Khan Kaitan battle wings, they could not surrender fast enough. Some few attempted to wheedle amnesty grants, but Caladan would have none of it, and banished them from the city walls with only what they could carry in two hands. This left a small bounty of supplies, gear, and animals, and Vidarian took some satisfaction in knowing that the Company would thus donate to the dwindling Val Imris food supply.

Exhaustion had long since taken root in Vidarian's bones, but was now declaring itself in the form of muddled thoughts and an aggressive headache. Merely remaining upright was a struggle demanding vigilance over his every muscle. Nonetheless, his tired mind sparked continuously with questions about the arrival of Empress Cetian.

The two women from Qui, older and younger, would have preferred to spend their time with the shapechangers, but understood that arriving unannounced in the capital city of an ancient adversary demanded certain protocols. To that end, they were closeted in Calphille's audience chamber, the rest of her usual retinue dismissed.

Calphille held her sleeping daughter while they talked, which had the desired effect of keeping the volume of their speech low as well as providing a common ground of motherhood on which to discourse. She and the Empress of Qui spoke at length about the health of babies and their mothers, winding from the relative value of *verali* milk to which vegetables were suitable for which age of child to the value of honey in a toddler's diet. It was a crucial bond that they were forming, but Vidarian couldn't help but rebel against the slowness of it.

When at last the opportunity arose, "How did you get back to Qui?" Vidarian asked, fatigued beyond the delicate fingertips of diplomacy.

Mey, sitting avidly at Calphille's feet, abruptly looked at the floor. She did not flush or show remorse, but neither would she meet their eyes.

Her mother's eyes widened. "*Mey*," she said, in exactly that tone reserved for mothers, and then she let forth a long and liquid stream of Qui syllables.

"My most profound apologies," the Empress said, and Vidarian tried to wrap his mind around a woman of her particular stature uttering those words. "My daughter has worn a bracelet imbued with great artifice since she was three years old. Regardless of distance, it allows her to communicate with a paired scrying bowl guarded by Asalet in the Grand Library. It is an heirloom dating back to the foundations of my family, so incredibly well crafted that its energy outlasted the Great Decline. I now understand that if she remained with you, it was because she concealed the existence of the bracelet." The Empress leveled a glare at her daughter that gave Vidarian new appreciation of her office's association with the burning firebird.

Mey continued to study the floor, and to not appear at all sorry. But she was wise enough not to argue, though it looked a struggle.

"Well," Calphille said lightly, breaking the silence that surrounded Vidarian's dull incredulity. "I should like to know if more such bracelets could be crafted in our current reawakened age."

Her subtle turn guided the conversation easily back onto the subject of ancient artifacts, and the two older women, at least, were off on another long exchange.

The next thing Vidarian knew, Calphille was standing beside him. He blinked, and his eyes slowly relinquished the rest of the room: Empress Cetian, her smile beatific as a passing summer cloud, held the young Imperial Princess Revelle in her arms. He was not quite ready to believe that he had fallen asleep, but his thoughts were betraying him.

"Go and rest," Calphille said gently, touching his elbow when he did not immediately reply. "That's an imperial order."

᷍᷍᷍

When he returned to the rooms he shared with Ariadel, she and Ailenne were already risen and gone. He had only a moment to regret this, and then a kind of relief kicked in at being so close to a place where sleep might be possible. The last few steps closed him across the room, and he fell onto the rumpled sheets.

᷍᷍᷍

Full rest, however, was not what the Starhunter had in mind.

He was aware again, though without pain, and with only the lingering memory of his intense fatigue. They were back in the same terrarium-filled chamber that the Starhunter had showed him when she had interrupted his passage to Shen Ti.

This time, thankfully, all of the globe worlds were covered in black cloth sprinkled with silver dust. Curtains had been drawn, also, lending the room a distinctively warmer touch. The head of the strange metallic black creature that the Starhunter had called a Milawan fear-beast still surveyed the room, its very presence ominous, but the remainder of the decor had been toned down.

The Starhunter herself was in a strange silver-white gown with a single shoulder strap and a pair of red-soled shoes whose heels suspended her high over the ground, an effect she exacerbated by providing her feet with just a touch of levitation. Strangely, these small things—the floating feet, the hypnotically red-violet color that she had stained her lips—unsettled him more than strange tiny worlds beneath glass cloches.

"You like it?" she preened. "I thought it would be a little old-school, nabbing you in your sleep." He started to answer, but she raised a painted fingernail to her lips, shushing. "You're doing so well," she said. "Now you've just gotta nail the dismount."

"Where did you come from?" he asked, out of a combination of lingering exhaustion and hard-won knowledge that, if the Starhunter ever answered any question, it had to be incredibly direct.

For a wonder, she answered, if cryptically. "My, we're feisty today! I came from a world inhabited by humans. From the world where you humans originated. Well, not *you*. Your great-great-great-great-great-great-great . . ."

"Through the gate," Vidarian interrupted.

"Your species can't keep track of anything," she snapped. "Let a couple of millennia slip by and it may as well have not happened at all!"

There was something different about her glib quips this time, perhaps even about the room itself. It felt more real, more distinct—as if, rather than being trapped in dream as he often felt, his movements restricted, he were actually present this time. He kept these thoughts to himself, as closely as he could, and tested out the newfound freedom again. "What did Ruby mean by 'immortality'?"

"What am I, a spy?"

He gave her a long look, until she exhaled in a theatrical *pbbbbbt*. But there was something more behind the derisive noise—a kind of sharpness. She was *enjoying* his autonomy.

"She thinks that stuffing herself in that box will make her immortal," she said. "It won't. Just long-lived and cranky." She watched Vidarian expectantly, her pupils slowly spinning and wavering until they became rotating gears. "Cranky. Get it? Because mechanical . . . oh, never *mind*."

"All right," he said, taking pity on her, though he wasn't entirely sure why. "Why did you bring me here?"

"What have we been *talking about* for the last century?" she exploded—for a split second, literally. A moment later she was back in the silver dress, though this time it seemed to be made out of snakeskin. "Rescuing Anake. Though for the life of me I can't imagine why. They're such a drag. Blah, blah, blah, Starhunter; 'you're the only real goddess, Starhunter'; 'you'll rue the day' . . . who *says* that?"

Quietly, Vidarian realized the source of his strengthened presence: the *sou-klehn*. Here, its constant unsettling vibration was gone, and in its place was that strange clarity, as if the world were in alignment. It raised a host of interesting questions, but he kept them to himself. "I'm really very exhausted," he said instead, without lying.

"You are *no* fun today," she said, and snapped her fingers.

When he woke, the pain between his eyes had dulled to a manageable ache. The tremor of the *sou-klehn* was back as well, but the memory of its existence in the Starhunter's strange parlor allowed him to "hear" it differently. Now that he understood how it was attuned, he realized that he'd been fighting its strange intonation, trying to make it "fit" the world he knew—and it never would.

Without opening his eyes, he drew a deep breath, listening—and worked to release that part of his mind that was fighting.

The tension eased, dropping away, and with it went a good measure of the lingering headache.

Encouraged, he opened his eyes—to darkness. At first he thought it was after nightfall, but as his eyes picked up what little light there was to be had, he saw that someone had entered the room—while he slept, unawares!—and covered the windows with thick blankets.

Suddenly concerned about how long he had slept, he levered himself out of the bed, and nearly stepped on Rai with both feet.

The wolf gave a soft bark of warning, then rolled to one side. His eyes, blue in the light, were discs of bright gold in the semidarkness. A stir of motion was the wolf's tail waving in greeting.

"How often have you waited like a nursemaid while I slept?" Vidarian asked, ruffling between Rai's ears. His answer was a wave of subtle emotion, warm and breeze-like—Rai enjoyed sleeping at Vidarian's bedside, but not as a puppy would.

The door to the attached washing room was closed, and when Vidarian opened it, light poured through, stinging his eyes even filtered through frosted glass. He muttered a complaint, but both light and the cold water in the stone pitcher there brought his mind to full wakefulness. And, in celebration of the city not being on fire, he availed himself of the covered cedar tub of hot water also, and scrubbed clean his entire body for the first time in longer than he cared to contemplate.

The brush of thought that Rai directed at him as they left the suite said that they would be expecting him, whenever he woke. Renard would hardly agree, but in fresh clothes, he felt presentable enough to find his way to the Empress Dowager's audience chamber. Rai's answer to this was a soft chuff; wolves worried far less about appearances. Although the wolf was fully capable of speaking in human language, Vidarian appreciated the effortless way they could communicate without it, even as it felt a strange thing to enjoy.

～～～

In the audience chamber, Ariadel had joined the Empress Dowager and was engaged in deep conversation with Iridan and Khalesh. Ailenne and Revelle were under the watchful eye of a birch-skinned dryad warrioress, playing with worn wooden Sky Knights.

Vidarian met the eyes of Iridan first, and then the Animator beside him. Both had had loved ones returned to them recently, after a fashion; he was compelled to ask after them, but neither seemed inclined to casual conversation. He suspected they were sensitive to the Calphille's presence. It had become easy to forget the weight of imperial power, Vidarian realized; Iridan, at least, had known Calphille before Revelle was born.

Rai spread himself out on the carpet between Ariadel and the children, which Raven, sitting at Ariadel's side, showed her approval of by whacking him in the face with a forepaw. It appeared that, beyond being two of the strongest shapechangers in memory living or dead, they were still also a cat and a dog.

"The city is secure," Khalesh was saying, "and we've added what measures we can to ensure it remains that way."

"At the very least, your beacons will give us some warning?" Calphille asked.

"As long as they remain functioning, they'll communicate with the Relay Room if they detect large expenditures of elemental energy," Khalesh agreed. "Iridan believes that they have enough of their own energy to remain vigilant for weeks." At this he looked to the automaton, who nodded agreement.

Vidarian hadn't realized how ravenous he was until he caught sight of the empty stew bowls at Calphille's elbow. She smiled when she noticed his attention, and made the smallest gesture with one finger. A steward brought a fresh bowl—lamb and root vegetables—to Vidarian, and set another in front of Rai. The wolf must have spoken to Raven when Vidarian had awakened.

Only the heat of the stew prevented him from swallowing the entire bowl in a handful of unhealthy gulps. Instead he ate carefully, listening to the discussion of the city's defenses.

As he finished, Calphille and Khalesh turned to him, silently inquiring.

He grimaced apologetically at what he was about to say. "We can't go on like this," he said, and their eyebrows lifted. "Waiting for the Company to act so that we can clean up what they destroy."

A moment of polite silence passed between them, and then Ariadel said, "I agree. I don't relish the idea of tracking this dragon to its lair," she gave an apologetic nod to Rai, and received an ear twitch in return, "but we're reacting, when action is necessary."

They looked to Calphille, and again Vidarian considered the strength of imperial power; the strength of an idea. She gave the smallest nod, the tension in her shoulders showing she also did not like the implications of Vidarian's suggestion, but would reluctantly agree to its necessity.

"*I believe I have deduced the focus of the Company's attention,*" Iridan said, startling them. "*Distilled from the device belonging to Justinian.*"

"Could you verify this with Veda?" Vidarian asked. He had been hesitant to raise the subject of the surrendered automaton to Iridan—particularly given his recent grief at his brother's destruction—but they could not afford an error.

Iridan's head tilted downward ever so slightly. "*She says that she does have information that would be of use,*" he admitted. "*But she says that she will speak only after swearing an oath to the human empress.*" Vidarian, Ariadel, and Khalesh all drew in breath at this. "*I admit to feeling cautious,*" Iridan added.

"Bring her to me," Calphille said.

Vidarian turned to her, too surprised, at first, to speak. Khalesh and Ariadel also seemed at a loss for words.

"Either we trust her or we do not," she replied to their unspoken questions. "If we do not, her information would be worthless anyway. But if you believe her to be sincere, bring her. I will welcome her as a citizen of Alorea."

Iridan stopped, perfectly still at these words. At length, he bent his head again. "*As you say, your majesty.*"

Chapter Twenty-Six

Autumn

The hackles on Thalnarra's neck stood nearly perpendicular to her spine as Vidarian explained what he was asking. She offered no other judgment, though the height of the feathers spoke louder than words. But she had said // *Of course,* // without hesitating, when he asked if she would guard Veda during her audience with the Empress Dowager.

Altair had also agreed, in spite of his own tenuous hold on his elemental abilities. There may have been stronger elementalists in the city among Thalnarra's flight, but Vidarian wanted no chances; only two gryphons would fit in the audience chamber, and he would have the two that he trusted completely.

Together, they went to the Arboretum and found Iridan preparing Veda. She was bound in restraints that would have curtailed even Ariadel's abilities, but none of them were sure what Veda—or Vidarian—could do if pressed.

"You have nothing to fear from me," Veda said. Vidarian looked into her gemstone eyes, the glittering graphite of her face. He could read nothing there, and so he only nodded without answering.

Guards lined the hallways along their path to the audience chamber, many of them recruited from the migratory militia that had taken to calling itself the Tesseract Legion. Vidarian did not know what he felt less comfortable with: the name, or that they followed him at all.

They entered the audience chamber without fanfare, and as Veda approached the Empress Dowager, Thalnarra and Altair took up close places to her right and left. Even as they walked, Vidarian could feel the subtle hum of fire energies, delicate and lace-like: Thalnarra, weaving some manner of protective shield.

Ariadel stood behind Calphille's chair, one hand resting upon its carved back. The chamber was not large enough for Raven's firebird shape, and so she was the ash-colored cat, curled around Ariadel's feet.

Caladan stood, half armored, on the other side of the Empress Dowager's chair, his sword loose in his scabbard. He must have known that he could do little should Veda attack, but there was no room for doubt in his steady gaze: he was ready to die for his empress.

The little imperial princess herself lay in a high-rimmed baby bed, snoring softly. Rai lay in front of it, for once allowing himself out of sight of Ailenne; Vidarian's daughter was in the care of the dryads.

"*Your majesty,*" Iridan said solemnly, and without hint of his own emotion. "*As you requested, I have brought you Veda, fourth automaton of Parvidian.*"

"*I greatly appreciate your understanding,*" Veda said. "*Loyalty is a subject of great importance to one such as I. I must transfer the loyalty I held to Justinian to you—and your daughter.*"

Calphille, radiant in the marl and rosewater makeup of an Alorean empress, extended her hand to Veda. "If loyalty is what you desire," she said, "pledge it to my daughter, and you will have mine in return."

Veda's eyes brightened, not as a human's would, but in actuality. Her hands were bound by the elemental restraints, but she lifted them together, and approached the Empress Regent.

The two figures touched hands, gingerly at first—and then Calphille withdrew sharply.

"*I do apologize,*" Veda said.

Slowly—so slowly it seemed at first an awkward kind of bow—Calphille slumped to the floor. Behind her, two of the dryad warrioresses did the same, choking.

The room erupted into chaos. Dryads—those still standing—drew weapons, stewards ran to find healers, guards shouted. Vidarian dove toward Calphille, hardly realizing what he was doing.

"Revelle," Calphille whispered.

Caladan rushed to the tiny bed, where Revelle was screaming. "She lives," he shouted.

Iridan turned toward Veda.

The world went black.

At first Vidarian was sure that Veda had unleashed some attack upon them all, but instead, it was Veda's voice that he heard rattling and choking around an objection.

Slowly, the room came back into focus, but shadowed and colorless.

Iridan's mind—was everywhere. As he had upon the *Jade Phoenix*, Vidarian could feel Iridan connecting them all together, spending energy wildly—and something more.

Vidarian could not move. He could observe, he could think—but he could not move his body or his metaphysical "hands"—his magic.

"*What have you done?*" Iridan asked quietly. Although his mind surrounded them, it was elsewhere—as though only he and Veda shared the room.

"*You know that this world would be much improved without these creatures of flesh,*" Veda said, and now venom seeped from her voice and posture. "*Their constant hunger, their weakness.*"

"*I did not expect such simple thinking from you,*" Iridan said. "*She was a powerful ally, an imperial ruler who would have granted us Alorean citizenship.*" Terrifyingly, there was no emotion in Iridan's voice, and so it seemed only half of him was there. Was the other half closeted away, or did it never exist? The gentle automaton who had seemed not only capable of compassion but weighed down by it in every moment?

Veda could not project her thoughts the way Iridan could, but the disdain that sizzled off of her needed no such projection. "*You are naive. They destroyed Modrian, and it is only a matter of time before they wreak similar animal wrath upon you and I. We are permitted to persist while we have use only.*"

A long silence clenched between them. Vidarian's heart pounded wildly in his chest. If he desired it, there was little doubt that Iridan could kill them all with a single thought.

"*She was my friend,*" Iridan said softly. The breath fled Vidarian's chest in an explosive gasp as he felt the weight of the automaton's attention release his body, and seize upon Veda.

"*This changes nothing,*" Veda said, her voice distorted. "*They have another.*"

The pressure upon her paused, promising relief. "*Where?*"

And Veda showed him. She showed them all, and Vidarian's heart sank.

Then Iridan crushed Veda's mind with his own. It was violent, physical—his mind pressing upon hers until whatever it was that made her "Veda" gave way. Thoughts, memories, sensations spilled out of her, rolling across their minds before evaporating like steam. Her metal body crashed to the floor as all sense left it.

The room returned then, sudden and bright. Vidarian could move. He breathed, gasping—staring at Calphille, whose eyes now were still and wide, desperately hoping she would stir again.

She did not.

"*I . . .*" Iridan stuttered. Vidarian turned to him, his eyes blurred and burning with tears. "*I'm so sorry.*"

He fled.

そそそ

In the courtyard, and in his heart, all was dark.

It was more than his own guilt. It was even more than grief. It felt, in that moment, that all of Alorea was lost. Vidarian knew, in the abstract, that somehow they would find a way of navigating—but he could not see it.

He had tried to follow Iridan, but knew that the automaton would be found only when he wished to be. With his formidable telepathic abilities, concealing himself would be easy as breathing. And so Vidarian had put up the effort for two sunmarks, in case a pursuit was what Iridan wanted, but then gave it up. Not wanting to return just yet to the palace proper, he had found this dark courtyard and hidden himself in it.

Like most people, he tried to think of death as little as he possibly could. It had become more difficult, oddly, not when he had faced terror after terror, but when Ailenne was born. He longed for her future with a passion that ached in his chest.

But he had seen, and been haunted by, too much death. His friends, even his enemies—it was easy enough to assume that the world was brutal and one should be at ease with its raw force, but that was not for him. He would never accept that the world must remain forever doomed to the messy mediocrity toward which it so often teetered. What kind of existence would that be?

Calphille had possessed that same defiance. She was immovable, untouchable—and now she was gone.

Beneath the well of guilt was a sharper rock, a loneliness. He missed her steadiness already, her clarity. Royal or not, she had been born to lead, though few truly expected it of her.

The loss would be even greater for Revelle. Vidarian had only seen glimpses of what Calphille had hoped for her daughter, and now none of them would be privy to those future visions. His hands clenched and unclenched of their own volition, until he forced his right hand around the hilt of his sword, brushing the stone embedded there.

Death is but a door, time is but a window . . .

Vidarian looked around, squinting into the dark leaves around him, but there was no other sign of the Starhunter.

"Not a good time," he mumbled into his free hand.

You called me, she huffed. *Honestly, I don't know what's gotten into you lately.*

He blinked, trying to discern if she were playing one of her games. "All right," he said. "Let's pretend I did and that you're a real goddess. Guide me."

Easy. Boss up and stop being so boring! she snapped. *Get back to work!*

The odd thing was that she was right. Whether he should return to their goal in Calphille's absence was unclear, but he *could*. And perhaps, in situations such as these, that was enough.

~~~

There was one person in the city who would know the weight and impossibility of what Veda had shown them. And so after Vidarian had numbly endured the wailing grief of the audience chamber, the chaos of the stewards and abandoned governors—after he had held his daughter, after he had taken refuge in Ariadel's arms and they had wept together—he went to find Marielle.

The distance to the hospital wing also seemed a distance between worlds. As real as the Starhunter's parlor had felt, the palace now felt unreal, as if it had become a ghost along with Calphille. It did not seem possible that the tragedy of Lirien's death could be followed so swiftly with hers. The hollow shell of Vidarian's grief was a glass wall between himself and the world, a lens that distorted even as it shielded.

Marielle, mercifully, had already heard the news when he arrived. It was a slender comfort that she seemed much recovered from her ordeal already—enough, perhaps, to eat that promised boar steak, though neither of them mentioned it.

It was not the way of sea-going people to linger long on talk of death. Nistra, glorious though she was, life-giver, was also a devourer, and claimed the lives of many a seafarer with impunity. Though Calphille would not be said to have gone to the sea, Marielle did not ask after the details of her death, and Vidarian thanked her silently for it.

"Veda showed us something," Vidarian said, after Marielle had held her arms out to him, and he had embraced her gently, careful of her still-tender lungs. "Before Iridan . . . destroyed her. She claimed that the Company had another device, that destroying her would not end the weapon's use."

He went on to describe what she had shown them: an archipelago surrounded by knife-reefs that reached high into the sky, so huge that they impacted the weather for miles. To the north was a glacier, and the icy wind that passed over it bombarded the region with vicious and unpredictable snowstorms. A siphon force—one that Vidarian now knew must have been elemental in origin—drew seawater up through the towering reefs, creating an environment for strange and deadly denizens that lived only in that forbidding place.

"You know where we need to go," he said.

"The Last Cove," Marielle whispered. "That's what they've been after all along . . ."

"Rivenwake," Vidarian answered, his heart sinking. "They were looking for the route. Ruby remembered the coordinates, but not how to get there."

"Even with a skyship, it would be dangerous," Marielle agreed, her voice distant, her mind working through the navigation.

The Last Cove had been a closely guarded secret of the ship culture of the West Sea. Before the formation of the West Sea Kingdom, a council had been formed composed of captains to whom the secret had been trusted. Every captain knew the coordinates of the Cove's location and how to get there by heart.

"The device is there," Vidarian said, "and so is Anake." He realized it only as he said it.

"The earth goddess?" Marielle said, startled. Vidarian realized that she would not yet know about the nature of the elemental goddesses—including Nistra. It would not be an easy conversation.

"I'll explain," he promised. "But we need to move quickly."

Chapter Twenty-Seven

The Last Cove

There was one ship that could take them to the Last Cove.

The *Jade Phoenix* had set off for Val Imris as soon as the attack on Rivenwake had proven impossible to repel. It had begun on a diplomatic mission, and so it would continue, filling its berths as heavily as it dared with refugees from the floating city and carrying them to what they hoped would be a rendezvous with the West Sea Queen in exile.

Captain Hao had come immediately to Marielle's bedside upon their arrival to swear his life to her. It was small compensation, he said, for what they had learned—that the *Jade Phoenix* had brought ruin to Rivenwake.

Marielle had rebuffed his guilt as she had Vidarian's, but had accepted the man's service on the condition that it not endanger the West Sea Kingdom's relations with Qui. Captain Hao had been confident that it would not; the emperor, he said, would be eager to pledge his own restitution, beyond Hao's service and the significant gift of the *Phoenix*. In the new age of awakened automata and relay spheres, news had traveled quickly—but Akeo Shisuno-mabari had already fled Shen Ti by the time word of his culpability had reached the emperor.

For his part, Emperor Ziao had other challenges on his hands. Rikan had invaded in earnest, crossing into the hill territory on the far side of the mountains that separated their coastal country from Qui. It was a move that would have been inconceivable mere decades before; the Rikani had clearly thrown themselves in with the Alorean Import Company in totality, and now brought their formidable resources to bear.

News of other unrest had also reached Val Imris, and it was clear that the defending armies of centaurs and shapechanger tribes had arrived only just in time. Velin to the north was fracturing into civil war, while more hostilities were breaking out across far Malu and Arafora.

The reasoning, to Vidarian, was as clear as it was disturbing: the Company was making every effort to foment as much disorder across Andovar as they could in the hopes of masking their death-stroke. Denied the focusing device protected by the Kala, they would use their weapon untuned, throwing the fate of all life in the world into a deadly dice roll.

Anake, too, was wrapped up in it. They intended to use her somehow—and that use would destroy her, along with, if Khalesh was correct, the minds of all those remaining earth elementalists.

In spite of all of this, or perhaps because of it, leaving Val Imris was no trivial task. Shiriki had agreed to carry word to her people and the rest of the *winjan*, the changing people, that they would guard Val Imris as they had pledged. Some would venture out into Alorea in the company of Sky Knight escorts to defend outlying towns and cities against rogue mercenary bands, and others would assist in the construction of a great hill-house on the out-skirts of Val Imris, a kind of gathering place and monument symbolizing the new treaty between the southern tribes and Alorea. None of them had expected that this act of diplomacy was to be Calphille's last; they mourned her as well, and the other tree-people who had fallen with her, their cousins.

Khan Zhenjin, for the most part, was content to follow this plan, as was Khan Kaitan. But once more the daughter of the khan declared her defiance.

"We will go with you," Qinde said. "Myself, and my father's most devoted guard."

It's dangerous, Vidarian wanted to say, but stopped himself, realizing that this was likely to make things worse in a colorful assortment of ways. He could hear Qinde's counterargument: you will bring your infant daughter with her, but not a queen of centaur warriors?

And it was true. The moment he had begun to suggest that Ariadel remain with Ailenne in Val Imris, she had given him a look that stopped him cold. The same arguments remained: Val Imris was hardly safe, and Ariadel was not prepared to entertain suggestions that she remain behind to make it safer.

"We'll be aboard a skyship for the journey," Vidarian began. "The snowstorms of the upper altitudes surrounding the cove . . . they dwarf the Everstorm." Though it had been far from their homeland, the centaurs knew of the Windsmouth and the incredible perpetual storm that had, until recently, blocked land passage between the southern and northern continents.

"We will fly where we can," Qinde answered, "and ride within the ship as we must. If Sky Knights and gryphons can do this, we can also."

Against this there remained little argument that would not endanger their new and still fragile alliance, and so Vidarian thanked her for her dedication—and hoped that the centaur's thirst for glory was not a fatal one.

For gryphons, the negotiation was simpler:

// *We've come with you this far,* // Thalnarra said, and there was a rare nutmeg spice to her voice. Her flight remained committed in its alliance with Alorea, and most of them were fulfilling purposes outside of the imperial city. They had set up a winged message network, not trusting to the relay spheres alone, and their scholars were making considerable inroads convincing the Alorean public that gryphons could be very good friends.

Two of Thalnarra's younger apprentices, however—Kaltak and Ishrak, harrier-gryphons, slim and tall but bulkier than he last remembered them—had requested to accompany Thalnarra. In truth, Vidarian was pleased to see them again, and their adventurous minds would be welcome on a long and dangerous voyage.

// *You're waking Anake?* // Altair had asked, then tilted his head thoughtfully in Thalnarra's direction.

She caught his meaning easily. // *Chayim was with my flight at the Qui-Alorean encampment,* // she said, and Vidarian recalled the vulture-gryphon. His bald and wattled face was a difficult one to forget. // *It will help to have a strong earth-wielder with us. When we explain what we seek, he will come.* //

~~~

The *Jade Phoenix*, being a cargo ship, was quickly adapted to its strange passenger list: five gryphons, three centaurs, three Sky Knight steeds, and half a dozen humans in addition to its crew. Khalesh had silently provided his gear for stowage; the Animator blamed himself overmuch for Veda's betrayal. The Sky Knights—Caladan and two of his lieutenants—had similar convictions. The mission, Caladan claimed, was in the name of his empress, and so he would go.

Marielle, for her sake, had no business in such dangerous enterprise with half-healed lungs, but she made it clear that if they were going to the Last Cove, she would see them there. And since the captain of their vessel could not countermand her, there was no discussion.

The *Phoenix* rose in the dead of night over Val Imris, floating serenely in a crystal clear sky. The stars grew brighter and more varied as they lifted away from the twinkling lights of the imperial city—the multicolored elemental lamps were an incongruous luxury amidst the city's privation, but they made for a spectacular sendoff. As they rose, a shadow passed below them, then drew alongside—Tephir, silent on owl's wings, wishing them farewell before he descended into a midnight patrol. It was a strange occupation for a scholar, but it seemed that the small gryphon's time in the south had planted in him a seed of adventurousness.

At Marielle's urging, Captain Hao flew the *Jade Phoenix* as high as she would fly, until the air became so thin that even birds did not dare it. When those atopships began to wheeze, the captain touched an elemental gem near the wheel, and a sphere of breathable air emanated out from the ship's center. Not without grounding was the Qui's pride in their history of elemental artifice.

They sailed through the night and day, reaching the eastern coast by the third morning—a feat that also would have been impossible in any Alorean skyship Vidarian had seen. The ship's shield of breathable air proved to extend far enough that the gryphons and winged centaurs could fly alongside—though only Altair could keep pace with the ship for long.

rvrvrv

After several days of flight filled only with discussion of what they might encounter, the storms that heralded the Last Cove became visible on the horizon. Captain Hao himself did not know of the cove's existence, and so relied solely on headings provided by Vidarian and Marielle; the captain's eyes were drawn as they took in the storm wall.

Whereas the Everstorm above the Windsmouth had broken apart and largely dissipated following the opening of the Great Gate, the cove's storm seemed to have increased in ferocity. The perpetual blizzard was legendary, but not beyond navigation; this storm seemed impossible.

Frost-knifed wind lashed at the ship, rattling its rigging, even as they drew in sail only less than a sea mile distant. When the ship kept moving, at first Vidarian thought it due to her smooth wind-lines and construction—until it became clear that they were not going to slow down.

Something that was not panic but was also not far from it broke out aboard the ship as the crew realized this as well: the Last Cove was *pulling* them toward itself.

The blizzard that wreathed the cove must have been creating a kind of suction between the still-unseen flying reef walls that created the cove's legendary reputation. They were being drawn into the eye—and would soon pass into the storm itself.

Between the pulling power of the storm and the *Jade Phoenix*'s own inertia, this meeting with the edge of the storm seemed quite likely to rip the ship apart.

Altair was the first of the gryphons to volunteer himself, and no one had the heart to countermand him. Kaltak and Ishrak might be younger, perhaps even stronger—but in flight an air gryphon could not be matched.

Vidarian's friend and mentor stood with his foreclaws on the rail, wings outspread to catch the wind. It was not one wind, but many, and a dozen such pulled at his primary feathers, striving to drag them this way and that.

Without warning, Altair dropped off of the rail, plummeting like fired artillery. All of the gathered sailors ran to the spot he had left and stared overboard—many of them were seasoned enough to stay away from a rail in a storm, but the sight of an air gryphon diving into the morass and then disappearing below was too tempting to miss.

Vidarian reached the rail just in time to see Altair slip into the white wall of the storm. Still the *Phoenix* was drawn toward it as though by a magnet—but, to Vidarian's relief, she did not seem to be accelerating.

Together they watched, hardly breathing, for Altair to return. Vidarian envisioned him exploding out of the cloudstuff with outstretched wings, his long throat extended to tell them of what wonders he had seen.

But he did not.

Vidarian was about to give up hope—to recklessly throw himself and Rai after Altair to fetch him, whatever condition he might be in—when the air gryphon plunged back into view.

His wingbeats were weak, intermittent—as if every lift of his muscles came at a cost of agony. Behind Vidarian, Captain Hao was rattling off a series of commands, and the ship turned abruptly toward the exhausted gryphon.

Under direct command, Hao's sailors were impeccable, and they fetched Altair out of the sky with agility and precision. When the large swallow-tailed gryphon panted out his story, the sailors gasped again: // *The storm is thick and wild,* // he said, his voice full but wavering with exhaustion. // *The ship will surely be pulled apart if it enters as it is. On the far side of the storm, peace—the Cove.* //

The *Phoenix,* as though she heard Altair's words, shuddered and groaned. They all looked up toward the blizzard wall, which was now scant ship-lengths away.

"Captain Hao," Vidarian asked, his mouth dry. "Can the *Jade Phoenix*'s air shield receive augmentation from another element?"

Hao blinked, taken aback by the question, and looked to his left and right, as if some counselor there could properly advise him. At length, he sighed, then nodded: "We believe that it can. But most of the oppositional elements would simply desire to be far from each other, and so we have never tried it."

"With your permission, sir," Vidarian said, dipping his head at Captain Hao without taking his eye off of the swiftly approaching edge of the storm.

The Captain ran his eye along the edge of the *Phoenix*'s hull, no doubt taking stock of her construction, reminding himself how much he loved his ship. "At this rate it's like to destroy us anyway. Permission granted."

Vidarian drew his sword and summoned his elements through it—fire, ocean, and the emptiness that ached between them. For a moment, the fire and water curved around each other like wary dogs as they had for most of Vidarian's experience—and then the between-energy asserted itself, yawning, and fire and ocean fled.

As he had not dared before that moment, Vidarian pulled the chaos energy close into him, guarding himself against its ravenous claws. It reached for him, for the center of his being, and he let it come close, but not beyond the hard armor he had forged around his soul. The Starhunter, at one time, had tried to invade him similarly with her mere presence; the *sou-klehn*'s energy, by contrast, was unfocused, mindless—easier to misdirect.

The *Jade Phoenix* plunged toward the storm-line, and Vidarian desperately forced the chaos energy to find a harmony with the ship's air shield.

Thalnarra was at his elbow, unannounced, her talons gripping the deck for purchase. // *Steady,* // she said, and her presence was an unwavering flame in his mind, a desperately welcome thread. // *You must weave the energy.* // He had seen her do this on several occasions, but he had never managed it himself. // *You can,* // she insisted, and the flame brightened. If she was repulsed by the chaos energy, she gave no sign. // *You must release part of yourself into the pattern. It is the only way.* //

The blizzard wall pulled at the ship, and now the mainmast began to bow toward it. A spiral arm of the snowstorm reached out toward them and lashed, knocking aside sailors and rattling ice across the deck.

The blasting snow seemed to cut around a figure perched on the rail, a female shape that became more distinct the closer they drew to the wall. The Starhunter— in an evening gown, carrying what appeared to be a champagne flute.

Vidarian ignored her, focusing instead on the wild magic that seemed to want to pour out of his grasp like an angry ferret. It bared its "teeth" at him, writhing—

He let it go, let it attack. He moved with it, following its mad movements like a hound chasing a rat.

At the last second, he saw where it could go—and made a single swift correction, directing it into the pattern he desired.

Energy sizzled through the *Jade Phoenix*'s shield, a wild fantastique of colors like the great polar radiance of Velin's winters. It touched the storm wall—and where it touched, the snow gave way.

Slowly, inexorably, the *Jade Phoenix* passed through, and when the blizzard had swallowed them completely, an eerie calm settled upon the ship. The shield's lights still played, and sweat coursed into Vidarian's eyes as he fought to keep his attention on the shield's energy.

When they passed through to the far side, he released the shield and fell to the deck, his palms flat on the snow-dusted boards. The breath came ragged in his chest, but the cold air was sweet.

// *Well done,* // Thalnarra murmured, brushing his shoulder with her beak.

Cautiously, Vidarian climbed back to his feet, pulling himself up by looping an arm around the rail.

The Last Cove laid itself out beneath them. They had passed within the black ring of the reef-walls—still obscured by blowing snow—and below them were five islands. The largest of the isles had been stripped to bare earth, and then some—excavated.

On the north side of the tiny island was a crystal wall, partly buried—and opposite it, a towering crystal cylinder, its surface winking even at this distance in a panoply of colors.

"Oh yeah," the Starhunter said. Thalnarra did not seem to hear or see her, a lack of reaction that prickled Vidarian's neck. "They built that for me. I told them that I appreciated the thought, but I just didn't think of them that way."

"You knew," Vidarian said. "You knew they were going to do all this."

Thalnarra turned an eye on him, but did not comment.

"Mass murder is such a buzzkill," the Starhunter yawned. "They were harshing my mellow."

Below, the tiny figures of distant men were continuing to excavate the crystal structures. Three of them worked on a large heap of dark metal that suddenly moved as they watched.

The metal shape's three-eyed head tilted upward.

"*Congratulations, Vidarian,*" Ruby said. "*You found the Last Cove.*"

CHAPTER TWENTY-EIGHT
IMMORTALITY

Ruby's words came with a titanic blast of water energy. The force of its creation pulled the *Jade Phoenix* toward her as she drew freezing elements from the blizzard wall.

There was no time to react. The burst struck the ship full on, tearing through the bowsprit, then the hull, splintering wood and ripping sail. The foremast tipped downward, shattering, and the blast exited to starboard. Had Ruby's aim been slightly to port, it would have torn clean through the forecastle. This fortune was difficult to appreciate, however, with the deck crumbling beneath Vidarian's feet. He leapt for firmer footing only to have more boards crumble away beneath him.

Sailors were screaming as they plummeted toward the sea and islands far below. A year ago, Vidarian would have been joining their panic; now, his thoughts were on the ship, and how to send it safely to one of the far islands before it could be attacked again.

His cause for bravery appeared above him, leathery wings first outstretched and then folded with the dragon's dive. Rai swooped past him, then banked, catching Vidarian neatly between his shoulders.

"The others!" Vidarian yelled, wrapping one hand around the leather harness as he slapped Rai's shoulder to signal that he was secure. The world spun as Rai rolled sideways, then straightened out into an angled dive.

The dragon caught first one sailor and then another in his outstretched claws; he dove again, then dipped up under a third. His wings labored under the burden, but they began to rise.

Vidarian had a split second to worry about another attack from Ruby before a searing column of fire hurtled toward the island from just outside the *Jade Phoenix*. It continued to burn, a tremendous strike, until Ruby's arms lifted up in front of her to protect her face.

Ariadel and Raven, acting in concert, let go of the energy, then dove to one side, streaking through the sky to put distance between themselves and the ship. Ruby would not be able to attack both, and could not afford to ignore them, even if she were so inclined.

As Rai labored up toward the ship, two smaller shapes dove toward Ruby. At first Vidarian thought they were gryphons—Kaltak and Ishrak, the only two unwise enough to attack Ruby directly—but a flash of hooves and upraised spears convinced him otherwise. Qinde was behind them, screaming a battle charge.

"Stop them!" Vidarian shouted, and Rai rumbled uncertainly—little he could do would be safe for the centaurs. "*QINDE!*" Vidarian called, and gasped with relief when her head turned back.

Ruby's head was tracking the firebird, and so her first knowledge of the Kaitan warrior was when he drove his spear into her neck. This did not go as he planned, and as the spear broke in half he spun in the air.

This did, however, earn him Ruby's full attention, and the handful of moments it took for her metal hand to rise, grasp his torso, and snap his spine.

Qinde and the other centaur both roared with grief and rage. Ruby's head turned toward them, and Rai bellowed, loosing a bolt of lightning into her face that staggered her for a moment. By now Rai had drawn up upon the *Jade Phoenix* and was dropping the sailors onto her swaying deck. The skyship was listing badly forward, but was not falling; its front wing-sails were crumpled, but having four such sails had saved it, in combination with the Qui ship's prodigious rudder-sail.

When the last sailor had been returned to the deck, "Go!" Vidarian shouted, and Rai dove toward Qinde. The dragon interposed his body between Ruby and the centaur, flaring his wings to obscure the automaton completely.

"Do not spend your life so cheaply!" Vidarian's voice thinned with emotion. Qinde darted downward, but Rai dropped with her, and after those crucial moments passed a kind of sense seemed to come back into Qinde's eyes. Vidarian met them, and his heart ached for her. "I know your mind. But dying this way is no solution."

"Dying in battle against such a monster is no dishonor!"

"You came here on a pledge to me. Will you fulfill it?"

This drew her up short, and once again her eyes focused on him instead of the battle beyond them.

"I need you to protect my daughter," he said, and continued quickly before she could decry him. "I brought her here. Please don't let her suffer for it. I am asking you." His throat closed, reacting to the constriction of his heart. He hoped that she understood it for what it was.

"I made a vow," Qinde said hoarsely, barely audible over the roar of storm and conflict. For an instant Vidarian thought she would launch herself at Ruby again, but she turned back toward the ship.

Behind them, Ariadel and Raven continued to bait Ruby. They were showing signs of fatigue, but still the pair danced lightly in the air, easily staying ahead of the slower automaton, drawing her away from the ship.

The *Jade Phoenix*, meanwhile, was slowly descending toward one of the outer islands, a shell-like arc of older reefs whose edges had been blunted by time and the sea. The three Sky Knights were leading the descent. Caladan lifted his lance at Vidarian when Rai turned toward them, and Vidarian raised his arm in return. They would descend safely.

Kaltak and Ishrak were flying swiftly around the islands, searching for enemies or weaknesses, Vidarian imagined. Thalnarra and Altair had engaged Ruby, loosing elemental attacks on her in a variety of forms, all only distractions—conserving their strength, for which Vidarian was grateful. After everything, it remained a wonder to watch them work: a sophistication of elemental touch that no human he knew possessed.

Without urging, Rai dove at Ruby, electricity crackling from his teeth and claws. His chest ballooned outward with a great inhalation of breath, and the *CRACK!* of lightning he loosed deafened Vidarian for several long moments.

Ruby's head turned toward them. Her body was tarnished and blackened from repeated battles and the crucible of the deep sea—all save the gemstones that covered her arms, shoulders, and face, which as yet exuded a malevolent glow. *"You will not take this from me, Vidarian."*

"I never sought to take anything from you, Ruby," he called.

"*You are blind. Everything I have ever asked of you, you have failed or denied me deliberately. No more.*"

Ruby turned from them then, and would not be moved, no matter the attacks that they directed at her back. "*I thought at first that your flesh caused you to fear,*" she said. "*But now I realize it is your spirit that clings to weakness.*" She opened a hatch beside the crystal wall, part of the strange unearthed structure. One huge hand dipped inside, and emerged—with a struggling silver automaton in its grip.

Arian . . . Rai thought, and Vidarian nodded grimly.

"*Veda was disturbed when Modrian had to be destroyed to create my body,*" Ruby said. "*She had a strange idea that automatons should be exempt from the same brutality that has ever ruled the living world.*"

Despite having no visible restraint, Arian seemed unable to speak, and so only redoubled her struggling when Ruby reached toward her head.

"*Stop,*" another automaton voice said.

"Iridan!" Vidarian turned, straining his neck to find the source of the voice. Rai turned in midair with him, and they looked back toward the *Jade Phoenix*.

Iridan had emerged from the ship, exiting out the broken hull where the foremast had once been. He held before him the triangular crystal fragment he had taken from Veda, which still glowed an unearthly blue.

As it had before, the world went dark again. Beneath him, Rai roared in protest.

"*That won't work on me, brother,*" Ruby said. "*Did you think Justinian would have forgotten those potent skills of yours?*"

Iridan released them, and light and color returned, blinding.

"Go to him," Vidarian murmured, and Rai growled agreement. They landed beside the *Jade Phoenix* just as Khalesh was emerging from the ship beside Iridan.

"*You seek to wake the earth goddess,*" Iridan said, and lifted the crystal. "*This will do so faster than Arian's life-source.*"

If it troubled Ruby to hear another automaton refer to the elemental crystals as a "life-source," she gave no sign.

"Wake her," Ruby said. Her head turned toward Vidarian. *"And we will finish this."*

Iridan turned to Rai. *"I would request your assistance, my friend."*

Rai dipped his head, then hunkered down toward the ground. Vidarian slid free from his shoulder, resting his hand on the dragon's flank as he landed. Rai reached back and brushed the hand reassuringly with his armored chin.

Iridan came to Rai, and the dragon picked him up delicately in his fore-claws. With a single hop they were airborne, and in a handful of wingstrokes had approached the center island. They landed beside Ruby, who set Arian on the ground, but did not release her.

Khalesh came to stand beside Vidarian, and together they watched, tense and uncertain.

"What is recorded about the gods and automata?" Vidarian asked quietly.

Khalesh looked uncomfortable. Vidarian gave him a look that if there were ever *not* a time for the protection of guild secrets, now was it. The Animator coughed. "It's very vague. Before the Dwindling began—during the wars—there were experiments intended to try to contain the chaos goddess. An alternative to the gate strategy. A . . . a device was created."

"A crystal."

"Anake, the earth goddess, was the gatekeeper to the vacant crystal," Khalesh agreed. "Without her, it doesn't function."

"They must be intending to use its power to amplify the device in Arian."

Khalesh gave him a miserable look that said he had come to the same conclusion. The Company would use the power of a goddess to end life across Andovar on an unimaginable scale.

As they watched, Iridan approached the crystal wall. Unlike Siane, most of the structure that was Anake was still buried. Iridan placed the crystal fragment he bore carefully, matching it to some pattern only he could see. A ripple of light passed across the wall.

Iridan withdrew then, and Rai planted his feet, claws digging into the earth. He drew back his head, inhaled, filling his lungs to their utmost.

The blast of lightning he released blinded them all; cries of surprise met its brightness. When vision returned, Rai's head was bent with exhaustion, his sides heaving.

The crystal triangle Iridan had set into place now shone too brightly to look upon directly—and its brightness was seeping throughout the wall. Beside Vidarian, Khalesh was mumbling something, some kind of prayer.

Iridan withdrew, and Rai followed him—but Ruby approached the wall. Her hands were raised in supplication, her metal face transfixed.

"*Who are you?*" Anake said. "*What have you done?*"

Without warning, the earth goddess released a blast of earth energy strong enough to crack the ground surrounding her. The island quaked and broke, not just around the wall but further from it, and along a line leading straight to Ruby. The bucking earth threw her across the island.

"*Unnatural,*" Anake whispered, her formidable attention passing over them all like spider's legs, but lingering on Ruby. "*You smell of death.*"

A mad rage took hold of Ruby then. She launched herself at the crystal wall, metal hands poised to tear it apart.

Rai roared, but had no energy left with which to resist Ruby.

A shadow passed over them, followed by a second, and a wall of flame rose between Ruby and Anake. Raven hovered above the wall, and Ariadel's hand was outstretched, trembling with exhaustion. Beside her, Thalnarra circled also, feeding the fire.

Ruby was about to walk through the flames when Vidarian drew his sword.

He had never worked at this distance before, but there was no time for hesitation. If Ruby destroyed Anake, millions of minds would be lost. He reached inside himself for the dissonant energy that coiled ever-present around his spine and pulled it free. As he did so, he realized that there was another way of addressing distance.

Closing his eyes, he saw the jump—drew the gate in the air, and leaped through it. In the next breath, he was falling just in front of Ruby—and he drove the sword into her chest.

Part of him knew that it was the only way to stop her. Most of him screamed that there must have been another way.

The gate energy had not faded, and it leached through Ruby's body, unmaking where it passed. Veins of nothingness crawled through her metal and tubing, exploding elemental gems and warping golden construction.

Vidarian released the hilt of the sword and fell, impacting the ground hard enough to knock the wind out of his chest. A second crash shook the earth just after he landed—Ruby, fallen.

Her metal hands twitched as she lay in the dirt, unable to move more of her body. The sword in her chest had cooled, its energy dissipating when Vidarian released it.

Vidarian pushed himself to his feet, then walked unsteadily toward the great head.

The prism key—he had known it as a sun ruby for most of his life—that contained Ruby herself, or what remained of her mind, still burned brightly, even as the others now lay cracked or extinguished. But its light was fading, beginning to flicker.

The blackened metal head turned toward Vidarian, and he jumped, unaware that she could still move. "*So it ends*," Ruby said. "*Consumed—hate.*" The prism key flickered.

"I don't hate you," Vidarian said, surprised by the sudden truth, and its weight. "I never hated you."

One of her hands lifted, and he did not move away.

"The Ruby I knew feared nothing," Vidarian said. He took Ruby's massive metal hand in his own, not knowing if she knew such a thing as touch in her automaton body. "She was—glorious. Unstoppable. Fearless." Memory and grief welled out from the hollow place inside him that he'd walled away when Ruby began down this dark path. She was the woman he had known again—heroine and friend. Hot tears filled his eyes and more, coursing down his cheeks. "I envied you. Part of me worshipped you. I could never be to my father what you were to your mother. We would never be so free. The Ruby I knew feared no man, woman, or goddess—not even death. *Especially* not death."

"*Nistra . . .*" Ruby said, and Vidarian did not know whether her broken mind and body saw him and answered, or whether she spoke directly to the goddess of the sea in entreaty.

"You are with her," Vidarian whispered. "The real you is with Nistra, Ruby." He coughed, struggling against the betrayal of his body. "I owe you so much, and have repaid so poorly—"

The ground rose up beneath Vidarian, throwing him to the side. He rolled, struggling, pushing himself to his knees, coughing at the dust thrown up by the shifting ground.

Justinian, his hands wreathed in green light, stepped over the rocks behind Ruby.

"I'm sorry, darling," Justinian said. "I can't have you sticking around after I've achieved immortality. That body of yours is terribly expensive—imagine the good it will do after you're gone." He reached down, and the green energy around his gauntleted hands pulled the sun ruby free from Ruby's metal face—then cracked it in half.

The lights in the prism key flickered; died.

"Now then," Justinian said. He turned, twisted his hand, and bands of earth rose up from the island, sealing the two of them—and Ruby's body—in a subterranean prison.

CHAPTER TWENTY-NINE
THE SHIELD

Justinian's face tilted upward and he smiled, watching the roof of earth close above him.

The sword was still embedded in Ruby's chest, but Vidarian avoided looking at it, lest he give away his only hope.

The stone dome shook, but Justinian only chuckled. As well he might; unless they could convince the disoriented earth goddess to assist them, there was little chance that anyone beyond could open the chamber without crushing Vidarian in the process.

Anyone.

"Help me," Vidarian whispered.

All you had to do, my dear, was ask.

Energy surged through Vidarian's body, burning, blinding. But there was no pain—not as he had known it. The world was made of energy: energy in his veins, energy in the stone, energy in the look of astonishment that Justinian was giving him.

Vidarian stood, and the stone above them crumbled away. He lifted his hand, freezing for a moment when he saw the glistening black plates of carapace-like armor that covered it:

"How can you stack whiskers on kittens up against the severed head of a Milawan fear-beast, honestly?" the Starhunter had said.

The black armor seemed to have been made from the insect-like hide of the beast whose head graced the Starhunter's parlor wall. Its venomous teeth studded the pauldrons and spiked the weapon-like point on each of his elbows. His head was heavy with a helmet, which he knew would imitate the death-eyed visage of that otherworldly creature.

Don't let it go to your head, she whispered.

With the stone dome crumbled away, the first thing Vidarian saw was a terrifying monster, clad like himself in glistening black armor. For a moment he thought the Starhunter had brought a living fear-beast to them, but then he noticed the flattened spines along its neck, the bluish tinge to the expansive wings. It was Rai—armored, also, helmeted in a many-tendriled fear-beast champron.

"Impressive," Justinian said, his voice shaking only slightly. He, too, stood, and brushed dust from his fine clothing.

"Do you fear death?" Vidarian asked. He lifted his hand again, and this time a sword filled it, long and quicksilver-bright, its damascene surface a prism of measureless worlds.

Justinian smiled. "Not fear," he said. "Who can fear what comes to us all?" Then, as if he feared Vidarian might answer, he raised a hand: "But more importantly: what is it that we all should do with life?"

I can see into his mind, a thought came—Iridan's.

Vidarian stopped himself from turning his head to look at the automaton. He stared at Justinian, who continued to speak.

"You know as well as I do that men like you and I are rare," Justinian said. "You can kill me, but another will take my place—and he will not be so kindly disposed toward you or those you care about."

He is going to put himself into the crystal intended for the Starhunter, Iridan whispered, and this time Vidarian had to force his body to remain still. *He does not intend to merely use the genocide device,* Iridan said. *He intends to become a god.*

Even as Iridan's words sank in, even as Vidarian came to believe Justinian's ambition in total, the truth of the man's words were juxtaposed atop his insane goal: if this was possible, and if Justinian knew how, killing him would not be enough. Another *would* take his place.

"We can usher in the world of peace I promised you," Justinian continued, and Vidarian looked hard into the man's blue eyes. The fervor in Justinian's face turned his stomach. He *believed* what he was saying with every fiber of his being—was unable to see any other reality.

But Vidarian had seen so many.

"There is a lesson in commerce," Justinian said, speaking carefully now, but earnestly. "If you have taken losses, your inclination will be to keep pursuing the same course for fear of losing all you have invested. But true mastery is to move beyond being driven by loss. You must take opportunities placed before you."

Show me how to stop him, Vidarian thought.

It is dangerous and uncertain, Iridan began. *The price—*

Show me.

He could see it then, in Justinian's eyes: fear. Fear that had driven him within the Company, fear that had led him to kill. Fear had made him, and paralyzed him now.

Vidarian seized upon the crystal with his mind. He closed his eyes.

∿∿

In the place between worlds that exists behind our eyes, Vidarian summoned the Starhunter.

She was there: indistinct, a figure of unseeable star and shadow. Her eyes were two points of infinite color.

"I need you to stop everything. I need to talk to her," Vidarian said.

The look in the Starhunter's eyes now was old, ancient. Tired.

"This is the last thing I'll ask of you," he said.

"Three minutes."

∿∿

They were in the Starhunter's impossible parlor. He was no longer clad in armor; neither of them were tattered or exhausted.

"What is this place?" Ariadel asked, turning slowly to take in the room, her eyes widening at the dome-worlds and the strange decorations.

"There's not much time," Vidarian said softly.

She turned to him, and now her face was slack with worry, denial.

"Iridan has seen that Justinian means to put his own mind into the vacant crystal intended for the Starhunter. There is only one way to stop anyone from doing the same, even if we could stop him."

Ariadel's hand went to her throat as she realized what he was saying. He thought of all that she was—her wit, her vibrancy, her love of knowledge and of life. All he could wish for, all he would never have known enough to wish for—all this, and the mother of their daughter. Hope for a future not dictated by those who desired only power and not life.

"I did this once without you," he said, fighting past the weakness in his heart. "I won't again. Not this time."

"If I stopped you, it would be for the wrong reason," Ariadel said, her eyes filling with tears. "It's just . . . We've had so little time . . ."

Vidarian touched her face, pressing his forehead against hers. "If we had eternity, I would want more time to know you."

She closed her eyes, tears streaming down her cheeks. "Go," she whispered.

He kissed her, the kind of kiss that would have to last an eternity.

∿∿∿

White.

The last words he heard were the Starhunter's.

You're going in there? she asked. *I wouldn't.*

"I know," Vidarian said.

∿∿∿

There was pain, at first. There was a moment when his body realized what was happening to it and protested. But it was brief, because the body's nerves saturate quickly, and then there was shock, a kind of separation from the body that wasn't yet real.

The crystal combed through his every memory, its nine hands brushing their fingertips through all he had ever been. Its touch was like the brush of goosedown, awakening every sensation he had ever experienced, every flash of inspiration or terror, every heart-stopping vista and moment of despair. It did not seem possible that some part of him retained these memories, trivial and profound, but one by one the crystal woke them up, brought them into the light, tucked them safely into a corner of itself.

It was like stepping from the dock onto a rowboat—and like that step, there was a moment when it was unwise to look down.

He looked down.

In that moment he was nothing and never had been. The infinite sweep of the universe was but an idea, a collision of possibilities in a dark and unknowable space, and no twisting nebula nor exploding comet could have such a thing as significance, much less a thing of such base elements as he.

All returns to liquid—

The words of the water priestess from the gateway to the Windsmouth came to him then, but where she had found them ecstatic, he found only gaping terror. He was unmade, not only in this moment but back through every moment, and the world itself was made of nothingness, one signal flickering at another in an everlasting absence. He was falling.

There was a small piece of him that remained Vidarian, and this piece reached out, wrapped itself around the throat of another.

Justinian.

The nothingness pulled Justinian down with it. There was enough of the businessman left to give a surge of victory—he thought that he was surging into the empty crystal, and so he was—

But between Justinian and his destiny was Vidarian, who looked into his face, a multiplying thing of extrapolating memory, and pulled them both down into the abyss.

Justinian reached for the crystal, reached for the immortality he had fought so hard to obtain, but Vidarian pushed it out of their reach. A nobleman, inheritor of privilege beyond a merchant captain's kin, Justinian had never known chaos, and had rarely known fear. The hounds of his personal darkness, therefore, were ferocious.

At last, when Justinian gave up the struggle for his goal, he turned to Vidarian. *"So destiny pairs us together for eternity."*

"No," Vidarian replied. *"It consumes us alone."* And he released Justinian into the void.

There was no air, no existence in which to scream or hear. In choosing solitude to condemn Justinian—to give him the one thing he feared most, which was to be alone with his own mind—Vidarian had indeed chosen the same fate. They would be two ghosts haunting the god-crystal. The path was lost.

Then someone else was there.

He was a bridge between worlds, a gateway to forever. Part of him touched the world that was, and parts of him touched worlds that would never be, an electric array of silver-white possibility that wreathed around him like lightning.

I'm coming with you, the wolf said.

You can't, Vidarian said.

I can, Rai replied calmly. *I am.*

They passed through the dark storm together, and this time it could not pull them into nothing. They stepped onto an insubstantial deck, a ship made of light and possibility.

ᶜᵛᶜ

Vidarian was wind over the West Sea. He was ice on the shadowed side of the mountain of a fire goddess. He was the last tear on his mother's face.

He was light.

EPILOGUE

In the time that they spent together Vidarian had come to understand how much he had underestimated the true size of Rai's spirit and mind. They should always have been equals. He wondered, had he remained human, if he would have been able to perceive this before his brief life found its conclusion.

It had taken several years before he was able to extend himself outside the crystal shell of the great prism that now contained them. He remembered the moment distinctly, as he now remembered all moments that he desired to: he had navigated through the permutations of potential energy and found a reality in which he could reach across the sand and tilt a black piece of fossilized coral from one side to the other. It was a good day.

Now the Last Cove, as it had been called, was no longer lost, and more of an island chain than a cove. It was still uninhabited, but he had gradually been able to flatten the knife-reefs that had encircled it for so long, banishing the perpetual blizzard.

But the isles were not always empty. In fact, today, a small skyship had arrived, a beautiful craft trim and well-made. In the last awakened age it must have been owned by a prominent merchant family.

Two women and a cat disembarked from the ship, carefully crossing the smooth rocks at the island's edge. A faint shimmer in the air rippled as they crossed one of the many signal shields placed around the island.

Ariadel carried her years handsomely, exchanging the smooth skin and silken hair of youth for worldly eyes and a lined face much used for smiling and contemplation. Ailenne, twenty-four years old, had become quiet as she grew older, no longer the garrulous child who could not be kept indoors and had a tendency to sing when she thought no one was looking. She was the youngest person to be declared a high priestess of Sharli in the temple's history, and was a trusted advisor to Revelle, High Empress of Alorea, as well as Mey Lin Song, Empress of Qui. One might suspect she had quite a lot on her mind.

Raven, the improbable firebird, had developed upon maturity a wild spectrum of colors: apricot and scarlet blazed at her crest, while her long and slightly curled primaries were layers of deep green and dark iridescent blue. Her long throat was covered in tiny feathers of metallic gold, scalloped like dragon scales. Fragments of memory told Vidarian that such a bird could exist only in legend, for the calculation of fire energy she represented was unprecedented in all the world. It was one of many spirals of thought that could remain transfixing, infinite, if he allowed it. In the beginning, Ariadel told him that he had lapsed into silence for days at a time. Now he had set aside a tiny corner of his mind to prickle his attention at intervals if a living creature were present nearby.

"Father," Ailenne greeted him, arriving just ahead of Ariadel.

"*Daughter*," he replied, affecting an aristocratic accent. She smiled, and his spirit lit within.

Not for the first time, he wished that she had been able to know a human father, or even a human-shaped one. Someday he might be able to project his former human image the way that Sharli could. Iridan had offered his mechanical body to him, but he had refused. The automaton had thought that his construction was strong enough to host both of them simultaneously, but Vidarian was unwilling to take the chance. Still the automaton had become a proxy of sorts—it was through Iridan that Ailenne had met a young man, an Animator, with whom Ariadel said she was in love.

"*How are your studies?*" Vidarian asked.

"Well enough," Ailenne said lightly, reminding him suddenly and warmly of Ariadel when he had first met her, coquettish in a distant way. "Fascinating to me, boring to you. Tephir sends his regards."

The memory of Ariadel on the docks of Val Harlon wanted to break free of the place where he kept it, but he resisted firmly. Memories were such fragile things, he could see now—touch them and their surfaces wore away like dust from a moth's wing.

Ariadel caught up with them then, and Ailenne excused herself. Vidarian suspected that she had come along this time primarily on a quest from her beau. He had met the boy once, but conversing had been difficult, as he'd been fixated on the notion of finding automaton relics elsewhere on the island. The Rockhunter Guild, an old and decrepit organization when Vidarian was born, had found new life in the unearthing of ancient but viable elemental devices, in which there was now a thriving trade.

"*My love,*" Vidarian said softly.

Ariadel smiled. She walked to the wall and sat beside it, leaning her back against the sun-warmed surface of the crystal.

As was their ritual, she brought him news of the world outside. It was not all new to him, per se—mechanisms in the crystal enabled him to gather impressions from all across Andovar if there were sentient beings there who carried elemental identities compatible with his. He knew quite a bit about the southern continent, peopled with the shapechanger tribes, and also quite a bit about another quasi-human population on the far side of the planet, whose magic was strange and as yet undiscovered by most of the human, gryphon, and centaur nations.

Ariadel described a circle around her own life—a noticeable one. When she had described enough of the goings-on of Revelle's court and the new priesthood—the rift that Endera had created had never quite healed—that she began repeating herself, Vidarian flickered, a kind of crystal equivalent of clearing his throat.

"*The nightmares,*" he said.

She nodded, a tiny movement.

"*It's been . . .*"

"Twenty-three years," she finished for him, smiling to take away the sting. She did keep track of time far better than he could.

"*A long time for such things,*" he said, and she nodded again. Two decades of the aftermath of his transition. She had described it to him once, and it was a strange experience, being haunted by one's own death through the conduit of a loved one. Her memory was of his lifeless body, falling, convulsing—later, of the sea burial. Justinian had fallen, too, and never awakened, his mind lost in trying to battle Vidarian for the crystal. He, too, haunted her, as for the first two years of Vidarian's inability to speak she had thought it had been Justinian that killed him. The Starhunter had spoken to her at the burial, but it had been—confusing. "*If I could . . . ?*"

He had asked many times if she would let go of the memories, allow him to keep them for her. Before, she had always refused, and refused quickly.

"I don't want you to have them," she said—a different answer.

"Then . . . perhaps Sharli?"

Ariadel straightened, then grew still, thoughtful. At last, she nodded again, and a wave of relief swept through him.

Vidarian remembered being human enough that the sensation was like closing his eyes, though he had none. More, he reached within himself, exploring a shadowed corner whose door radiated outward—and Sharli was there, bright and other. He saw her now as few humans could, her radiant beauty, a rose of infinite petals, each a mind touched by her presence.

She wants to forget, he said, each word a thousand concepts, and Sharli knew them immediately.

He drew a circle of light around one of the many pieces of the crystal that served sensory functions. Ariadel pressed her hand to it, and he touched Sharli again with his mind. She reached *through* him and into Ariadel—a kind of communion that she could do without touch, but this would help to preserve every memory.

When it was done, Ariadel sagged against the wall, drawn with exhaustion. But a tension had gone out of her, and with it, out of Vidarian. The moments they had, an eyeblink in the span of what his memory would be, were too precious to be diminished by dark visions.

As the sun sank toward the ocean, casting the sky in kaleidoscope shades of violet and orange, Ailenne crested one of the dunes to the west and emerged, a silhouette against the fiery sky. Her arms were full of rocks. Perhaps this time there would in fact be a device embedded in one of them, but Vidarian was skeptical.

"I looked away, and our little girl was gone," Ariadel said.

"*I remember every moment of her*," Vidarian said. "*I will remember*."

And he did.

~~~

AUTHOR'S NOTE

How do you end a story?

This is one of the great puzzle-box questions in storytelling, and one I think about quite a lot. How many great books have you read that consume your whole existence only to fall over in the end like a flan in a cupboard, as Eddie Izzard would say? I endeavored not to deliver one of those.

There are so many people to thank:

My husband, Jay, to whom the book is dedicated. He read this book as it was written, nudged when I needed nudging, and mostly convinced me that I was not (too) crazy;

My editor, Lou Anders, for believing in this story and this world. I am happy to exist in the same blink of geological time as Pyr;

The team at Prometheus Books (including, this time, Jill Maxick, Lisa Michalski, Catherine Roberts-Abel, Jacqueline Cooke, Jade Zora Scibilia, and Bruce Carle), whose love of books, reason, and excellence is so humbling and inspiring;

Gabrielle Harbowy for fine copyediting, and the ladies of Di'Quinasev, especially Brenda Cobbs, Kristin Jett, and Anni Fahlstrom;

The Homeless Moon, whose conversation and support are a constant solace, and again Scott H. Andrews of Beneath Ceaseless Skies specifically for purchasing another Andovar story;

My family—parents, grandparents, brothers and sisters, who still seem to think this is all pretty cool;

Dehong He, whose amazing cover art for this book knocks me out again;

And the Andovar fans: your emails, Facebook® notes, tweets, and more are a constant source of inspiration and energy. I am so humbled and honestly still a little astonished at your love not just of Andovar but of all stories and fantastical worlds. That love is the most delicious thing I know. Forget thumbs—a sense of wonder is what makes us human.

There is an appearance of a strange non-Andovar gryphon in this book, courtesy of the Starhunter, of course. He belongs to Melody Pena, artist extraordinaire, who blew my mind by agreeing to paint two of her griffin statues to look like Thalnarra. I've been an admirer of Melody's amazing dragon, griffin, and other statues since I was a kid, and it was an honor to work with her, John, and her terrific Windstone team. You can check out photos of the Thalnarra Windstone® on the Andovar Facebook page (www.facebook.com/andovarworld), and find more of Melody's amazing worlds and work at windstoneeditions.com. Watch out for your wallets.

Some have asked what comes next for Andovar, and the truth is that I'm not sure! Rather, I designed Andovar specifically to be a world in which virtually any kind of story could be told, and I plan to stick to my goal of proving that out. There will be more short stories, and eventually more novels (hint: who are your favorites from the next generation?)—and other things, like text online worlds, a medium my heart can never seem to let go of.

It's certainly not the end. There are no ends.

Thank you for coming with me.

ABOUT THE AUTHOR

Erin Hoffman is a video-game designer, author, and essayist on player rights and modern media ethics. She lives in northern California with her husband, two parrots, and two excessively clever dogs. For more about her work, and the world of Andovar, visit www.erinhoffman.com.